Peter Temple is Australia's most acclaimed crime and thriller writer, and is the only author to have won the Ned Kelly Prize five times. He received the 2007 CWA Gold Dagger for *The Broken Shore*, while his ninth and most recent novel, *Truth*, was awarded the 2010 Miles Franklin Award. Peter Temple lives with his family in Ballarat, Australia.

Also by Peter Temple

An Iron Rose
Shooting Star
In the Evil Day
Truth

The Jack Irish Novels

Bad Debts
Black Tide
Dead Point
White Dog

PETER TEMPLE

The Broken Shore

Quercus

First published in Great Britain in 2006 by Quercus
First published in Great Britain in paperback in 2007 by Quercus
This paperback edition published in 2011 by

Quercus
21 Bloomsbury Square
London
WC1A 2NS

A CIP catalogue record for this book is available
from the British Library

ISBN 978 0 85738 349 5

Printed and bound in Great Britain by Clays Ltd, St Ives plc

10 9 8 7 6 5

*To Anita: for the
laughter and the loyalty.*

CASHIN WALKED around the hill, into the wind from the sea. It was cold, late autumn, last glowing leaves clinging to the liquidambars and maples his great-grandfather's brother had planted, their surrender close. He loved this time, the morning stillness, loved it more than spring.

The dogs were tiring now but still hunting the ground, noses down, taking more time to sniff, less hopeful. Then one picked up a scent and, new life in their legs, they loped in file for the trees, vanished.

When he was near the house, the dogs, black as liquorice, came out of the trees, stopped, heads up, looked around as if seeing the land for the first time. Explorers. They turned their gaze on him for a while, started down the slope.

He walked the last stretch as briskly as he could and, as he put his hand out to the gate, they reached him. Their curly black heads tried to nudge him aside, insisting on entering first, strong back legs pushing. He unlatched the gate, they pushed it open enough to slip in, nose to tail, trotted down the path to the shed door. Both wanted to be first again, stood with tails up, furry scimitars, noses touching at the door jamb.

Inside, the big poodles led him to the kitchen. They had water bowls there and they stuck their noses into them and drank in a noisy way. Cashin prepared their meal: two slices each from the cannon-barrel dog sausage made by the butcher in Kenmare, three handfuls each of dry dog food. He got the dogs' attention, took the bowls outside, placed them a metre apart.

The dogs came out. He told them to sit. Stomachs full of water, they did so slowly and with disdain, appeared to be arthritic. Given permission to eat, they looked at the food without interest, looked at each other, at him. Why have we been brought here to see this inedible stuff?

Cashin went inside. In his hip pocket, the mobile rang.

'Yes.'

'Joe?'

Kendall Rogers, from the station.

'Had a call from a lady,' she said. 'Near Beckett. A Mrs Haig. She reckons there's someone in her shed.'

'Doing what?'

'Well, nothing. Her dog's barking. I'll sort it out.'

Cashin felt his stubble. 'What's the address?'

'I'm going.'

'No point. Not far out of my way. Address?'

He went to the kitchen table and wrote on the pad: date, time, incident, address. 'Tell her fifteen-twenty. Give her my number if anything happens before I get there.'

The dogs liked his urgency, rushed around, made for the vehicle when he left the building. On the way, they stood on station, noses out the back windows. Cashin parked a hundred metres down the lane from the farmhouse gate. A head came around the hedge as he approached.

'Cop?' she said. She had dirty grey hair around a face cut from a hard wood with a blunt tool.

Cashin nodded.

'The uniform and that?'

'Plainclothes,' he said. He produced the Victoria Police badge with the emblem that looked like a fox. She took off her smudged glasses to study it.

'Them police dogs?' she said.

8

He looked back. Two woolly black heads in the same window.

'They work with the police,' he said. 'Where's this person?'

'Come,' she said. 'Dog's inside, mad as a pork chop, the little bugger.'

'Jack Russell,' said Cashin.

'How'd ya know that?'

'Just a guess.'

They went around the house. He felt the fear rising in him like nausea.

'In there,' she said.

The shed was a long way from the house, you had to cross an expanse of overgrown garden, go through an opening in a fence lost beneath rampant potato-creeper. They walked to the gate. Beyond was knee-high grass, pieces of rusted metal sticking out.

'What's inside?' Cashin said, looking at a rusted shed of corrugated iron a few metres from the road, a door half open. He felt sweat around his collarbones. He wished he'd let Kendall do this.

Mrs Haig touched her chin, black spikes like a worn-down hair brush. 'Stuff,' she said. 'Junk. The old truck. Haven't bin in there for years. Don't go in there.'

'Let the dog out,' he said.

Her head jerked, alarmed. 'Bastard might hurt im,' she said.

'No,' he said. 'What's the dog's name?'

'Monty, call them all Monty, after Lord Monty of Alamein. Too young, you wouldn't know.'

'That's right,' he said. 'Let Monty out.'

'And them police dogs? What bloody use are they?'

'Kept for life-and-death matters,' Cashin said, controlling his voice. 'I'll be at the door, then you let Lord Monty out.'

His mouth was dry, his scalp itched, these things would not have happened before Rai Sarris. He crossed the grassland, went to the left of the door. You learned early to keep your distance from potentially dangerous people and that included not going into dark sheds to meet them.

Mrs Haig was at the potato-creeper hedge. He gave her the thumbs up, his heart thumping.

The small dog came bounding through the grass, all tight muscles and yap, went for the shed, braked, stuck its head in the door and snarled, small body rigid with excitement.

Cashin thumped on the corrugated iron wall with his left hand. 'Police,' he said loudly, glad to be doing something. 'Get out of there. Now!'

Not a long wait.

The dog backed off, shrieking, hysterical, mostly airborne.

A man appeared in the doorway, hesitated, came out carrying a canvas swag. He ignored the dog.

'On my way,' he said. 'Just had a sleep.' He was in his fifties perhaps, short grey hair, big shoulders, a day's beard.

'Call the dog, Mrs Haig,' Cashin said over his shoulder.

The woman shouted and the dog withdrew, reluctant but obedient.

'Trespassing on private property,' said Cashin, calmer. He felt no threat from the man.

'Yeah, well, just had a sleep.'

'Put the swag down,' Cashin said. 'Take off your coat.'

'Says who?'

'I'm a cop.' He showed the fox.

The man folded his bluey, put it down on his swag, at his feet. He wore laced boots, never seen polish, toes dented.

'How'd you get here?' Cashin said.

'Walking. Lifts.'

'From where?'

'New South.'

'New South Wales?'

'Yeah.'

'Long way to come.'

'A way.'

'Going where?'

'Just going. My own business where I go.'

'Free country. Got some ID? Driver's licence, Medicare card.'

'No.'

'No ID?'

'No.'

'Don't make it hard,' Cashin said. 'I haven't had breakfast. No ID, I take you in for fingerprinting, charge you with trespass, put you in the cells. Could be a while before you see daylight.'

The man bent, found a wallet in his coat, took out a folded sheet of paper, offered it.

'Put it in the pocket and chuck the coat over.'

It landed a metre away.

'Back off a bit,' Cashin said. He collected the coat, felt it. Nothing. He took out the piece of paper, often folded, worn. He opened it.

Dave Rebb has worked on Boorindi Downs for three years and is a hard worker and no trouble, his good with engines, most mechanic things. Also stock. I would employ him again any time.

It was signed Colin Blandy, manager, and dated 11 August 1996. There was a telephone number.

'Where's this place?' said Cashin.

'Queensland. Near Winton.'

'And this is it? This's your ID? Ten years old?'

'Yeah.'

Cashin found his notebook and wrote down the names and the number, put the paper back in the coat. 'Scared the lady here,' he said. 'That's not good.'

'No sign of life when I come,' said the man. 'Dog didn't bark.'

'Been in trouble with the police, Dave?'

'No. Never been in trouble.'

'Could be a murderer,' said Mrs Haig behind him. 'Killer. Dangerous killer.'

'Me, Mrs Haig,' said Cashin, 'I'm the policeman, I'm dealing with this. Dave, I'm going to drive you to the main road. Come back this way, you'll be in serious trouble. Okay?'

'Okay.'

Cashin took the two steps and gave the man back his coat. 'Let's go.'

'Charge him!' shouted Mrs Haig.

In the vehicle, Dave Rebb offered his hands to the dogs, he was a man who knew about dogs. At the T-junction, Cashin pulled over.

'Which way you going?' he said.

There was a moment. 'Cromarty.'

'Drop you at Port Monro,' Cashin said. He turned left. At the turnoff to the town, he stopped. They got out and he opened the back for the man's swag.

'Mind how you go now,' Cashin said. 'Need a buck or two?'

'No,' said Rebb. 'Treated me like a human. Not a lot of that.'

Waiting to turn, Cashin watched Rebb go, swag horizontal across his back, sticking out. In the morning mist, he was a stubby-armed cross walking.

'NO DRAMA?' said Kendall Rogers.

'Just a swaggie,' said Cashin. 'You doing unpaid time now?'

'I woke up early. It's warmer here, anyway.' She fiddled with something on the counter.

Cashin raised the hatch and went to his desk, started on the incident report.

'I'm thinking of applying for a transfer,' she said.

'I can do something about my personal hygiene,' Cashin said. 'I can change.'

'I don't need protecting,' she said. 'I'm not a rookie.'

Cashin looked up. He'd been expecting this. 'I'm not protecting you from anything. I wouldn't protect anybody. You can die for me anytime.'

A silence.

'Yes, well,' Kendall said. 'There are things here to be resolved. Like the pub business. You drive back at ten o'clock at night.'

'The Caine animals won't touch me. I'm not going to go to an inquiry and explain why I let you handle it.'

'Why won't they touch you?'

'Because my cousins will kill them. And after that, they'll be very nasty to them. Is that a satisfactory answer, your honour?' He went back to the report but he felt her eyes. 'What?' he said. 'What?'

'I'm going to Cindy's. Ham and egg?'

'I'll let you face the savage bitch? On a Friday morning? I'll go.'

She laughed, some of the tension gone.

When she was at the door, Cashin said, 'Ken, bit more mustard this time? Brave enough to ask her?'

He went to the window and watched her go down the street. She had been a gymnast, represented the state at sixteen, won her first gold medal. You would not know it from her walk. In the city, off duty, she went to a club with a friend, a photographer. She was recognised by a youth she had arrested a few months before, an apprentice motor mechanic, a weekend raver, a kicker and a stomper. They were followed, the photographer was badly beaten, locked in his car boot, survived by luck.

Kendall was taken somewhere, treated like a sex doll. After dawn, a man and his dog found her. She had a broken pelvis, a broken arm, six broken ribs, a punctured lung, damaged spleen, pancreas, crushed nose, one cheekbone stove in, five teeth broken, a dislocated shoulder, massive bruising everywhere.

Cashin returned to the paper work. You could get by without identification but Rebb had been employed, there might be some tax record. He dialled the number for Boorindi Downs. It rang for a while.

'Yeah?'

'Victoria Police, Detective Cashin, Port Monro. Need to know about someone worked on Boorindi Downs.'

'Yeah?'

'Dave Rebb.'

'When's that?'

'1994 to 1996.'

'No, mate, no one here from then. Place belongs to someone else now, they did a clear-out.'

'What about Colin Blandy.'

'Blands, oh yeah. I know him from before, he got the

bullet from the Greeks, went to Queensland. Dead, though.'

'Thanks for your time.'

Cashin thought that he had made a mistake, he should have fingerprinted Rebb. He had cause to, he had allowed sympathy to dictate.

Could be a murderer, said Mrs Haig. Killer.

He rang Cromarty, asked for the criminal investigation man he knew.

'Got a feeling, have you?' said Dewes. 'I'll tell them to keep a lookout.'

Cashin sat, hands on the desk. He had threatened Rebb with this, the fingerprinting, the long wait in the cells.

'Sandwich,' said Kendall. 'Extra mustard. She put it on with a trowel.'

An ordinary shift went by. Near the end, the word came that the first electronic sweep found no David Rebb on any government database in the states and territories. It didn't mean much. Cashin knew of cases where searches had failed to find people with strings of convictions. He clocked off, drove out to the highway, turned for Cromarty.

Rebb had walked twenty-three kilometres. Cashin pulled in a good way in front of him, got out.

He came on, a man who walked, easy walk, stopped, a tilt of shoulders, the tilted cross.

'Dave, I've got to fingerprint you,' Cashin said.

'Told you. Done nothing.'

'Can't take your word, Dave. Can't take anyone's word. Got to charge you with trespass,' Cashin said.

Rebb said nothing.

'That's so we can take your prints.'

'Don't lock me up,' said Rebb, softly, no tone. 'Can't go in the cells.'

Cashin heard the fear in the man's voice and he knew that once he would not have cared much. He hesitated, then he said, 'Listen, you interested in work? Dairy cows, cow stuff. Do that kind of thing?'

Rebb nodded. 'Long time ago.'

'Want some work?'

'Well, open to offers.'

'And garden stuff, some building work maybe?'

'Yeah. Done a bit of that, yeah.'

'Well, there's work here. My neighbour's cows, I'm clearing up an old place, might rebuild a bit, thinking of it. Work for a cop?'

'Worked for every kind of bastard there is.'

'Thank you. You can sleep at my place tonight. There's a shed with bunks and a shower. See about the job tomorrow.'

They got into the vehicle, Rebb's swag in the back. 'This how they get workers around here?' he said. 'Cops recruit them.'

'All part of the job.'

'What about the fingerprints?'

'I'm taking your word you're clean. That's pretty dumb, hey?'

Rebb was looking out of the window. 'Saved the taxpayer money,' he said.

CASHIN WOKE in the dark, Shane Diab on his mind, the sounds he made dying.

He listened to his aches for a time, tested his spine, his hips, his thighs – they all gave pain. He pushed away the lovely warm burden of the quilts, put feet in the icy waiting boots, and left the room, went down the passage, through Tommy Cashin's sad ballroom, into the hall, out the front door. It was no colder out than in, today the mist blown away by a strong wind off the ocean.

He pissed from the verandah, onto the weeds. It didn't bother them. Then he went inside and did his stretching, washed his face, rinsed his mouth, put on overalls, socks, boots.

The dogs knew his noises, they were making throat sounds of impatience at the side door. He let them in and the big creatures snuffled around him, tails swinging.

Thirsty, he went to the fridge and the sight of the frosted beer bottles made him think he could drink a beer. He took out the two-litre bottle of juice, eight fruits it said. Only a dickhead would believe that.

He held the plastic flagon in both hands, took a long drink, a tall glass at least. He took the old oilskin coat off the hook behind the door, picked up the weapon. When he opened the door to the verandah, the dogs pushed through, bounded down the steps, ran for the back gate. They jostled while they watched him come down the path, shrugging into the coat as he walked. Gate open, they ran down the path, side by side, reached the open land and made for the trees, jumping over the big tufts of grass, extravagant leaps, ears floating.

Cashin broke the little over-and-under gun as he walked, felt in his side pockets and found a .22 slug and a .410 shell, fed the mouths. He often had the chance to take a shot at a hare, looked through the V-sight at the beautiful dun creature, its electric ears. He didn't even think of firing, he loved hares, their intelligence, their playfulness. At a running rabbit, he did take the odd shot. It was just a fairground exercise, a challenge. He always missed – his reaction too slow, the .410's cone of shot not big enough, too soon dissolved and impotent.

Cashin walked with the little weapon broken over his arm, looking at the trees, dark inside, waiting for the dogs to reach them and send the birds up like tracer fire.

The dogs did a last bound and they were in the trees, triggering the bird-blast, black shrapnel screeching into the sky.

He walked over the hill and down the slope, the dogs ahead, dead black and light-absorbing, heads down, quick legs, coursing, disturbing the leaf mulch. On the levelling ground, on the fringe of the clearing, a hare took off. He watched the three cross the open space, black dogs and hare, the hare pacing itself perfectly, jinking when it felt the dogs near. It seemed to be pulling the dogs on a string. They vanished into the trees above the creek.

Cashin crossed the meadow. The ground was level to the eye but, tramping the long dry grass, you could feel underfoot the rise and fall, the broad furrows a plough had carved. The clearing had once been cultivated, but not in the memory of anyone living. He had no way of knowing whether his ancestor Tommy Cashin had planted a crop there.

It was a fight to get to the creek through the poplars and willows, thousands of suckers gone unchecked for at least thirty years. When he reached the watercourse, a trickle between pools, the dogs appeared, panting. They went straight in, found the deepest places, drank, walked around, drank, walked around, the water eddied weakly around their thin, strong legs, they bit it, raised pointed chins, beards draining water. Poodles liked puddles, didn't like deep water, didn't like the sea much. They were paddlers.

Across the creek, they began the sweep to the west, around the hill, on the gentle flank. In the dun grass, he saw the ears of two hares. He whistled up the dogs and pointed to the hares. They followed his arm, ran and put up the pair, which broke together and stayed together, running side by side for ten or fifteen metres, two dogs behind them, an orderly group of four. Then the left hare split, went downhill. His dog split with him. The other dog couldn't bear it, broke stride, swerved left to join his friend in the pursuit. They vanished into the long grass.

After a while, they came back, pink of tongues visible from a long way, loped ahead again.

Walking, Cashin felt the eyes on him. The dogs running ahead would soon sense the man too, look around, turn left and make for him. He walked and then there were sharp and carrying barks.

The man was out of the trees, the dogs circling him, bouncing. Cashin was unconcerned. He saw the hands the man put out to them, they tried to mouth them, delighted to see their friend. He angled his path to meet Den Millane, nearing eighty but looking as he had at fifty. He would die with a dense head of hair the colour of a gun barrel.

They shook hands. If they didn't meet for a little while, they shook hands.

'Still no decent rain,' said Cashin.

'Fuckin unnatural,' said Millane. 'Startin to believe in this greenhouse shit.' He rubbed a dog head with each hand. 'Bugger me, never thought I could like a bloody poodle. Seen the women at the Corrigan house?'

'No.'

They both had boundaries with the Corrigan property. Mrs Corrigan had gone to Queensland after her husband died. No one had lived in the small redbrick house since then. The weather stripped paint from the woodwork, dried out the window putty, panes fell out. The timber outbuildings listed, collapsed, and grass grew over the rotting pieces. He remembered coming for a weekend in summer in the early nineties, hot, he was still with Vickie then, a big piece of roof had gone, blown off. He asked Den Millane to contact Mrs Corrigan and the roof was fixed, in a fashion. Roofs decided whether empty houses would become ruins.

'The Elders bloke brung em,' said Den, not looking up. 'He's a fat cunt too. The one's got short hair, bloke hair. Like blokes used to have. Then they come back yesterday, now it's three girls, walkin around, they walk down the old fence. Fuckin lesbian colony on the move, mate.'

'Spot lesbians? They have them in your day?'

Millane spat. 'Still my bloody day, mate. Teachers in the main, your lessies. Used to send the clever girls out to buggery, nothin but dickheads there couldn't read a comic book. Tell you what, I was a girl met those blokes, I'd go lessie. Anyway, point is, you ever looked at your title?'

Cashin shook his head.

'Creek's not the boundary.'

'No?'

'Your line's the other side, twenty, thirty yard over the

creek.' Millane passed a thumb knuckle across his lower lip. 'Claim the fuckin creek or lose it, mate. Fence that loop or say goodbye.'

'Well,' Cashin said, 'you'd be mad to buy the place. House needs work, ground's all uphill.'

Millane shook his head. 'Seen what they're payin for dirt? Every second dickhead wants to live in the country, drive around in the four-wheel, fuckin up the roads, moanin about the cowshit and the ag chemicals.'

'No time to read the real estate,' Cashin said. 'Too busy upholding the law. Still need someone to take the cows over to Coghlans?'

'Yeah. Knee's getttin worse.'

'Got someone for you.'

'There's a bit of other work, say three days, that's all up. No place to stay, though.'

'I'll bring him over.'

Den was watching the dogs investigating a blackberry patch. 'So when you gonna leave the fancy dogs with me again?'

'Didn't like to ask,' Cashin said. 'Bit of a handful.'

'I can manage the fuckin brutes. Bring em over. Lookin thin, give em a decent feed of bunny.'

They said goodbye. When Cashin was fifty metres away, Den shouted, 'Ya keep what's bloody yours. Hear me?'

THE CALL came at 8.10 am, relayed from Cromarty. Cashin was almost at the Port Monro intersection. As he drove along the coast highway, he saw the ambulance coming towards him. He slowed to let them reach the turn-off first, followed them up the hill, around the bends and through the gates of The Heights, parked on the forecourt.

A woman was standing on the gravel, well away from the big house, smoking a cigarette. She threw it away and led the paramedics up the stairs into the house. Cashin followed, across an entrance hall and into a big, high-ceilinged room. There was a faint sour smell in the air.

The old man was lying on his stomach before the massive fireplace, head on the stone hearth. He was wearing only pyjama pants, and his thin naked back was covered with dried blood through which could be seen dark horizontal lines. There was blood pooled on the stones and soaked into the carpet. It was black in the light from a high uncurtained window.

The two medics went to him, knelt. The woman put her gloved hands on his head, lifted it gently. 'Significant open head injury, possible brain herniation,' she said, talking to her companion and into a throat mike.

She checked the man's breathing, an eye, held up his forearm. 'Suspected herniation,' she said. 'Four normal saline, hyperventilate 100 per cent, intubation indicated, 100 mils Lidocaine.'

Her partner set up the oxygen. He got in the way and Cashin couldn't see what was happening.

After a while, the female medic said, 'Three on coma scale. Chopper, Dave.'

The man took out a mobile phone.

'The door was open,' said the woman who had been waiting on the steps. She was behind Cashin. 'I only went in a step, backed off, thought he was dead, I wanted to run, get in the car and get out of there. Then I thought, oh shit, he might be alive and I came back and I saw he was breathing.'

Cashin looked around the room. In front of a door in the left corner, a rug on the polished floorboards was rucked. 'What's through there?' he said, pointing.

'Passage to the south wing.'

A big painting dominated the west wall, a dark landscape seen from a height. It had been slashed at the bottom, where a flap of canvas hung down.

'He must have gone to bed early, didn't use even half the wood Starkey's boy brought in,' she said.

'See anything else?'

'His watch's not on the table. It's always there with the whisky glass on the table next to the leather chair. He had a few whiskies every night.'

'He took his watch off?'

'Yeah. Left it on the table every night.'

'Let's talk somewhere else,' Cashin said. 'These people are busy.'

He followed her across a marble-floored foyer to a passage around a gravelled courtyard and into a kitchen big enough for a hotel. 'What did you do when you got here?' he said.

'I just put my bag down and went through. Do that every day.'

'I'll need to take a look in the bag. Your name is...?'

'Carol Gehrig.' She was in her forties, pretty, with blonded hair, lines around her mouth. There were lots of Gehrigs in the area.

She fetched a big yellow cloth bag from a table at the far end of the room, unzipped it. 'You want to dig around?'

'No.'

She tipped the contents onto the table: a purse, two sets of keys, a glasses case, makeup, tissues, other innocent things.

'Thanks,' Cashin said. 'Touch anything in there?'

'No. I just put the bag down, went to the sitting room to fetch the whisky glass. Then I rang. From outside.'

Now they went outside. Cashin's mobile rang.

'Hopgood. What's happening?' He was the criminal investigation unit boss in Cromarty.

'Charles Bourgoyne's been bashed,' he said. 'Badly. Medics working on him.'

'I'll be there in a few minutes. No one touches anything, no one leaves, okay?'

'Gee,' Cashin said. 'I was going to send everyone home, get everything nice and clean for forensic.'

'Don't be clever,' said Hopgood. 'Not a fucking joking matter this.'

Carol Gehrig was sitting on the second of the four broad stone steps that led to the front door. Cashin took the clipboard and went to sit beside her. Beyond the gravel expanse and the box hedges, a row of tall pencil pines was moving in the wind, swaying in unison like a chorus line of fat-bellied dancers. He had driven past this house hundreds of times and never seen more than the tall, ornate chimneys, sections of the red pantiled roof. The brass plate on a gate pillar said The Heights, but the locals called it Bourgoyne's.

'I'm Joe Cashin,' he said. 'You'd be related to Barry Gehrig.'

'My cousin.'

Cashin remembered his fight with Barry Gehrig in primary school. He was nine or ten. Barry won that one, he made amends later. He sat on Barry's shoulders and ground his pale face into the playground dirt.

'What happened to him?'

'Dead,' she said. 'Drove his truck off a bridge thing near Benalla. Overpass.'

'I'm sorry. Didn't hear about that.'

'He was a deadshit, always drugged up. I'm sorry for the people in the car he landed on, squashed them.'

She found cigarettes, offered. He wanted one. He said no.

'Worked here long?'

'Twenty-six years. I can't believe it. Seventeen when I started.'

'Any idea what happened?'

'Not a clue. No.'

'Who might attack him?'

'I'm saying, no idea. He's got no enemies, Mr B.'

'How old is Mr Bourgoyne?'

'Seventy something. Seventy-five, maybe.'

'Who lives here? Apart from him?'

'No one. The step-daughter was here the day before yesterday. Hasn't been here for a long time. Years.'

'What's her name?'

'Erica.'

'Know how to contact her?'

'No idea. Ask Mrs Addison in Port Monro, the lawyer. She looks after business for Mr Bourgoyne.'

'Anyone else work here?'

'Bruce Starkey.'

Cashin knew the name. 'The football player?'

'Him. He does all the outside.' She waved at the raked gravel, the trimmed hedges. 'Well, now his boy Tay does. Bit simple, Tay, never says a word. Bruce sits on his arse and smokes mostly. They come Monday, Wednesday and Friday. And when he drives Mr B. Sue Dance makes lunch and dinner. Gets here about twelve, cooks lunch, cooks dinner, leaves it for him to heat up. Tony Crosby might as well be on a wage too, always something wrong with the plumbing.'

The male paramedic came out. 'There's a chopper coming,' he said. 'Where's the best place to land?'

'The paddock behind the stables,' said Carol. 'At the back of the house.'

'How's he doing?' Cashin said.

The man shrugged. 'Probably should be dead.'

He went back inside.

'Bourgoyne's watch,' said Cashin. 'Know what kind it was?'

'Breitling,' said Carol. 'Smart watch. Had a crocodile-skin strap.'

'How do you spell that?'

'B-R-E-I-T-L-I-N-G.'

Cashin went to the cruiser, got Hopgood again. 'They're taking him to Melbourne. You might want to have a yarn with a Bruce Starkey and his young fella.'

'What about?'

'They're both part-time here.'

'So?'

'Thought I'd draw it to your attention. And Bourgoyne's watch's probably stolen.' He told him what Carol had said.

'Okay. Be there in a couple of minutes. There's three cars coming. Forensic can't get a chopper till about 10.30.'

'The step-daughter needs to be told,' Cashin said. 'She

was here the day before yesterday. You can probably get an address from Cecily Addison in Port Monro, that's Woodward, Addison & Cameron.'

'I know who Cecily Addison is.'

'Of course.'

Cashin went back to Carol. 'Lots of cops coming,' he said. 'Going to be a long morning.'

'I'm paid for four hours.'

'Should be enough. What was he like?'

'Fine. Good boss. I knew what he wanted, did the job. Bonus at Christmas. Month's pay.'

'No problems?'

Eyes on him, yellow flecks in the brown. 'I keep the place like a hospital,' she said. 'No problems at all.'

'You wouldn't have any reason to try to kill him, would you?'

Carol made a sound, not quite a laugh. 'Me? Like I'd kill my job? I'm a late starter, still got two kids on the tit, mate. There's no work around here.'

They sat on the steps in the still enclosure, an early winter morning, quiet, just birdsounds, cars on the highway, and a coarse tractor somewhere.

'Jesus,' said Carol, 'I feel so, it's just getting to me...I could make us some coffee.'

Cashin was tempted. 'Better not,' he said. 'Can't touch anything. They'd come down on me like a tanker of pigshit. But I'll take a smoke off you.'

Weakness, smoking. Life was weakness, strength was the exception. Their smoke hung in sheets, golden where it caught the sun.

A sound, just a pinprick at first. The dickheads, thought Cashin. They were coming with sirens.

'Cromarty cops'll take a full statement, Carol,' he said. 'They'll be in charge of this but ring me if there's anything you want to talk about, okay?'

'Okay.'

They sat.

'If he lives,' said Cashin, 'it's because you got to work on time.'

Carol didn't say anything for a while. 'Reckon I'll keep getting paid?'

'Till things are settled, sure.'

They listened to the sirens coming up the hill, turning into the driveway, getting louder. Three squad cars, much too close together, came into the forecourt, braked, sent gravel flying.

The passenger door of the first car opened and a middle-aged man got out. He was tall, dark hair combed back. Senior Detective Rick Hopgood. Cashin had met him twice, civil exchanges. He walked towards them. Cashin stood.

The whupping of a helicopter, coming out of the east.

'End of shift,' said Hopgood. 'You can get back to Port.'

Irrational heat behind his eyes. Cashin wanted to punch him. He didn't say anything, looked for the chopper, walked around the house to the far hedge and watched it settle on the paddock, a hard surface, a dry autumn in a dry year. The local male medic was waiting. Three men got out, unloaded a stretcher. They went around the stables and into the house through a side door.

'Take offence?'

Hopgood, behind him.

'At what?' said Cashin.

'Didn't mean to be short,' said Hopgood.

Cashin looked at him. Hopgood offered a smile, yellowing teeth, big canines.

'No offence taken,' said Cashin.

'Good on you,' said Hopgood. 'Draw on your expertise if needed?'

28

'It's one police force,' said Cashin.

'That's the attitude,' said Hopgood. 'Be in touch.'

The medics came out with the stretcher, tubes in Bourgoyne. They didn't hurry. What could be done had been done. After the stretcher was loaded, the local woman said a few words to one of the city team, both impassive. He would be the doctor.

The doctor got in. The machine rose, turned for the metropolis, flashed light.

Cashin said goodbye to Carol Gehrig, drove down the curving avenue of Lombardy poplars.

'CAUGHT him yet?'

'Not as far as I know, Mrs Addison,' said Cashin. 'How did you hear?'

'The radio, my dear. What's happening to this country? Man attacked in his bed in the peaceful countryside. Never used to happen.'

Cecily Addison was in her after-lunch position in front of the fireplace in her office, left hand waving a cigarette, right hand touching her long nose, her brushed-back white hair. Cecily had been put out to graze in Port Monro by her firm in Cromarty. She arrived at work at 9.30 am, read the newspapers, drank the first of many cups of tea, saw a few clients, mostly about wills, bothered people, walked home for lunch and a few glasses of wine.

On the way back to the office, she dropped in on anyone who wasn't quick enough to disappear.

'Sit down,' she said. 'Don't know what the world's coming to. Read the paper today?' She pointed at her desk.

Cashin reached for the Cromarty *Herald*. The front-page headlines said:

**ANGER MOUNTS
ON CRIME WAVE**
Community calls for curfew

'Curfew, mind you,' said Cecily. 'That's not the way we want to go. Can't have Neighbourhood Watch calling the shots. Old buggers with nothing better to do than stickybeak. Neighbourhood bloody Nazis.'

Cashin read the story. Outrage at public meeting. Call for curfew on teenagers. Epidemic of burglaries and car thefts. Five armed robberies in two months. Sharp rise in assaults. Shop windows broken in the Whalers Mall. Lawless element in community. Time for firm action.

'Aimed at the Abos,' said Cecily, 'always is. Every few years they get on to it again. You'd think the white trash were all at choir practice of a Saturday night. I can tell you, forty-four years in the courts in Cromarty, I've seen more Abos fitted up than I've had hot dinners.'

'Not by the police, surely?' said Cashin.

Cecily laughed herself into a coughing fit. Cashin waited.

'I hate to say this,' Cecily said, taking the newspaper. 'Don't mind telling you I've voted Liberal all my life. But since this rag changed hands its mission in life is to get the Libs back in Cromarty. And that means bagging blacks every chance they get.'

'Interesting,' said Cashin. 'I want to ask you about Charles Bourgoyne. I gather you pay his bills.'

Cecily didn't want to change the subject.

'Never thought I'd say something like that,' she said. 'Hope my dad's not listening. You know Bob Menzies didn't have a house to live in when he left Canberra?'

'I didn't know that, no. I'm a bit short of time.'

A lie. Cashin knew how hard the ex-Prime Minister had done it because Cecily told him the story once or twice a month.

'Paid for his own phone calls, Bob Menzies. Sitting up there in the Lodge in Canberra, when he rang his old mum, he put a coin in a box. Little money box. When it was full, he gave it to Treasury. Went into general revenue. Catch today's pollies doing that? Take a coin out more likely. Rorters and shicers to a man. Did I tell you they wanted me to stand for Parliament? Told em, thanks very much, I'm already paid for being involved with crooks.'

'Charles Bourgoyne,' said Cashin. 'I've come about him. You pay his bills.'

Cecily blinked. 'Indeed I do. Known Charles for a very long time. Clients of the firm, Dick and Charles, Bourgoyne & Cromie, we did all their work.'

'Bourgoyne & Cromie's a bit before my time. Who's Dick?'

'Charles's dad. Bit of a playboy, Dick, but he ran the firm like a corner shop, argue the toss over a couple of quid. Not that he needed to. Go anywhere in this country, all the Pacific, bloody New Zealand, B&C engines everywhere. Put the lights on all over the outback. Powered the shearing stands, made a mint after the war, I can tell you. Whole world crying out for generators.'

'What happened?'

'Dick kicked the bucket and Charles sold the business to these Pommy bastards. They never intended to keep the factory going. Just wanted to cut out the competition.'

Cecily was staring out of the window, smoke curling through her fingers. 'Tragedy,' she said. 'I remember the day they told everyone. Half Cromarty out of work at one fell swoop. Never worked again, most of them.'

She scratched where an eyebrow had been. 'Still, can't blame Charles. They gave him assurances. No one blamed him.'

'About the bills.'

'Bills, yes. Since old Percy Crake had his stroke. Attend to matters on his behalf. Not that Charles couldn't do it himself. Just likes to pretend he's got better things to do.'

Cecily took a final vicious drag on her cigarette and, without looking, inserted the butt into the vase of flowers on the mantelpiece. A hiss, the sound of silk brushing silk. Mrs McKendrick, her ancient secretary, put flowers in the two rooms twice a week, first emptying urns full of foul beer-dark water and Cecily's swollen cigarette ends.

'Who'd try to kill him?' said Cashin.

'Some passing hoon, I suppose. Country's turning into America. Kill people for a few dollars, kill them for nothing. Thrills.' A bulge moved in her cheeks, suggested something trying to escape. 'Drugs,' she said. 'I blame it on drugs.'

'What about close to home? Someone who knew him?'

'Around here? If Charles Bourgoyne departs, it'll be the biggest funeral since old Dora Campbell kicked it, now that was a send-off. A lovely man, Charles Bourgoyne, lovely. They don't make gentlemen like that any more. He was a catch, I can tell you. Still, the girls all had long teeth by the time he married Susan Kingsley. They say old Dick told him to get married or kiss the fortune goodbye. Said he'd give it to the Cromarty old-age home.'

'What happened to Erica's father?'

'Erica and Jamie's father. Bobby Kingsley. Car smash. Had another woman with him unfortunately.'

'Charles have enemies?'

'Well, who knows? Bourgoyne Trust's put hundreds of kids through uni. Plus Charles shells out to anyone comes along. Schools, art gallery, the Salvos, the RSL, you name it. Bailed out the footy club umpteen times.'

'How does attending to Bourgoyne matters work?'

'Work?'

'The mechanics of it.'

'Oh. Well, all the bills come here, credit card, everything. Every month, we send Charles a statement, he ticks them off, sends it back, we pay them out of a trust account. Pay the wages too.'

'So you've got a record of all his financial dealings?'

'Just his bills.'

'From how far back?'

'Not long. I suppose it's seven, eight years. Since Crake's stroke.'

'Can I see your records?'

'Confidential,' she said. 'Between solicitor and client.'

'Client's been bashed and left for dead,' said Cashin.

Cecily blinked a few times. 'Not going to get me in trouble with the Law Institute this? Don't want to have to ask bloody Rees for advice.'

'Mrs Addison, it's what you have to do. If you don't, we'll get a court order today.'

'Yes,' she said, 'I suppose that changes things a bit. I'll tell Mrs McKendrick to make copies. Can't see what help it'll be. You should be out looking for bloody druggies. What's stolen from the house?'

'The people who work at Bourgoyne's,' said Cashin, 'what about their pay now?'

Cecily raised her pencilled eyebrows. 'He's not dead, you know. They'll be paid until someone instructs me to stop. What would you expect?'

Cashin got up. 'The worst. That's what police life teaches you.'

'Cynical, Joe. In my experience, and I say that with...'

'Thank you, Mrs Addison. I'll send someone for the copies. Where's Jamie Bourgoyne?'

'Drowned in Tasmania. Years ago.'

'Not a lucky family then.'

'No. Money can't buy it. And it ends if Charles dies. The line's broken. The Bourgoyne line's ended.'

The street was quiet, sunlight on the pale stone of the library. It had been the Mechanics' Institute when it opened in the year carved above the door: 1864. Three elderly women were going up the steps, in single file, left hands on the metal balustrade. He could see their delicate ankles. Old people were like racehorses – too much depending on too little, the bloodline the critical factor.

The Cashin bloodline didn't bear thinking about.

'I CAN'T fix stuff like this for you, Bern,' said Cashin. 'I can't fix anything. Sam's in shit because he's bad news and now he has to cop it.'

They were in a shed like an aircraft hangar at his cousin Bern Doogue's place outside Kenmare, a town twenty kilometres from Port Monro with a main street of boarded-up shops, two lingering pubs, a butcher, a milk bar and a video hire.

Farmland had once surrounded the village of Kenmare like a green sea. Long backyards had run down to paddocks with milk cows oozing dung, to potato fields dense with their pale grenades. Then the farms were subdivided. Hardiplank houses went up on three-acre blocks, big metal sheds out the back. Now the land produced nothing but garbage and children, many with red hair. The blocks were weekend parking lots for the big rigs that rumbled in from every direction on Saturdays – Macks, Kenworths, Mans, Volvos, eighteen-speed transmission, 1800-litre tank, the owners' names in flowery script on the doors, the unshaven, unslept drivers sitting two metres off the ground, spaced out and listening to songs of lost love and loneliness.

The truckies had bought their blocks when land was cheap, fuel was cheap, freight rates were good and they were young and paunchless. Now they couldn't see their pricks without a mirror, the trucks sucked fifty-dollar notes, the freight companies screwed them till they had to drive six days, some weeks seven, to make the repayments.

Cashin stood in the shed door and watched Bern splitting wood on his new machine, a red device that stood on splayed legs like a moon lander. He picked up a section of log, dropped it on the table against a thick steel spike, hit the trigger with a boot. A hydraulic ram slammed a splitter blade into the wood, cleaving it in half.

'Well, Jesus,' said Bern, 'what's the use of havin a fuckin copper in the family, I ask you.'

'No use at all,' Cashin said.

'Anyway, it's not like it's Sam's idea. He's with these two Melbourne kids, city kids, the one breaks the fuckin car window with a bottle.'

'Bern, Sam's got Buckley's. I'll ring a lawyer, she's good, she'll keep him out of jail.'

'What's that gonna cost? Fuckin arm?'

'It'll cost what it costs. Otherwise, tell him to ask for the duty solicitor. Where'd you get this wood?'

Bern put fingers under his filthy green beanie, exposed his black widow's peak, scratched his scalp. He had the Doogue nose – big, hooked. It was unremarkable in youth, came with age to dominate the male faces.

'Joe,' he said, 'is that a cop kind of question?'

'I don't care a lot about wood crime. It's good-looking stuff.'

'Fuckin prime beef, mate. Beefwood. Not your rotten Mount Gambier shit.'

'How much?'

'Seventy.'

'Find your own lawyer.'

'That's a special fuckin family price. Mate, this stuff, it runs out the fuckin door.'

'Let it run,' Cashin said. 'Got to go.' He walked.

'Hey, hey, Jesus, Joe, don't be so fuckin difficult.'

'Say hello to Leeane for me,' Cashin said. 'Christ knows what she did to deserve you. Must be something in another life.'

'Joe. Mate. Mate.'

Cashin was at the door. 'What?'

'Give and take, mate.'

'Haven't been talking to my mum, have you?'

'Nah. Your mum's too good for us. How's sixty, you tee up the lawyer? Split, delivered, that's fuckin cost, no labour, I'm takin a knock.'

'Four for two hundred,' Cashin said. 'Neatly stacked.'

'Shit, takin food out of your own family's mouths. He's up next week Wednesday.'

'I'll ring with an appointment time.'

Bern smacked on another log, stamped on the trigger. There was a bang, bits of wood went everywhere. 'Fuck,' he said. He pulled a big wood sliver out of the front of his greasy army surplus jumper.

'This place's a model of workplace safety,' Cashin said. 'Be on my way.'

He went out into the grey day, into Bern's two-acre backyard, a graveyard of cars, utes, trucks, machinery, windows, doors, sinks, toilet bowls, basins, second-hand timber, bricks. Bern followed him to his vehicle, parked in a clearing.

'Listen, Joe, there's somethin else,' he said. 'Debbie says the Piggot kid, I forget his name, there's hundreds of em, she says he's sellin stuff at school.'

Cashin got in, wound down the window. 'Got something against drugs, Bern? Since when?'

Bern screwed up his eyes, scratched his head through the beanie with black-rimmed nails. 'That's totally fuckin different, we're talking about sellin hard stuff to kids here.'

38

'Why'd she tell you?'

'Well, not me. Told her mum.'

'Why?'

Bern cleared his throat and spat, bullethole lips, a sound like a peashooter. 'Leeane found some stuff. Not Debbie's, just holdin it for this other girl bought it from a Piggot.'

Cashin started the vehicle. 'Bern,' he said, 'you don't want your cousin the cop cracking down on teenage drug-taking in Kenmare. Think about it. Think about the Piggots. There's an army of them.'

Bern thought about it. 'Yeah, well, that's probably the strength of it. Mark me for the dog straight off, wouldn't the bastards. Boong dog. Mind you, comes to Doogues against Piggots, they wouldn't take a round off us.'

'We don't want it to come to that. I'll call you.'

'Wait, wait. You can do somethin else for me.'

'What?'

'Put the hard word on Debbie. She won't listen to her mum and I'm a fuckin non-starter.'

'I thought she was just holding the stuff?'

Bern shrugged, looked away. 'To be on the safe side,' he said. 'Can't hurt, can it?'

Cashin knew there was no way out. Next he would be reminded of how Bern had risked death by jumping onto the back of mountainous, cretinous Terry Luntz and hung on like a chimp on a gorilla, choking the school bully with a skinny forearm until he relaxed his deadly squeeze.

'What time's she get back from school?' Cashin said.

'About four.'

'I'll come round one day, point out the dangers.'

'You're a good bloke, Joe.'

'No, I'm not. I just don't want to hear about fucking Terry Luntz again. He would've let me go.'

Bern smiled his sly, dangerous Doogue smile. 'Never. Blue in the face, tongue stickin out the side of your mouth. You had fuckin seconds left.'

'In that case, what took you so long?'

'Prayin for guidance, mate. What excuse you cunts got for takin so long to catch our beloved Mr Charlie Bourgoyne's killer?'

'The victim's not being squeezed by a fat boy. There's no hurry. What've you got against Bourgoyne?'

'Nothin. The local saint. Everyone loves Charlie. Rich and idle. You know my dad used to work there, Bourgoyne & Cromie? Charlie sold it out under em. Shot the fuckin horse.'

Cashin passed three vehicles on the way home, knew them all. At the last crossroads, two ravens pecking at vermilion sludge turned on him the judgmental eyes of old men in a beaten pub.

IT WAS darkening when Cashin reached home, the wind ruffling the trees on the hill, strumming the corrugated iron roof. He got the fire going, took out a six-pack of Carlsberg, put on *L'elisir d'amore,* Donizetti, sank into the old chair, cushion in the small of his back. Tired in the trunk, hurting in the pelvis, pains down his legs, he swallowed two aspirins with the first swig of beer.

Life's short, son, don't drink any old piss.

Singo's advice, Singo always drank Carlsberg or Heineken.

Cashin sat and drank, stared at nothing, hearing Domingo, thinking about Vickie, about the boy. Why had she called him Stephen? Stephen would be nine now, Cashin could make the calculation, he knew the day, the night, the moment. And he had never spoken to him, never touched him, never been closer than twenty metres to him. Vickie would not bring him to the hospital when Cashin asked her to. 'He's got a father and it isn't you,' she said.

Nothing moved her.

All he wanted was to see him, talk to him. He didn't know why. What he knew was that the thought of the boy ached in him like his broken bones.

At 7 pm, on the second beer, he put on the television.

In what is feared to be another drug underworld killing, a 50-year-old Melbourne accountant, Andrew Gabor, of

Kew, was this morning shot dead in front of his fifteen-year-old daughter outside exclusive St Theresa's girls' school in Malvern.

Footage of a green BMW outside the school, men in black overcoats beside it. Cashin recognised Villani, Birkerts, Finucane.

Two gunmen fled the scene in a Ford Transit van, later found in Elwood.

A van being winched onto the police flatbed tow truck to be taken to the forensic science centre.

Police appealed to anyone who saw two men wearing dark clothing and baseball caps in the van or at or near the scene around 7.30 am to contact CrimeStoppers.

It is believed that police today questioned Mr Gabor's nephew, Damian Gabor, a rave party and rock concert entrepreneur. In 2002, Mr Gabor was found not guilty of assaulting Anthony Metcalf, a drug dealer later found dead in a rubbish skip in Carnegie. He had been shot seven times.

On the monitor behind the news reader Cashin saw The Heights filmed from the television helicopter, vehicles all over the forecourt, the search of the grounds in progress.

Following another crime of violence, the seventy-six-year-old head of one of the state's best-known families is tonight fighting for his life in an intensive-care unit after being brutally assaulted at his home outside Cromarty.

Charles Bourgoyne was this morning found near death in the sitting room of the family mansion. He was flown to King George's Hospital by helicopter.

Mr Bourgoyne, noted for his philanthropy, is the son

of Richard Bourgoyne, one of the founders of Bourgoyne
& Cromie, legendary engine manufacturers. Charles
Bourgoyne sold the family firm to British interests in
1976. His twin older brothers both died in World War II,
one of them executed by the Japanese.

Homicide investigators believe Mr Bourgoyne, who was
alone in the house, may have been the victim of a burglary
turned vicious. Items of value are missing from the house.

Hopgood on camera, outside The Heights, wind
moving his straight hair.

'This is a savage attack on a much-loved and defenceless
man.

We are committing all our resources to find those
responsible for this terrible act and we appeal to anyone
with information to come forward.'

King George's Hospital tonight said that Mr
Bourgoyne's condition was critical.

Cashin reached for the envelope with the business
statements from Cecily Addison. This has nothing to do
with me, he thought. I'm the station commander in Port
Monro, staff of four.

Old habits, curiosity. He started with the most recent
statement. Then he heard the name.

Australia's newest political party, United Australia, today
elected lawyer and Aboriginal activist Bobby Walshe to
lead it into the federal election.

Cashin looked at the television.

The new party, a coalition of Greens, Democrats and
independents that has drawn support from disaffected

43

Labor and Liberal supporters, will field candidates in all electorates.

Bobby Walshe appeared on camera. Handsome, sallow, hawk-nosed, just a hint of curl in his dark hair.

'It's a great honour for me to be chosen by so many dedicated and talented people to lead United Australia. This is a watershed day. From now on, Australians have a real political choice. The time when many Australians saw voting for one of the small parties as a waste of a vote are over. We're not small. We're not single-issue. We offer a real alternative to the tired, copycat policies of the two political machines that have dominated our political lives for so long.'

Bobby Walshe had been the smartest kid in Cashin's class at primary school and that hadn't stopped him being called a boong and a coon and a nigger.

The Bourgoyne payment statements didn't make any sense. Cashin's attention wandered, he put them back in the file, opened another drink and thought about what to eat.

THE HILL was lost in morning mist, a damp silence on the land. Cashin took a route towards the Corrigan boundary, visibility no more than thirty metres, the dogs appearing and disappearing, bounding patches of dark in the pale-grey world.

At the fence, there was a path, overgrown. He had walked it often as a boy, it was the direct way to the creek. In childhood memory, the creek was more like a river – broader, deeper, thrillingly dangerous in flood. The dogs were behind him when he made his way through the vegetation, crossed the puddles. On the other side, he whistled for them and they rushed by and led the way up the slope to the old Corrigan house.

Trespassing, Cashin thought.

The dogs had their heads down, a new place, new scents, interested-puzzled flicks of tails. He walked around the house, looked through the windows. Doors, skirting boards, floorboards, mantelpieces, tiles – all seemed intact. The place hadn't been looted like Tommy Cashin's ruined house. If there were new owners, they wouldn't need to spend much to get it liveable.

They walked through the yellow grass as far as Den Millane's fence, went down. Above the creek, Cashin found the remains of a fence, rusted wire, a few grey and riven posts lying down, possibly the boundary Den talked about. It was around two hundred metres, a bit more perhaps.

Did he want to claim this line?

Ya keep what's bloody yours.

Yes, he did want to claim it.

He walked across the creek, down the narrow twisting path through the poplars, into the rabbit grounds, then turned for home. It was fully light when they approached the house, but still an hour before the sun would burn off the mist. He was thinking about Kendall. What did being raped do to you? A male cop, off-duty, had been grabbed by three men in Sydney, out in the western suburbs, taken to an old drive-in. They handcuffed him to a screen pylon, cut off his jeans with a Stanley knife, carved swastikas into his buttocks, his back.

Then they raped him.

A cop called Gerard told Cashin the story one night, in the car. They were parked, eating kebabs.

The bloke never came back to work. Went to Darwin. They say he topped himself up there.

Gerard, dark-faced and handsome, dead-black hair, a mole on his cheek.

Got the cunts but. Done it through a ring, big fucking stupid lead thing, home-made ring. Melted sinkers. The cop could draw it.

What'd they get?

Death penalty. The one drowned in the river. Homebush. Other two, murder-suicide. Very ugly scene.

Gerard had smiled. When he smiled he showed some inner-lip, an intimate colour, vaginal.

Before Cashin did, the dogs saw Rebb sitting on the old garden bench. They charged.

Rebb was smoking a hand-rolled, flat, as much paper as tobacco. He was shaven, hair damp.

The dogs were all wag and twist, they liked Rebb, but then they liked most people.

'Put stuff in the wash machine,' Rebb said, cigarette in

46

the corner of his mouth, a big hand for each dog. 'That okay?'

'Any time,' said Cashin. 'Up early?'

'No.'

'I'll make some breakfast when I've showered.'

'Got food,' said Rebb. He didn't look at Cashin, he was intent on the dogs. He had said the same thing the night before.

'Scrambled eggs,' said Cashin. 'You make it for one, might as well make it for ten.'

When he was clean and dressed, he put cutlery, bread and butter, Vegemite, jam, on the table, cooked the food, found Rebb outside with the dogs. Rebb didn't eat like a swaggie. He kept his elbows at his sides, ate with his mouth closed, slowly, ate every morsel.

'Good,' he said. 'Thank you.'

'Fill up on the bread.'

Rebb cut a thick slice. He spread butter, put on a coal-dark seam of Vegemite.

'You can stay here if you like,' Cashin said. 'Won't cost you. Ten minutes' walk to the cow job.'

Rebb looked at him, nothing, black eyes. He nodded. 'Do that then.'

They drove around to Den Millane's, not a word spoken. Den heard them coming, he was at the gate. He shook hands with Rebb.

'Pay's nothin fancy,' he said. 'Do it myself, bloody knee wasn't crook. Know cows?'

'A bit, yeah.'

Cashin left them, drove to his mother's house, twenty minutes. The roads were thin strips of pot-holed bitumen, lacy at the edges, room for one vehicle, someone had to give way, put two wheels on the rutted verge. But, generally, both vehicles did, and local drivers raised their hands to each other. He passed potato fields and dairy farms where the sliding-jawed animals turned soft eyes. From Beacon Hill, the land sloped to the sea, peaty soil the colour of chocolate when ploughed, lying naked before the south-westerly wind and the wild winter gales off the Southern Ocean. Early settlers planted cypress trees and hedges as windbreaks around their houses. It worked to some extent but the displaced wind took its revenge. Trees, shrubs, sheds, tanks, windmills, dunnies, dog kennels, chickenhouses, old car bodies – everything in its path sloped to leeward.

Cashin parked in the driveway, went around the back, saw his mother through the kitchen window. When he opened the back door, Sybil said, 'I've been thinking about you, living in that ruin. After what we put in with you kids, your dad and me.'

She was arranging flowers in a large squarish pottery jug, brown and purple. 'That vase,' Cashin said. 'Could that be a rejected prototype for storing nuclear waste?'

His mother ignored the question. Outside, his stepfather appeared from the shed, wearing white overalls, gloves, a full-face mask, a tank on his back. He began spraying the rose arbour. Mist drifted.

'Do the roses like Harry bombing them with Agent Orange?' Cashin said.

She stood back to admire her work, a small, trim woman, strong swept-back hair. All the size genes in Cashin and his brother, Michael, came from their father, Mick Cashin.

'Charles Bourgoyne,' she said. 'What are you doing about that?'

'Doing what can be done.'

'I'll never understand humans. Why didn't they just take what they wanted? Why did they have to bash an old man? What could he do to resist them?'

'I've giving up on the understanding part,' said Cashin. 'The question you want answered isn't why, it's who.'

His mother shook her head. 'Well, on another matter,' she said, eyes on the arrangement, moving her fingers. 'Michael's bought a unit in Melbourne. Docklands. On the water. Two bedrooms, one-and-a-half bathrooms.'

'A clean person, Michael,' said Cashin. 'Very clean. What do you do in the half bathroom?'

'Pour the tea,' she said. 'Just made.'

He poured tea into handmade mugs that tilted when at rest. His mother bought things at outdoor markets: terrible watercolour paintings, salt and pepper cellars in the shape of toadstools, placemats woven from plastic grocery bags, hats made of felted dog hair.

'Michael's in Melbourne so much he says he might as well have somewhere to keep his clothes,' she said.

'The spare set of clothes that would be.'

His mother sighed. 'Give credit where it's due, that's what you haven't learned, Joseph.'

'Take credit where it's offered, I've learned that. Why do roses need that chemical shit Harry's spraying?'

'You never swore. Michael picked it up at school, the first day, came home and said a swearword. I went down there, gave that Killeen man a few words of my own. Never trusted him and proved right. Mother's instinct.'

'I should have learned to swear early,' said Cashin. 'By now I might have half a bathroom at Docklands. I'm going to fix up the house.'

'Are you mad? Why?'

'To live in. As a step up from living in a ruin.'

'It's haunted.' She shuddered in a theatrical way. 'Built by a madman. Leave it alone. You should sell it.'

'I like the place. I'm going to clear up the garden.'

'I thought this was temporary? For you to get better.'

Cashin finished his tea. 'Life's pretty temporary. How's uni?'

'Don't change the subject. I should have gone earlier. Wasted years.'

'Wasted how?'

She came to the kitchen table and patted his cheek twice, gave it a final sharp slap. 'I only want the best for you,' she said. 'You set your sights so low. The police force, I ask you. Stay here a moment longer than you need to, you'll be stuck forever. Game over.'

'Where do you get that from?'

'What?'

'Game over?'

'Old before your time,' she said. 'Why don't you sign up for a course at uni? Be among young people. Stay fresh.'

'I'll kill myself first,' Cashin said.

Sybil put fingers to his mouth. 'Don't say that. The closed mind. It's the older generation's supposed to have that.'

'Got to go,' he said. 'Be among young people. Arrest them.'

'Turn it into a joke, you get that from your father, that's pure Cashin. Even a tragedy's only a tragedy for five minutes, then it's a joke.'

They went out. Harry was misting the arbour, the cattle dog standing behind him, looking up, faithfully breathing in the fumes.

'So the dog's expendable?' said Cashin. 'Collateral damage.'

At the gate, his mother said, 'It's a pity you don't have children, Joseph. Children settle people down.'

The sentences stopped Cashin in his tracks, filled him with wonder. How could she of all people say that?

'How do you know I don't have children?' he said.

'Oh, you.' She held his arms and he bent to kiss her on the cheek. For many years, he could not kiss her.

'Did I ever tell you I thought you were going to be the bright one?' she said.

'I am the bright one,' he said. 'You're confusing me with the rich one. One of Bern's boys is in trouble in Melbourne.'

'It'll be that Sam, right?'

'Right.'

'What kind of trouble?'

'Theft from a parked car. Him and two others.'

'What can you do?'

'Nothing probably.'

'The Doogues. I always thank the Lord I've got no ties with them.'

'You're a Doogue. Bern is your nephew. He's your brother's son. How can you not have ties with them?'

'Ties, dear, ties. I don't have any ties with them.'

'Game over,' said Cashin. 'Bye, Syb.'

'Bye, darling.'

Harry waved a gloved hand at him, slowly, like a polar explorer saying a final sad goodbye.

DRIVING TO Port Monro on a cold day, overcast, Cashin thought about his mother in the caravan, saw her sitting at a fold-down table topped with marbled green Formica edged with an aluminium strip. She had a plastic glass in one hand, yellow wine in it, a cigarette in the other hand, a filter cigarette held close to her fingernails, which were painted pink, chipped. Her nose was peeling from sunburn. There were blonde sunstreaks in her hair and it was heavy with salt from swimming, pieces fallen apart, he could see her scalp. She drank from the glass and liquid ran out of her mouth, down her chin, fell on her teeshirt. She wiped her chest with her cigarette hand and the cigarette touched her face, the glowing tip dislodged, stuck to her shirt. She looked down at the burn opening like a flower. She seemed to wait forever, then she carefully tilted her glass, poured wine over it. He remembered the smells of burnt cotton and burnt skin and wine filling the small space and how he felt sick, went out into the sub-tropical night.

Some time after Cashin's father's death, he didn't know how long, his mother had packed two suitcases and they left the farm outside Kenmare. He was twelve. His brother was at university on his scholarship. At the first stop for petrol, his mother told him to call her Sybil. He didn't know what to say. People didn't call their mothers by their names.

They spent the next three years on the road, never

staying anywhere for long. When he thought about those times later, Cashin realised that in the first year Sybil must have had money: they stayed in hotels and motels, in a holiday shack near the beach for a few months. Then she started taking jobs in pubs, roadhouses, all sorts of places, and they lived in rented rooms, granny flats in people's backyards, on-site caravans. In his memory, she always seemed to be drinking, always either laughing or crying. Sometimes she forgot to buy food and some nights she didn't come home till long after midnight. He remembered lying awake, hearing noises outside, trying not to be frightened.

The turn-off to Port Monro. Light rain falling.

Cashin's shift started at noon, there was time for coffee. He bought the paper at the service station, parked outside the Dublin, hadn't been there for a while. You couldn't go to the same place too often, people noticed.

The narrow room was empty, summer over, the long cold peace on the town. 'Medium black for the cop who pays,' said the man sitting behind the counter. 'My customer of the day.'

His name was Leon Gadney, a dentist from Adelaide whose male lover had been found knifed to death in a park near the river, possibly killed by one of the sexual crazies for which Adelaide was famous, possibly killed by policemen who thought the crazies were doing a public service when they killed homosexuals.

'You could close in winter,' said Cashin. 'Save on electricity.'

'What would I do?' said Leon.

'Go to Noosa, chat to other rich retired dentists. It's warm up there.'

'Fuck warm. And I'd like to go on record that I'm not a retired dentist. Ex-dentist, former dentist, now impoverished barista and short-order cook.'

He delivered the coffee. 'Want a nice almond bickie?'

'No, thanks. Watching the weight.'

Leon returned to his seat, lit a cigarette. 'In a certain light, you're not bad looking,' he said. 'And here we are, virile single men marooned on an island of old women in sandals.'

Cashin didn't look up. He was reading about police corruption in the city, in the drug squad. The members had been selling drugs they'd confiscated. They had originally supplied the ingredients to make the drugs. 'You're very distinguished, Leon,' he said. 'But I've got too much going on, I couldn't concentrate.'

'Well, think about it,' said Leon. 'I've got good teeth.'

Cashin went to work, dealt with a complaint from a man about a neighbour's tree, a report of a vandalised bench in the wetlands. A woman with a black eye came in – she wanted Cashin to warn her husband. At 2.15, the primary school rang to say a mother had seen someone lurking on the block across the road.

He parked a way from the school, went down a driveway and looked over the fence. High yellow grass. Someone had thrown a concrete slab and got no further, weeds covering the heap of building sand. There was a small shed, a panel van parked behind it.

Cashin walked back down the drive and onto the block, approached the vehicle. The windows were fogged glass, no one visible in the cab. He rapped on the roof with knuckles.

Silence. He bounced his fist.

'Fuck off!' A male.

'Police,' said Cashin.

The vehicle moved. He stood back and he could see a figure climbing over the bench seat. The driver's window came down a few centimetres: eyes, dark eyebrows, strands of black hair.

54

'Just takin a nap.'

'This your property, sir?' Cashin was showing his badge.

'I'm the builder.'

'Not much building going on.'

'Startin soon as he gets his finance.'

'You local, sir?'

'Cromarty.'

'I'd like you to step out of the vehicle, sir, and show me some ID.'

'Listen, takin a nap on a buildin job, what's the fuckin crime?'

'Out of the vehicle, please, sir. With your ID.'

The man turned, reaching backwards. Cashin saw skin colour, the man was half-naked, he was looking for his pants.

Cashin stood well back, hand inside his jacket, eased the gun in the clip.

The man moved, struggled, he couldn't get his pants on. 'Listen,' he said through the gap. 'Somethin a bit private goin on here, y'know. Gissus a break, will you?'

'Get out and put your pants on,' said Cashin. 'Sir.'

The door opened. A thin man, late twenties. He moved his legs out, open flannel shirt over a teeshirt, no shoes, hole in a red sock, one leg in his denims, stood in the weeds to pull them up, zip. He had a pimple on a thigh.

He reached inside, found a wallet, offered it. 'Driver's, credit, all kinds of shit.'

'Put it on the roof,' Cashin said, 'and stand against the shed.'

'Jesus, mate, I'm just a fuckin brickie.'

He obeyed. Cashin took the wallet, looked at cards. Allan James Morris, an address in Cromarty. He wrote it down. 'Phone number?'

He gave Cashin a mobile number.

'Now if you'll help the person with you get out, I'd like some ID there too,' said Cashin.

Morris walked back to the van, opened the back door, there was an exchange. A girl in jeans and a short pleated pink jacket got out. She was no more than fifteen, dark hair, pretty, it wouldn't last. Her lips were puffy, lipstick smeared.

'ID, please,' said Cashin.

She opened a wallet, offered a card. Cashin looked at it.

'Not you,' he said, flicked the card back across the bonnet. 'Got some real ID? We can do this at the station. Get your mum and dad in.'

She pouted, eye-flick to Morris, produced another card, school ID with a photograph: Stacey-Ann Gettigan.

'Fourteen, Stacey,' he said. 'In the back of a van with a grown man.'

'Just waggin,' she said. She folded her arms under her breasts. 'Not a crime.'

'What do you reckon, Allan?' Cashin said. 'Crime to be jumping a fourteen-year-old in your van?'

'Just kissin and that,' said Morris.

'Take your pants off to kiss? Kissing with your bum? You married, Allan?'

Morris scratched his head. He was in sunlight and Cashin saw dandruff motes fly into the still air. The girl was looking down, biting on a painted nail. 'Listen,' said Morris, 'no harm done, I swear.'

'Married, Allan?'

'Yeah. Sort of.'

'Sort of? They got that now? Do a sort of ceremony in church?'

Morris didn't want to look at Cashin. Cashin motioned to the girl to follow him. They went around the shed. He said, 'Got a complaint you'd like to make

56

against this man, Stacey? Made you do something against your will? Threaten you? This's your chance.'

She closed her eyes, shook her head. 'No. Nothin.'

'Sure? I'm going to write all this down, that I asked you. Want to talk somewhere else, on your own? A woman cop?'

'No,' she said.

Cashin went back and beckoned to Morris, walked down the block a few paces. The man came, not easy in his skin, a rabbitty look. They stood in the weeds. White clouds moved across the pools of rain on the concrete slab.

'What's she to you, then?' said Cashin.

'Cousin, some kind, I dunno exactly.'

'Yeah?'

'She's on at me all the time, come to me work even. I done nothin. Today's the first… anyway, nothin happened. I swear.'

'Not Deke Gettigan's granddaughter, is she?'

Morris scratched his head with both hands as if suddenly attacked by lice. 'Mate, they'll fuckin kill me,' he said. 'Please, mate.'

'Don't bring any more kids here to root, Allan,' said Cashin. 'Nowhere near here. There's an alert on your van from now on. And you're not the builder here, are you?'

'Me mate, he's kind of, he's the…'

'You come down this way to do a bit of building, that's building I'm talking about, not fucking under-age girls, you let me know, Allan. Then I'll tell the school they don't have to worry about a man with his cock out, he's just having a piss. Okay?'

'Right, sure. Thanks.'

Cashin looked back as he walked away. The girl held his eyes. She knew she was out of this, he wasn't going to dob them, and she smiled at him, bold, sexual, ancient wisdom.

AT THE station, Carl Wexler came out of the front door making flexing bodybuilder's movements. He was a year out of the academy, not stupid, third in his course, but a city boy, resentful about being posted away from the action.

Cashin lowered his window.

'Cromarty rang, boss,' Wexler said. 'Senior Hopgood for you.'

Cashin went in and rang.

'Your mate Inspector Villani sends his love,' said Hopgood. 'How is it that wogs have taken over this force?'

'Natural selection,' said Cashin. 'Survival of the best dressed.'

'Yeah, well, he's given me the benefit of his wog opinions. He wants you to ring.'

Cashin didn't say anything. Hopgood put the phone down.

The city switch put Cashin straight through.

'How's retirement?' said Villani. 'I went down there once. Very nice. I hear the surfies call it the Blue Balls Coast.'

'Wimps,' Cashin said. 'What?'

'Joe, listen, this Bourgoyne was news to me but the media put that right. Then Commisioner Wicken yesterday explains to me how connected the step-daughter

58

is, senior partner at Rothacker Julian, the Labor Party's legal wing.'

'That now carries some weight in a homicide?'

'I'm finding out all kinds of stuff. Today Mr Pommy Commissioner Wicken gives me hints on conducting myself in public. Fashion tips too. What suit, what shirt, what shoes. I enjoyed that so very much.'

'So?'

'I want you on this.'

'I'm the cripple running Port Monro now. Send that prick Allen.'

'Joe, we are thinner than the Durex Phantom. Jantz, Campbell and Maguire, all retired in one month. DePiero quit, Tozer's on stress leave, your mate Allen, his wife buggered off with a butcher from Vic Market, took the kids. Now he's found some mystical shit, living in the fucking moment. I wouldn't send him to a Buddhist domestic.'

A pause.

'Also,' said Villani, 'when the newspapers get down there in a few days, you'll see the former drug squad's criminal mates are again killing each other. The big boss woman's supposed to have sacked all the dirtbags and elevated the cleanskins but whoopy do, here we go again. So I've got a number of people committed to the utterly pointless shit of trying to find out which particular cunt killed some other cunt for whose death we should be grateful. As a city. As a state. A country. As a fucking world.'

'I think you're over-excited,' said Cashin. 'On Bourgoyne, what's to show for the forensic geniuses you had here?'

'Bugger all. The alarm was off. No break-in, no prints, no weapon. No strange DNA. Don't know what's gone except the watch. There's locked drawers broken open in the study and his bedroom.'

'And him?'

'It's likely to be murder. Lives, he's a cabbage.'

'Did you ever ask yourself why they hit on the cabbage? What about the carrot? How about the Brussels sprout?'

'Let's leave the philosophy for the pub, gentlemen.'

It was a Singo saying, from the time before Rai Sarris.

'So what am I supposed to do?' said Cashin.

'This Rothacker Julian connection, we need a senior officer on the job. I don't want any fuck-ups. I'm new in the tower, Joe, I can feel the wind. This'll end up some dumb *In Cold Blood* thing, I feel it in my dick, it's just the in-between shit we have to manage.'

'What about Cromarty?'

'Fuck them. This is the commissioner speaking.'

'And I say no?'

'Listen, son, you are still a member of homicide. You're a member on holiday. Remember duty?'

'Some things about it, yes.'

'I'm glad I don't have to say any more.'

'You arsehole.'

'Come around to my office and repeat that to a senior officer,' said Villani. 'First, a talk with Ms Bourgoyne, the step-daughter. She's been asked to go down and take a look, should be there in about an hour. Cromarty's opening the place.'

'She's been interviewed?'

'Not really. What we need is for you to be with her when she sees the house. Find out what was in the drawers, if she can see anything else missing, anything unusual while she was there, any ideas she can give us.'

'Sure you need a senior officer? Why don't you just give your marvellously detailed instructions to some prick from traffic?'

'Sorry, sorry, sorry. Jesus, don't be so touchy.'

'What about other family?'

'No one close. There was a step-son, Erica's brother. She says he drowned in Tassie a long time ago.'

'She says?'

'We'll verify that. Okay? We'll get some prick from traffic to check that out. Give him detailed instructions.'

'Just asking.'

CASHIN DROVE out to the Bourgoyne house, up the steep road from the highway, through the gates, down the winding poplar drive, and parked in the same place as before. The gravel showed the marks of many vehicles.

He parked and waited, listened to the radio, thought about being on the road with his mother, the other children he met, some of them feral kids, not going to school, beach urchins, the white ones burnt dark brown or freckled and always shedding pieces of papery skin. He thought about the boy who taught him to surf, in New South Wales, it might have been Ballina. Gavin was the boy's name. He offered the use of a board with a big piece out of it.

'Shark, mate,' said Gavin. 'Chewed the bloke in half. He don't need it no more, you can have a lend of it.' When they left, Gavin gave him the board. Where was Gavin now? Where was the board? Cashin had loved that board, covered the gap with tape.

I'm bored here, love. We're going.

His mother had said before every move further north.

Cashin got out of the car to stretch his spine, walked in a circle. A vehicle was coming.

A black Saab came around the bend, parked next to the cruiser. The driver eased himself out, a big man, cropped hair, wearing jeans and a leather jacket, open.

'Hi,' he said. 'John Jacobs, Orton Private Security Group. I'm ex-SOG. Mind if I see the ID?'

Police Special Operations Group membership was supposed to bestow some kind of divinity that transcended being kicked out for cowardice or for turning out to be a violent psychopath.

Cashin looked at the cruiser. 'That's my car. Your idea is I could be a dangerous person stole a cop car?'

'Don't take anything for granted,' Jacobs said. 'Used to be standard police practice.'

'Still is,' said Cashin. 'And I'm the one who asks for ID. Let's see it.'

Jacobs gave him a closed-lips smile, then a glint of left canine while he took out a plastic card with a photograph. Cashin took his time looking at it, looking at Jacobs.

'You're keeping the lady waiting,' said Jacobs. 'Need better light? Sure you don't want back-up?'

'What's your job today?' said Cashin.

'I'm looking after Ms Bourgoyne. What do you reckon?'

Cashin gave back the card. Jacobs went around the car and opened the passenger door. A woman got out, a blonde, tall, thin, the wind moved her long hair. She raised a hand to control it. Early forties, Cashin guessed.

'Ms Bourgoyne?'

'Yes.' She was handsome, sharp features, grey eyes.

'Detective Cashin. Inspector Villani spoke to you, I understand.'

'Yes.'

'Do you mind if we have a look around? Without Mr Jacobs, if that's okay?'

'I don't know what to expect,' she said.

'It's always difficult,' said Cashin. 'But what we'll do is walk through the house. You have a good look, tell me if anything catches your eye.'

'Thank you. Well, let's go in the side door.'

She led the way around the verandah. On the east side was an expanse of raked gravel dotted with smooth boulders, ending in a clipped hedge. She opened a glass door to a quarry-tiled room with wicker chairs around low tables. There wasn't any sun but the room was warm.

'I'd like to get this over with as soon as possible,' said Erica.

'Of course. Did Mr Bourgoyne keep money on the premises?'

'I have no idea. Why would he?'

'People do. What's through that door?'

'A passage.'

She led the way into a wide passage. 'These are bedrooms and a sitting room,' she said and opened a door. Cashin went in and switched on the overhead light. It was a big room, curtains drawn, four pen-and-ink drawings in black frames on the walls. They were all by the same hand, suggestions of street scenes, severe, vertical lines, unsigned.

The bed was large, white covers, big pillows. 'There's nothing to steal here,' Erica said.

The next two rooms were near-identical. Then a bathroom and a small sitting room.

They went into the large hall, two storeys high, lit by a skylight. A huge staircase dominated the space. 'There's the big dining room and the small one,' said Erica.

'What's upstairs?'

'Bedrooms.'

Cashin looked into the dining rooms. They appeared undisturbed. At the door to the big sitting room, Erica stopped and turned to him.

'I'll go first,' he said.

The room smelled faintly of lavender and something else. The light from the high window lay on the carpet in front of where the slashed painting had hung. The blood-stain was hidden by a sheet of black plastic, taped down.

Cashin went over and opened the cedar armoire

against the left wall: whisky, brandy, gin, vodka, Pimms, Cinzano, sherries, liqueurs of all kinds, wine glasses, cut-glass whisky glasses and tumblers, martini glasses.

A small fridge held soda water, tonic, mineral water. No beer.

'Do you know what was kept in the desk?'

The small slim-legged table with a leather top stood against a wall.

Erica shrugged.

Cashin opened the left-hand drawer. Writing pads, envelopes, two fountain pens, two ink bottles. Cashin removed the top pad, opened it, held it up to the light. No impressions. The other drawer held a silver paperknife, a stapler, boxes of staples, a punch, paperclips.

'Why didn't they take the sound stuff?' she said.

Cashin looked at the Swedish equipment. It had been the most expensive on the market once.

'Too big,' he said. 'Was there a television?'

'In the other sitting room. My step-father didn't like television much.'

Cashin looked at the shelves of CDs beside the player. Classical music. Orchestral. Opera, dozens of disks. He removed one, put it in the slot, pressed the buttons.

Maria Callas.

The room's acoustics were perfect. He closed his eyes.

'Is this necessary?' said Erica.

'Sorry,' said Cashin. He pushed the OFF button. The sound of Callas seemed to linger in the high dark corners.

They left the room, another passage.

'That's the study,' she said.

He went in. A big room, three walls covered with photographs in dark frames, a few paintings, and the fourth floor-to-ceiling books. The desk was a curve of pale wood on square dark pillars tapering to nothing. The chair was modern too, leather and chrome. A more comfortable-looking version stood in front of the window.

The drawer locks of two heavy and tall wooden cabinets, six drawers each, had been forced, possibly with a crowbar. They had been left as found on the morning.

'Any idea what was in them?' said Cashin.

'No idea at all.'

Cashin looked: letters, papers. He walked around the walls, looked at the photographs. They seemed to be arranged chronologically and, to his eye, span at least seventy or eighty years – family groups, portraits, young men in uniform, weddings, parties, picnics, beach scenes, two men in suits standing in front of a group of men in overalls, a building plaque being unveiled by a woman wearing a hat.

'Which one's your step-father?' he said.

Erica took him on a tour, pointed at a smiling small boy, a youth in school uniform, in cricket whites, in a football team, a thin-faced young man in a dinner jacket, a man in middle age shaking hands with an older man. Charles Bourgoyne had aged slowly and well, not losing a single brushed hair.

'Then there are the horses,' she said, pointing. 'Probably more important than the people in his life.'

A wall of pictures of horses and people with horses. Dozens of finishing-post photographs, some sepia, some tinted, a few in colour. Charles Bourgoyne riding, leading, stroking, kissing horses.

'Your mother,' said Cashin. 'Is she still alive?'

'No. She died when I was young.'

Cashin looked at the bookshelves: novels, history, biography, rows of books about Japan and China, their art, culture. Above them were books about World War II, the war against Japan, about Australian prisoners of the Japanese.

There were shelves of pottery books, technical titles, three shelves.

They moved on.

'This is his bedroom,' said Erica Bourgoyne. 'I've never been into it and I don't think I'll change that now.'

Cashin entered a white chamber: bed, table, simple table lamp, small desk, four drawers open. The lower ones had been broken open. Through a doorway was a dressing room. He looked at Bourgoyne's clothes: jackets, suits, shirts on hangers, socks and underwear in drawers, shoes on a rack. Everything looked expensive, nothing looked new.

There was a red lacquered cupboard. He opened it and a clean smell of cedar filled his nostrils. Silken garments on hangers, a shelf with rolled-up sashes.

He thought of asking Erica to come in.

No.

Beyond the dressing room was a bathroom, walls and floor of slate, a wooden tub, coopered like a barrel, a toilet, a shower that was just two stainless-steel perforated plates, one that water fell from, one to stand on. There were bars of pale yellow soap and throwaway razors, shampoo. He opened a plain wooden cupboard: three stacks of towels, six deep, bars of soap, bags of razors, toilet paper, tissues.

He went back to Erica. They looked at another bedroom, like a room in a comfortable hotel. It had a small sitting room with two armchairs, a fireplace. There was another bathroom, old-fashioned, revealing nothing. At the end of the passage was a laundry with a new-looking washing machine and dryer.

Beyond it was a storeroom, shelves of heavy white bed linen and tablecloths, napkins, white towels, cleaning equipment.

They went back they way they had come. 'There's

another sitting room here,' said Erica. 'It's the one with the television.'

Four leather armchairs around a fireplace, a television on a shelf to the left, more Swedish sound equipment to the right. Cosy by the standards of this house, thought Cashin.

'Well,' said Cashin, 'that's it. We needn't go upstairs, I gather it's undisturbed.'

There was a moment when she looked at him, something uncertain in her eyes.

'I'd like to go up,' she said. 'Will you come with me?'

'Of course.'

They crossed the house to the entrance hall, walked side by side up a flight of broad marble stairs to a landing, up another flight. All the way, he shut down his face against the pain, did not wince. At the top, a gallery ran around the stairwell, six dark cedar doors leading off it, all closed. They stood on a Persian rug in a shaft of light from above.

'I want to get some things from my mother's room, if they're still there,' said Erica. 'I've never had the nerve before.'

'How long have you waited?'

'Almost thirty years.'

'I'll be here' said Cashin. 'Unless...'

'No, that's fine.'

She went to the second door on the left. He saw her hesitate, open the six-panel door, put out a hand to a brass light switch, go in.

Cashin opened the nearest door and switched on the light. It was a bedroom, huge, twin beds with white covers, two wardrobes, a dressing table, a writing table in front of the curtained window. He walked on a pale pinkish carpet, lined like a quilt, and parted the curtains. The view was of a redbrick stable block and of treetops beyond, near-leafless, limbs moving in the wind, and then of a low hill stained with the russet leaves of autumn.

He went back to the gallery and went to the balustrade and looked down the stairwell at the entrance hall, felt a flash of vertigo, an urge to throw himself over the barrier.

'Finished,' said Erica behind him.

'Find what you wanted?'

'No,' she said. 'There's nothing there. It was stupid to think there might be.'

They went back to the sunroom and sat with a glass-topped table between them.

'Notice anything worth mentioning?' said Cashin.

'No. I'm sorry, I'm not much use. I'm pretty much a stranger in this house.'

'How's that?'

She looked at him sharply. 'Just the way it is, detective.'

'Everything locked at night, alarm switched on?' he said.

'I don't know. I haven't been here at night for a very long time.'

Time to move on. 'About your brother, Ms Bourgoyne.'

'He's dead.'

'He drowned, I'm told.'

'In Tasmania. In 1989.'

'Went for a swim?'

Erica shifted in her seat, crossed her legs in corduroy pants, twitched a shiny black boot. 'Presumably. His things were found on a beach. The body wasn't found.'

'Right. So you were here on Tuesday morning.'

'Yes.'

'Visit your step-father often?'

She rubbed palms. 'Often? No.'

'You don't get on?'

Erica pulled a face, looked much older, lined. 'We're

not close. It's our family history. The way I grew up.'

'And the reason for this visit?'

'Charles wanted to see me.'

'Can you be more specific?'

'This is intrusive,' she said. 'Why do you need to know?'

'Ms Bourgoyne,' said Cashin, 'I don't know what we need to know. But if you want me to record that you preferred not to answer the question, that's fine. I will.'

She shrugged, not happy. 'He wanted to talk about his affairs.'

Cashin waited until it was clear that she wasn't going to say any more. 'On another subject. Who'll inherit?'

Widened eyes. 'No idea. What are you suggesting?'

'It's just a question,' Cashin said. 'You didn't discuss his will?'

A laugh. 'My step-father isn't the kind of person who would talk about his will. I doubt whether he's ever given dying a thought. It's for lesser beings.'

'Assuming that he knew the person who attacked him...'

'Why would you assume that?'

'One possible line of inquiry. Who might want to harm him?'

'As far as I know,' she said, 'he's a much respected person around here. But I don't live here, I haven't since... since I was a child. I've only been a visitor.'

She looked away. Cashin followed her gaze, looked out at the disciplined gravel that ran to the hedge. Nothing lifted the spirits about the grounds of The Heights – hedges, lawns, paving, gravel, they were all shades of green and grey. It came to him that there were no flowers.

'He had all the garden beds ripped out,' she said, reading his mind. 'They were wonderful.'

'A last thing. Do you know of anything in your step-father's life or your life that might have led to this?'

'Such as?'

'This may become a murder investigation.'

'What does that mean?'

'Nothing will be left private in the life of anyone around your step-father.'

She straightened, gave him the unfazed gaze. 'Are you saying I'll be a suspect?'

'Everyone will be of interest.'

'What about perfect strangers?' she said. 'Is there a chance that you might take an interest in perfect strangers who got into the house and attacked him?'

He wanted to echo her sarcastic tone. 'Every chance,' he said. 'But with no sign of forced entry, we have to consider other possibilities.'

'Well,' she said, looked at her watch, a slim silver band, 'I'd like to get going. Are you a local policeman?'

'I'm down here for as long as it takes.'

There was truth in this. There was some truth in almost anything people said.

'May I ask you why you brought the bodyguard?' said Cashin.

'It's a work-related thing. Just a precaution.' Erica stood up.

Cashin rose. 'You've been threatened?'

Erica held out her right hand. 'Work-related, detective. In my work, that makes it confidential. Goodbye.'

They shook hands. The ex-SOG man, Jacobs, walked onto the forecourt to see him go. In the mirror, Cashin saw him give a mocking wave, fingers fanned, right hand held just beside his tough-guy smile.

Cashin gunned the cruiser, showered Jacobs with gravel, saw him try to protect his face.

CASHIN DROVE out on the road behind Open Beach, turned at the junction with the highway, went back through Port Monro, got a coffee. He parked above Lucan Rocks, below him a half-dozen surfers, some taking on the big breakers, some giving it a lot of thought.

It was a soothing thing to do: sit in a warm car and watch the wind lifting spume off the waves, see the sudden green translucence of a rising wall of water, a black figure's skim across the melting glass, the poetic exit into the air, the falling.

He thought about Gavin's shark-bitten board, paddling out on it, the water warm as a bath. The water he was looking at was icy. He remembered the testicle-retracting swims when he was a boy, when they had the family shack above Open Beach and the Doogue shack was over the next dune, rugged assemblages of corrugated iron, fibro sheet, salvaged weatherboards. In those days, the town had two milkbars, two butcher shops, the fish and chip shop, the hardware, a general dealer, one chemist, one doctor. Rich people, mostly sheep farmers, had holiday houses on the Bar between the sea and the river. Ordinary people from the inland had shacks above Open Beach or in South Port or in the streets behind the caravan park.

Cashin remembered his father stopping the Falcon on

the wooden bridge, looking down the river at the yachts moored on both sides.

'This place's turning into the bloody Riviera,' his father said.

'What's a Riviera?' said Joe.

'Monaco's on the Riviera,' said Michael.

Mick Cashin looked at Michael. 'How'd you know that?

'Read it,' said Michael. 'That's where they have the grand pricks.'

'Grand pricks?' said Mick Cashin. 'You mean the royal family? Prince Rainier?'

'Don't be rude, Mick,' said Cashin's mother, tapping his father's cheek. 'It's pronounced pree, Michael. It means prize.'

Every year there had been more city kids on the beach. You knew city kids because of their haircuts and their clothes and because the older ones, boys and girls, wore neck chains and smoked, didn't much care who saw them.

Cashin thought about the winter Saturday morning they had driven up to their shack and Macca's Shacca next door was gone, vanished, nothing there except disturbed sand to show where the low bleached building had stood, gently leaning backwards.

He had walked around, marvelling at the shack's absence. There were marker pegs in the ground, and the next time they came a house was half-built on a cement slab.

That summer was the last in their shack, the last summer before his dad's death. Years later, he asked his mother what became of the place.

'I had to sell it,' she said. 'There wasn't any money.'

Now you would have to be more than just rich to own a place in the teatree scrub on the Bar and no shacks broke the skyline above Open Beach; on the once worth-less dunes stood a solid line of houses and units with wooden decks and plateglass windows. Nothing under six hundred grand.

A fishing boat was coming in, heading for the entrance.

Cashin knew the boat. It belonged to a friend of Bern's who had a dodgy brother, an abalone poacher. Just six boats still fished out of Port Monro, bringing in crayfish and a few boxes of fish, but it was the town's only industry apart from a casein factory. Its only industry if you didn't count six restaurants, five cafes, three clothing boutiques, two antique shops, a bookshop, four masseurs, an aromatherapist, three hairdressers, dozens of bed-and-breakfast establishments, the maze and the doll museum.

He finished his coffee and went to work the long way, through Muttonbird Rocks, no one in the streets, most of the holiday houses empty. He drove along two sides of the business block, past the two supermarkets, the three real-estate agents, three doctors, two law firms, the newsagent, the sports shop, the Shannon Hotel on the corner of Liffey and Lucas Streets.

In the late 1990s, a city drug dealer and property devel-oper had bought the boarded-up, gull-crapped Shannon. People still talked about a bar fight there in 1969 that needed two ambulances from Cromarty to take the injured to hospital. The new owner spent more than two million dollars on the Shannon. Tradesmen took on apprentices, bought new utes, gave their wives new kitchens – the German appliances, the granite benchtops.

Two men in beanies were coming out of the Orion, Port's surviving bloodhouse, still waiting for its developer. In Cashin's first week in charge, three English backpackers drinking there at lunchtime gave some local hoons cheek. The one took a king hit, went down and stayed down, copped a few boots. The others, skinny kids from Leeds, were headbutters and kickers and they got into a corner and took out several locals before Cashin and his offsider got there.

The bigger man on the pavement was giving Cashin the eye. Ronnie Barrett had various convictions – assault, drink-driving, driving while suspended. Now he was on the dole, picking up some cash-in-hand at an auto wreckers in Cromarty. His ex-wife had an intervention order against him, granted after he extended his wrecking skills to the former marital home.

Cashin parked outside the station, sat for a while, looking at the wind testing the pines. Winter setting in. He thought about summer, the town full of spoilt-rotten city children, their blonde mothers, flabby fathers in boat shoes. The Cruisers and Mercs and Beemers took all the main street parking. The men sat in and outside the cafes, stood in the shops, hands to heads, barking into their mobiles, pulling faces.

But the year had turned, May had come, the ice-water rain, the winds that scoured skin, and just the hardcore left – the unemployed, under-employed, unemployable, the drunk and doped, the old-age pensioners, people on all kinds of welfare, the halt, the lame. Now he saw the town as you saw a place after fire, all softness gone: the outcrops of rock, the dark gullies, the fireproof rubbish of brown beer bottles and car skeletons.

Ronnie Barrett, he was Port in winter. They should put him in an advertisement, on a poster: GET TO KNOW THE REAL PORT MONRO.

Cashin went in, talked to Kendall. It was overlap time, the two of them on duty for a few hours. He wrote the report on his visit to The Heights, sent it to Villani, printed two copies for the file.

Then he rang homicide and spoke to Tracy Wallace, the senior analyst.

'Back in harness, are you?' she said. 'I gather it's titsoff down there.'

Cashin could see the flag, plank-stiff in the arctic wind. 'Nonsense. Only people with over-sensitive parts say that. What's the word on Bourgoyne?'

'Unchanged. If you're recovered, please come home. The place is filling up with young dills.'

'Be patient. They'll turn into older dills.'

THE SHIFT went by.

Cashin went home, along the country roads. Newly milked dairy cows, relieved for a time of their swaying burdens, turned to look at him, blessed him with dark, glossy eyes.

No sign of Dave Rebb.

He walked the dogs, made something to eat, watched television, all the time the pain getting worse. It took revenge for the hours he was upright. For a long time after he left hospital, he had been unable to cope without resorting to pethidine. Getting off the peth, the lovely peth, that was the hardest thing he had ever done. Now aspirin and alcohol were the drugs of choice and they were a poor substitute.

Cashin got up and poured a big whisky, washed down three aspirins. Callas, Bergonzi and Gobbi always helped. He went to the most expensive thing he owned, two thousand dollars worth of stereo, and put on a CD. Puccini, Tosca. The sound filled the huge room.

He owed opera and reading to Raimond Sarris, the mad, murderous little prick. Opera had just been rubbish arty people pretended to like. Fat men and women singing in foreign languages. Books were okay, but reading a book took too long, too many other things to do. There were few spaces in Cashin's days before Vickie and, afterwards, he left home early, came back in the dark, ate at his desk, sitting in cars, in the street. His spare time he spent sleeping or someone, a cop, would hoot outside and they'd go to the races, the football, fishing, stand in some cop's backyard eating charred meat, drinking beer, talking about work.

Then came Rai Sarris.

After Rai, he had many hours of the day and night in which he had no capacity to do anything except read or watch television. At night, when they were trying to wean him off painkillers, the aches in his back, his pelvis, his thighs, would always give him a moment to drop into sleep. He would fall away from himself for a while, to a deep and dreamless place. The pain would wake him slowly, pain as a sound, far away but insistent, as with a crying baby, part of a dream of hearing something unwelcome. He would move, not fully awake, lie every way, trying to find a position that lessened the pain. Then he would give up and lie on his back – sweaty, now aching from neck to knees – and switch on the light, prop up, try to read. This happened so many times in a night, they blurred.

One day a nurse called Vincentia Lewis brought him a CD player and two small speakers and a box of CDs, twenty or thirty. 'My father's,' she said, 'he doesn't need them anymore.' They sat on the bedside cabinet untouched for a long time until, waiting for the dawn one morning, pain shimmering, Cashin put on the light, picked out a disk, any disk, didn't look at it, put it on, put on the headphones, put out the light.

It was Jussi Björling.

Cashin did not know that. He endured a few moments, gave it a minute, another. In time, the day leaked in under the cream blind, the morning-shift nurse came and ran it up. 'Look a bit more peaceful today,' she said. 'Better night?'

What did Rai Sarris call himself now? For months, they had tapped everyone Rai knew. He never called anyone.

Cashin got up with difficulty and poured another whisky. A few more and he'd sleep.

THEY WALKED around the western side of the house, through the long grass, dogs ahead, jumping up, hanging stiff-legged in the misty air, hoping to see a rabbit.

'Where'd you grow up?' Cashin said.

'All over,' said Rebb.

'Starting where?'

'Don't remember. I was a baby.'

'Right, yes. Go to school?'

'Why?'

'Most people know where they went to school.'

'What's it matter? I can read, I can write.'

Cashin looked at Rebb, he didn't look back, eyes front. 'Like a good yarn, don't you? Big talker.'

'Love a yack. How come you walk like you're scared you'll break?'

Cashin didn't say anything.

'Confide in anyone comes along, don't you? Why's the place's like this?'

The dogs had vanished into the greenery. Cashin led the way down the narrow path he'd cut with hedge clippers. They came to the ruins. 'My great-granddad's brother built it, then he dynamited this part of it. He was planning to blow the whole thing up but the roof fell on him.'

Rebb nodded as if dynamiting a house was an unexceptional act. He looked around. 'So what do you want to do?'

'Clear up the garden first. Then I thought I might fix up the house.'

Rebb picked up a piece of rusted metal. 'Fix this? Be like building that Chartres cathedral. Your kids'll have to finish the job.'

'You know about cathedrals?'

'No.' Rebb looked through an opening where a window had been.

'I thought we could do it in bits,' said Cashin without enthusiasm. He was beginning to see the project through Rebb's eyes.

'Easier to build a new place.'

'I don't want to do that.'

'Be the sensible thing.'

'Well, maybe cathedrals didn't look like a sensible thing.'

Rebb walked beside the wall, stopped, poked at something with a boot, bent to look. 'That was religion,' he said. 'Poor buggers didn't know they had a choice.'

Cashin followed him, they fought their way around the building, Rebb scuffing, kicking. He uncovered an area of tesselation, small octagonal tiles, red and white. 'Nice,' he said. 'Got pictures of the place?'

'They say there's a few in a book in the Cromarty library.'

'Yeah?'

'I'll get copies.'

'Need a tape measure. One of them long buggers.' Rebb mimed winding.

'I'll get one.'

'Graph paper too. See if we can work up a drawing.'

They walked back the long way, it was clearing now, pale blue islands in the sky, dogs ranging ahead like minesweepers.

'People live here before you?' said Rebb.

81

'Not really. A bloke leased it, ran sheep. He used to stay here a bit.'

'Cleaning up the garden's going to take a while,' said Rebb. 'Before you start the big job.' He found the makings, rolled a smoke as he walked, turned his back to the wind to light up, walked backwards. 'How long you planning on taking?'

'They know how long a cathedral would take?'

'Catholic?'

'No,' said Cashin. 'You?'

'No.'

The dogs arrived, came up to Cashin as if to a rendezvous with their leader, seeking orders, suggestions, inspiration.

'Met this priest done time for girls,' said Rebb. 'He reckoned religion's a mental problem, like schizophrenia.'

'Met him where?'

Rebb made a sound, possibly a laugh. 'Travelling, you meet so many priests done time for kids, you forget where.'

They were at the front entrance.

'Help yourself to tucker,' said Cashin. 'I'm getting something in town.'

Rebb turned away, said over his shoulder, 'Want to leave the dogs? Take them to Millane's with me, stay in the yard. He likes them. He told me.'

'They'll be your mates for life. Den's has to be better than the copshop.'

Cashin drove to Port Monro down roads smeared with roadkill – birds, foxes, rabbits, cats, rats, a young kangaroo with small arms outstretched – passed through pocked junctions where one or two tilted houses stood against the wind and signs pointed to other desperate crossroads.

In Port, Leon made him a bacon, lettuce and avocado to take away. 'Risking the wrath of Ms Fatarse here, are we?' he said. 'I'm thinking of having a sign painted. By appointment, supplier of victuals to the constabulary of Port Monro.'

'What's a vittle?'

'Victuals. Food. In general.'

'How do you spell that?'

'V-I-C-T-U-A-L-S.'

'I find that hard to accept.'

Cashin ate his breakfast at Open Beach, parked next to the lifesaving club, watching two windsurfers skimming the wave tops, bouncing, taking off, strange bird-humans hanging against the pale sky. He opened the coffee. There was no hurry. Kendall was acting station commander while the Bourgoyne matter was on. Carl Wexler didn't like that at all, but the compensation was that he could bully the stand-in sent from Cromarty, a kid even rawer than he was.

Bourgoyne.

Bourgoyne's brother was executed by the Japs. How could you be interested in Japanese culture when your brother was executed by the Japs? Did executed mean having his head cut off? Did a Jap soldier cut off his head with a sword, sever the neck and spine with one shining stroke?

Some fucking *In Cold Blood* thing. How did Villani know about Truman Capote? He couldn't have seen the movie. Villani didn't go to the movies. Villani didn't read books either, Cashin thought. He's like me before Rai Sarris. He doesn't have the standstill to read books.

Before Rai, he wouldn't have known what *In Cold Blood* meant either. Vincentia gave him the book. She was doing a literature degree part-time. He read the book in a day and a night. Then she gave him *The Executioner's Song* by Norman Mailer. That took about the same time. He asked her to buy him another book by

Mailer and she came in with *The Naked and the Dead*, second-hand.

'All about dying?' he said. 'I think I can read other kinds of stuff.'

'Try it,' she said, 'it's about a different kind of senseless killing.'

Shane Diab shouldn't have been there. Nothing could change that. He was just a keen kid, he was in awe, so rapt at being in homicide he would have done anything, gone anywhere, worked twenty-three-hour days, then got up early.

There was no point in thinking about Shane. It served no purpose, cops got killed in all sorts of ways, he could just as easily have been shot by some arsehole brain-dead on Jack Daniels and speed. That was the job.

Cashin's mobile rang.

'Joseph?' His mother.

'Yes.'

'Michael rang. I'm worried.'

'Why?'

'It's the way he sounds.'

'How's that?'

'Strange. Not like him.'

'Rang from where?'

'Melbourne.'

'The one-and-a-half bathrooms?'

'I don't know, what does it matter?' Irritated.

'How does he sound?'

'He sounds low. He never sounds low.'

'Everyone gets low. Life's a seesaw. Up, down, brief level bit if you're lucky.'

'Rubbish, Joseph. I know him. Will you ring? Have a chat?'

'What do I say? Your mother asked me to ring you? We don't have chats. We don't have any chat.'

Silence. A windsurfer was in the air, hanging beneath his board. He disconnected, man and board vanished behind the wave as if dropping into a slot.

'Joe.'

'Yes.'

'It's Mum, not your mother. I brought both of you into the world. Will you do that for me? Ring him?'

'Give me the number.'

'Hang on, I'll find it. Got a pen?'

He wrote the number in his book, said goodbye. The windsurfer had reappeared. I'll ring Michael later, he said to himself. After a few drinks, I'll make up a reason. We'll have a chat, whatever the fuck that is.

In the main street, Cashin bought groceries, milk, onions and carrots, half a pumpkin and four oranges and a hand of bananas. He put the bags in the vehicle, walked down to the newsagency. It was empty except for Cecily Addison looking at a magazine. She saw him, replaced it on the stand.

'Well, what's happening?' she said. 'What's taking you so long?'

'Investigation progressing.' Cashin picked up the Cromarty *Herald*. The front-page said:

RESORT COULD BRING 200 NEW JOBS

'They call the man a developer,' said Cecily. 'Might as well call hyenas developers. Hitler, there's a developer for you. Wanted to develop Europe, England, the whole damn world.'

Cashin had learned that when Cecily got going, you didn't have to say anything. Not even in response to questions.

'Going to the mouth since I don't know when,' said Cecily. 'My dear old dad made little cane rods for us, two bricks and a biscuit high the two of us. There's that little spit there, a bit of sand, perfect to cast a line. Mind you, you had a walk. Park the Dodge at the Companions camp, best part of twenty minutes over the dunes. Seemed like a whole day. Worth it, I can tell you.'

She paused to breathe. 'What do you think this Fyfe jackal is slinging the pinkos?'

'I'm not quite with you, Mrs Addison.'

Cecily pointed at the newspaper.

'Read that and weep. The socialists are talking about letting Adrian Fyfe build at Stone's Creek mouth. Hotel, golf course, houses, brothel, casino, you name it. If that's not enough, this morning I find my firm, my firm, is acting for the mongrel. No wonder people think we're lower than snakes' bellies.'

'Why does he need lawyers?'

'Everyone needs lawyers. He'll have to buy the Companions camp from Charles Bourgoyne. Well, could be the estate of Charles Bourgoyne now. What this rag doesn't say is buying Stone's Creek mouth's no use unless you can get to it. And the only way's through the nature reserve or through the camp.'

'Bourgoyne owns the camp?'

'His dad gave the Companions a forty-year lease. Peppercorn. That's history, been nothing there since the fire. Companions are history too.'

Cashin's mobile rang. He went outside. Villani.

'Joe, Bourgoyne. Two kids tried to sell a Breitling watch in Sydney yesterday.'

86

CASHIN SAT at a pavement table. 'You heard this when?' he said.

'Five minutes ago,' said Villani. 'Cash Converters kind of place. Your pawnshop, basically. The manager did the right thing, sent his offsider out after them and he got a rego, reported it. And that lay on some dope's desk till now.'

'So?'

'Toyota ute, twincab. Martin Frazer Gettigan, 14 Holt Street, Cromarty.'

'Jesus,' said Cashin, 'not another Gettigan.'

'Yes?'

'A clan. Lots of Gettigans.'

'What are we talking? Aboriginal?'

'Some are, some aren't.'

'Like Italians. Find out about this ute without spooking anybody? Can't trust the Cromarty turkeys. Turkeys and thugs.'

Cashin thought about the building site, the trembling panel van. 'I'll have a go.'

'From a distance, understand?'

'Not capiche? Out of fashion, is it?'

Villani said, 'Don't take too long about this. Minutes, I'm talking.'

'Whatever it takes,' said Cashin.

He rang the station, got Kendall. 'Listen, there's an

incident report on Allan James Morris, me, complaint from the primary school. His mobile number's there.'

It took more than a minute for Morris to answer. Pulling up his pants on a building site somewhere, thought Cashin.

'Yeah.'

'Allan?'

'Yeah.'

'Detective Sergeant Cashin from Port Monro. Remember me?'

'Yeeaah?'

'You can help me with something. Okay?'

'What?'

'Martin Frazer Gettigan, 14 Holt Street. Know him?

'Why?'

'I'm in a hurry, son. Know him?'

'Know him, yeah.'

'Is he in town?'

'Dunno. Don't see him much.'

Cashin said, 'Allan, I want you to do something for me.'

'Jeez, mate, I'm not doin fuckin cop's work...'

'Allan, two words. Someone's grand-daughter.'

Cashin heard the sounds of a building site: a nailgun firing, hammer blows, a shouted exchange.

'What?' said Morris.

'I want to know who's driving Martin's Toyota ute.'

'How'm I supposed to fuckin...'

'Do it. You've got five minutes.'

Cashin drove to Callahan's garage at the Kenmare crossroads, filled up. Derry Callahan came out of the service bay, cap pulled down to his eyebrows, unshaven. Cashin knew him from primary school.

'You blokes got nothin to do except drive around?' he said. He wiped a finger under his nose, darkened the existing oil smear. 'What's happenin with the Bourgoyne business?'

'Investigation proceeding.'

'Proceeding? You checkin out the boongs? Curfew on the whole fuckin Daunt, that's what I say. Barbed wire around it, be a start. Check em comin and goin.'

'Lateral thinking,' said Cashin. 'Why don't you write a letter to the prime minister? Well, spelling'd be a problem. You could phone it in.'

Derry's eyebrows disappeared beneath his cap. 'They got that?' he said. 'Talkback?'

The mobile rang while Cashin was paying Derry's sister, fat Robyn, slit eyes, mouth permanently hooked into a sneer. He let it ring, took his change and went into the cold, stood at the vehicle, in the wind, looking across the highway at the flat land, the bent grass, pressed the button on the phone.

'Well, he's here,' said Allan Morris. 'Workin over at his old man's place.'

'The ute?'

'Had to make up a fuckin stupid story.'

'Yes?'

'Says he lent it to Barry Coulter and Barry's kid buggered off in it. He's not fuckin happy, I kin tell you.'

A sliver of pain up from his left leg, the upper thigh, into his hip. He knew the feeling well, an old friend. He shifted his weight. 'What's the kid's name?'

'Donny.'

'That's Donny Coulter?'

'What else?'

'Buggered off where?'

'Sydney. He rang. Got another kid with him, Luke Ericsen. He's the driver. They're cousins. Sort of. Donny's not too bright.'

'Been in trouble, these kids?'

'Black kids? In this town? Ya phonin from Mars?'

'Yes or no?'

'Dunno.'

'We never had this talk,' said Cashin.

'Shit. And I'm plannin to go around tellin everyone about it.'

Cashin rang Cromarty station, got Hopgood, gave him the names.

'Donny Coulter, Luke Ericsen,' said Hopgood. 'I'll talk to the boong affairs adviser. Call you back.'

Cashin pulled away from the pumps, parked at the roadside, waited in the vehicle thinking about a smoke, about having another try at getting Vickie to let him see the boy. Did she doubt the boy was his? She wouldn't discuss the subject. He's got a father, that was all she said. When they had their last, unexpected one-night stand, she was seeing Don, the man she married. Seeing, screwing, there were men's clothes in the laundry, muddy boots outside the back door. A vegetable patch had been dug in the clay, seed packet labels impaled on sticks – that sure as hell wasn't Vickie.

You'd have to be blind not to know who the father was. The boy had Cashin written on his forehead.

His mobile.

'Typical Daunt black trash,' said Hopgood. 'They've got some minor form. Suspected of doing some burgs together. Means they did them. Luke's older, he fancies he's a fighter. Donny's a retard, tags along. Luke's Bobby Walshe's nephew.'

'How old?'

'Donny seventeen, Luke nineteen. I'm told they might be brothers. Luke's old man fucked anything moving. Par for the boong course. What's the interest?'

'Looks like one of them tried to sell a watch like Bourgoyne's in Sydney.'

A pause, a whistle. 'Might have fucking known it.'

'New South's got an alert for a Toyota ute registered to Martin Gettigan, 14 Holt Street. The boys are in it.'

'Well, well. Might go around and see Martin,' said Hopgood.

'That would be seriously fucking stupid.'

'You're telling me what's stupid?'

'I'm conveying a message.'

'From on fucking high. Suit yourself.'

'I'll keep you posted,' said Cashin.

'Gee, thanks,' said Hopgood. 'Do so like to be in the fucking loop.'

Cashin rang Villani.

'Jesus,' said Villani. 'Plugged in down there, aren't you? I've got news. Vehicle sighted in Goulburn, three occupants. Looks like your boys are coming home.'

'Three?'

'Given someone a lift, who knows.'

'You should know Luke Ericsen is Bobby Walshe's nephew.'

'Yes? So what?'

'I'm just telling you. Going to pick them up?'

'I don't want any hot-pursuit shit,' said Villani. 'Next thing they're doing one-eighty on the Hume, they wipe out a family in the Commodore wagon. Only the dog survives. Then it's my fault.'

'So?'

'We'll track them all the way, if I can get these rural dorks to take KALOF seriously and not spend the shift keeping a look out for skirt to pull over.'

'If they come back here,' said Cashin, 'it'll be Hopgood's job.'

'No,' said Villani. 'You're in charge. You've done

enough malingering. I want to avoid a Waco-style operation by people watched too much television. Understand?'

'Capiche,' said Cashin. 'Whatever that means.'

'Don't ask me. I'm a boy from Shepparton.'

AT 3 PM, Hopgood rang.

Cashin was in Port Monro, looking at the gulls scrapping in the backyard, no dogs to chase them away.

'These Daunt coons are on their way,' Hopgood said. 'Don't stop somewhere for a bong, they should be here about midnight.' He paused. 'I gather you're the boss.'

'In theory,' said Cashin. 'I'll be there in an hour or so.'

He went home, fed the dogs. They didn't like the change in routine; food came after the walk, that was the order of things. There was no sign of Rebb. He left a note about the dogs, drove to Cromarty.

Hopgood was in his office, a tidy room, files on shelves, neat in and out trays. He was in shirtsleeves, a white shirt, buttoned at the cuffs. 'Sit,' he said.

Cashin sat.

'So how do you want this done?' Hopgood affected boredom.

'I'll listen to advice.'

'You're the fucking boss, you tell me.'

Cashin's mobile rang. He went into the passage.

'Bobby Walshe's nephew,' said Villani. 'I take your point. We do this thing by the book. There's a bloke coming down to you, on his way now. Paul Dove, detective sergeant. Transferred from the feds, done soft stuff, no one wanted him but he's smart so I took him. He's learning, takes the pains.'

Takes the pains. That was a Singo expression. They were both Singo's children, they used his words without thinking.

'He's taking over?' said Cashin.

'No, no, you're the boss.'

'Yes?'

'Yes what?'

'Oh come on,' said Cashin.

'He's Aboriginal. The commissioner wants him there.'

'I'm lost here. Night has fallen.'

'Don't come the naïve shit with me, kid,' said Villani. 'You told me about Bobby Walshe. Plus Cromarty's record's fucking appalling. Two deaths in cells, lots of other suspicious stuff.'

'Go on.'

'So. When these boys get there, they'll be knackered. Let them go home. You want them asleep. Go in two hours after they pack it in, more. Gently. I cannot say that too strongly.'

The conversation ended. Cashin went back into Hopgood's office.

'Villani,' he said. 'He wants the boys lifted at home.'

'What?'

'At home. After they've gone to bed.'

'Jesus Christ,' said Hopgood, running both hands over his hair. 'Heard everything now. You don't just go into the fucking Daunt at night and arrest people. It's Indian territory. Excellent chance we end up being attacked by the whole fucking street, the whole fucking Daunt, hundreds of coons off their fucking faces.'

Hopgood got up, went to the window, hands in pockets. 'Tell your wog mate I want confirmation that he's taking all responsibility for this course of action. The two of you both.'

94

'What's your advice?' said Cashin.

'Lift the cunts on the way into town, that's no risk, no problem.'

Cashin left the room and rang Villani. 'The local wisdom,' he said, 'is that going into the Daunt for something like this is inviting a small Blackhawk Down. Hopgood says to lift them on the way in is easy. I say let him run it.'

Villani sighed, a sad sound. 'You sure?'

'How can I be sure? The Daunt's not the place it was when I was a kid.'

'Joe, the commissioner's on my hammer.'

Cashin was thinking that he wanted to be somewhere else. 'I think you might be over-dramatising,' he said. 'It's just three kids in a ute. Can't be that hard to do.'

'So you'll be the one on television explaining what happened to Bobby Walshe's relation?'

'No,' said Cashin. 'I'll be the one hiding in a cupboard and letting your man Dove explain.'

'Fuck you,' said Villani. 'I say that in a nice way. Do it then.'

Cashin told Hopgood.

'Some sense,' said Hopgood, face in profile. 'That's new.'

'They're sending someone down. The commissioner wants an Aboriginal officer present.'

'Jesus, not enough coons here,' said Hopgood. 'We have to import another black bastard.'

'Is there somewhere I can sit?' said Cashin.

Hopgood smiled at him, showed his top teeth, a small gap in the middle. 'Tired, are we? Should've taken the pension, a fucked bloke like you. Gone up where it's warm.'

Cashin willed his facial muscles to be still, looked in

the direction of the window, saw nothing, counted the numbers. There would be a day, there would be an hour, a minute. There would be an instant.

IT WAS the usual mess: desks pushed together, files everywhere, a draining board full of dirty mugs. Someone had left a golf bag in a corner, seven clubs, not all of one family.

Cashin was eating a pie, meat sludge, when Hopgood showed Dove in.

'The supervisor's arrived,' he said and left.

Dove was in his early thirties, tall, thin, light-brown head buzz-cut in homicide style, round rimless glasses. He put his briefcase on a desk. They shook hands.

'I'm here because they want a boong present when you arrest Bobby Walshe's nephew,' Dove said. He had a hoarse voice, like someone who'd taken a punch in the voicebox.

'You can't be plainer than that,' said Cashin.

Dove looked at Cashin for a while, looked around the room. 'Heard about you,' he said. 'Where do I sit?'

'Anywhere. You eaten?'

'On the way, yeah.' Dove took off his black overcoat, underneath it a black leather jacket. 'Got stuff to catch up on,' he said, opening his briefcase.

Cashin didn't mind that. He wrapped the remains of the pie, put them into the bin, went back to Joseph Conrad. *Nostromo*. He was trying to read all Conrad's books, he didn't know why. Perhaps it was because Vincentia told him that Conrad was a Pole who had to learn to write in English. He thought that was the kind of book he needed – writer, reader, they were both in foreign territory.

Cashin's mobile rang.

'Michael called again.' His mother.

'Bit hectic here, Syb. I'll do it first chance I get. Yes.'

'I'm worried, Joe. You know I'm not a worrier.'

Cashin wanted to say that he knew that very well.

'You could do it now, Joe. Won't take a minute. Just give him a ring.'

'Soonest. I'll ring him soonest. Promise.'

'Good boy. Thank you, Joseph.'

Ring Michael. Michael came to see him in hospital, once. He stood at the window, spoke from there, did not sit down, answered three phone calls and made one. 'Well,' he'd said when he was leaving, 'chose a dangerous occupation, didn't you.' He had a thin smile, a boss smile. It said: I can't get close. One day I may have to sack you.

Hopgood stuck his head in. 'Cobham. The BP servo. Three in the ute.'

The boys were 140 kilometres away.

Cashin went out for a walk, bought cigarettes, another surrender. A cold night, rain in the west wind, the last of the leaves flirting with bits of paper in the streetlights. He lit up, went down the street of bluestone buildings, past the sombre courthouse, the place where young men finally found the stern father they'd been looking for. Around the corner, uphill, past dark shops to the old Commonwealth Bank on the next corner, now a florist and a gift shop and a travel agency.

Here on the heights of Cromarty the rich of the nineteenth century and after – traders in wool and grain, merchants of all kinds, the owners of the flour mill, the breweries, the foundries, the jute bag factory, the ice works, the mineral water bottling plant, the land barons of the inland and the doctors and lawyers – built houses of stone and brick.

Coming to town was a big thing when Cashin was a boy. The four of them in the Kingswood on a Saturday morning, his father with a few shaving cuts on his face, black hair combed and shining, his mother in her smart clothes, only worn for town. Cashin thought about her touching the back of his dad's head, the tongue-pink varnish on her nails.

He turned the corner at the Regent pub, a noise like a shore-break behind the yellow windows. When the shopping was done, Mick Cashin met his brother Len at the Regent for a drink before they went home. He dropped Sybil and the two boys on the waterfront and went to the pub. They bought chips at the little shop and walked out on the long pier, looking at the boats and the people fishing. Then they went up through the town, up the street he was now walking down. Cashin remembered that Michael always kept his distance from them, hanging back, looking in shop windows. It wasn't hard to find the car, always near the pub. They got in and waited for Mick Cashin. Michael had his school case, he did homework, it would have been maths. His mother read from a book of riddles. Joe loved those riddles, got to know them off by heart. Michael didn't take part.

Mick Cashin crossing the road with Uncle Len, laughing, hand on Len's shoulder. Len was dead too, an asthma attack.

Cashin felt the wind on his face, the salt smell in his head. He was a boy again, the child lived in him. He turned the corner and went back to the stale air of the station, two elderly people at the counter, the duty cop looking pained, scratching his head. Someone in the cells was making a sad singing-moaning sound.

Hopgood and four plainclothes were in the office. One of them, a thin, balding man, was eating a hamburger and dipping chips into a container of tomato sauce, adding them to the mix. Dove was at the urn, running boiling water into a styrofoam cup.

'Welcome, stranger,' said Hopgood. 'The bloke at Hoskisson's just logged the ute. We've got fifty minutes or so.'

Hopgood made no introductions, went to the white-board stained with the ghosts of hundreds of briefings and drew a road map.

'I'm assuming these pricks are going to Donny's house or Luke's,' he said. 'Makes no difference, a block apart. They're coming down Stockyard Road. We have a vehicle out there, it's had a breakdown, it'll tell me when they pass. When they get to Andersen Road, that's here, the second set of lights, they can turn right or they can carry on to here, go down to Cardigan Street and turn right.'

Hopgood's pen extended the road out of Cromarty. 'That's too hard. So we have to take them here where it's still one lane.' He pointed at an intersection. 'Lambing Street and Stockyard Road.'

He put an X further down the road. 'Golding's smash-repair place. Preston and KD, you'll wait here, facing town. You're group three. I'll let you know when to get going so you'll be in front of the ute. When you get to the Lambing lights, they'll be red. They'll stay red till we're done. With me so far?'

Everyone nodded. The hamburger-eater burped.

'Now when the ute pulls up behind you,' he said, 'you blokes sit tight. Wait, okay? Lloyd and Steggie and me, that's group one, we'll pull up behind them in the Cruiser and we'll be out quick smart.'

Hopgood ran a finger under his nose. 'And Lloyd and Steggie,' he said, 'I hereby say to you and everyone else

I have received a message from on high and nothing, that's absolutely nothing, can happen to these... these dickheads.'

He looked from face to face, didn't look at Cashin or Dove.

'Right,' he said. 'Anything stupid happens, we run away and hide. We will starve the pricks out. This is not some kind of SOG operation. Detective Senior Sergeant Cashin, you want to say something?'

Cashin waited a few seconds. 'I've given Inspector Villani and the crime commissioner an assurance that seven trained officers can pick up three kids for questioning without any problems.'

Hopgood nodded. 'Detectives Cashin and Dove, you will be group two in the second vehicle behind the ute. Your services are unlikely to be needed. Any questions? No? Let's get going. I'll be talking to all of you. Code is Sandwich. Sandwich. Okay?'

'If they've got a scanner?' said Preston. He had a big nose and a small, sparse moustache, the look of a rodent.

'Have a heart,' said Hopgood. 'These are Daunt dickheads.'

A uniformed cop came in. 'The third one in the ute,' he said, 'it might be another cousin. Corey Pascoe. He's been in Sydney for a while.'

They put on their jackets and went out to the carpark behind the station, a small paved yard carved out of the stone hill.

'Take the Falcon,' said Hopgood to Cashin. 'It's in better nick than it looks.'

They drove out in a convoy, Hopgood's Landcruiser in front, then Cashin and Dove, behind them the cops called Preston and KD in a white Commodore. It was raining heavily now, the streets running with the lights of cars and the neon signs of shops, blurs and pools of red and

101

white, blue, green and yellow. They crossed the highway and drove out through the suburbs, past the racecourse and the showgrounds, turned at the old meatworks. They were on Stockyard Road. The boys were out there, coming towards them.

'This bloke know what he's doing?' said Dove. His chin was down in his overcoat collar.

'We hope,' said Cashin. The car smelled of cigarette smoke, sweat and chips cooked in old oil.

'Sandwich,' said Hopgood on the radio. 'Group three, station's coming up, should hear from me again inside twenty-five minutes.'

'Group three, roger to that,' said a voice, possibly KD.

Golding's Smash Repair came into sight on the right, a big tin building, a scarlet neon sign. In the rearview, Cashin saw the white Commodore turn off.

The rain was heavier now. He upped the wipers' speed.

'Sandwich group one,' said Hopgood. 'Turning left.'

'Group two, roger to that,' Cashin said. He followed the Cruiser into a dirt side road, muddy. It stopped, he stopped. It did a U-turn, so did he. It stopped. He pulled up behind it, killed the lights.

A knock on his window. He ran it down.

'Keep the motor running, follow us when we go,' said Hopgood. 'No more radio talk from now.'

'Right.'

'Don't like this fucking rain,' said Hopgood and went into the dark.

Window up. They sat in silence. Cashin's pelvis ached. He settled into his breathing routine but he had to shift every minute or two, try to transfer the weight of his torso onto less active nerves.

'Okay if I smoke?' said Dove.

'Join you.'

He punched the lighter, took a cigarette from Dove, dropped his window a centimetre or two. Dove lit their smokes with the glowing coil. They smoked in silence for a while, but nicotine loosens the tongue.

'Do a lot of this?' said Cashin.

Dove turned his head. Cashin could only see the whites of his eyes. 'Of what?'

'Be the Aboriginal representative.'

'This is a favour for Villani. He says he's been leaned on about the Bobby Walshe connection. I quit the feds because I didn't want to be a showpiece boong cop.'

'I was in primary school with Bobby Walshe,' said Cashin and regretted it.

'I thought he grew up on the Daunt Setttlement.'

'No school there then. The kids came to Kenmare.'

'So you know him?'

'He wouldn't remember me. He might remember my cousin. Bern. They teamed up on kids called them names.'

Why did I start this, thought Cashin? To ingratiate myself with this man?

A long silence, no sound from the engine. Cashin touched the pedal and the motor growled.

'What kind of names?' said Dove.

'Boong. Coon. That kind of thing.'

More silence. Dove's cigarette glowed. 'Why'd they call your cousin that?'

'His mum's Aboriginal. My Aunty Stella. She's from the Daunt.'

'What, so you're a boong-in-law.'

'Yeah. Sort of.'

In the hospital, he had begun to think about how he'd never stood with his Doogue cousins, with Bobby Walshe and the other kids from the Daunt when the whites called them boongs, coons, niggers. He'd walked away. No one was calling him names, it wasn't his business. He remembered telling his dad about the fights. Mick Cashin was working on the tractor, the old Massey Ferguson, big fingers winding out sparkplugs. 'You don't have to do anything till they're losing,' he said. 'Then you better get in, kick some heads. Do the right thing. Your mum's family.'

By the time his Aunty Stella took him in, no one called any Doogue kid anything. They didn't need help from anyone. They were big and you didn't get one: they came as a team.

Cashin watched the main road. A vehicle crossed. No move by the Cruiser. Not the one. He put on the wipers. The rain was getting harder. Now was the time to call this thing off, you couldn't do stuff like this in a cloudburst.

Another vehicle flicked by.

Glare of taillights on. Hopgood moving.

'Here we go,' said Cashin.

IT WAS raining heavily, the Falcon's wipers weren't up to it.

Hopgood didn't hesitate at the junction, swung right.

Cashin followed, couldn't see much.

They were at fifty, eighty, ninety, a hundred, the Falcon went flat, it couldn't do more than that, something wrong.

He felt a front wheel wobble, thought he'd lose control, slowed.

Hopgood's taillights were gone into the sodden night.

This wasn't smart, this wasn't the way to do it.

'Get Hopgood,' said Cashin. 'This is bullshit.'

Dove took the handset. 'Sandwich two for Sandwich one, receiving me. Over.'

No reply.

Golding's Smash Repairs on the left, neon sign a red smear in the wet night. Car one, group three, Preston and KD, they would have pulled out, they would be ahead of the ute now, closing on the traffic lights.

'Abandon,' said Cashin. 'Tell him.'

'Sandwich one, abandon, abandon, received? Please roger that.'

Four vehicles, speeding in the rain on a pitch-black night.

The lights would be red. Preston would stop.

The ute would stop behind him. Three kids in a

twincab. Tired from a long trip. Yawning. Thinking of home and bed. Were they Bourgoyne's attackers? At least one of them would know who took the watch off the old man's wrist.

'I say again, abandon, abandon,' Dove said. 'Roger that, roger that.'

'Say again, Sandwich two, can't hear you.'

Coming up to the last bend, driving rain, the Lambing Street intersection coming up. Cashin couldn't see anything except the yellow glow of street lights beyond.

'Sandwich one, abandon, abandon, received? Please roger that.'

Cashin slowed, in the bend now.

Red glare. Cruiser taillights.

Stopped.

Cashin braked, the Falcon's back wanted to slide away, he had to go with it, straighten out gently.

'Fucking hell,' said Dove. 'Sandwich one, abandon, abandon, I say again, abandon. Roger that, roger that.'

Cashin stopped behind the Cruiser, couldn't see anything. Three doors open.

'Let's go,' he said, something badly wrong here.

Dove was around the car first, Cashin bumped into him, they almost fell, both blind in the pouring rain.

A vehicle had slammed into the traffic lights on the wrong side of the road. A ute. He could see three or four figures, milling about.

Gunshots.

Someone shouted: 'PUT THE FUCKIN THING...'

A shotgun fired, the muzzle flame of a shotgun, reflected by the wet tarmac.

'DROP IT, DROP THE FUCKIN GUN!'

'BACK OFF, BACK OFF!'

Two more bangs, handgun, tongue-tips of flame, quick, SMACK-SMACK.

Silence.

'Fuck,' said Dove. 'Oh my sweet fuck.'

Someone was moaning.

Hopgood shouted, 'KD, GISSUS THE FUCKING SPOTLIGHT!'

A few seconds and the light came on, the world turned hard white, Cashin saw the broken ute, thousands of glass fragments glittering on the road.

Three men standing. A body behind the ute, a shotgun beside it.

He walked across the space, wiping rain from his face.

Lloyd and Steggie, guns out, pale faces. Steggie's mouth moved, he was trying to say something. Then he was sick, a column of fluid. He went to his knees, to all fours.

'Get an ambo!' Cashin shouted. 'Maximum fucking speed!'

He went to the person on the ground, a slim youth, his mouth was open. He was shot in the throat. Cashin saw a glint of teeth, heard a gurgling sound. The youth coughed, blood poured out of him, ran in the road, thicker than the rain.

Cashin took the youth's shoulders in his hands, raised him, knew he was going to die, felt it in the thin arms, the little shakes, heard it in the rasping sounds.

'The fucking idiot,' said Hopgood from behind him.

Cashin let the boy down. There was no help he could give. He got up and went to the ute. The driver was pinned by the steering wheel and the dashboard, his face covered in blood, blood everywhere.

Cashin put a finger on his neck, felt the faintest pulse. He tried to open the door, couldn't. He went to the other side. Dove was there. The passenger was another boy, he had blood flowing from his mouth but his eyes were wide.

'Oh fuck,' he said softly. He said it again and again.

They got him out, laid him down. He would live.

The ambulance arrived, then another, the second with a doctor, a woman. She'd never done gunshot but it didn't matter, it was always too late.

When they lifted the boy, Cashin saw a shotgun in a black puddle beside him, single-barrel pumpgun, sawn off.

The driver was still alive when they got him into the ambulance. The cops stood around.

'Nobody touches anything here,' said Cashin. 'Not a fucking thing. Close the road.'

'Who the fuck do you think you are?' said Hopgood. 'This's Cromarty, mate.'

VILLANI put the tape in the machine and gave the remote control to Hopgood. 'This is the media conference two hours ago,' said Villani. 'Be on telly at lunchtime.'

The assistant crime commissioner's pink baby face appeared on the monitor. He was prematurely bald. 'It's my sad duty to report that two of the three people involved in the incident outside Cromarty late yesterday have succumbed to injuries received,' he said. 'The third person has a minor injury and is in no danger. The events are now the subject of a full investigation.'

A journalist said, 'Can you confirm that police fired on three young Aboriginal men at a roadblock?'

The commissioner remained blank. 'It was not a roadblock, no. Our understanding is that police officers were fired upon and responded appropriately.'

'If it wasn't a roadblock, what was it?'

'The persons involved are suspects in an inquiry and an attempt was made to apprehend them.'

'That's the Charles Bourgoyne attack?'

'Correct.'

'Did both victims die of gunshot wounds?'

'One of them. Unfortunately.'

The journalist said, 'And is that Luke Ericsen, the nephew of Bobby Walshe?'

'I'm not yet in a position to answer that,' said the commissioner.

'And the other boy? What did he die of?'

'Injuries sustained in a vehicle accident.'

Another journalist said, 'Commissioner, the officers involved, were they uniformed police?'

'There were uniformed police at the scene.'

'So if it wasn't a roadblock, was this a chase gone wrong?'

'It was not a chase. It was an operation designed to avoid any danger to everyone involved and…'

'Can you confirm that two police vehicles were travelling behind the vehicle that crashed. Can you confirm that?'

'That's correct, however…'

'Excuse me, commissioner, how is that not a chase?'

'They were not pursuing the vehicle.'

'It wasn't a roadblock and it wasn't a chase and you have two dead Aboriginal youths?'

The commissioner scratched his cheek. 'I'll say again,' he said. 'It was an interception operation designed to minimise the possibility of injury. That is always the intent. But police officers in danger have the clear right to act to protect themselves and their colleagues.'

'Commissioner, Cromarty has a bad reputation for this kind of thing, doesn't it? Four Aboriginal people dead in matters involving the police since 1987. Two deaths in custody.'

'I can't comment on that. To my knowledge, the officers involved in this incident, and that includes a highly respected Aboriginal police officer, behaved with the utmost respect for protocol. Beyond that, we'll wait for the coroner's verdict.'

Villani gestured to Hopgood to switch off the monitor. Cashin was standing at the window, looking at the noonday light on the stone building across the street, having trouble focusing. He was thinking about the crushed boy in the ute. Shane Diab looked like that, the life squeezed out of him.

Pigeons and gulls were walking about, some drowsing, apparently living in amity. Then full-on violence broke out on the parapet – wings, beaks, claws. The peace had only been a lull.

'The position is,' said Villani, rubbing his face with both hands, ageing himself, 'that this operation has brought upon me, upon you, upon this station and upon the entire fucking police force an avalanche of shit. We are buried in shit, the guilty and the innocent.'

'With respect,' said Hopgood, 'how can you know that a driver will be so dumb? What kind of stupid cunt swerves around a car at red lights and loses control?'

'You can't,' said Villani. 'But you wouldn't have had to if you'd listened to me and taken them at home. Now you'd all better pray these kids are the ones attacked Bourgoyne.'

'Ericsen had no reason to fire on us,' said Hopgood. 'He's a violent little arsehole, he'd likely have done the same if we'd waited till they were home in the Daunt.'

'My understanding,' said Villani, 'is that Ericsen's in an accident, he gets out, sees two civilians jump out of an unmarked car and come at him. Could be mad hoons. Three years ago four such animals did exactly the same thing, beat two black kids to pulp, the one's in a wheelchair for life. Also in this town a year ago a black kid walking home was chased down by a car. He tried to run away and the car mounted the pavement and collected him. Dead on arrival.'

Villani had been looking around the room. Now he stared at Hopgood. 'You familiar with those incidents, detective?'

'I am, boss. But...'

'Save the buts, detective. For the inquiry and the inquest. Where you will need all the buts you can find.' Villani sighed. 'Two dead black kids,' he said. 'Bobby Walshe's nephew. Shit.'

'Walshe's never been near his nephew,' said Hopgood. 'He's too good for his fellow Daunt...'

He didn't say the word. They all knew what the word was.

'I wish I was more distant,' said Villani. 'Mars, that would be good. Maybe not far enough.'

Cashin coughed, it caused a scarlet flash of pain.

'I'm just a country cop,' said Hopgood, 'but it's not clear to me that the presumption of innocence lies with arseholes who try to run red lights, hit a pole, climb out with an unlicensed sawn-off pumpgun and fire on police officers.'

He rubbed the stubble on his upper lip with a big finger. 'Or is it different when they're related to fucking Bobby Walshe?'

'That's well put,' said Villani. 'The presumption of innocence. You might think about retraining for the law. For something anyway.'

He took out cigarettes, flicked the pack, lipped one, lit it. There was a sign prohibiting smoking. His smoke stood in the dead air.

'The procedure here is going to be a model for future cock-ups,' said Villani. 'Two feds plus ethical standards officers plus the ombudsman's office. They're here. All officers involved are now on holiday. Any contact, that's the phone call, the little chat, the fucking wink over the bananas in the supermarket, those concerned will turn in the wind. Understand? The family, the brotherhood, that shit, that is not going to operate. Understood?'

Cashin said, 'Could you go over that again?'

Villani said, 'Well, that's it, you can go. Cashin stay.'

Hopgood and Dove left.

'Joe,' said Villani, 'I don't appreciate smart shit like that.'

He smoked, tapped ash into his plastic cup. Cashin looked away, watched the birds across the street. Sleep, shuffle, shit, fight.

'For presiding over this cock-up, I am branded,' said Villani.

'It was my advice. What else could you do?'

'You passed on Hopgood's considered opinion. That's what you did. Passed it on. I decided.'

Villani closed his eyes. Cashin saw his tiredness, the tiny vein pulsing in an eyelid.

'I shouldn't have brought you in,' said Villani. 'I'm sorry.'

'Bullshit. No sign of Bourgoyne's watch?'

'No. Probably flogged it somewhere else. They're looking. They haven't found Pascoe's place in Sydney.'

'Sydney detection at its best,' said Cashin.

'I wouldn't point the finger,' said Villani. 'Not me.'

Silence. Villani went to the window, forced it open, shot his stub at the pigeons, crashed the window down.

'I've got a little media appearance to do,' he said. 'How do I look?'

'Ravishing,' said Cashin. 'Nice suit, ditto shirt and tie.'

'Advised by experts.' At the door, Villani said, 'If it were me, I'd say as little as possible. Innocent stuff comes back to haunt you. And this cunt Hopgood, Joe. Don't do him any favours, he'll sell you without a blink.'

113

IT WAS mid-afternoon before Cashin's turn.

In an overheated interview room, audio and video running, he sat on a slippery vinyl chair before two feds, a fat senior sergeant from ethical standards called Pitt and his puzzled-looking offsider Miller, and a man from the police ombudsman's office.

Cashin took the first chance to say that he'd had to convince Villani to approve the operation.

'Well, that's a matter for another time,' said Pitt. 'Not the matter at hand.'

The feds, a man and a woman, both stringy like marathon runners, took Cashin through his statement twice. Then they picked at it.

'And I suppose,' said the man, 'with hindsight, you'd see that as an error of judgment?'

'With hindsight,' said Cashin, 'I see most of my life as an error of judgment.'

'Are you taking the question seriously, detective?' said the woman.

Cashin wanted to tell her to fuck off. He said, 'In the same circumstances, I'd make the same decision.'

'It resulted in the deaths of two young men,' she said.

'Two people died,' Cashin said. 'The courts will decide who's to blame.'

Silence. The interrogators looked at one another.

'What was your initial opinion of conducting an operation like this in heavy rain?' said the woman.

'You can't choose the weather. You take what you get.'

'But the wisdom of it? What was your opinion?'

'I had no strong opinion until it was too late.'

It had been too late. He had waited too long.

'And then you say you instructed Dove to call Hopgood and order the operation abandoned?'

'I did.'

'You believed you had the authority to order the operation abandoned?' said the man from the ombudsman's officer.

'I did.'

'You still think so?'

'I thought I was in overall command, yes.'

'You thought? It wasn't made clear who was in command?'

'I'm in charge of the Bourgoyne investigation. This operation flowed from it.'

They looked at one another. 'Moving on,' said the woman. 'You say you made three attempts to call it off?'

'That's correct.'

'And they weren't acknowledged?'

'No.'

'Dove asked for the calls to be acknowledged?'

Cashin looked away. He was in pain, thinking of home, whisky, bed. 'Yes. Repeatedly. After the first message, Hopgood asked for a repeat, said he couldn't hear us."

'That surprised you?'

'It happens. Equipment malfunctions.'

'To go back to the moment you rounded the vehicle,' said the male fed. 'You said you heard shots.'

'That's correct.'

'And you saw a muzzle flash beside the ute?'

'Yes.'

'You heard a shot or shots and then you saw the muzzle flash?'

Cashin thought: he's asking whether Luke Ericsen was fired on and fired back.

'An instant in a cloudburst,' he said, 'I heard shots, I saw a muzzle flash at the ute. The order, well…'

'It's possible the muzzle flash was Ericsen firing after the other shots?' said Pitt.

'I can't make that judgment,' Cashin said.

'But is it possible?'

'It's possible. It's possible the shotgun fired first.'

'I'm sorry, are you changing your statement?' The woman.

'No. I'm clarifying.'

'A person of your experience,' said the male fed. 'We'd expect a little more precision.'

'We?' said Cashin, looking into his eyes. 'Does we mean you? What the fuck do you know about anything?'

That didn't help. It was another hour before he could go home. He drove carefully, he was tired, nerves jangling. At the Kenmare crossroads, he remembered milk and bread and dog food, there was only a bit of the butcher's sausage left. He pulled in to Callahan's garage and shop.

The shop was unheated, smelling of sour milk and stale piecrust, no one behind the counter. He got milk, the last carton, went to the shelves against the wall to get dog food. One small can left.

'Back again.'

Derry Callahan, oil smears on his face, was standing behind him, close up. He was wearing a nylon zipped-up cardigan, taking strain over his belly.

'Good to see you blokes earnin yer fuckin money for a change,' he said.

Cashin looked around, smelled alcohol and poisonous

breath, saw Callahan's pink-rimmed eyes, the greasy strands of hair hand-combed over his pale spotted scalp.

'How's that?' he said.

'Takin out those two Daunt coons. Pity it wasn't a whole fuckin busload.'

There was no thought, just the flush. Cashin had the can of Frisky Dog, Meaty Chunks in Marrow Gravy, in his right hand. He turned his hips and brought his arm around close to his body and hit Derry in the middle of his face, not a lot of travel, they were close. The pain made him think he had broken his fingers.

Callahan went backwards, two short steps, dropped slowly to his knees, at prayer, hands coming to his face, blood getting there first, dark red, almost black, it was the fluorescent lighting did that.

Cashin wanted to hit him again but he threw the carton of milk at him. It bounced off his head. He stepped over to kick Callahan but something stopped him.

At the vehicle, Cashin realised that he was still holding the dog food can. He opened his hand. The can was dented. He threw it onto the back.

Rebb heard him arrive, a beam of light, the dogs jumping, big ears flapping, running for him. He fondled their ears, hand hurting. Dogs went between his legs, came around for more.

'Thought you'd buggered off,' said Rebb. 'Leaving me with your mad dogs and your debts.'

THE DOGS woke Cashin a good way out from dawn and, blind, he crossed the space, let them into the cold, dark room, went back to bed. They snuffed the kitchen for dropped food, gave up, jumped onto the bed, spoilt rotten.

Cashin didn't care. They sandwiched him, pushed against him, lay their light heads on his legs. He went back to sleep, woke with a start, a sound in his memory, a scrape, metal against metal. Head raised, neck tense, he listened.

Just a sound in a dream. The dogs would hear anything unusual long before he did. But sleep was over. He lay on his back, fingers of his right hand hurting, hearing the sad whimpering pre-dawn wind.

The boys in the ute.

In the same circumstances, I'd make the same decision. It resulted in the deaths of two young men.

Until that moment in the stale room, it had not fully dawned upon him that the line ran directly from the bleeding and dying boys to him on the phone talking to Villani.

I think you might be over-dramatising. It's just three kids in a ute. Can't be that hard to do.

Would it have been different if Hopgood had spoken to Villani? Would Villani have rejected the advice if it came directly from Hopgood?

No matter how much they might have botched raids on the boys at their homes, there wouldn't be two dead.

He tried to think about something else.

Rebuilding Tommy Cashin's blown-up house, lying ruined since just after World War I. How stupid. It would never be done, he'd waste his spare time for a while, then he'd give it away. He'd never done anything with his hands, built anything. How had the idea come to him?

It had somehow developed on his walks with the dogs as they returned to the house in its tangled wilderness. And then one morning on the way to work he met Bern at a crossroads. A load of uncleaned old red bricks was on the back of his Dodge. Sitting beside Bern was a local ancient called Collo who cleaned his bricks, sat outside in all weathers covered in a grey film of cement dust, whistling through the gaps between his teeth, utterly absorbed in chipping at mortar.

They pulled onto the verges, got out. Bern crossed the road, smoke in his mouth.

'Bit early for you,' said Cashin. 'Pull down a house in the dark?'

'What would you cunts know about honest labour?' said Bern. 'All got these fat flat arses.'

'Student of arses, are you?' Cashin said. And then he said the fateful words. 'How many bricks you got there?'

'Three thousand-odd.'

'How much?'

'What's it to you?'

'How much?'

'For a valued customer, forty a hundred, clean.'

'Let's say twenty-five.'

'I'll sell you bricks for twenty-five, I can get forty? Know how scarce old bricks are? Antiques, mate.' He spat neatly. 'No, you don't know. You know fuck all.'

'Say thirty.'

'Whaddaya want with bricks?'

'I'm fixing Tommy Cashin's house,' said Cashin. The words came from nowhere.

Bern shook his head. 'You're another fuckin Cashin loony, you know that? Done at thirty. Delivery extra.'

Now the bricks were stacked near the ruin.

Cashin got up, pulled on clothes, made tea. On the edge of dawn, he set out for the beach with the dogs, a fifteen-minute drive, the last few on a dirt track. Under a sky of streaked marble, he walked barefoot on hard rippled sand against a freezing wind.

His father's view had been that you didn't wear footwear on the beach no matter what you were doing there. Not thongs, not anything. If the sand was hot, well, shut up or go home. Cashin thought about the summers of having his soles burnt, cut from broken glass and sharp rocks. He must have been seven or eight when he stood on a fish hook. He hopped and sat down hard, tears of pain flowing.

His father came back, lifted the foot. The hook was in the soft flesh behind the pad of his big toe.

'No bloody going back with hooks,' Mick Cashin said and pushed the hook through.

Cashin remembered the barb coming out of his skin. It looked huge, his father took it between finger and thumb and pulled the whole thing through. The skin bulged before the eyelet emerged. He remembered the feeling of the length of pale nylon gut being drawn through his flesh.

The dogs liked the beach, weren't keen on the sea. They chased gulls, chased each other, snapped at wavelets, ran from them, went up the dunes to explore the marram grass and the scrub for rabbits. Cashin looked at the sea as he walked, his face turned from the grit blowing off the dunes.

A strong rip was running parallel to the beach, just beyond the big breakers. They went all the way to the mouth of Stone's Creek. The outgoing tide had divided the stream into five or six shallows separated by sandbars, perfect finger biscuits of different widths. This was where Cecily Addison told him Adrian Fyfe planned to build his resort.

Hotel, golf course, houses, God knows what else. Brothel, casino, you bloody name it.

On a wild polar day like this, the idea was lunacy.

The dogs went to the first rivulet, wet their feet, thought about crossing to the first biscuit. Cashin whistled and they looked, turned, ready to go home for breakfast.

When he had fed them, showered, found a clean shirt, he went in to Port Monro to clear his desk. There was no knowing how long the suspension would last. Forever, he thought.

Outside the station, a woman sat in an old Volvo wagon, two young children imprisoned in the back. He parked behind the building and by the time he unlocked the back door, she had her finger on the buzzer.

He looked through the blinds before he raised them: thirtyish, many layers of garments, weak and dirty hair striped in red and green, a sore at the corner of her mouth.

Cashin unlocked.

'Keep fucking easy hours here,' she said. 'This a copshop or what?'

'Not open for another half an hour. There's a sign.'

'Jesus, like fucking doctors, people only allowed to get sick in office hours, nine to fucking five.'

'Missed an emergency, have we?' He went behind the counter.

'I've fucking had it with this town,' she said. 'I go into

the super last night, they reckon they seen me taking frozen stuff out of me trackie at the car. So I'm gonna walk around with fucking frozen peas down me trackie, right? Right?'

'Who said that?'

'The Colley slut, she's history, the bitch.'

'What did she do?'

'Sees me coming in, she reckons I'm banned. Half the fucking town there, hears her.'

'Which super are we talking about?'

'Supa Valu, the one on the corner.'

'Well,' Cashin said, 'there's always Maxwell's.'

She thrust her chin at him. 'That's your fucking attitude, is it? I'm guilty without trial? On their fucking say so?'

Cashin felt the tiny start of heat behind his eyes. 'What would you like me to do, Ms...?'

'Reed, Jadeen Reed. Well, tell that Colley bitch she's got no right to ban me. Tell her to get off my case.'

'The store has the right to refuse admittance to anyone,' Cashin said. 'They can tell the prime minister they don't want his business.'

Jade widened her eyes. 'Really?' she said, a grim smile. 'Fucking really? Don't give me that crap. You telling me I park a Mercedes wagon outside the fucking super the bitch would try this on? Reality fucking check, mister.'

Hot eyes now. 'I'll note your complaint, Ms Reed,' he said. 'You might also like to take your problem up with the Department of Consumer Affairs. The number's in the phone book.'

'That's it?'

'That is it.'

She turned, walked. At the door, she turned again. 'You wankers,' she said. 'Looking after the rich, that's your fucking job, isn't it?'

'Got a record, Jadeen?' said Cashin. 'Any form? Been in trouble? Why don't you sit down, I'll look you up?'

'You cunt,' she said, 'you absolute fucking cunt.'

She left, tried to slam the door but it wasn't that kind of door.

Cashin went to his desk and worked through the papers in his in-tray, looked for matters that needed his attention. The dogs were walking around the enclosure like prisoners in an exercise yard, walking because it was less boring than the alternative.

I'm not suited to this work, Cashin thought. And if I can't handle this station, I'm not suited to any kind of police work. What else did Rai Sarris do to me? It wasn't just the body. What neural cobweb did the mad prick cause to fizzle? Once I had patience, I didn't get hot eyes, I didn't punch people, I thought before I did things.

Constable Cashin is good at dealing with people, particularly in circumstances where aggression is involved.

Sergeant Willis wrote that on Cashin's first assessment, showed it to him before he sent it. 'Don't get up your fucking self about this, son,' he said. 'I say it about all the girls.' At his cubicle, he turned. 'Course, in my day, a report like this, they'd say put the wuss on traffic.'

Kendall arrived. She was making tea, her back to him, when she said, 'The business in Cromarty.'

'Yes. A monumental stuff-up. I'm now on holiday. You're in charge. The relief kid'll stay on.'

'How long?'

'Who knows? Till ethical standards get the blame sorted out. It could be permanent.'

'They the Bourgoyne ones?'

'Looks like it. Them or someone they know.'

'Good riddance then,' she said.

Cashin looked out the window at the sky, hated Kendall for a while, her quick stupidity. He saw the sparks, the crushed ute, the rain, the blood in the puddles. The boys, broken, life leaking away. He thought about his son. He had a boy.

'It only looks like it, Ken,' he said. 'Nobody should die because we think they might have done something wrong. Nobody gave us that power.'

You fucking hypocrite, he thought.

Kendall went to her desk.

He finished, took the files and his notes and went over, put them in her in-tray. 'Pretty much up to date,' he said.

She didn't look at him. 'I'm sorry I said that, Joe,' she said. 'It just, shit, it just came out, I wanted to say…'

'I know. Solidarity. That's a good instinct. Call me if you need anything.'

He was at the back door when she said, 'Joe, feel like a bit of company. Well, any time. Yes.'

'Take you up on that,' he said, went out.

He walked around to the Dublin. A new four-wheel-drive was parked outside and Leon had two customers, a middle-aged couple having breakfast. Soft-looking leather jackets hung on the backs of their chairs.

'Takeaway black,' said Cashin. 'The overdose.'

'Either you sit down or you get one of those vacuum cups,' said Leon. 'Polystyrene does nothing for expensive coffee.'

Cashin had no interest. 'I'll bear that in mind,' he said.

Leon went to the machine. 'Your muscle boy was in yesterday. Very fetching but not keen on paying. Long and pregnant pause before he shelled out.'

Cashin was looking across the street at Cecily Addison talking to the woman outside the aromatherapy shop. 'He's a city lad,' he said. 'They treat officers of the law differently there. Like royalty.'

'Message received. Roger. Do you say that? Roger?'

'We say Roger, we say Bruce, we say Leon, it all depends. Case by case.'

Leon brought the container to the counter, capped it. 'Bringing in reinforcements for the march?'

'The march?'

'Could be ugly. Feral greenies, rich old farts pulling up the drawbridge.'

'I could be missing something here,' Cashin said. He had no idea what Leon was talking about.

'The march against the Adrian Fyfe resort? Been away, have we?'

'Can't keep up with events in this town. It's all go, go, go. Anyway, I'm on holiday.'

'Why don't you try Noosa, chat to rich retired drug cops? It's warm up there.'

'Don't care for the victuals in Noosa,' Cashin said. As he said the word, he saw the strange spelling. 'Listen, an ordinary old toasted cheese and tomato?'

Leon raised his right arm in a theatrical way, drew fingers across his forehead as if wiping away sweat. 'I take it you don't require sheep-milk fetta with semi-dried organic tomatoes on sourdough artisan bread?'

'No.'

'I suppose I can find a gassed tomato, some rat-trap cheese and a couple of slices of tissue-paper white.'

Cashin bought the city newspaper and drove to Open Beach. One surfer out on a big, heaving sea.

The headline on page three said:

TWO DIE IN CHASE
CRASH, GUNFIGHT

It had happened too late for the previous morning's newspaper. The three youths were much younger in the photographs. The captions didn't mention that. And the reporter didn't buy the interception line. It was a chase gone wrong. Luke Ericsen, he said, 'apparently died in a hail of gunfire'. The conduct of seven officers was under investigation.

Another story was headlined:

UNITED AUSTRALIA LEADER SLAMS POLICE

Bobby Walshe was quoted:

Shock and grief, they are my emotions. Luke Ericsen is my sister's boy, a bright boy, everyone had great hopes for him. I don't know exactly what happened but that doesn't really matter. Two youngsters are dead. That's a tragedy. And there's been far too many of these tragedies. Right across Australia, it's a police culture problem. Indigenous people get the sharp end. Who needs courts when you can hand out punishments yourself? And I'm not surprised this happened in Cromarty. The present federal treasurer entrenched the culture there when he was state police minister. He helped the local police to cover up two Aboriginal cell deaths. I'll remind him of that disgraceful episode in the election campaign. Often. That's a promise.

The toasted sandwich wasn't bad. Flat and tanned, leaking cheese, something yellow anyway.

Would Derry Callahan complain? Punched with a can of dog food. Cashin thought that he didn't care. Hitting him was worth the damage to his fingers. He should have kicked him too, it would have been a good feeling.

His mobile rang. It took time to find it.

'Taking it easy?' said Villani. 'Lying on the beach in the thermal gear. The striped long johns.'

'I'm reading the paper. Full of good news.'

'I'll give you good news. The pawnshop bloke, he's ID'd Pascoe and Donny.'

The surfer paddled on a great wall of water. It seemed unwilling to break, then it curled, he stood, an upsurge from a sandbar caused it to crash. He shot out the back, towed by his board.

'I just talked to the commissioner,' said Villani. 'Actually, he talked to me. Non-stop. The spin doctors say we're playing into our enemies' hands. I think that means Bobby Walshe and the media. So it's just Lloyd and Steggles suspended. You are no longer on holiday. And Dove's coming back to you, he'll be your offsider.'

'What about the rest?'

'Preston to Shepparton, Kelly goes to Bairnsdale.'

'And Hopgood?'

'Stays on the job.'

'So the idea is to load the other ranks?'

'The commissioner's decision, Joe. He's taken advice.'

'That's what I call leadership. In Sydney, the pawnshop, it was just Pascoe and Donny?'

'Ericsen was probably waiting outside.'

'So what happens to Donny?'

'He's still in hospital, under observation, but he's okay, bruises, cuts. He'll be charged with attempted murder, interview at 10 am, lawyer present.'

'On this? Well, excuse fucking me, that's a pretty thin brief.'

'With luck, he'll plead it,' said Villani. 'If not, we'll see. You'll see.'

'This is the post-Singo attitude? Winging it?'

'It's what we have to do, Joe,' said Villani, a flatness in his tone.

THEY SAT in the interview room, waiting. Cashin hadn't worn a suit since coming to Port Monro.

'In a very short time, I've grown to hate this town,' said Dove. His forearms were on the table, cuffs showing, silver cufflinks, little bars. He was looking at his hands, his long fingers stretched.

'The weather's not great,' said Cashin.

'Not the weather. Weather's weather. There's something wrong with the place.'

'Big country town, that's all.'

'No, it's not a big country town. It's a shrunken city, shrunk down to the shit, all the shit without the benefits. What's the hold-up here? Since when do you sit around waiting for the prisoner?'

A knock, a cop came in, followed by the youth Cashin had seen in the passenger seat of the ute at the fatal crossroads, then another cop. Donny Coulter had a thin, sad face, a snub nose, down on his upper lip. It was a child's face, scared. He was puffy-eyed, nervous, licking his lips.

'Sit down, Donny.'

Another knock, the door was behind Cashin.

'Come in,' he said.

'Helen Castleman, for the Aboriginal Legal Service. I represent Donny.'

Cashin turned. She was a youngish woman, slim, dark

128

hair pulled back. They looked at each other. 'Well, hello,' he said. 'It's been a while.'

She frowned.

'Joe Cashin,' he said. 'From school.'

'Oh, of course,' she said, unsmiling. 'Well, this is a surprise.'

They shook hands, awkward.

'This is Detective Sergeant Dove,' said Cashin.

She nodded to Dove.

'I didn't know you lived here,' said Cashin.

'I haven't been back long. What about you?'

'I'm in Port Monro.'

'Right. So who's in charge of this?'

'I am. You've had an opportunity to speak to your client in private.'

'I have.'

'Like to get going then?'

'I would.'

Cashin sat opposite Donny. Dove switched on the equipment and put on record the date, the time, those present.

'You are Donald Charles Coulter of 27 Fraser Street, Daunt Settlement, Cromarty?'

'Yes.'

'Donny,' said Cashin, 'I'm going to tell you what rights you have in this interview. I must tell you that you are not obliged to do or say anything but that anything you say or do may be given in evidence. Do you understand what I've said?'

Donny's eyes were on the table.

'I'll say it again,' said Cashin. 'You don't have to answer my questions or tell me anything. But if you do, we can tell the court what you said. Understand, Donny?'

He wouldn't look up. He licked his lips.

'Ms Castleman,' said Cashin.

'Donny,' she said. 'Do you understand what the policeman said? Do you remember what I told you? That you don't have to tell them anything.'

Donny looked at her, nodded.

'Will you say that you understand, please, Donny,' said Cashin.

'Understand.' He was drumming his knuckles on the table.

'I must also tell you of the following rights,' said Cashin. 'You may communicate with or attempt to communicate with a friend or a relative to inform that person of your whereabouts. You may communicate with or attempt to communicate with a legal practitioner.'

'At this point,' said Helen Castleman, 'I'd like to say that my client has exercised those rights and he will not be answering any further questions in this interview.'

'Interview suspended 9.47 am,' said Cashin.

Dove switched off the equipment.

'Short and sweet,' Cashin said. 'Would you care to step outside with me for a moment, Ms Castleman?'

They went into the corridor. 'Bail hearing at 12.15,' Cashin said. 'If Donny was to tell his story, there might not be opposition to bail.'

Her eyes were different colours, one grey, one blue. It gave her a look somehow fierce and aloof. Cashin remembered studying her face in the year twelve class photograph long after he left school.

'I'll need to get instructions,' she said.

Dove and Cashin went down the street and bought coffee at a place called Aunty Jemimah's. It had checked tablecloths and Peter Rabbit pictures on the walls.

'Old school mates,' said Dove. 'Lucky you.'

'She was too good for me,' said Cashin. 'Old Cromarty money. Her father was a doctor. The family used to own the newspaper. And the iceworks. The only reason she didn't go to boarding school was she wouldn't leave her horses.'

On the way back, Dove opened his cup and sipped. 'Jesus, what is this stuff?' he said.

'Some of the shit you get without the benefits.'

Helen Castleman was outside the station, talking on her mobile. She watched them coming, looked at them steadily. They were near the steps when she said, 'Detective Cashin.'

'Ms Castleman.'

'Donny's mother says he was at home on the night of the Bourgoyne attack. I'll see you in court.'

'Look forward to it.' Cashin went in and rang the prosecutor. 'Bail is strenuously opposed,' he said. 'Investigations incomplete. Real danger accused will interfere with witnesses or abscond.'

At 11.15, Dove and Cashin headed for the station door.

'Phone for you,' said the cop on the desk. 'Inspector Villani.'

'What's wrong with your mobile?' Villani said.

'Sorry. Switched off.'

'Listen, the kid gets bail.'

'Why?'

'Because that's what the minister told the chief commissioner, who told the crime commissioner, who told me. It's political. They don't want to take the chance Donny so much as gets a nosebleed in jail.'

'As their honours please.'

'Donny's bail not opposed,' Cashin said to Dove.

'Pissweak,' said Dove. 'That is capitulation, that is so pissweak.'

The desk cop pointed at the door. 'Got a reception committee. Television.'

Cashin went cold. Somehow he hadn't thought of this. 'You speak to them,' he said to Dove. 'You're from the city.'

Dove shook his head. 'Hasn't taken you long to turn into a flannelshirt, has it?'

They went out, into camera flashes and the shiny black eyes of television cameras, furry microphones on booms thrust at them. At least a dozen people came at them, jostling.

'What's Donny Coulter charged with?' said a woman in black, blonde hair immobilised with spray.

'No comment,' said Dove. 'All will soon be revealed.'

They made their way down the stairs and the camera crews ran ahead and filmed them walking down the winter street under a grey tumbling sky. Rounding the bend, they saw the crowd outside the court.

'Ms Castleman's spread the word,' said Dove.

The crowd parted, allowed them a narrow corridor. They walked side by side between the hostile faces, silence until they neared the top of the stairs.

'You murderers,' said a man wearing a rolled-up balaclava on Cashin's left. 'All you cunts are good for, killin kids.'

'Bastards,' said a woman on Dove's side. 'Mongrels.'

The lobby was crowded, the small courtroom was full. They made their way to the prosecutor, a senior constable. 'Change of mind,' said Cashin. 'Not opposing bail for Coulter.'

She nodded. 'I heard.'

They took their places on the Crown's seats. Dove looked around. 'Just the two of us representing the forces of law and order,' he said. 'Where's Hopgood, the friendly face of community policing?'

'Probably on the firing range breaking in the replacements for KD and Preston,' said Cashin.

Dove looked at him for a second, the round glasses flashed.

Helen Castleman arrived with an older woman. Cashin thought he saw a resemblance to Donny.

At 12.15 exactly, Donny was brought up from the cells to a hero's welcome from the spectators. He didn't look at anyone except the woman with Helen Castleman. She smiled at him, winked, a brave face.

The audience were told to be silent, then to stand. The magistrate came in and sat down. He had a chubby pink face and the grey strands combed over his bald scalp made him look like an infant suffering from a premature-ageing disease.

The prosecutor identified Donny, said he was charged with attempted murder. The audience had to be hushed again.

'This is obviously a show-cause situation, your honour,' she said, 'but there is no objection to bail.'

The magistrate looked at Helen Castleman and nodded.

She rose. 'Helen Castleman, your honour. I represent Mr Coulter and would like to apply for bail. My client has no criminal record, your honour. He has been charged in the most tragic circumstances imaginable. A few days ago, he saw his cousin and a close friend die in an incident involving the police...'

Applause from the gallery, a few shouts. More silencing by the clerk of the court.

'In this court, Ms Castleman,' said the magistrate, a baby with a gruff voice, 'it is not a good idea to grand-stand.'

Helen Castleman bowed her head. 'That was not my intention, your honour. My client is just an innocent boy, the victim of circumstances. He is traumatised by what has happened and he needs to be at home with his family. He will give and honour all undertakings the court may require. Thank you, your honour.'

The magistrate frowned. 'Bail is granted,' he said. 'The accused is not to leave his place of residence between the hours of 9 pm and 6 am and must report to the Cromarty police once a day.'

Applause again, more shouts, more silencing.

Cashin looked at Helen Castleman. She tilted her head, gave him a suggestion of a smile, lips just parted. Cashin felt like the teenage boy he once was, full of lust and full of wonder that a beautiful and clever rich girl would kiss him.

THEY WALKED past Helen Castleman being inter-viewed on the court steps and the television crews caught up with them before they reached the station. Dove declined to answer questions.

'There's a room organised, boss,' the desk cop said to Cashin. 'Upstairs, turn left, last door on the right.'

When they got there, Dove looked around, shook his head. 'Organised?' he said. 'They unlocked the fucking junk room, that's organised?'

Tables pushed together, two computers, four bad chairs, piles of old newspapers, scrap paper, drifts of pizza boxes, hamburger clams, styrofoam cups, plastic spoons, uncapped ballpoints, crushed drink cans.

'Like a really bad sitting room in an arts students' shared house,' Dove said. 'Disgusting.' He went to a window, unlatched it, tried to pull the bottom half up, failed, banged both sides of the frame with fists, tried again. Cords showed in his neck. The window didn't move.

'Shit,' he said. 'Can't breathe in here.'

'Need the nebuliser?'

It was provocative and it worked. 'I don't have fucking asthma,' Dove said. 'I have a problem with breathing air circulated ten thousand times through people with bad teeth and rotten tonsils and constipation.'

'Didn't mean anything. People have asthma.' Cashin sat down. He had to live with Dove.

Dove pulled a chair out, sat, put his polished black shoes on the desk. The soles were barely worn, insteps shiny yellow and unmarked. 'Yeah, well,' he said, 'I don't have asthma.'

'Glad to hear it. I'm assuming what will happen here is the defence will want Luke Ericsen loaded with Bourgoyne. Luke's dead, it's not a problem for him.'

'If Donny was there, he'll share the load.'

'Placing Donny there,' said Cashin. 'That's a challenge. And if it happens, the story then will be led astray by his older cousin, didn't take part, that sort of thing.'

A crash, his heart jumped. Unlatched by Dove, its sash cords rotten, the top half of the window had waited, dropped. The big panes were vibrating, wobbling the outside world.

Cold air came in, the sea – salty, sexual.

'That's better,' said Dove. 'Much better. Delayed action. Smoke?'

'No thanks. Always fighting the urge.'

Dove lit up, moved his chair back and forth. 'I'm new to this but if you don't place Donny at the house, all you have is he went to Sydney with Luke and they tried to sell Bourgoyne's watch. A half-way solid story about where he was on the night, tucked up in bed, he'll walk.'

'I suppose he should. That's the system.'

Dove eyed him briefly, narrow eyes. 'The smartarses who walk. You see them look at their mates, little smirk. Outside, it's the high fives. How easy was that? Fucking shithead cops, let's do it again.' Pause. 'What's Villani say? Your mate.'

Cashin felt a powerful urge to smack Dove down. He waited. 'Inspector Villani says nothing,' he said. 'The solicitor says Donny's mum's giving the alibi. There may be others to confirm it.'

Dove's head was back. 'Some women amaze me. They

spend their whole lives covering up for men – the father, the husband, the sons. Like it's a woman's sacred duty. Doesn't matter what the bastards do. So what if my dad beat my mum, so what if my hubby fucked the babysitter, so what if my boy's a teenage rapist, he's still my...'

'We don't have anything that says Donny was there on the night,' Cashin said.

'Anyway, it's academic,' Dove said. 'Hopgood's right. Bobby Walshe's made them go soft-cock on this. First it's bail, next they drop the charges.'

'You should tell Hopgood that. He'll want you on the Cromarty team. You could be spokesperson.'

Dove smoked in silence, eyes still on the ceiling. Then he said, 'I'm black so I'm supposed to empathise with these Daunt boys. Is that what you're saying?'

There was a gull on the sill – the hard eyes, the moulting head, it reminded Cashin of someone. 'The idea is to keep an open mind until the evidence convinces you of something.'

'Yes, boss. I'll keep an open mind. And in the meantime, I have to live in the Whaleboners' Motel.'

'The Whalers' Inn.'

'Could very well be.' Cigarette in his mouth, Dove looked at Cashin. 'Just tell me,' he said. 'I accept reality. I'll read a book until it's time to go home.'

'The job is to build the case against Donny and Luke,' said Cashin. 'I don't have any other instructions.'

'I'm not talking about instructions.'

The sagging chair wasn't doing anything for Cashin's aches, his mood. He got up, took off his coat, spread an old newspaper on the floor, lay down and put his legs on the chair, tried to get into a Z shape.

'What's this?' said Dove, alarmed. 'Why are you doing that?'

Cashin couldn't see him. 'I'm a floor person. We'll have to see where we can get with Donny's mum.'

Dove appeared above him. 'What's the point?'

'If she's going to lie for the boy, she'll be worried. They don't know what we've got. Getting Donny to plead guilty to something would be a good outcome.'

Cashin heard the door open.

'Just you, sunshine?' said Hopgood. 'Where's Cashin?'

Dove looked down. Hopgood came around the table and studied Cashin as if he were roadkill.

'What the fuck is this?' he said.

'We missed you in court,' said Cashin.

Hopgood's chin went up. Cashin could see the hairs in his nose. 'Not my fucking business.'

'We need to talk to Donny's mum.'

'Thinking about going to the Daunt, are you?'

Cashin didn't fancy the idea. 'If we have to. Can't see her presenting here.'

'Well, it's your business,' Hopgood said. 'Don't call us.'

'I need to talk to the Aboriginal liaison bloke.'

'Ask the desk where he's currently doing fuck all.'

A phone rang. Dove picked up one, wrong, tried another. 'Dove,' he said. 'Good, boss, yeah. Went off okay, yeah. I'll put him on.'

He offered Cashin the phone. 'Inspector Villani,' he said, impassive.

Cashin reached up. 'Supreme commander,' he said.

'Joe, we are talking a cooling-off period,' said Villani.

'Meaning?'

'Let things settle down. I saw your court crowd today, our television friends showed us their pictures for the evening news. The word is no more turbulence like that is wanted.'

'Who said that?'

'I can tell you I don't quote the bloke at the servo.'

'The kid's been charged on close to zero. Now you're saying you don't want us to find any actual evidence or try to get a plea out of him?'

'Nothing is to be done to inflame this situation.'

'That's a political order, is it?'

Villani expelled breath as a whistle. 'Joe, can't you see the sense?' he said.

Cashin felt Dove and Hopgood looking at him, a man lying on the floor, talking on a phone, his calves on a chair.

'I'd like to say, boss,' he said, 'that we have a short time here when we might shake something loose. We let that pass, we will need jackhammers.'

Silence.

Cashin focused on the ceiling, yellow, creased and spotted like the back of an elderly hand. 'That is my common sense,' he said. 'For what it's worth.'

Silence.

'For what it's worth, Joe,' said Villani, 'taking Shane Diab parking outside Rai Sarris's place was your idea of common sense.'

Cashin felt the cold knife inside him, turning. 'Moving on,' he said. 'How long is a cooling-off period? For example.'

'I don't know, Joe, a week, ten days, more.' Villani spoke slowly, like someone talking to an obtuse child. 'We'll need to use our judgment.'

'Right. Some of us will use our judgment.' Cashin was looking at Dove. 'In the meantime, what's Paul Dove do?'

'I need him back here for a while. I want you to take some time off. Handle that?'

'Is that suspension again, boss?'

'Don't be a prick, Joe. I'll call you later. Put Dove on.'

Cashin handed up the handset to Dove.

'What's he say?' said Hopgood.

'He says there's a cooling-off period over Donny.'

'Is that right?' said Hopgood, something like a smirk in his voice, on his lips. 'You won't be needing this comfortable office then.'

In light rain, Dove and Cashin walked up to the Regent, got beers in the bar and sat in the dim cooking-fat-scented bistro, the only customers.

Dove read the laminated menu, ran his index finger down the list.

'Twelve main courses,' he said. 'You need at least three people in the kitchen to do that.'

'In the city,' said Cashin. 'Three bludgers. Here we do it with a work-experience girl.'

'A steak sandwich,' said Dove. 'What can they do to that? How badly can they fuck that up?'

'They meet any challenge.'

A worn woman in a green coverall came out of a back door and stood over them with a notepad, sucked her teeth, sounds like the last dishwater going down a blocked drain.

'Two steak sandwiches, please,' said Cashin.

'Only in the bar,' she said, her gaze on the wall. 'No sangers here. The bistro menu here.'

'Cops,' said Cashin. 'Need a bit of privacy.'

She looked down, smiled at him, crooked teeth. 'Right, well, that's okay. Know all the cops. You here for the Bourgoyne thing then?'

'Can't talk about work.'

'Black bastards,' she said. 'Two down, why don't you nail the bloody lot of them? Bomb the place. Like that Baghdad.'

'Could you cut the fat off?' said Dove. 'I'd appreciate that.'

'Don't like fat? No worries.'

'And some tomato?'

'On a steak sandwich?'

'It's a boong thing,' said Dove.

At the kitchen door, she glanced back at Dove. Cashin saw the uncertainty in her eyes. Across the gloomy space, he saw it.

'An attractive woman,' said Dove. 'So many attractive people around here, it must be something in the white gene pool.' He looked around. 'Stuff like the other night bother you? Still bother you? Ever bother you?'

'What do you think?'

'Well, you're fairly hard to read, if I may say so. Except for the lying on the floor stuff, that's a real window into the soul.'

Cashin considered telling him about the dreams. 'It bothers me.'

'Shooting the kid.'

'Somebody shoots at you, what do you do?'

'What I'm getting at,' said Dove, 'is whether the kid fired first. Did you tell them that?'

Cashin didn't want to answer the question, didn't want to consider the question. 'You'll know what I told them when we get to the coroner.'

'Cross your mind we were set up? Hopgood puts us together in a dud car, claims he can't hear the radio.'

'Why would he do that?'

'Leave himself and his boys a bit of slack if anything went wrong.'

'That may be too far-sighted for Hopgood. You missing the feds?'

Dove shook his head in pity. They talked about nothing, the sandwiches came, the woman fussed over Cashin.

'Could this be whale steak?' said Dove after a bout of chewing. 'I don't suppose they honour the whaling treaty here.'

Walking back in drizzle and wind, Dove said, 'Cooling-off period my arse. This thing's in the freezer and it's staying there. Still, I escape the fucking Whaleboners' Tavern.'

'Whalers' Inn.'

'That too.'

On the station steps, Dove offered a long hand. 'Strong feeling I won't be back. I'll miss the place so much.'

'So good, the whale steak, Miss Piggy's coffee.'

'Aunty Jemimah's.'

'You feds are trained observers,' said Cashin. 'See you soon.'

DEBBIE DOOGUE was sitting at the kitchen table, school books spread, mug of milky tea, biscuits, cartoon show on television. The room was warm, a wood heater glowing in the corner.

'This's the place to be,' said Cashin.

'Want tea?' she said.

She was a pale gingerhead, ghosts of freckles, her hair pulled back. She looked older than fourteen.

'No, thanks,' Cashin said. 'Full of tea. How's school?' It was a pointless question to ask a teenager.

'Okay. Fine. Too much homework.' She moved her bottom on the chair. 'Dad's in the shed.'

Cashin went to the sink, wiped a hole in the fogged window. He could see rain speckling the puddles in the rutted mud between the house and the shed. Bern was loading something onto the truck, pushing it with both hands. He had a cigarette in his mouth.

'He's worried about the stuff your mum found,' said Cashin, turning, leaning against the sink.

Debbie had her head down, pretending to be reading. 'Well, had to dob me, didn't he?' she said.

'What's to dob? I thought it wasn't yours?'

She looked up, light blue Doogue eyes. 'Didn't even know what it was. She just gave me this box, said, hang on to this for me. That's all.'

'You thought it was what?'

143

'Didn't think about it.'

'Come on, Debbie, I'm not that old.'

She shrugged. 'I'm not into drugs, don't want to know about them.'

'But your friends are? Is that right?'

'You want me to dob in my friends? No way.'

Cashin stepped across, pulled out a chair and sat at the table. 'Debbie, I don't give a bugger if your friends use drugs, wouldn't cross the road to pinch them. But I don't want to see you dead in an alley in the city.'

Her cheeks coloured slightly, she looked down at her notepad. 'Yeah, well, I'm not...'

'Debbie, can I tell you a secret?'

Uneasy, side to side movements of her head.

'I wouldn't tell you if you weren't family.'

'Um, sure, yeah.'

'Keep it to yourself?'

'Yeah.'

'Promise?'

'Yeah.'

The inside door opened violently and two small boys appeared, abreast, fighting to be first in. Debbie turned her head. 'Geddout, you maggots!'

Eyes wide in their round boy faces, mouths open, little teeth showing. 'We're hungry,' said the one on the left.

'Out! Out! Out!'

The boys went backwards as if pulled by a cord, closed the door in their own faces.

Debbie said, 'I promise.'

Cashin leaned across the table, spoke softly. 'Some of the people selling stuff to your friends are undercovers.'

'Yeah?'

'Understand what that means?'

'Like secret agents.'

144

'That's right. So the drug cops know all the names. If your friend bought that stuff, his name's on the list.'

'Not my friend, her friend, I don't even know him.'

'That's good. You don't want to know him.'

'What would they do with the names?'

'They could tell the school, tell the parents. They could raid the houses. If you were on the list, they could knock on the door any time.'

Cashin rose. 'Anyway, got to go. I wanted to tell you because you're family and I don't want to see anything bad happen to you. Or to your mum and dad.'

At the door, he heard her chair scrape.

'Joe.'

He looked back.

Debbie was standing, hugging herself, now looking about six years old. 'Scared, Joe.'

'Why's that?'

'I bought the stuff. For my friend.'

'The girl friend?'

Reluctant. 'No. A boy.'

'From a Piggot?'

'Yeah.'

'Which one?'

'Do I have to say?'

'I won't do anything. Not my line.'

'Billy.'

'You tabbing?'

'No. Well, just the one, didn't like it.'

He looked down, looked into her eyes, waited.

'Smoking?'

'No. Don't like it either.'

A chainsaw started outside, the roar, bit into something hard, a savage-toothed whine.

'They won't, will they?' she said. 'Tell on me? Come here?'

'Out of my control,' Cashin said. 'I can talk to them, I suppose. What do you reckon I could say?'

She gave him some hints about what he could say.

Cashin went out to the shed, mud attaching itself to him. At the back, in the gloom, Bern was on his haunches, applying a blowtorch to an old kitchen dresser. Layers of paint were blackening and blistering under the blue flame. The smell was of charring wood and something metallic.

'I smell lead,' Cashin said. 'That's lead paint you're burning.'

Bern turned off the torch, stood up. Paint flakes were stuck to his beard stubble. 'So?' he said.

'It's toxic. It can kill you.'

He put the torch on the dresser. 'Yeah, yeah, everythin can kill you. How'd you pricks manage to kill those kids?'

'Accident,' Cashin said. 'No harm intended.'

'That Corey Pascoe. He was in Sam's class. Bound for shit from primary.'

'Bit like Sam then.'

'No harm in Sam. Led astray. You talked to Debbie?'

'Gave her a message, yeah.'

'What's she say?'

'Seemed to get it.'

Bern nodded. 'Well, you can only fuckin hope. I'd say thanks except I give you that wood. Dropped it off today. There's a bloke there, helpful.'

'Dave Rebb. Going to help me with the house.'

'Yeah? Where'd you find him?'

'In a shed over at Beckett. Mrs Haig. A swaggie.'

Bern shook his head, rubbed his chin stubble, found the paint flakes and looked at them. 'Point about swaggies,' he said, 'is they're not real strong on work.'

'We'll see. He's giving Den Millane a hand, no complaints so far.'

'Seen him somewhere, I reckon. Long time ago.'

They walked to the vehicle. Cashin got in, lowered the window. Bern put dirty hands on the sill, gave him a look.

'I hear someone punched out that cunt Derry Callahan,' he said. 'Stole a can of dog food too. You blokes investigatin that?'

Cashin frowned. 'That right? No complaint that I know of. When it happens, we'll pull out all the stops. Door-to-door. Manhunt.'

'Let's see your hand.'

'Let's see your dick.'

'C'mon. Hiding somethin?'

'Fuck off.'

Bern laughed, delighted, punched Cashin's upper arm. 'You fuckin violent bastard.'

On the way home, the last light a slice of lemon curd, Cashin reflected that his lies to Debbie would probably keep her straight for about six months, tops.

Still, six months was a long time. His lies generally had a much shorter shelf life.

FOR REASONS Cashin didn't understand, Kendall Rogers wanted him to be in charge of policing the march.

'I'm on leave,' he said.

'Just be an hour or so.'

'Nothing's going to happen. This is Port Monro.'

It was the wrong thing to say.

'I'd just appreciate it,' she said, not quite looking at him. 'It would be a favour to me.'

'Favour, now you're talking. The favour bank.'

The demonstrators assembled at the post office in the main street. Kendall was at Cashin's end, Moorhouse Street. Carl Wexler was handling traffic at the Wallace Street intersection, not a taxing job at 11 am, winter, Port Monro. He was making a big thing of it, studied movements, like an air hostess pointing out the exits. Cashin thought it was easy to pick the blow-ins, those who had bought into Port at a high price and now wanted the drawbridge up. They had good haircuts and wore expensive outdoor clothes and leather shoes.

At the march's advertised starting time, the fat photographer from the Cromarty *Herald* was looking with sadness at the crowd, about thirty people, more than half women. The primary school came around the corner, all in rain gear, a multicoloured crocodile led by the principal, a thin balding man holding the hands of a girl and boy. The children carried signs written on white cardboard and tacked to lengths of dowel, no doubt a full morning's work in the art class:

KEEP AWAY FROM OUR MOUTH
DONT SPOIL OUR BEACHES
NATURE'S FOR EVERYONE NOT JUST THE RICH

Three shire councillors Cashin knew arrived. The *Herald* reporter got out of his car and signalled to the photographer, who went into sluggish action. Then two small buses banked up at Carl's end of the street. He directed them on with flourishes. A minute or two later, the occupants came back, walking in a group – about thirty people, all ages from about fifteen. To one side was Helen Castleman, talking on a mobile. She put it away, came past Cashin, gave him a nod.

'Good day, Detective Cashin.'

'Good day, Ms Castleman.'

Cashin watched her talking to the organiser, Sue Kinnock, a doctor's wife. She'd come to the station to show the shire permit for the march. 'We'll assemble at the post office, march down Moorhouse Street, cross Wallace, turn right into Enright, left into the park,' she'd said.

The sunlight had caught the pale yellow down on her cheeks. She had big teeth and a clipped way of speaking. Cashin put her down as the Pommy nurse who got the Aussie doctor, to the envy of her better-looking colleagues.

She came over with Helen Castleman. 'I gather you know each other, detective. Helen's WildCoast Australia president in Cromarty.'

'A person of many parts, Ms Castleman,' said Cashin.

'And you, detective. One minute, you're homicide, the next you're crowd control.'

'Multiskilling. These days we turn our hands to anything. How's Donny?'

'Not good. His mum's worried about him. How's your investigation?'

'Moving along. The way this parade should be.'

'The Channel 9 chopper's on the way, they're giving Bobby Walshe a lift. If you don't mind, we'll wait for them.'

'A reasonable wait I don't mind,' said Cashin. 'What's reasonable?'

'Fifteen minutes? They're landing on the rec reserve.'

'We can do that.'

Helen Castleman went over and helped a young man in a green WildCoast windcheater organise the marchers: children in front, the rest in ranks of five. She stood back and took a look, went over to the school principal. They talked. He didn't look happy but agreed to something. Helen chose six kids and eight of the oldest locals. They were arranged in two rows, four adults and three children in each, holding hands. Then came the school crocodile and the other marchers.

When he was finished, Helen went to Sue Kinnock. Sue raised her loudhailer. 'We'll be off in a few minutes. Please be patient.'

A helicopter thrummed over, dropped below the line of pines. The occupants arrived soon after in one of the small buses. Carl waved them through. They parked outside the library. The door slid open and Bobby Walshe got out, followed by a young man in a dark suit. Cashin saw a woman in the front seat move the rearview mirrow to fine-tune her lipstick.

Bobby Walshe was in casual gear: light blue open-necked shirt, dark blue jacket. He kissed Helen Castleman, he knew her, you could see that by the way they laughed, the linger of his hands on her arms. Cashin felt envy, shook it away.

'Right everybody,' said Sue Kinnock, amplified. 'Sorry to keep you waiting. Banners up, please. Thank you. And ready, set, off we go.'

Cashin looked across the street. Cecily Addison was lecturing Leon, a hand raised. Leon caught Cashin's eye, nodded in a knowing way. The vinegary couple from the newsagency were in their shop doorway, mouths curving southwards. Triple-bypassed Bruce of the video shop was beside saturated-fat dealer Meryl, the fish and chip shop owner. At the kerbside bicycle rack, shivering in yellow teeshirts, three young women, the winter staff of Sandra's Café, had an argument going. The spiky-haired one with the nose rings was taking on the others.

Outside the Supa Valu supermarket stood seven or eight people in anoraks, tracksuits. An old man in a raincoat had a beanie pulled over his ears.

Cashin walked along the pavement. 'Didn't know we had so many cops,' said Darren from the sports shop. 'Out in force.'

It began to drizzle at the instant the marchers broke into thin and ragged song: *'All we are saaaying, is saaave our coast.'*

The children had gone by when two men came out of the bar of the Orion. Ronnie Barrett and his mate, a slighter shaven-headed figure in a yellow and brown striped tracksuit, small tuft of hair on his chin.

Barrett came to the pavement edge, made a megaphone with his hands: 'Fuck off wankers! Don't give a shit about jobs, do ya?'

The other man joined him, 'Rich bastards pissouta Port!' he shouted. He took a step backwards, then another, unbalanced, almost fell over.

Cashin saw Barrett gesture at someone in the march, step off the kerb, all drunken belligerence. His companion followed.

A man stepped out of the column, a black beret on the back of his head, said something to Barrett.

Cashin got moving. Carl Wexler was trotting down the street, a TV cameraman behind him. They weren't close when Barrett lunged at the marcher with his left hand, trying to hold him for a punch.

The marcher, loose-looking, took a step forward, allowed Barrett to touch him. Barrett swung with his right, the man was inside the fist, he blocked it casually with his left forearm, stood on Barrett's left foot and hit him under the chin with the heel of his right hand.

It wasn't a hard blow, there was contempt in it, but it knocked Barrett's head back, and the marcher's left hand punched him in the ribs, several quick, professional punches.

'Break it!' shouted Carl.

Barrett was down, making sounds, his friend backing off, no more interest in a fight.

The marcher turned his head, looked at Cashin, went back into the ranks, expressionless, adjusted his beret. An old man next to him patted him on the arm.

The march had stopped. Cashin turned his back on the camera, he didn't want to be on television again. 'Let's get moving here,' he said loudly. 'Move on, please.'

The crocodile moved.

'Arrest, boss?' said Carl.

'Who?'

'The greenie.'

Cashin stood over Barrett. 'Get up and fuck off,' he said, 'See you again today, mate, you're sleeping over.'

To Carl, he said, 'It's over. Back to work.'

At the park, Sue Kinnock stood on the bandstand and made a short speech about people despoiling the beauties of nature, not wanting Port Monro to end up like Surfers Paradise. Cashin looked at the storm clouds boiling in the south, saw the cold drizzle falling on umbrellas, on dozens of little raincoat hoods. Like Surfers Paradise? Please God, could the weather part of that be arranged?

Sue Kinnock introduced Helen Castleman.

'As you may know,' Helen said, 'WildCoast is dedicated to preserving what remains of Australia's unspoilt coastline and to keeping it open to everyone. We came here today to say: If you want to stop developers ruining everything that makes your place special, well, we'll stand with you. We'll fight this project. And we'll win!'

Loud applause. Helen waited for silence, nodding.

'And now I'd like to introduce someone who identifies with our concerns and who's made a huge effort to be with us today. Please welcome the leader of Australia's newest political party, someone who grew up in this area, Bobby Walshe of United Australia.'

Walshe stepped up. The crowd was pleased to see him. Sue Kinnock tried to hold a big golf umbrella over him. He motioned her away, said his thanks, paused.

'Silverwater Estuary. Wonderful name. Brings to mind a place where a clean river meets the sea.'

Walshe smiled. 'Well, the reality is that Silverwater Estuary will end up as a place where a landscape and an ecosystem have been wrecked in the name of profit.'

He held up a newspaper.

'The Cromarty *Herald* is pretty excited about the project. Two hundred and fifty new jobs. How can that be bad? Well, let me tell you that these people always get the local paper excited about creating jobs. New jobs. It's the magic phrase, isn't it? Justifies anything. But all over Australia there are once beautiful places now ugly. Hideous. Ruined by projects like Silverwater Estuary.'

Bobby Walshe paused. 'And the developers and the local papers sold every single one of these projects as a job creation scheme.'

He ran fingers through his wet, shiny hair. 'We also have to ask what jobs did they actually create? I'll tell you. Jobs for part-time cleaners and dishwashers and waiters. Jobs that pay the minimum wage and come and go with the seasons and airline strikes and events thousands of kilometres away.'

Applause.

'And while I'm at it, let's talk about so-called local papers. Local? No, they're not. Take this newspaper.'

He waved the Cromarty *Herald*.

'This local paper is owned by Australian Media. The head office of AM is in Brisbane. That's pretty local, isn't it? The editor of this local paper arrived three months ago from New South Wales, where he edited another AM local paper. Before that he was in Queensland, doing what he's been sent to Cromarty to do. And what's that?'

Bobby waited.

'To boost advertising revenue. Make more money. Because, like the people behind Silverwater Estuary, money is all that matters. And this environmentally dangerous project means large amounts of advertising money for the paper. As for the company behind this, well, they're just flakcatchers. It'll be sold to other people once they get planning permission.'

Walshe was wet now, rain was running down his face, his shirt was dark.

'The state government can shut the door on this project in a second,' he said. 'They show no sign of doing that. It's not in the coastal reserves, they say. It's a matter for the shire council, they say. Does that mean that areas outside the coastal reserve are fair game for any shonky developer who comes along? I'm here today to say to hell with that bureaucratic rubbish. United Australia will support you in this fight. In all the fights like this going on all over our country. And that includes the cities.'

Bobby brushed water from his hair, put his hands in the air. 'One last thing,' he said. 'Do you know what a project like this is? I'll tell you what it is. It's an insult to the future.'

Applause. Bobby Walshe shook his head and rain droplets flew.

Cashin thought that Walshe knew how this would look on television: a handsome politician standing in the rain for a cause more important than his comfort.

To long applause, Bobby stood down. There followed a bad speech by a man with a bad haircut and a bad beard, shire councillor Barry Doull. When the hard rain came, Sue shut him up, said the thanks, directed people to the Save the Mouth fighting fund booth.

The crowd broke up, people wanted to shake Bobby Walshe's hand and he shook every one offered, bent to talk to an old lady and she kissed him, the camera on them. The school crocodile re-formed, set off, taking the short route home.

Cashin walked back with Kendall. 'A spunk,' she said. 'He's got my vote. I didn't know he was local.'

'Make sure it's his policies you like,' Cashin said.

In the main street, Bobby Walshe did a short on-camera interview with the woman who'd arrived with him. Now Cashin recognised her from when he and Dove were leaving the Cromarty station to go to court. She had asked the question.

Bobby talked to Helen Castleman. They were animated. He looked over his shoulder, met Cashin's eyes, said something to Helen. They came over.

'I know you,' said Walshe. 'Joe Cashin. Bern Doogue's cousin. From primary school.'

'That's right.'

Walshe put out a hand, they shook.

'How's Bern?' he said.

'Fine. Good.'

'What's he do now?'

'Well, this and that.'

'I couldn't have survived primary school without Bern,' said Walshe. 'The best kid on your side in a fight.'

'Some aptitude there, yes,' said Cashin.

Walshe laughed. 'You see him?'

'No week goes by.'

'Luke and Corey,' said Walshe. 'You were there.'

'Unfortunately.'

'It's a pretty sad business.'

'Kids go around carrying shotguns, there's always the chance things will turn sad.'

Walshe shrugged. 'Well, the inquest will decide whether it was his weapon, who fired first. Give Bern my regards. Tell him I haven't forgotten.'

'I'll tell him.'

They shook hands again.

'Don't forget to vote United Australia,' said Walshe.

'Can you vote for a soccer team?'

Walshe laughed, Helen gave Cashin a downturned smile. They went back to the vehicle and the television woman spoke to Walshe again.

Walking back to the station, Kendall said. 'You didn't say you knew him.'

'He knows me. Listen, Billy Piggot. What's he mean to you?'

'Don't know a Billy. There's a Ray Piggot that's a piece of work.'

'What's he done?'

'Ripped off a rep staying at the motel. Five hundred-odd bucks. The bloke came in the next morning. Cromarty handled it.'

'Ripped off how?'

'He had a story, the rep, but it was probably...' She made a sign with her right hand, the wiggle.

'Pillars of society, the Piggots,' said Cashin. 'Well, I'm off, two weeks to life, starting in five minutes.'

'And we're fully staffed. If you call a musclebound beach boy and a work-experience kid staff.'

'With your guidance, they'll grow,' said Cashin. 'Be fair but firm. Brunette but soft.'

She gave him a little nudge in the back with a fist, an act of disrespect given his rank, insubordination really.

LATE IN the day, a man in his seventies called Mick arrived from outside Kenmare and towed a mower around Tommy Cashin's wilderness, broke bottles, mangled metal, bumped over solid obstacles hidden in the grass.

'Should charge you bloody danger money,' he said when he'd loaded the tractor and the mower onto his truck. 'Can't, can I? Cause I'm doin this for nothin and you're givin me sixty bucks to pass on to the charity of my choosin.'

'I'm a cop,' said Cashin. 'Sworn to uphold the tax laws of our country.'

'Make it fifty,' said Mick.

Cashin gave him a note. He folded it and tucked it into the sweatband of his hat. People in this part of the world had an aversion to collecting the goods and services tax on behalf of the government.

While the dogs hunted the cleared area, much taken with the smells released by the mowing, Dave Rebb and Cashin walked around the the ruined building, measuring it. Cashin held the end of the tape and Rebb wrote down the distances and drew on a pad of graph paper. At the end, they sat on a piece of wall and Rebb showed him what he had recorded.

'Big,' said Cashin. 'Never thought it was that big.'

'Rich bugger, was he?'

'He made money on the goldfields, blew it all on the house. Also breeding horses, I think.'

A wind had come up, flattening the grass beyond. They could smell the land it had run over, smell the cold sea.

'He must've gone nuts early,' said Rebb. 'Could've built it somewhere warm.'

'It's about showing off,' said Cashin. 'He had to do it here. The Cashins had bugger all before that. Bugger all after that too.'

Rebb finished making a smoke, lit it, spat tobacco strands off his bottom lip. 'So you want to do that again, more showing off?'

'I do. What now?'

'Asking me? What do I know?'

They sat for a while, stood, the wind stronger now, pushing at them. They watched the dogs. The animals sensed their eyes, looked around, ran over and visited briefly, went back to work. Cashin thought about the stupidity of the project. This was the moment to quit, no harm done.

'What about the picture?' said Rebb. 'There's a whole piece missing, blown to buggery. Also we need a shelter, keep stuff dry.'

They walked back, the dark ponding in the valley. Days ended quickly now, twenty minutes from full light to ink black. Cashin's body ached from the bending.

Near the shed, Rebb said, 'Old bloke give me a bunny. In the fridge. See that?'

'No.'

'Bin there two days. Better cook it tonight.'

Cashin didn't say anything. He didn't feel like cooking.

'I can do it,' said Rebb. 'A bunny stew.'

A moment of hesitation. A cop meets a swaggie, the swaggie goes to live on his property, cooks meals. The locals would take a keen interest in this. Poofs, mate. Detective Poof and his swaggie bumchum.

Cashin didn't care. 'Sounds good,' he said. 'Go for your life.'

He fed the dogs, made a fire, got out beers, sat down, some relief from the pain. Rebb cooked like someone who'd done it before, cutting up the rabbit, chopping the wilted vegetables, browning the meat.

'This wine?' said Rebb, pointing at a bottle on the shelf. 'Saving it for something?'

'There's a corkscrew hanging there.'

Rebb opened the wine, poured some into the pot, added water. 'That's done,' he said. 'Be back.'

He went to the side door and the dogs roused themselves and followed him out. Cashin read the newspaper, drowsed. Rebb came back, dogs in first, they came to greet Cashin as if they'd been to the North Pole, thinking of him all the way there and back.

Cashin thought it was a very good stew, piled on rice. He ate in front of the fire and the television. Dave ate at the table, reading the newspaper. The news came on. The Port Monro march was item number six:

United Australia leader Bobby Walshe was in the seaside town of Port Monro today to speak at a rally against a proposed resort development.

The rally had things television liked: kids holding hands with the elderly, singing, the brief fistfight.

'That bloke's lucky to escape an assault charge,' said Cashin without looking at Rebb.

'Self defence,' said Rebb. 'He didn't hurt him much.'

'You swaggies know how to handle yourselves.'

'Just a drunk,' said Rebb. 'No challenge there.'

They watched the snatches of Bobby Walshe's speech.

He looked good wet, there was a close-up, raindrops running down his face. They saw the old lady kiss him, his kind smile, his hand on her elbow.

Walshe did a brief interview. Then the camera followed him and Helen Castleman going over to Cashin and Kendall and Wexler. The camera zoomed.

Cashin shuddered. He hadn't seen the lens pointing, he would have turned away. The woman with the freeze-dried hair said: 'Bobby Walshe also took the opportunity to speak to Detective Joe Cashin. Cashin was one of the police present at the death on Thursday of Walshe's nephew Corey Pascoe and another Aboriginal youth, Luke Ericsen, both from the Daunt Settlement outside Cromarty.'

Bobby Walshe again, running a hand through his damp hair: 'Just saying hello to the officer. I went to primary school with him. My hope is we'll find out exactly what happened that night and we'll get justice for the dead boys. I say I hope. Aboriginal people have lived in hope of justice for two hundred-odd years.'

Rebb got up, went to the sink, washed his plate, his knife and fork. 'You shoot that kid?' he said, neutral tone.

Cashin looked at him. 'No. But I would have if he'd pointed the shotgun at me.'

'I'll be off then.'

'You've got a touch with a dead bunny,' said Cashin. 'Bring one around any time.'

At the door, dogs trying to go out with him, Rebb said, 'When's the chainsaw coming?'

'Tomorrow. Bern reckons he'll drop it off with the water tanker first thing. That could be sparrow, could be midnight.'

'Also. We need stuff – cement, sand, timber, all that. I wrote it down by the sink there.'

'How much cement?'

Cashin thought he saw pity in Rebb's eyes. 'Make it six bags.'

'Need a cement-mixer?'

Rebb shook his head. 'Not unless you planning to bring in a few more innocent blokes you find on the road.'

'I'm always looking,' said Cashin.

He rang Bern and then, tired, hurting, sad, he went to bed early. Sleep came, a nightmare woke him, a new one. Dark and rain and garish light and screaming, people everywhere, confusion. He was trapped, held by something octopus-like, he fought it, it was crushing him, the space was shrinking, no air, he was suffocating, dying, terrified.

Awake in the big chamber, thin green light from the radio clock, feeling his heart in his chest and hearing the wind planing over the corrugations.

He got up. The dogs heard him and barked and he let them in. They ran for the bed, bumping, jumped, snuggled down. Cashin put on the standing lamp, threw wood into the stove, wrapped himself in a blanket and sat down with *Nostromo*.

Always an army chaplain – some unshaven, dirty man, girt with a sword and with a tiny cross embroidered in white cotton on the left breast of a lieutenant's uniform – would follow, cigarette in the corner of the mouth, wooden stool in hand, to hear the confession and give absolution; for the Citizen Saviour of the Country (Guzman Bento was called thus officially in petitions) was not averse from the exercise of rational clemency. The irregular report of the firing squad would be heard, followed sometimes by a single finishing shot; a little bluish cloud of smoke would float up above the green bushes...

He fell asleep in the big shabby chair, woke in early light, two dogs nudging him, their tails crossing like furry metronomes. The phone on the counter rang when he was filling the kettle.

'Constable Martin, Cromarty, boss. I'm instructed to tell you that Donny Coulter's mother rang a few minutes ago to says he's missing. She doesn't know since when. She saw him in bed at 11 pm last night.'

Cashin put a hand over the mouthpiece and cleared his throat. 'He hasn't done anything till he doesn't clock in. Tell his mum to check his mates, see if anyone else's gone. Call me on the mobile.'

He went outside, had a piss, looking at the hillside. The scarlet maples came and went through the mist like spot fires. He moved his shoulders, trying to ease the stiffness.

Donny wasn't going to sign the bail book at 10 am. He knew that.

'DONNY DIDN'T show,' said Hopgood. 'The mother says the little prick's been weepy.'

In misty rain, Cashin and Rebb had just started clearing the path that led to the former front door, uncovering red fired tiles, the colour still bright.

'She's had a look around?' said Cashin.

'I gather.'

'What about his mates?'

'Sounds like they're accounted for. Fastafuckingsleep like the rest of the boongs.'

'Take anything? Bag, clothes?'

'I would've said.'

Cashin was watching Rebb digging into the deep layer of couch grass, weeds, earth. He swung the long-handled spade tirelessly, scooping, scraping the hidden tiles. It made Cashin feel feeble, his own excavations meagre things.

'You might be on holiday but you're still in charge,' said Hopgood. 'We await instructions.'

'Bail violation,' said Cashin. 'Matter for the uniforms. The liaison bloke can work with Donny's mum, get the locals to search the whole Daunt. Every garage, shed and shithouse.'

'The locals are going to find Donny? You off the medication?'

Cashin looked at the sky. 'Keep me posted,' he said.

Back to digging his side of the path, feeling hollow in the stomach, as if he hadn't eaten for a long time. He was four or five metres along, Rebb as far as that ahead of him, when the water trailer arrived, a battered tank towed by Bern's Dodge truck, equally dented and scarred. Bern got out, unshaven, greasy overalls, cigarette in mouth. He looked around, unpleased by what he saw.

'Jesus, you're nuts,' he said. 'Cash on delivery.'

'Half past eleven?' said Cashin. 'This's first thing?'

'First thing I'm deliverin to you today. One-twenty bucks for the chainie, all tools included, owned by an old lady cut flowers with it, twenty for the corrie iron, twenty a week for the tanker, four weeks minimum hire, ten for delivery. Water, free first time, that's generous, refills ten. Let's say two hundred, throw in the first top-up. Present to you since you're family and a fuckwit.'

Cashin walked around the water tanker. It had been crudely sprayed black with aerosol paint. But before that rust had set in where markings had been erased, probably with a steel brush on a grinder. The rust was bubbling the new paint.

'Where'd you get this?' he said.

Bern flicked his cigarette end. 'Listen,' he said, 'you go in the McDonald's drive-in, you ask the kid where'd you get the mince?'

Cashin did another circuit of the tanker. 'The army reserve complaint,' he said. 'They were down the other side of Livermore, in the gorge, buggering about, rooting under canvas, went into town for a few beers. The next day they couldn't find two water tankers and a big tent and some tarps and gas bottles. Missing in action.'

'In the army reserve,' said Bern, 'takes three to wipe one arse. Bloke brung this in the yard. Says he's coming back to talk money. Never seen him before, never see him again.' He spat. 'What more can I say?'

'Don't say anything that could be used against you in a court of law,' said Cashin. He got out his wallet, offered four fifties.

'What, no argument?'

'No.'

Bern took three fifties. 'Jesus, you bring out the Christian in me.'

'Be a small Christian. Like a garden gnome Christian. We need some building hardware here. The trowels and the spirit levels, that sort of thing.'

Bern looked at Rebb, leaning on his spade, gaze elsewhere. 'Hey, Dave,' he shouted. 'Know a bit more about buildin than this bloke?'

Rebb turned, shrugged. 'I wouldn't know what he knows.'

'Yeah, well, I suggest you blokes come around,' said Bern. 'I got some brickie's stuff. Not cheap, mind you, hard to find. Take their gear to the grave, brickies.'

'There was a burg at Cromarty Tech,' said Cashin. 'They got into the building department storeroom.'

'Well, whoopy fuckin doo. Another thing I never heard of. You make up this shit, don't you?'

'I don't want to buy anything on the list of items missing,' said Cashin.

'Where you get your ideas I dunno. Not a stain on me. Your mates come down on me, that fuckin Hopgood, him and a footy team of pricks. An hour of fuckin around, messin up my place, they go off empty-handed, not so much as a fuckin sorry.' Bern spat. 'Anyway, give us a hand with this iron,' he said. 'You got any good corrie iron stories?'

They unloaded the corrugated iron. Bern got into the truck. 'Dave, been meanin to ask,' he said. 'Don't I know you from somewhere?'

Rebb was examining the chainsaw. 'Well, I don't know

you,' he said. 'But I know a buggered chainie when I see one.'

They got back to work. When Rebb reached the house, he turned and began digging on Cashin's side, coming towards him.

Cashin's mobile.

'For your information,' said Hopgood. 'No Donny. They checked every square inch of the place.'

Cashin was looking at the blisters on his left palm, one pale pregnant bump for each finger. 'Stage two,' he said. 'Probably should have done that in the first place.'

'Talking about us or you?'

'Just talking.'

'The alert's been out since before 9 am. We didn't wait for your say so. They tell you Bourgoyne's on the way out?'

'No.'

'Maybe you're out of the loop.'

When they were nearing each other on the path, casting the last sods into the green wildness, Rebb said, 'That Bern. He's your cousin?'

'Right.'

'Through your old man?'

'My mum. His dad's my mum's brother.'

Rebb gave Cashin a full stare and went back to work. After a while, he said, 'This was a serious garden. Got pictures of it too?'

'I'm going to Cromarty, I'll see,' said Cashin. He wasn't thinking about gardens, he was thinking about Donny and the dead boys and Hopgood.

HELEN CASTLEMAN was in court, said her firm. Cashin walked around the block, had just sat in the courtroom when she rose, all in black, silky hair.

'As your honour knows, the Bail Act of 1977 does not give us a definition of exceptional circumstances...'

The magistrate stopped her with a raised finger. 'Ms Castleman, don't tell me what I know.'

'Thank you for your guidance, your honour. The defendant has no history of involvement with drugs. He has two convictions for minor offences involving second-hand goods. He has four children under twelve. The family's only income is the defendant's scrap-metal business. Mrs O'Halloran cannot care for the children and run the business without her husband.'

The magistrate was looking in the direction of the windows.

'Your honour,' Helen Castleman said, 'I'm told that my client's trial is at least three months away. I submit with respect that these factors do add up to the exceptional circumstances demanded by the Act and I ask for him to be granted bail.'

'In this community,' the magistrate said, 'heroin possession is regarded as an extremely serious offence.'

'Attempted possession, with respect, your honour.'

Cashin could see the magistrate's jaw muscles knot. 'Possession of heroin is regarded as an extremely serious offence in this community. Perhaps that wasn't the case in Sydney, Ms Castleman.'

The magistrate made a croaking noise and looked around for appreciation, showed yellow dog teeth. The prosecutor smiled, her eyes dead. The magistrate came back to Helen, teeth still showing.

'The points I wish to make, your honour,' said Helen, 'are that my client, if convicted, faces a penalty at the bottom of the scale, and that his circumstances make the prospect of bail violation remote.'

The magistrate stared at her.

'If your honour wishes,' said Helen, 'I will address the subject, including the recent judgment by Mr Justice Musgrove in the Supreme Court on an appeal against a magistrate's court's refusal of bail.'

He took out a tissue and blew his nose. 'I don't require any instruction from the depths of your inexperience, Ms Castleman. The conditions are as follows.'

The magistrate set bail conditions.

'Your honour,' said Helen. 'With respect, I submit that $20,000 is so far beyond the defendant's capacity as to constitute a denial of bail.'

'Oh really?'

'May I address the court on precedent?'

He heard her without interjection. Then, silver motes of spittle catching the light, he reduced bail to $5,000.

When Cashin came out, a criminal investigation unit cop he knew called Greg Law was leaning against the balustrade, smoking a cigarette in fingers the colour of the magistrate's teeth.

'Jesus, that woman's cheeky,' Law said. 'You're supposed to lick his arse, not threaten to ram an appeal judgment up it.'

'When to lick and when to kick,' said Cashin. 'The central problem of life in the criminal courts.'

Law's eyes were on the street. Cashin followed them to a rusting orange Datsun with one blue door. The driver was slumped like a fat crash-dummy, her beefy right arm hanging out of the window, a cigarette in fat fingers. She lifted it to mouth. Cashin could see three big rings, knuckledusters.

'Gabby Trevena,' said Law. 'The lord knows, she's overdue. Broke a woman's jaw outside the Gecko Lounge, she's pregnant like a balloon. When she's down, Gabby puts in the slipper, cracks four ribs. What a piece of fucking work.'

A man in middle age and a youth came down the street, came up the steps, looking at Greg Law. The man was thin faced, faded ginger hair, mildewy suit from long ago, looser on him now than when he wore it to the wedding. The youth looked like his father, with longer ginger hair, bright with life, and a gold ring in an earlobe.

'Straight on, with you in a moment,' said Law, twinkling fingers at them. 'The story is the woman pinched these plants Gabs had growing in the roof. At crop time.'

'A roof garden,' said Cashin. 'Up in the ceiling of the fibro, a few deckchairs, plants in pots, Gabs sunbathing. I can see it.'

'Today the fat bitch walks. Complainant can't be found. Might need an excavator to find her.'

Law levered himself away from the railing. 'Talking licking and kicking, I hear Hopgood's your best mate.'

'Yeah?'

Law shot his cigarette into the street. 'Gabby Trevena's not the most dangerous person in this town. Almost but not quite.'

'What's that mean?'

'What do you think? Got to go.'

Helen Castleman came down the stairs. Cashin

stepped forward. 'Good day,' he said. 'Can I have a word?'

'If you want to walk with me. I'm late for a client.'

They went down the steps, turned left.

'Get my complaint about Donny being harassed?' she said.

'No. I'm on leave. Harassed how?'

'I complained to your Mr Hopgood. Patrol cars driving by the house, shining spotlights. What kind of shit is that? Are you surprised he's taken off? That was the aim, wasn't it?'

'I don't know about this.'

'You simply don't have a case, that's your problem.'

'We've got a case,' Cashin said. It was a lie.

Two skateboarders were coming, in line, the front one too old to be having fun. Cashin moved left, the pair rolled between them.

'Tell that to the two dead kids,' said Helen.

'No sane cop wants to shoot kids, shoot anyone actually. But normal kids don't get out of a wreck with a shotgun.'

'Well, that's your story, that's not a matter of fact. What do you want from me?'

Cashin didn't want her to dislike him. 'It would help if we knew he'd done a runner.'

Helen shook her head in a musing way. 'Do you think I'd tell you if I knew?'

'What would it hurt to tell me?'

'If I knew, it would be knowledge gained in representing him. How could I pass that on to you? I cross here.'

They stood at the corner, waiting for the lights, not looking at each other. Cashin wanted to look at her, looked. She was looking at him.

'I don't remember you as being so tall and thin,' she said.

'Late growth spurt. But you're probably thinking of someone else.'

Green light. They crossed.

'No,' she said, 'I remember you.'

Cashin felt a blush. 'Returning to the present,' he said. 'You're an officer of the court. There's no ethical problem.'

No reply. They walked in silence, stopped at her office, a bluestone building.

'I'm told you were city homicide,' she said.

'Been there, yes.'

He saw the shift of her head, readied himself.

'So it's your experience that lawyers tell you things about their clients?'

'I don't generally ask lawyers things about their clients. But your client's violated his bail. All I'm asking you is that if you know he's left the area, you save us the trouble of looking for him here. It's not a big ask.'

'I'm prepared to say that I don't know any more than you do.'

'Thank you, Ms Castleman.'

'My pleasure, Detective Cashin. Any time. By the way, I found out yesterday that we're to be neighbours.'

'How's that?'

'I've bought the place next door. The one with the old house. Mrs Corrigan's property.'

'Welcome to the shire,' said Cashin. Today we fence that boundary, he thought.

He walked back to the station. Hopgood wasn't there, out on the matter of a body in the ashes of a house in Cromarty West.

Cashin left a short message, drove to the library for the photograph. Closed, the librarians' day off. On the way home, he thought about the night in his last year at school, the final days. Tony Cressy drove out to pick him up in a Merc, a car from Cressy's Prestige Motors on the highway. Tony was the full back in the Cromarty High team, he had no pace, could hardly get his body off the ground, but he was big and he intimidated the opposition.

The four of them in the car, driving to the Kettle, to the Dangar Steps, two males and Helen Castleman and Susan Walls, he had not spoken more than a few words to either of the girls before that night.

The steps had long been fenced off, warning signs put up, but that only encouraged people. He helped Helen climb the wire, made a stirrup with his hands. She had no trouble with stirrups, she was a show jumper, people said she could go to the Olympics. They walked across the rock, along the worn path, in the footsteps of Mad Percy Hamilton Dangar, who spent twelve years cutting the narrow steps that began close to the entrance and ran around the walls, going down to the high-tide waterline. Everyone knew the story. Perhaps a hundred steps remained, unsafe lower down, gnawed by sea and spray and wind.

That night, they didn't descend far. They sat with backs against the cliff, the boys smoking, passing a bottle of Jim Beam, taking burning sips, not really drinkers, any of them. It was just for show. You had to do it. Cashin and Helen sat on the step below Tony Cressy and Susan. Tony kept them laughing, he could make anyone laugh, even the stern teachers.

Cashin remembered the feel of a breast touching his bare arm when Helen laughed, rocked sideways.

She wasn't wearing a bra.

He remembered the huge waves breaking against the entrance, the thunder, the white spray rising, the heart-stopping moments when the water exploded into the round chamber beneath them, surged up the limestone sides. There was no certainty it would stop – it came up and up and you thought that this one would pluck you from your perch, take you down into the hole, falling, falling into the boiling Kettle.

But it didn't.

It climbed the cliff to within five or six metres, fell back, tongues of water spat from the rock caves. The Kettle frothed and surged, then the big hole drained and it was calm.

He remembered the jokes, the next-time-it's-us-mate jokes.

They dropped Susan first, parked half a block from Helen's house. Joe walked her to the gate. She kissed him quickly, unexpectedly, looked at him, then she kissed him again, a long kiss, her hands in his hair.

'You're nice,' she said, went in her gate.

He walked back to the car, heart pumping. 'Now that,' said Tony Cressy, 'now that is class. And you're a lucky boy.'

IT WAS almost dark, the wind up, when they finished digging the rotten timber out of the last posthole. Cashin ached everywhere, it hurt to stand upright.

'Get it done by night tomorrow,' said Rebb. 'Given we got the materials.'

'Bern'll bring everything in the morning,' said Cashin. 'He's got a better understanding now of what's meant by first thing.'

They shouldered the tools, began to climb the hill for home. Cashin whistled and black heads appeared at the creek, together, looking up.

The house roof was in sight when his mobile rang, a feeble sound in the soughing wind. He stopped, put down the spade, found the phone. Rebb kept going.

'Cashin.'

Static. No reply. He killed it.

Cashin followed Rebb up the slope, every step an effort. On the flat, the phone rang again.

'Cashin.'

'Joe?' His mother.

'Yes, Syb.'

'You're faint, can you hear me?'

'I can hear you.'

'Joe, Michael tried to commit suicide, they don't know...'

'Where?' A feeling of cold, of nausea.

'In Melbourne, in his unit, someone rang him and they realised there…'

'What hospital?'

'The Alfred.'

'I'll go now. Want to come?'

'I'm scared, Joe. Did you ring him? I asked you to ring him.'

'Syb, I'm leaving now. Want to come?'

'I'm too scared, Joe. I can't face…'

'That's fine. I'll call you when I've seen him.'

'Joe.'

'Yes.'

'You should have spoken to him. I told you, I asked you twice, Joe. Twice.'

Cashin was looking at Rebb and the dogs. They were almost at the house, dogs criss-crossing in front, noses down. They had the air of point men, at the sharp end of a dangerous mission. At the gate, they would look back, each raise a paw, give those watching the all-clear.

'I'll ring, Syb,' he said. 'Call me if you hear anything.'

It was full dark when he came to the Branxholme junction and turned for the highway and the city. The headlights swept across a peeling house, a car on its axles, lit up devil-green dog eyes beside a bleeding rainwater tank.

CASHIN FELT a near-panic as the doctor led him down the long room, between the curtained cubicles. He knew the smell, of disinfectant and scented cleaning fluids, the computer-pale colour of everything and the humming, the incessant electronic humming. It came to him that a nuclear submarine would be like this, lying in a freezing ocean trench, hushed, run by electronics.

As they passed the stalls, Cashin saw bodies attached to tubes, wires. Tiny lights glowed, some pulsed.

'Here,' said the doctor.

Michael's eyes were closed. His face, what showed of it around the oxygen mask, was white. Strands of hair, black as liquorice, were drawn on the pillow. Cashin remembered his hair as short, neat – salesman's hair.

'He'll be okay,' said the doctor. 'The guy who rang him called emergency. Lucky. Also, the paras weren't far away, coming from a false alarm. So we had a small window of time.'

He was young, Asian, skin of a baby, a private-school voice.

'Took what?' said Cashin. He wanted to be gone, into the open, breathe cleansing traffic fumes.

'Sleeping pills. Benzodiazepine. Alcohol. Lots of both, a lethal amount.'

The doctor felt his jaw with a small hand. He was very

177

tired. 'He's just come off the dialysis. Feel like hell when he wakes up.'

'When will that be?'

'Tomorrow.' He looked at his watch. 'It's arrived already. Come around noon, he should be talking then.'

Cashin left the building and rang his mother, kept it short. Then he drove to Villani's house in Brunswick, parked in the street and walked down the driveway. He'd rung on the way. 'Tony's room's open, next to the garage,' Villani had said. 'I think it's been disinfected recently.'

The room was papered with posters of football players, kick-boxers, muscle cars, a music stand stood in a corner, sheet music on it. A cello case leant against the wall. Cashin looked at the photographs pinned to the corkboard above the desk. He saw his own face in one, long before Rai Sarris, a younger Cashin, looking at the camera, in the pool at someone's house, holding up a small Tony Villani. The boy was the adult Villani shrunken, retouched to take away the frown lines, to restore some hair at the temples.

That's how old my boy is now, Cashin thought, and sadness rose in him, to his throat. He sat on the bed, took off his shoes and socks, slumped, elbows on knees, head in hands, tired and hurting. After a while, he looked at his watch: 2.25 am.

A car in the driveway. A few minutes later, a tap on the door.

'Come in,' Cashin said.

Villani, in a suit, tie loosened, bottle in one hand, wine glasses in the other. 'The news?'

'He's going to be okay. They got him in time.'

'That's worth a drink.'

'Just the one bottle?'

'You're supposed to be fucking frail. Although, personally, I think it's all been wanking.'

178

Villani sat in his son's desk chair, gave Cashin a glass, poured red wine. 'Serious attempt?' he said.

'The doctor says so.'

'That's a worry. Know the why?'

'He rang my mum a few times, feeling down. She asked me to talk to him. I didn't.'

'That's like a summary of a short story.'

'What the fuck would you know about short stories?'

Villani looked around the room. 'Been reading a bit. Can't sleep.' He ran wine around his mouth, eyes on the posters. 'This isn't just any grog,' he said. 'But wasted on some. Smoke?'

'Yes, please.'

'I'm giving up tomorrow. Because you've given up.'

The nicotine hit Cashin the way it used to after a surf – raw, eye-blinking. He drank some wine.

'Definitely not your 2.30 am cask piss,' he said. 'Somehow I can tell that.'

'Bloke gave it to me, I couldn't say no.'

'Work needed on that before you front up to ethical standards. Is this early rising or late to bed?'

'Remember Vic Zable?'

'Amnesia is not the problem.'

'Yeah, well, Vic got it tonight, carpark at the arts centre, can you believe that? The guy doesn't know an art from a fart. In his ribs, couldn't get closer range unless you stick it up his arse. The shooter was sitting next to him, the silver Merc Kompressor, quadraphonic radio on, heater's going, he gives Vic the whole magazine. One little fucker bounces around inside Vic, comes out behind his collarbone, hits the roof.'

Cashin took a sip. 'How many left-handed friends has Vic got?'

'You're like a cop in a movie. Two we know so far. One's in Sydney, the other one's not home. I've just been there. There was a moment when I thought we'd get lucky.'

'Gangland hit arrest. Cop hailed.'

'In my dreams.'

'How's Laurie?'

'Good. The same. Pissed off at me. Well, we're mutually pissed.'

'What's wrong?'

Villani took a drag, his cheeks hollowed, pulsed out three, four smoke rings, perfect circles rolling in the dead air. 'Both of us having... affairs.'

'I thought you just looked?'

'Yeah, well, not much joy at home, if I'm not knackered, Laurie is. She's got all these night functions, the races, corporate catering, sometimes we don't see each other for days. We don't talk anymore, haven't talked for years. Just business, the bills, the kids. Anyway, I met this woman and the next day I actually wanted to see her again.'

'And Laurie?'

'I found out about her little adventure. Don't leave your mobile account lying around.'

'Cancel out then, don't they? Two little adventures?'

'It's a question of who went first, cause and effect. I'm said to be the cause of her rooting this cameraman dickhead. She's with him now, in Cairns, catering for some moron television shit. Probably on the beach, fucking under a tropical moon.'

'Grown poetic,' said Cashin. He didn't want to hear any more, he liked Laurie, he had lusted after her. 'Is that what being the boss does?'

Villani poured wine. 'I just pedal. I've got this pommy cunt Wicken on my back, he's cut out Bell, report directly to him. Don't understand the politics, don't fucking want to. I want Singo back, I was happy then.'

He sighed.

'We were both happy then,' said Cashin. 'Happier. I'll drop in on him in the morning.'

'Shit, I've got to get out there, there's never a fucking minute in the day. Well, what's with Donny?'

'The lawyer says there's been harassment, cars keeping the family awake. Why didn't you tell me about Hopgood?'

'Thought you knew the history of bloody Cromarty. Still, Donny might turn up.'

'Or not,' said Cashin. 'And we never had a fucking thing on him. Nothing.'

Villani shrugged. 'Yeah, well, we'll see. Forward, what do you do about your brother?'

It had been on Cashin's mind. 'Failed suicides. I know bugger all about it.'

'Wayne's alive, failed suicide. Needs to put in more effort. Bruce's dead. Well done, Bruce. Your brother's the family success, is he?'

'No,' Cashin said. 'He's just clever and educated. Plus the money.'

Villani filled the glasses. 'And the happiness, in spades. Not married?'

'No.'

'Someone?'

'No idea. The last time I saw him was when I was in hospital. He didn't sit down, took a few calls. I don't blame him, we don't know each other. Just doing his duty.'

'Sounds like Laurie on me and the family. If he wants a shrink, there's this bloke Bertrand saw when he went sad after that Croat cunt stabbed him. Not a cop shrink.'

'The Croat's the one needed the shrink. Bertrand needed a panelbeater.'

They had shared a life, they talked, smoked, Villani

went into the night and came back with another bottle, open. He poured. 'You think about the job? A person of leisure. Time to think.'

'What else was I good for?' Cashin was feeling the long drive, the hospital, the drink.

'Anything. You've got the brain.'

'Don't know about that. Anyway, I never thought, I didn't know what to do, stuffed around, surfed, then I just joined. Lots of fuckwits but... I don't know. It didn't feel like a job.' Cashin drank. 'Getting introspective, are we?'

Villani scratched his head. 'I never felt the worth of it till I got to homicide. The robbers, well, that was full-on excitement, us against the crooks, like a game for big kids. But homicide, that was different. Singo made me feel that. Justice for the dead. He say that to you?'

Cashin nodded.

'Singo could pick the right people for the squad. He just knew. Birkerts was bloody hopeless at everything but Singo picked him. Bloke's a star. Now I pick people like Dove. University degree, all chip and no shoulder. Doesn't want to be black, doesn't want to be white.'

'He'll be okay,' Cashin said. 'He's smart.'

'And now,' said Villani, 'I'm trying to get justice for drug scumbags got knocked before they could knock some other arseholes. Plus I get lectures on politics and fucking dress sense and applying the right spin. I now know why Singo blew a brain fuse.'

They drank most of the bottle before Villani said, 'You're more knackered than I am. Set the alarm if you want to. I'd have a fucking decent sleep myself.'

Before bed, Cashin slid open the window, got under the duvet on the narrow bed. The smell of cigarette smoke lingered. He thought of being seventeen, in the room he shared with Bern, lying on their backs in the dark, passing a smoke between the single beds before sleep.

When he woke, the clock said 8.17 am. He rose, dizzy for a moment. He had slept as if clubbed, felt clubbed now.

An envelope under the door.

Joe: Back door key. Eggs and bacon in the fridge.

Cashin ate breakfast at a small place on Sydney Road. It was either Turkish or Greek. The eggs were served by a wide man with eyes the colour of milk stout.

'I know you,' he said. 'You come after they shoot Alex Katsourides next door. You and a small one.'

'That's a long time ago,' said Cashin.

'You never catch them.'

'No. Maybe one day.'

A big sniff. 'One day. You never catch them. Gangland killers. That bloke on the radio, he says police useless.'

Cashin felt the blood coming to his face, the heat in his eyes. 'I'm eating,' he said. 'You want to talk to a cop, go down to the station. Where's the pepper?'

MICHAEL WAS out of intensive care, in a single room on the floor above. He was awake, pale, darkly stubbled.

Cashin went to the bed and touched his brother's shoulder, awkward. 'Gave us a scare, mate,' he said.

'Sorry.' Hoarse, breathless voice.

'Feeling okay?'

Michael didn't quite look at him. 'Terrible,' he said. 'I feel like such a creep, wasting people's time. There are sick people here.'

Cashin didn't know where to go. 'Serious decision you took,' he said.

'Not actually a decision. It just happened, sort of. I was pretty pissed.'

'You hadn't been thinking about it?'

'Thinking about it, yes.' He closed his eyes. 'I've been pretty low.'

Time went by. Michael seemed to go to sleep. It allowed Cashin to study him, he had never done that. You didn't usually look at people closely, you looked into their eyes. Animals didn't stare at each other's noses or chins, foreheads, hairlines. They looked at the things that gave signals – the eyes, the mouth.

He was looking when Michael said, eyes closed, 'Sacked three weeks ago. I was running a big takeover and someone leaked information and the whole thing went pear-shaped. They blamed me.'

'Why?'

Eyes closed. 'Photographs of me with someone from the other side. The other firm.'

'What kind?'

'Nothing sordid. Just a kiss. On the steps outside my place.'

'Yes?'

Michael opened his black eyes, blinked a few times, he had long lashes, turned his head enough to look at Cashin.

'It was a he,' he said.

Cashin wanted a smoke, the craving came from nowhere, full strength. It had never entered his mind that Michael was queer. Michael had been engaged to a doctor at one time. Syb had showed him a photograph taken at an engagement party, a thin blonde woman, snub nose. She was holding a champagne flute. She had short nails.

'A kiss?' he said.

'We were in a meeting late, eleven, we met again in the carpark, he came back to my place for a drink.'

'Sex?'

'Yes.'

'Did you tell him stuff?'

'No.'

'Well,' said Cashin, 'I've heard of worse shit.'

His brother had closed his eyes again, there were deep furrows between his eyebrows. 'He killed himself,' he said. 'The day after his wife left him, took the three kids. Her father's a judge, he went to law school with my head of firm.'

Cashin shut his eyes too, put his head back and listened to the sounds – low electronic humming, the sawing of traffic below, a far-away helicopter whupping the air. He stayed that way for a long time. When he opened his eyes, Michael was looking at him.

'You all right?' he said.

'Fine,' said Cashin. 'That is serious shit.'

'Yes. They told me you were here in the small hours. Thanks, Joe.'

'Not a matter for thanks.'

'I haven't been much of a brother.'

'Two of us then. Want to talk to someone? A shrink?'

'No. I've been to shrinks, I've made shrinks rich, I've helped shrinks buy places in Byron Bay, there's nothing they can do. I'm a depressive. Plain and simple. It's in me. It's a brain disorder, it's probably genetic.'

Cashin felt an unease. 'Drugs,' he said. 'They've presumably got the drugs.'

'Turn the world into porridge. If you're on anti-depressants, you can't work sixteen-hour days, plough through mountains of documents, see the holes, produce answers. My kind of depression, well, it's not like the tent collapses on you. It's just there. I can work, that's the thing that keeps it at bay, you don't want an idle moment. But there's no joy. You could be, I don't know, washing dishes.'

Michael was crying silently, tears running down his cheeks, crystal streams on each side.

Cashin put a hand on his brother's forearm, he did not squeeze. He did not know what to do, he had no physical language for comforting a man.

Michael said, 'They told me about the photograph and Kim's death at the same time. I walked out, got on a plane, drank and slept and drank, and it got worse and then I took the pills.'

He tried to smile. 'I think that's more than I've said to you at one time in our whole lives.'

A nurse was in the doorway. 'Keeping up the fluids?' she said, stern. 'Important, you know.'

'I'm drinking,' said Michael. He swallowed. 'Is it too early for a gin and tonic?'

She shook her head at his flippancy. Cashin could see she liked the look of Michael. She went away.

'Who took the picture?' he said.

A shrug. 'I don't know. There was a whole sequence, five or six shots. From across the street, I think.'

'Someone watching you or him. Who'd do that?'

Another shrug.

'When was the leak? Before or after?'

Michael put a hand to his hair. 'You're a cop. I forgot that for a while. After. In the next day or so. They knew what happened at a meeting our team had the morning after. Anyway, it doesn't matter now. Kim's dead, I don't have a career, everything's gone, twenty years of grind wasted.'

'Dangerous occupation you chose.'

Michael remembered. He smiled, a sad smile.

'You'd better come down and stay with Sybil for a while,' said Cashin. 'Help the husband napalm the roses.'

'No, I'll be all right. I'll stay with a friend, she's got lots of room. Get back on the medication. Avoid the drink. Exercise, take some exercise. I'll be okay.'

Silence.

'I'll be fine, Joe. Really.'

'What can I do?' said Cashin.

'Nothing.' Michael put out his left hand. Cashin took it, they held hands awkwardly.

'Don't get depressed, do you?' said Michael.

'No.' It was a lie.

'Good, that's good. You've escaped the curse of the Cashins.'

'The what?'

'Dad, me. Probably a long line before us. Tommy Cashin for sure. Mum says you're rebuilding his house. We're all the same, he was just at the extreme edge. Wanted to take his house with him.'

'What about Dad?'

Michael took his hand away. 'Mum's told you?'

'What?'

'She said she'd tell you when you were older.'

'What?'

'About Dad.'

'What?'

'That he committed suicide.'

'Oh,' said Cashin. 'That. Yeah, I know about that.'

'Okay. Listen, tell Mum I'm fine, Joe. Tell her it was all a silly mistake. Accidental overdose. Do that?'

'Sure.'

'Give her my love. Tell her I'll ring her tomorrow. Don't feel up to it today.'

Cashin said goodbye, kissed his brother on the forehead, a taste of salt, caught the lift with a family of four, near-adult children, everyone sombre. On the ground floor, he found the toilets, went into a booth and sat down, slumped, hands between his thighs. It was peaceful. From time to time, the urinal cleansed itself, a wash of water.

He saw himself in the Holden, a boy sitting next to his mother, on the way to strange places, for a reason unknown.

His father. No one ever told him. They all knew and no one ever told him.

THE NURSING home was a yellow brick veneer island in a sea of bitumen and concrete, not a blade of grass. A nurse in a dark blue skirt and spotted white shirt showed him to the room.

Singo was wearing a checked dressing-gown, sitting in a wheelchair in front of a glass door. The view was of a concrete strip and a high metal fence the colour of dried blood.

'Someone to see you, Dave,' she said. 'You've got a visitor.'

Singo didn't react.

'I'll leave you,' said the nurse.

Cashin moved the chair in the room, sat facing Singo's profile, moved the chair closer. 'G'day, boss,' he said. 'It's Joe.'

Singo turned his head. Cashin thought he'd aged since he'd last seen him, the paralysed side of his face now younger than the other.

Singo made a sound. It could have been 'Joe', it was a short sibilant sound.

'Looking much better, boss,' said Cashin. 'You're on the mend. Villani says to please come back. He'll tell you himself, he'll be out to see you soon. Snowed under. You'll know about that.'

Singo's lips worked, he made another sound, spitty, but Joe thought he was amused, something in his eyes.

He raised his left arm, the working arm, stretched his fingers. He seemed to be offering his hand to be held.

Not shaken. Held.

You could not hold Singo's hand, no. Singo could not possibly want that. He wasn't brain damaged, not that way, he was hindered, bits of him didn't work. Singo was in there, the hard man was there under the slack muscle, the disobedient tendons.

Cashin didn't know what to do, the second time in two hours.

Perhaps the hard man wasn't there anymore. Perhaps there was just a helpless and hopeless man reaching out.

Cashin thought about his father and he put out his right hand and touched Singo's.

Singo knocked his hand away.

Not reaching out. A mistake.

'Sorry, boss,' said Cashin. 'Water? Want some water? Anything?'

Singo blinked his left eyelid repeatedly. His eyes were saying something. He released another moist splutter of sound.

'Watching the TV, boss?' There was a television on the wall, no sign of a remote control. They would decide what he saw and for how long.

A nod, it could be a nod.

'Villani's got his hands full, see that?' said Cashin.

Singo raised his hand again, the fingers stretched.

Oh shit, thought Cashin, he's pointing.

He looked. There was a pad on the bedside cabinet and a pen, a fat pen. He fetched them, put the pad on Singo's tray, offered the pen to the left hand. Singo took it, clumsily, shakily, moved it in his big fingers.

'Why didn't she tell me you could write, boss? The nurse?'

Singo was trying to write on the pad, he was concentrating, the pen would not obey him, the pad shifted, veins stood out on his forehead,

Cashin reached out and moored the pad. Singo made scratch marks on it, possibly a C, possibly an R, a scribble of lines. His strength seemed to leave him, the hand slumped, his eyes closed.

Cashin waited.

Singo was asleep.

Cashin stood up and went to the door. He turned and said, not loud, 'Be back, boss. We're on your case. Get you out of here.'

He could see Singo reflected in the glass door and he thought he saw his eyes looking at him. He went back. Singo's eyes were closed. He moved the pad from under the big hand, long hairs on the fingers, and tore off the page.

'See you, boss,' he said, took his life in his hands and said, 'Love you.'

He sat in the vehicle for a while before he switched on, trying to make sense of Singo's marks. Then he put on music, shut his mind against the hours ahead, drove. Near home, exhausted, pains down both legs, the mobile rang.

'Found someone,' said Hopgood. 'Want to be there?'

CASHIN WALKED down the pier in the last light, stood behind the half-dozen watchers, cold salt westerly gale in his face. He saw the cat heel around the breakwater, stern down, twin engines howling. A man in yellow was at the wheel, two figures behind him, standing, dark wetsuits.

Hopgood, in a black leather jacket, turned his head, edged back through the group.

'Bloke in a plane saw a body outside the Kettle,' he said. 'In the Rip.'

For a moment Cashin thought that he would be sick, that he would spew over Hopgood.

'You're looking ratshit,' said Hopgood. 'Even more ratshit.'

'Bad pie.'

'What's the other kind?'

Cashin had heard of bodies being pushed into the sea caves by the powerful surges. Sometimes it was days, weeks, before they were sucked out of the holes, out of the Kettle and into the Rip.

Close in, the helmsman throttled back, the craft died in the water, rose and fell in a trough, motored to the pier and snarled to turn broadside at the pontoon. Two men were waiting, casual toss of a line, the boat was secured bow and stern.

They carried the body up wrapped in an orange nylon sheet, a man at each corner, the bottom ones fearful. On the pier, they put the burden down on the rough planks, gently, stood back, unwrapped it. Hopgood leaned over.

Cashin caught a glimpse of a bloated face, a bare foot, jeans torn to shreds. He didn't want to see any more, he'd seen enough of dead people, crossed to the shore-side railing and looked at the lights of the town above, not bright in the gloom. Cars flicked by at the two round-abouts on Marine Parade, people going home. People with families waiting. Children.

He wished he had a cigarette.

'In his pocket,' said Hopgood, behind him. 'In the jacket.'

Cashin turned. Hopgood offered him a grey nylon wallet, zipped. 'Torch here,' he said.

A torch came on, crossed the pier. Hopgood took it, shone it on Cashin's hands.

Cashin unzipped the wallet, found a card, a photograph in the corner. He strained to look at it, put it back.

Then a grey booklet, a prancing unicorn on the cover, inside it a plastic envelope.

Daunt Credit Union.

It was almost dry, water-stained only along the edges.

Perhaps twenty entries on two pages, smudged printer type, small sums in and out.

Donny Coulter drowned in the Kettle with $11.45 in his account.

Cashin put the passbook back in the wallet, zipped it, gave it to Hopgood.

'That's probably the full stop,' he said. 'I'm going home now. I'm supposed to be on leave.'

'Time to smarten up,' said Hopgood. 'Here it comes.'

A television crew was on the pier, coming towards them, already filming.

'Tip them off yourself?' said Cashin. 'Or have you got some suckhole does it for you?'

'Transparency, mate. That's the way it is now.'

'Bullshit. Told Donny's mum?'

'Told her what? She'll have to ID him.'

'Is that before she sees this on television?'

'This still your investigation? Your wog friend hasn't told me.'

'This has got nothing to do with the investigation,' said Cashin. 'And there never was any fucking investigation.'

He walked, straight at the television crew. The frozen-haired woman recognised him and said something to the sound recordist. Then she blocked his way.

'Detective Cashin, can we have a word, please?'

Cashin walked, he didn't reply, went around her. His shoulder knocked aside a furred microphone, the holder said, 'Steady on.'

'Fuck off,' said Cashin.

He drove the last stretch with Callas full blast on the player, roared down the dark and jolting roads with her beautiful voice filling the cab. The Kettle. A body floating outside the Kettle. In the big, foaming, shifting Rip.

They went to see it for the first time when he was six or seven, everyone had to see the Kettle and the Dangar Steps. Even standing well back from the crumbling edge of the keyhole, the scene scared him, the huge sea, the grey-green water skeined with foam, sliding, falling, surging, full of little peaks and breaks, hollows and rolls, the sense of unimaginable power beneath the surface, terrible forces that could lift you up and suck you down and spin you and you would breathe in icy salt water, swallow it, choke, the power of the surge would push you through the gap in the cliff and then it would slam you against the pocked walls in the Kettle, slam you and slam you until your clothes were threads and you were just tenderised meat.

It was called the Broken Shore, that piece of the coast. When Cashin was little, he had heard it as one word – the Brokenshaw. At some point, someone told him the first sailors to see the coast called it that because of the massive pieces of the limestone cliff that had broken away and fallen into the sea. Perhaps the sailors saw it happen. Perhaps they were close in and they saw the edge of the earth collapse, join the sea.

Home, thank god, the headlights passing across Rebb's shed.

He parked close to the building and sat, the pains in him, all over. Lights off. Reluctant to move. It would not be a hardship to sleep where he was. A little sleep.

Knocking, he heard knocking, came upright, full of alarm.

Two dog heads at the window, the wash of light from a torch. He wound down the glass.

'You okay?' said Rebb.

'Yeah, just tired.'

'Brother okay?'

'He's okay.'

'That's good. Dogs had their tucker. Finish the fence tomorrow.'

Rebb walked away. Cashin and the dogs went inside. He rang his mother. She wanted more than he had to give. He cut her off, washed down codeine tablets with a beer, poured a big whisky. He sat in the upright chair and sipped and waited for the relief.

It came. He drank more whisky. Before he went to bed, he watched the local news.

Police will not comment on speculation that the body found in the sea outside Cromarty's notorious Kettle, scene of many suicides over the years, is that of eighteen-year-old Donny Coulter, charged with the attempted murder of local identity Charles Bourgoyne. Detective Senior Sergeant Joe Cashin left Long Pier without comment after the body was brought to shore.

He saw himself coming down the pier – slit-eyed, shoulders set, hair being whipped around a stone face. Hopgood was next, pious-looking. There was something of the priest about his face, the mask of sadness and sincerity assumed for an occasion. 'Always bad to find a body,' Hopgood said. 'We have no other comment at this time.'

The reporter said: 'Donny Coulter's mother, Mrs Lorraine Coulter, spoke out tonight about police treatment of her son, missing since Tuesday.'

Donny's mother standing in front of a brown brick veneer house with a threadbare lawn, concrete wheel strips running to a carport. 'They hound him. Ever since the bail. They come by every night, put the spotlight on the house, right on Donny's window, they sit out there. He went to sleep in the back, he couldn't stand it no more. Drivin us all mad, Donny had enough to worry about, the boys the cops killed, all that...'

Cashin went to bed without eating and fell asleep instantly, did not wake until the dogs complained and the cold world was fully lit, no cloud in the sky.

REBB HAD the square redgum corner posts in, buttressed with diagonals notched into the strainers. Star posts were lying along the line of the new fence. In the middle was another strainer post.

'Bern give you a hand?' said Cashin.

'Didn't need a hand. Not much of a fence.'

'By my standards, it's much of a fence. What now?'

'Get the stars in. Line em up.'

'We'll need string.'

'Don't need string. Eye's good enough.'

'My eye?'

'Any prick's eye.'

Cashin squinted over the corner post, moving Rebb back and forth until he held each star post in line with the three strainer posts. Rebb used a sledgehammer to tap in the posts, held it in one hand as if it had no weight. Then he marked a pole with the height of the strainers and sent Cashin down the line to chalk the height on the lower part of each star post. Rebb came behind him, hammering the posts until they reached the mark. He swung with a fluid grace, a full overhead swing, no sign of effort, hit the small target cleanly, never a mishit. The sound was a dull ring and it went across the valley and came back, sad somehow.

After that they strung wire, four strands, bottom strand first, working from the middle strainer post, using a wire strainer, a dangerous-looking device. Rebb showed Cashin the knot used to tie off the bowstring-taut wire around the post.

'What's that called?'

'What?'

'The knot, the wire knot.'

'What's it matter?'

'Well,' said Cashin, 'no names, the world's all grunts and sign language.'

Rebb gave him a long sidelong look. 'Called a strainer hitch, you've got no use for that name. Have a look for mine?'

Cashin hesitated. You didn't talk about things like this. 'Your name? Had a look, yeah. That's my job.'

'Find anything?'

'Not yet. Covered your tracks well.'

Rebb laughed. It was the first time.

They worked. The dogs came, interested, bored, left, other things to do. When they were finished, it was almost mid-afternoon, no food eaten. Cashin and Rebb stood at the high point and looked down the line. It ran true, the posts straight, the low light singing silver off the new wire.

'Pretty good fence,' said Cashin.

He felt pride, it had not often been given to him to feel pride in work. He was tired and hurting in the pelvis and up his back but he felt happy, a kind of happy.

'It's a fence,' said Rebb. He was looking away. 'This the new neighbour?'

Cashin didn't recognise the woman coming down the grassy slope. Her hair was loose and she was in jeans and a leather jacket. She lost her footing a few times, narrowly avoided falling on her backside.

'I'll take the stuff up,' said Rebb. 'Milking time.'

Helen Castleman.

Cashin walked down the fence to meet her.

'What's this?' she said, out of breath. She looked scrubbed. It made him aware of how sweaty he was.

'Just fixing the fence,' said Cashin. 'Replacing the fence. I'm not asking you to pay half.'

'Generous of you. I understand the creek to be the boundary.'

'The creek?'

'Yes.'

'That's not so. Who told you that?'

'The agent.'

'The agent? A lawyer relied on the agent?'

Helen's cheekbones coloured, an autumn shade.

'Of all the people you might rely on,' said Cashin, 'the real estate agent...'

'That'll do, thank you. Having a good run, aren't you, Mr Cashin? Feeling pretty smart. You drive the poor frightened kid to suicide, now you don't have to make any case, he's made the case for you. And everyone else's dead, all suspects dead. Because you and your fucking mates killed them.'

She turned and began the climb, slipping.

All day, seeing a boy on the Dangar Steps, a brown boy in cheap jeans, nylon anorak, broken runners, standing on a crumbling limestone ledge, the salt spray rising like a mist to bathe him, looking down at the churning water.

'Listen,' he said, 'give me a break, it's...'

Her head came around, her hair swung. 'You don't deserve a break and I'll have a survey done, we'll see about this fucking boundary.'

Cashin watched her climb the slope. She had a few slips, a few slides. Half-way, she turned and looked down at him.

'What are you looking at?' she shouted. 'Why don't you just fuck off?'

In the shower, thinking about what he should have said, the phone rang. No towel. He went, dripping.

'Draw a line under this then,' said Villani. 'They switched off Bourgoyne. We're never going to know exactly what happened that night.'

'Exactly?' said Cashin. He was shivering, the place was a giant fridge. 'We never had the vaguest fucking idea.'

'The watch, Joe, the watch. Not found in a lucky dip at the church fete. Someone took it off an old bloke… anyway, what the fuck, it's over.'

Cashin wanted to say more but he caught himself, his gaze fell on his shrivelled penis, lying in the wet crinkly hair like something in a tidal pool.

'The harassment stuff,' he said, 'there's something about that…'

'Cromarty should have been purged long ago,' said Villani. 'They had the chance after the deaths in custody. But no, they moved the boss and put in a cleanskin, made his name in traffic, traffic dynamo. And presto, six months later Hopgood and his cocksucker offsiders were running the show again.'

'I'm not happy,' said Cashin.

'Nor am I,' said Villani. 'I'm at home. They say I'm never here. That's right, that's the way it is. So I make an effort tonight to eat with my kids and there's no one here. How's that?'

'I have no sympathy. Go back to gangland. I'm always home alone.'

In the night Cashin woke, tried to hypnotise himself with the measured breathing, the words to stifle thought. He was falling when he saw the Kettle, the clouds parting, a full moon lighting the world silver-grey, huge waves coming in, fretting at the top, exploding through the keyhole, pure untrammelled murderous power.

CASHIN ROSE early, unease in him like a stomach ache, took the dogs on the long route. They crossed the creek high up and walked back on the path below the shining new fence, on Cashin land, now demarcated.

After they had all breakfasted, he loaded the dogs and set off for his mother's house. Near the coast, he took the road that ran between the two volcanic hills, their caldera lakes home to swans, ducks, swamp hens, wicked-eyed bickering gulls by the hundreds. The lakes were never known to dry up. Cashin thought about the swims in them when he was living with the Doogues. They rode out on bicycles, five or six boys. They waded out in the black water, cold mud oozing through their toes, shivering on the hottest days. They walked around the dead tree trunks, avoided the branches that lay almost submerged like big snakes, green with moss and slime, streaked with birdshit.

At a shout, they would all throw themselves in and swim. In the middle, they crowded together, treading water, feeling the black and sucking deep beneath them. The idea was to dive and come up with a handful of grey mud. But no one wanted to be the first. Eventually, the boldest duck-dived. They would wait for him to come up before anyone else went down. Once Bern dived and swam away under water, rose silently behind a dead tree.

They waited for him to appear. They looked at one

another. Then they panicked. Cashin remembered that, no signal given, they all made for the shore, swam for their lives, abandoned Bern.

When they were standing in the shallows, Bern shouted: 'Cowardly bastards. How'd you know I wasn't stuck down there?'

The news came on.

Four people, including a policewoman, are in hospital after what Cromarty police claim was an attack on a patrol car in the Daunt Settlement outside the city last night. Police said a car on routine patrol was stoned shortly after 10 pm. Two other cars went to the scene. They found the first car on fire and a hostile crowd blocking the street.

The officers attempted to drive through the crowd to reach their colleagues, a police spokesperson said. However, they were forced to leave their vehicles and shots were fired before order was restored.

Police Minister Kim Bourke today defended the police actions.

'Of course this will be fully investigated but it's clear that it was an extremely dangerous situation. The officers' lives were in danger and they feared for the lives of their colleagues. They took what action was necessary.'

A forty-six-year-old man, a young woman and a youth from the Daunt Settlement were admitted to Cromarty Base Hospital with injuries. They are in a stable condition. A policewoman with head injuries is also said to be off the danger list. Two other people were treated and discharged.

A routine patrol? Through the Daunt on the night they found Donny Coulter? What kind of station commander didn't tell them to keep out of the Daunt?

*You drive the poor frightened kid to suicide, now you
don't have to make any case, he's made the case for you.
And everyone else's dead, all suspects dead. Because your
fucking mates killed them.*

His mother and Harry were having breakfast in the
kitchen, muesli and fruit, eating out of lopsided purple
bowls.

'Had breakfast?' said his mother.

'Not yet.'

'Probably nothing to eat in that ruin.' Sybil got up and
filled another bowl with muesli from a glass jar, poured
the remains of the tin of mixed fruit into it.

Cashin sat down. She put the bowl in front of him,
brought the milk jug closer. He poured and ate. It was
surprisingly edible.

'Michael rang,' she said. 'He's fine, very chipper.'

Harry nodded. 'Very chipper.' He was a repeater, it
was his role in the marriage.

'Good,' said Cashin.

'An accident,' said Sybil. 'All that stress he's under in
the job. So high-powered, it's not a good life.'

Cashin's eyes were on the bowl. What were the black
bits? Pips?

'He's coming down soon to have a bit of a rest.'

'Bit of a rest,' said Harry.

'Chance for you to spend some time together,' said his
mother. 'He was very warm about you, very apprecia-
tive.'

'I love being appreciated,' said Cashin. 'It's so rare in
my life.'

Harry laughed but he caught Sybil's eye and he choked
it, gazed into his bowl.

'Probably been over-appreciated,' said Sybil. 'The love
and care that's been bestowed on you.'

Cashin thought about drunk Sybil in the caravan, the nights of waiting for her to come back. He ate a piece of peach and a piece of something else, pinkish. The same taste.

'Disgraceful business in the Daunt last night,' said Sybil. 'It's turning into Israel, police provoking the dispossessed into violence. Manufacture of deviance.'

'Manufacture of what?'

'Of deviance,' said Sybil. 'You're part of that. You produce the justification for your existence.'

'Me?'

'The machinery of control. You're an unselfconscious part of it.'

'You get this from uni?'

'I've always felt it. Uni gives you the intellectual back-up.'

'I think I could use some intellectual back-up. What's this course called?'

'Finish your food, I don't want that muesli wasted. It's organic, cost the earth, I bought it at the farmers' market.'

'The farmers' market,' said Harry, and smiled, he had the smile of a mother's boy.

Sybil came with him to the vehicle. The dogs went berserk. 'They don't like me,' she said.

'Barking's not a judgment on you. It's just barking.'

Sybil kissed him on the chin. 'Keep in touch with Michael, will you, dear,' she said. 'Ring him. Promise?'

'Why didn't you tell me Dad killed himself?'

She took a pace back, clutched herself. 'He didn't. He fell. He slipped and fell.'

'Where?'

He saw water in her eyes.

'Fishing,' she said.

'Where?'

'Where?'

'Yes. Where?'

'At the Kettle.'

Cashin didn't say anything. He got into the vehicle and drove, didn't wave goodbye.

JUST AFTER noon, on his way back from Cromarty, the photographs of Tommy Cashin's house finally copied, Cashin registered that he was near the turnoff that led to the Bourgoyne place.

He slowed, turned, went up the hill. There was no thought behind it. He could turn left at the top, take the road around the hill, go through Kenmare, say hello to Bern.

He turned right, went around the bends and through the gates of The Heights.

He had no idea why he was doing this except that it seemed the way to close the business, where it began. He parked and walked around the house, clockwise. At least a dozen cops would have walked the south side, in a line, moving in slow-motion, studying the ground, picking up twigs, looking under leaves.

Today, there were few leaves. Everything was trim, the local football legend and his son were obviously still employed, had been on the job recently, plucking weeds, mowing grass, raking gravel. He went by the kitchen entrance, through an arbour, leafless but with branches so intricately twined as to deny the light.

Single-storeyed redbrick outbuildings to the left, a paved courtyard, old pink bricks in a herringbone pattern, sagging in places, depressions holding saucers of water.

Cashin walked between two buildings, looked through an ornate cast-iron gate into a drying yard, washing lines strung between wooden crosses, enough to dry the washing of an army. He went on, to where mown grass ran to a rustic post-and-rail fence, fifty metres away. Beyond that was a big paddock, its boundary a line of tall pines. The road lay beyond them.

He went back, around the south-west corner of the house. This was a clean space, a long empty rectangle bordered with lemon trees in big terracotta pots. Many of them looked unhappy, leaves yellow.

They'd had four lemon trees at the old house, out the back. You needed to piss on lemon trees, around the trunk. His father had often taken him out to do that after tea. They went from tree to tree, Mick Cashin had enough for all four, the last one got a little less. Joe ran out early but he carried on, stood with his father, aiming his small empty hose at the ground.

'Some places, it's all they get,' said his father. 'Dry countries. Nothin wrong with piss. Filtered by the body. Mind's the same. Hangs onto the bad stuff.'

Across the courtyard was a long double-storeyed brick building, doors and windows on the ground floor, sash-hung windows above. Cashin crossed and tried the big double door in the middle. It opened onto a corridor running the width of the building.

A door on the right was ajar. He went in a short way.

It was a big room, well lit from windows on two sides, a pottery studio – two big wheels, a smaller one, trestle tables, several steel trolleys lined up, bags stacked against the far wall, shelving holding small bags and tins of all sizes, implements of various kinds laid out. There were no pots to be seen. The place was neat and clean, like a classroom swept and tidied after the students each day.

Cashin went down the corridor to the door on the left.

It opened on darkness. He felt for a light switch, found several, clicked them.

Spotlights came on, three rows in the roof. It was a gallery, windowless, the floor of stone, dull-grey, smooth, the bare walls a pale colour.

A narrow black table ran almost the width of the room. On it, at regular intervals, stood – Cashin counted them – nine vessels. They were big, more than half a metre high, the shape of eggs with their tops cut off, tiny lips. Cashin thought it was a beautiful shape, the shape pots might want to be if potters would let them.

He went closer, looked at them from both sides. Now he saw small differences in shape, in bulge and taper. And the colours. The pots were streaked and lined and blotched and speckled in blacks that seemed to absorb light, in reds that looked like fresh blood leaking through tiny fissures, in the sad and lovely blues and browns and greys and greens of the earth seen from space.

Cashin ran a hand down a pot. There were smooth parts and then rough, like moving from a woman's cheekbone to a late afternoon stubble. And ice cold, as if the hellish passage through fire had conferred a permanent immunity to warmth.

Was this Bourgoyne's entire output as a potter? All that he kept? There were no pots in the house. Cashin picked one up carefully, turned it upside down: the letters C B and a date, 11/6/88.

He replaced the pot and went to the doorway. He stood looking at the pots. He did not want to kill the lights and leave them in the dark, their colours meaningless, wasted.

He killed the lights.

The rest of the building was an anticlimax. Upstairs, there were empty rooms on one side, living quarters on the other comfortably furnished, perhaps in the 1970s, a sitting room, a bathroom, a kitchen. He opened a door: a small bedroom, a stripped double bed, a bedside table, a wardrobe. The view from the window was across the paddocks, nothing for kilometres.

At the door to the corridor, he looked back into the sitting room. There was a bolt on the bedroom door. He went downstairs, out the back door onto a stone-paved terrace, looked at mown lawn, old elms, an oak wood beyond a picket fence. Straight ahead was the horse barn and the paddock where the helicopter landed.

A concrete path led off from a ramp at the left edge of the terrace. Cashin followed it, went through a gate in the fence and into the dense wood. The oaks were huge, no doubt planted by a Bourgoyne ancestor, trees to climb into, branches arranged in ladders. They were still heavy with brown leaves in spite of the thick new layer on the ground.

The land sloped up gently, the path twisted through the trees, its route dictated by the plantings. He was thirty or so metres along it when he caught himself enjoying the walk, a stroll in a wood on an early winter day, and was about to turn back.

A sound. He stopped. It was hollow, mournful, someone blowing into a cowrie shell.

He went on, the sound growing louder. The oaks stopped, a firebreak and then old eucalypts, towering. They thinned and there was a clearing on a gentle slope. The path veered left around a pile of split wood under a tin roof.

There was the smell of a hardwood fire, long dead.

Cashin stopped, uneasy. He went on, rounded the wood stack.

In the clearing stood a tunnel-like structure of cement-coloured bricks. It tapered in both dimensions, the narrower and lower end pointed at an opening in the trees, at the sea a few kilometres away. At the back was a square chimney.

He went closer. The earth at the base of the walls had a crust like bread. Low along the flank were square steel-shuttered openings, the bricks around them blackened. The chimney had a steel plate sticking out of it, a damper, Cashin thought, it could be moved in and out to regulate the flow of hot air. On the other side were more shuttered windows.

The front was open. On his neck, Cashin felt the westerly blowing straight into the mouth of the chamber, making the hollow sound. This was Bourgoyne's kiln, the furnace from which the pots emerged.

Blackened bricks were neatly stacked around the mouth. He stooped to look: beyond the scorched entrance were three tiers, like a short hierarchy of broad altars. There was a strong smell of things heated, vaguely chemical.

The wind off the sea would blow into the burning kiln like breath into a trumpet. Was it alight at night? The kiln would hum, the fire holes would glow white. It would have to be fed at intervals to maintain the heat.

Suddenly Cashin wanted to leave the clearing with its sad sound and smell of dead fires. He became conscious that the wind was cold, rain in the air. He went back through the trees, down to the buildings, continued his walk around the house, looking, thinking about what it would be like to approach the buildings at night, where the place would be to break in.

A few metres down the the north-western side of the house was a door, half glass, four panes. He looked in: a small room, tiled floor, benches on either side, coats and hats on pegs.

He turned. The severely tended garden ran for at least two hundred metres to a picket fence, then there were paddocks fenced with hedges, stands of trees, glints of water.

Perhaps a whim, half-pissed kids driving by, one of them given an idea by the big gates and the headlights catching the brass plate. It would have sent a message, as if in neon lights: RICH PEOPLE LIVE HERE.

Driving by? Going where? Heading back to the Daunt after fishing and drinking on the beach, you might take this route. It would be less risky than the main road.

Did the boys park a vehicle somewhere along the road, climb a fence, walk to the house? A kilometre in the dark, crossing paddocks, opening gates? No, they hadn't done that.

They would have parked near the gates and walked up the driveway, a dark passage, no lights in the grounds, the massive poplars, still in leaf, blocking the moonlight.

The boys, standing in the dark at the end of the drive, looking at the house. Were there lights on? Bourgoyne's bedroom was at the back of the house. He wasn't in bed. Where was he? In the study? Did they walk around, see the study and bedroom lights? If so, they would have broken in as far away as possible.

Thieves didn't break into occupied houses where there were lights on. The householder might have a gun.

What did they use to beat Bourgoyne? Did they bring it with them, take it away? There would be a post-mortem on him now, the pathologists would have an opinion, but it might be no more useful than ruling out faceted instruments or round ones bigger than a golf club shaft.

There was a noise. A door from the sunroom opened and Erica Bourgoyne came out. She was in soft-looking clothes, shades of grey, younger looking today, she could have passed for thirty.

'What's this about?' she said.

'Just having another look,' said Cashin. 'I'm sorry about your step-father.'

'Thank you,' said Erica. 'What's the point of looking around now?'

'The matter isn't closed.'

A man came out behind her, prematurely grey curly hair. He was just taller than short, tanned, dark suit, pale shirt and blue tie. 'What's happening?' he said.

'This is Detective Cashin,' said Erica.

He came around Erica, held out a hand. 'Adrian Fyfe.'

When Cashin felt the hard grip, the real man's grip, he gave Fyfe the dead fish, took his hand away. This was Adrian Fyfe the solicitor-developer who wanted to build a resort at the Stone's Creek mouth. Cashin remembered Cecily Addison's outrage that morning in the newsagency. *What this rag doesn't say is buying Stone's Creek mouth's no use unless you can get to it. And the only way's through the nature reserve or through the camp.*

'He would have been convicted, wouldn't he?' said Erica. 'Donny Coulter.'

'That's not certain,' said Cashin.

'What about the watch?'

'We have someone who says two of the suspects tried to sell it to him. We don't know how they got it.'

'Don't know?' said Adrian Fyfe. 'Pretty bloody obvious, isn't it?'

'There's no obvious in these things,' said Cashin.

'Anyway, it's over,' said Fyfe. 'The whole thing. Some justice done.'

'So pointless,' said Erica, listless now. 'To kill an old man for a watch and a few dollars, whatever it is they took. What kind of people do that?'

Cashin didn't try to answer. 'We'd like access to the buildings if you don't mind.'

A moment's pause. 'No, I don't mind,' she said. 'I

won't be coming again. The place will be sold at some point. There's a big bunch of keys in the kitchen. Dozens of keys. Give them to Addison when you're finished.'

She followed him around the house. They shook hands.

The same security man was leaning against the Saab, smoking. 'That gravel stunt,' he said to Cashin. 'One day I'll rip your head off, stick it up your arse.'

'You threatening a police officer?' said Cashin. 'Above the law, are you?'

The man turned his head away in contempt, spat on the gravel. Cashin looked back. Erica hadn't moved. He returned, climbed the steps.

'By the way,' he said. 'Who inherits?'

Erica looked at him, blinked twice. 'I do. What's left after the bequests.'

REBB WAS laying bricks, rebuilding the fallen north-east corner of the house. Cashin watched him for a while – the slicing pick-up of the mortar, the icing of the brick, the casual placement, the tapping with the trowel handle, the removal of the excess.

'Supervising?' said Rebb, eyes on the job. 'Boss.'

Cashin wanted to say it but he couldn't. 'What do I do?' he said.

'Mix. Three cement, nine sand, careful with the water.'

Cashin was full of care. Then he ruined the mixture by flooding it.

'Same again,' said Rebb. 'Half spades now.' He came over and put in the water, a slop at a time, took the spade, cut and shuffled the mortar. 'That's the pudding,' he said.

The dogs arrived from a mission in the valley, greeted Cashin with noses and tongues, then left, summoned to some emergency – a rabbit rescue perhaps, the poor creature trapped in a thicket.

Cashin carried bricks, watched Rebb, got the mixture more or less right the next time. The trick was extreme caution. The work moved to the opposite corner, a string was strung, tight enough to ping.

'Ever laid a brick?' said Rebb.

'No.'

'Have a go. I need a leak.' He left.

Cashin laid three bricks. It took a long time and they looked terrible. Rebb came back and, saying nothing, undid the work, cleaned the bricks. 'Watch,' he said.

Cashin watched. Rebb relaid the bricks in a minute. 'Got to keep the perps the same width,' he said. 'Otherwise it looks bad.'

'Want to eat?' said Cashin. 'Then I'll work on my perps. Whatever the fuck a perp is.'

It was after 3 pm. He had bought pies from the less bad bakery in Cromarty. Beef and onion. They ate them sitting in the lee of the brick pile, in the diluting sunlight.

'Not bad,' said Rebb. 'There's some meat.' He chewed. 'The problem here is the doors and windows,' he said. 'We don't know where they are.'

'We do. I've got the pictures. I forgot.'

When Cashin got back with the photographs, Rebb had made a cigarette. He looked at the pictures. 'Jesus, there's bits missing here all right. This is a serious proposition.'

'Yes,' said Cashin. 'It's not a proposition at all. I should have said.'

He had known the moment he looked at the old photographs. In one, Thomas Cashin and six men, builders, stood in front of the house. Thomas could have been Michael in an old-fashioned suit.

They sat in silence. In the valley, one dog gave the high-pitched hunting bark, then the other. An ibis rose, another, they flapped away like prehistoric creatures. Rebb got up, walked beyond the brick pile and held up the picture. He looked at his newly repaired piece of building, looked at the picture. He came back and sat.

'Bit like putting in twenty mile of fence, I suppose,' he said. 'You just think about the bit to the next tree.'

'No,' said Cashin. 'It's a stupid idea.'

He was relieved that the lunacy was over. It was as if

a fever had peaked, leaving him sweaty but lucid. 'House's fucked, it should stay that way.'

Rebb scuffed the earth with a boot heel. 'Well, I dunno. You could do worse. Least you're building something.'

'I don't need to. There's no point.'

'What's got a point?'

'It's a stupid idea. I admit it, let's leave it at that.'

'Well, got all this stuff here. Bit of a waste to stop now.'

'I'm making a judgment.'

'You can be too quick making judgments.'

Cashin felt the flash. 'I've had a bit more practice making judgments than your average swaggie,' he said and regretted his policeman's voice.

'I'm an itinerant labourer,' said Rebb, not looking at him. 'People pay me to do jobs they don't want to do themselves. Like the state pays you to keep property safe for the rich. The rich call, you come with the siren going. The poor call, well hang on, there's a waiting list, we'll get around to it some time.'

'Bullshit,' said Cashin. 'Bullshit. You've got no fucking idea what you're talking about...'

'Those dead boys,' said Rebb. 'That the judgment you talking about?'

Cashin felt his anger drain, the taste of tin in his mouth.

'The difference between us,' said Rebb, 'the difference is I don't have to stay on the job. I can just walk.'

In the silence, the dogs came with licks and nudges, as if, in the valley probing the undergrowth, they had heard the violence in the voices of their friends and had come in haste to calm them.

'Anyway, it's not as if I have a right to speak my opinion to you,' said Rebb. 'Being a swaggie.'

Cashin had no idea what to say, the ease that had grown between them over the days was gone and they had no history of arguments – won, lost, drawn, abandoned – to fall back on.

'Milking time,' said Rebb.

He rose and walked, left the spade stuck in the mound of sand, his bricklaying implements in the bucket, handles sticking out of silver water.

The dogs went with him, down the slope, even blacker against the sere grass. They trotted along happily. Then they stopped, turned, dark eyes on Cashin sitting on the bricks.

Rebb marched on, hands in his pockets, head down, shoulders sloped.

The dogs were torn.

Cashin wanted to tell them to go with Rebb, to say to them, you faithless things, I took you in, I saved you, you'd be in a concrete backyard now, knee-deep in your own droppings, you would not know a rabbit from a takeaway barbecue chicken. But I was only ever a meal-ticket and a soft bed, legs to lie on.

So go. Fuck off. Go.

The dogs bounded back to him, the lovely bouncing run, the ears afloat. They jumped up, put their paws on him and spoke to him.

He shouted, 'Dave.'

No response. 'DAVE.'

Rebb turned his head, didn't stop walking.

'OKAY, WE'LL FIX THE FUCKING THING!'

Rebb walked on, but he raised his right arm and gave a thumbs-up.

THE PHONE rang when he was making toast.

'Joe, time to leave this,' said Villani. 'It's over.'

'How did we get to over?' said Cashin. 'Because Donny tops himself? That's not a confession, that's an indictment of these local deadshits.'

'Did you see Bobby Walshe last night?'

Cashin sat down at the table. 'No.'

'Stay in touch with the world, son. We have apparently crucified three innocent black children. It's Jesus and no thieves, everyone's clean.'

'Can I say…'

'And another matter,' said Villani. 'Someone spoke to someone who spoke to the deputy who spoke directly to me. It concerns your visit to the Bourgoyne house yesterday.'

'Yes?'

'I'm asked why we are still hanging around The Heights.'

'Just doing the job. That's a complaint from Erica, is it?'

'The place's been x-rayed. What the fuck were you doing there?'

'Having a sniff. Remember having a sniff? Remember Singo?'

'It's too late for sniffing. Let it rest, will you?'

'There's no certainty the boys did it,' said Cashin. He had not planned to say that.

Villani whistled, rueful. 'Well, Joe, I've got a lot on the plate, it's a full plate. Every day. And night. What say we talk about this insight of yours later? I'll give you a call. First free moment. Okay?'

'Okay. Sure.'

'Joe?'

'Yes.'

'A cop, Joe, don't forget that. You don't obsess. You do your best and then you move on.'

Cashin could hear the voice of Singo.

'No one's done their best about this,' he said. 'No one's done a fucking thing.'

'Have a relaxing day,' said Villani. 'Did I say your holiday's been extended? The deputy wants you to take the full five weeks you're owed. He's worried about your health and wellbeing. He's like that. Caring. I'll get back to you.'

You don't obsess. Words chosen to remind, to caution. To hurt.

Cashin felt the nausea rising and the pain in his shoulders that would move up his neck into his head. In the worst times, these symptoms had signalled the coming of the frozen images, the ghostly negatives that lingered on the retina after he looked away from things. It had seemed clear to him then that he was going mad.

He took three tablets, sat in the big chair, head back, eyes closed, concentrating on his breathing, waiting. The pain did not reach its former heights, the nausea receded. But it was almost an hour before he could get up. He washed his face and hands, brushed his teeth and gargled, drove down empty roads to Port Monro. The cattle were indifferent to his passing.

He parked outside the post office. Four letters in the mailbox, nothing personal. No one wrote to him. Who would write to him? Not a single soul in the world. He walked around the corner to the station.

Kendall was on the desk. 'Can't live with it, can't et cetera,' she said. 'Boss.'

'Keeping the sovereign's peace?'

'Yes, sir. Spread the word to the locals that in the event of bad behaviour you'd come back.'

Cashin went to his desk, read the log, the official notices, sat looking at the backyard.

'While you're here, can I do some personal business, boss?' said Kendall.

'On your way,' said Cashin.

She had been gone a minute when a whippet-thin young man came in the door, looked around like a first-time bank robber. Cashin went to the counter. 'Help you?'

'They reckon I should talk to youse.' He pulled down on the rounded visor of his cap.

'Yes? Your name?'

'Gary Witts.'

'What can we do for you, Mr Witts?'

'Problem with the girlfriend. Yeah.'

Cashin gave him the compassionate nod. 'The girlfriend.'

'Yeah. Don't want to get her in no trouble. She's me girlfriend.'

'And the problem?'

'Well, it's me ute.'

'The girlfriend and your ute?'

'It's not like I wanna lay a charge.'

'Your girlfriend? No, you wouldn't.'

'Don't mean I'm not pissed off. I'm no fuckin rug, mat, whatever. Not me.'

'What's she done?'

'Went to Queensland in me ute. With this mate of hers from Cromarty, they're hairdressers, apprentices. You know that place WowHair? That's where.'

'So she took your ute without your permission?'

'Nah. Gave her a lend of it. Now she reckons she's not comin back. Met this Surfers Paradise bloke, Carlo, Mario, some wog name, he's got three saloons, offered her a job. Now she reckons I owe her the ute.'

'Why's that?'

Gary tugged at his visor again until Cashin couldn't see his eyes. 'She loaned me the deposit.'

Cashin knew. 'And she's been making the payments?'

'Just tempory. Pay her back. Got a job now.'

'How long did she make the payments?'

'Jeez, I dunno. A while. Year, bit more. Could be two. Yeah.'

'So what do you want?' Cashin said.

'I thought, like, you could get the cops up there, they could tell her to bring it back. Lean on her a bit. Y'know?'

Cashin put his forearms on the counter, laced his fingers, looked under Gary's visor. 'Gary, we don't do that kind of thing. She hasn't committed a crime. You lent her the ute. You owe her lots of money. Best thing you can do is go up there, pay her what you owe her, drive the ute home.'

'Well, fuck,' Gary said, 'can't do that.'

'Then you'll have to see a lawyer. Take some kind of civil action against her.'

'Civil?'

'A lawyer'll explain it to you. Basically, they write her a letter, tell her to hand over the ute or else.'

Gary nodded, scratched an ear. 'She's pretty scared of cops. Wouldn't take much to scare her, I can tell you.'

'We're not in the scare business, Gary.'

Gary went to the door, disappointment in his shoulders. He hesitated, came back, sniffed. 'Nother thing,' he said. 'How come you blokes don't do nothin about the fuckin Piggots?'

'What should we do something about?'

'Getting fuckin rich on drugs.'

'What's the point here, Gary?'

'Well, the mate she went with. She's fuckin thick with the Piggots. I reckon they dropped off a bag on the way, who's gonna check two chicks, right?'

'You know this, do you?'

Gary looked away. 'Won't say I do, won't say I don't.'

'What's her name? The friend?'

'Lukie Tingle.'

'An address and a phone number for you, Gary.'

'Nah. Don't wanna be involved. See you.'

'Gary, don't be dumb. I'll find you in five minutes, park outside your house, come in for a cup of tea, how's that?'

'Shit, gissus a break, will you?'

He gave an address and a phone number, left without another word, passed Kendall at the door.

On the way home, a man on the radio said:

'The state government's problem is that if it's seen as soft on law and order in Cromarty, it risks losing the white vote and the seat at the next election. And it needs every seat. So there's a real quandary. For the federal government, Janice, the mileage Bobby Walshe has got out of Cromarty is a nightmare. But of course a huge plus for United Australia.'

'Exactly how much mileage, Malcolm?'

'Bobby's performance last night was amazing, the passion, his sadness. He got on every TV news in the country, huge radio airplay. Bobby's given Cromarty a kind of symbolic status, and this is very important, Janice. The bit about the three crucified black boys, it had so much power, I can tell you it spoke to all kinds of people. Biblical. The talkback today has been amazing.

222

People crying, even from the redneck belts. Those words struck a major chord, they resonated.'

'But will that translate nationally, I mean...?'

'These are interesting times, Janice. The government's fear isn't just about losing Cromarty. The government can live without Cromarty. No, now it's a real fear that United Australia will split the vote all over the place. Become a genuine coalition of the disaffected. And the big shiver is that Bobby Walshe will roll the Treasurer in his own seat. It used to be rusted on. Now it'll take nine per cent and Bobby might be able to do that, Janice.'

'Thank you Malcolm. Malcolm Lewis, our political editor on the big issues driving political life today. Did I say life? Excuse me. My next guest knows about life, he almost lost his in a...'

Cashin found the classical station. Piano. He was coming around to the classical piano – the quick-fingered tinkling, the dramas, the final notes that floated like the perfume of women you'd lusted after. Most of all, he liked the silences, the gaps between what had been and what was to come.

THEY WORKED on the building again. By milking time, they had laid bricks to the first doorway to windowsill height.

'Stone sills in the picture,' said Rebb. 'Be stone lintels too, probably. Huge bloody door here.'

'I'll talk to Bern,' said Cashin. 'He may well have stolen them in the first place.'

Rebb left. Cashin worked on the garden for an hour, took the dogs for a short walk in the cold dusk. Tonight, he had only twinges of pain. He was tired but not hurting. Feed dogs, shower, make the fire, open a beer, water on for pasta.

Rebb knocked, came in, the dogs were on him.

'Surveyors down there,' he said, he was half in shadow, menacing. 'At the fence. Two blokes. When I went to milking.'

'She's unhappy,' said Cashin. 'Wasting her money. The agent is the snake, she should survey him. There's pasta on the way here.'

'Ate with the old bloke, he gets a bit lonely, doesn't want you to go. Not that he'd admit it. Wouldn't admit a croc's hanging off his leg.' He paused. 'About the house.'

'What?'

'We can get it up till you can see your way to going on yourself,' said Rebb.

Cashin felt the pang of loss anticipated. 'Listen,' he

said, 'this's about that swaggie thing? I'm sorry. I'll say sorry.'

'No,' said Rebb. 'I'm a swaggie, swaggie's got to keep moving. We're like sharks. Tuna, we're more like tuna.'

'The old bloke'll miss you.'

Cashin knew that he was speaking for himself.

Rebb was looking down, fondling dog heads. 'Yeah, well, everything passes. He'll find someone else. Night then.'

Cashin ate in front of the television, the dogs on the couch, limp as cheetahs, a head at each end. He refuelled the fire, made a big whisky, sat thinking.

Michael the fag. Did his mother know Michael was queer? Bisexual, he was bisexual. She knew. Women always knew. What did it matter what Michael was? Vincentia Lewis the nurse who gave him her father's CDs was a lesbian. Given the chance, he'd have married her, lived in hope. What hope? What did men have to offer? They died calling out for their mothers.

Mick Cashin drowned in the Kettle. *Took his life.* There was something terrible about that expression.

To take your life. That was the ultimate assertion of ownership – to choose to go into the silence, to choose sleep with no prospect of the dawn, of birdsong, of the smell of the sea on the wind.

Mick Cashin and Michael both made the choice.

This was not something to think about.

His father was always laughing. Even after he'd said something serious, scolding, he would say something funny and laugh.

Why did his mother still say it was an accident? She told Michael she would tell him his father had killed himself. And she couldn't, after all this time. She had probably changed her mind about what happened. Sybil had mastered reality. No need to tolerate the uncomfortable bits.

But why had no one else told him? He had come back and lived in the Doogue house, they all knew, they never said a word, never mentioned his father. The children must have been told not to speak about Mick Cashin. No one ever said the word *suicide*.

In the hospital, in the early days, when he had no idea of time, Vincentia had sat with him, held his hand, run fingers up his arm to the elbow. She had long fingers and short nails.

The Cashin suicide gene. How many Cashins had killed themselves? After they'd reproduced, created the next generation of depressives.

Michael hadn't done that. He was a full stop.

So am I, Cashin thought, I'm another dead end.

But he wasn't. The day he saw the boy walking from the school gate he knew he was his own beyond question – his long face, the long nose, the midnight hair, the hollow in his chin.

His son carried the gene. He should tell Vickie. She should know.

Rubbish. He wasn't a depressive. He felt low sometimes, that was all. It passed, as the nausea passed and the pain and the ghostly frozen images passed. He'd been fine before Rai Sarris. Now he was someone recovering from an accident, an assault. A murderous attack by a fucking madman.

Rai Sarris. Afterwards, in the hospital, he began to see how obsessed he'd become with him. Sarris wasn't an ordinary killer. Sarris had burnt two men to death in a lock-up near the airport. Croatian drug mules. He tortured them and then he burnt them alive. It took five years to get to the point when there was enough evidence to charge him.

And then Sarris vanished.

Where was Rai at this moment? What was he doing? Pouring a drink in some gated canal estate in Queensland, the boat outside, the whole place owned by drug dealers and white-collar criminals and slave-brothel owners and property crooks?

Had Rai been prepared to die the day he drove his vehicle into them? He was mad. Dying had probably never entered his mind.

Cashin remembered sitting with Shane Diab in the battered red Sigma from surveillance, looking at the grainy little monitor showing the two-metre-high gates down the street.

When they began to slide apart, he felt no alarm.

He remembered seeing bullbars, the nose of a big four-wheel-drive.

He didn't see the station wagon coming down the street, the chidren in the back, strapped into their seats.

The driver of the tank didn't care about station wagons with children in them.

Watching the monitor, Cashin saw the tank gun out of the gate and swing right.

There was a moment when he knew what was going to happen. It was when he saw the face of Rai Sarris. He knew Rai Sarris, he had spent seven hours in a small room with Rai Sarris.

But by then the Nissan Patrol was metres away.

Forensic estimated the Nissan was doing more than sixty when it hit the red car, rolled it, half-mounted it, rode it through a low garden wall, across a small garden, into the bay window of a house, into a sitting room with a piano, photographs in silver frames on it, a sentimental painting of a gum tree on the wall behind it.

The vehicles demolished that wall too, and, load-bearing structures having been removed, the roof fell on them.

Slowly.

The driver of the station wagon said the four-wheel-drive reversed out of the ruins, out of the suburban front garden, and drove away. It was found six kilometres away, in a shopping centre carpark.

Shane Diab died in the crushed little car. Rai Sarris was never found. Rai was gone.

Cashin got up and made another big whisky, he was feeling the drink. Music, he needed music.

He put on a Callas CD, settled in the chair. The diva's voice went to the high ceiling and came back, disturbed the dogs. They raised their heads, slumped back to sleep. They knew opera, possibly even liked it.

He closed his eyes, time to think about something else.

How many people like Dave Rebb were there out there, people who chose to be ghosts? One day they were solid people with identities, the next they were invisible, floating over the country, passing through the state's walls. Tax file numbers, Medicare numbers, drivers' licences, bank accounts, they had no use for them in their own names. Ghosts worked for cash. They kept their money in their pockets or in other people's accounts.

Did Dave ever have an earthly identity? He was more like an alien than a ghost, landed from a spaceship on some dirt-brown cattle station where the stars seemed closer than the nearest town.

An imperfect world. Don't obsess. Move on.

Sensible advice from Villani. Villani was the best friend he'd had. Something not to be forgotten. Best friend in a small field. Of how many? Relations excluded, relations didn't qualify as friends. Not many.

Cashin had never sought friends, never tried to keep friendships in good repair. What was a friend? Someone who'd help you move house? Go to the pub with you, to the football? Woody did that, they'd drunk together, gone to the races, the cricket. On the day before Rai Sarris, they'd eaten at the Thai place in Elwood. Woody's new ambition, Sandra, the high-cheekboned computer woman, was looking at Woody and laughing and she ran her bare stockinged foot up Cashin's shinbone.

Instant erection. That was the last time he'd felt anything like that.

Woody came to the hospital a few times but, afterwards, Cashin didn't see him, they couldn't do the same things as before. No, that wasn't it. Shane Diab lay between them. People thought he was responsible for Shane's death.

They were right.

Shane was dead because Cashin had taken him along to see if his hunch was right that Sarris would come back to the house of his drug-trader partner. Shane had asked to come. But that didn't exonerate Cashin. He was a senior officer. He had no right to involve a naïve kid in his obsession with finding Sarris.

Singo never blamed him. Singo came to see him once a week after he was out of danger. On the first visit, he put his head close and said: 'Listen, you prick, you were right. The bastard came back.'

More drink. Think about the present, he told himself. People wanted Donny and Luke to be Bourgoyne's killers. If they were, it justified the deaths of Luke and Corey. And Donny's suicide, it explained that – the act of a guilty person.

Innocent boys branded as the killers of a good man, a decent, generous man. Two injustices. And whoever did it was out there, like Rai Sarris – free, laughing, sneering. Cashin closed his eyes and he saw the boys, unlined faces, one barely breathing, chest crushed, one gasping, spraying a dark mist, dying in the drenched night, the lights gleaming off the puddles of rain, of blood.

He had another drink, another, fell asleep in the chair and woke in alarm, freezing, fire low, rain heavy on the roof. The microwave clock said 3:57. He took two tablets with half a litre of water, put out the lights and went to bed fully clothed.

The dogs joined him, one on each side, happy to have been spared the middle passage of exile to their quarters.

THE LIGHT came back to a freezing world, wind from the west, bursts of rain, hail spits the size of pomegranate pips.

Cashin didn't care about the weather. He was beyond weather, felt terrible, in need of punishment. He took the dogs to the sea, walked to the mouth in a whipping wind, no sand blowing, the dunes soaked, the beach tightly muscled.

Today, Stone's Creek was strong, the inlet wide, the sandbars erased. On the other side, a man in an old raincoat, a baseball cap, was fishing with a light rod, casting to the line where the creek flow met the salt, reeling. A small brown dog at his feet saw the poodles and rushed to the creek's edge, barking, levitating on stiff legs with each hoarse expulsion.

The poodles stood together, silent, front paws in the water, studying the incensed animal. Their tails moved in slow, interested scientific wags.

Cashin waved to the man, who took a hand off his rod. There was little of him to see – a nose, a chin – but Cashin knew him from Port, he was an odd-job man for the elderly, the infirm, the inept, replaced tap washers, fuses, patched gutters, unblocked drains. How is it, he thought, that you can recognise people from a great distance, sense the presence of someone in a crowd, know their absence in the instant of opening a door?

On impulse, he turned left, walked along the creek, threading his way through the dune scrub. The dogs approved, brushed past him, went ahead and found a path worn by human feet over a long time. The land rose, the creek was soon a few metres below the path, glass-clear, shoals of tiny fish flashing light. They walked for about ten minutes, the path diverging from the creek, entering a region of dunes like big ocean swells. At the top of the highest one, the coastal plain was revealed. Cashin could see the creek winding away to the right, a truck on the distant highway, and, beyond it, the dark thread that was the road climbing the hill to The Heights.

Below, the path ran in a gentle curve to a clearing of several hectares, cut from bushland now coming back. It led to a roofless building, to the remains of other struc-tures, one a tapering chimney standing amid ruins, a brick finger sticking out of a black fist.

The dogs reached the scene well ahead of Cashin, stopped, eyed the place, tails down. They looked back at him, got the signal, kicked off, running for a pile of bricks and rubble. Rabbits unfroze, scattered, bewildered the dogs for choice.

Cashin walked to the edge of the settlement, stood in the spattering rain. The flat area to the left had been a sports field. Three football posts remained, sunk in long grass, paint gone, wood bleached white. He became aware of the sounds the wind was making as it passed through the ruins – a tapping noise, a creaking like a nail being pulled from shrunken hardwood, a variety of low moans.

He went to the roofless timber structure, four rooms, a passage between them, looked in a window socket, saw a vandalised, pillaged space where fires had been made and people had defecated on bare earth once covered by floor-boards. Fifty metres beyond it stood the chimney. He crossed to it, went around to the highway side. Once the brickwork had housed two stoves in big recesses, between them an oven. The cast-iron door lay rusting on the brick hearth, broken from its hinges.

The dogs were running around frantically, demented by rabbit scents everywhere. But the rabbits were gone, safe beneath the broken bricks and rusted sheets of corrugated iron. Behind the kitchen, in the grass on the other side of an expanse of cracked concrete, Cashin found the brick footings of a long building, two rooms wide. The top bricks were blackened and, inside the footings, he stumbled over a charred floor joist.

That's history, been nothing there since the fire. Companions are history too.

Cecily Addison's words.

Cashin whistled, a chirpy sound in the forlorn place. The dogs appeared, joined at the mouths by something, tugging at it. He made them sit and release the object.

It was a leather belt, stiff and cracked – a boy's belt, a size to span a waist no bigger than a football. Cashin picked it up. On the rusted buckle, he could make out a fleur-de-lis and parts of words: B Prepa .

Be Prepared. It was a boy scout buckle.

He raised his arm to cast it away and then he could not. He walked across the overgrown playing field and bent the small hard belt around a goalpost, buckled it, let it slide into the grass.

On the highest dune, Cashin looked back. The wind was moving the goalposts, waving the grass. From the highway came the sound of a truck's airhorn, lonely somehow, nocturnal. He called the dogs and walked.

They drove home on empty roads, past houses sunk in their hollows, greenwood smoke being snatched from chimneys. The age of cheap dry wood from a million ringbarked trees was over.

He thought about Bourgoyne. Short of a startling piece of luck, it would never be known who bashed him, killed him. But it would always be stuck on the boys, their families, stuck on the whole Daunt, and even on people like Bern and his kids. Bourgoyne's killing was ammunition for all the casual haters everywhere.

Takin out those two Daunt coons. Pity it wasn't a whole fuckin busload.

Most of Derry Callahan's customers would have said Fuckin A to that.

Don't obsess, he thought. Listen to Villani, leave the business alone.

Rebb was waiting, out of the wind, he had heard the vehicle. He walked across, flat cigarette in mouth. Cashin got out, released the dogs. Rebb held his hands low, palms up, the dogs went to them and didn't jump, waggled their whole bodies.

'Listen,' he said, 'you going to town today?'

'I am,' said Cashin, deciding in the instant. 'You eaten?'

'No, just come from the cows.'

'We can eat somewhere. Give me ten, I need to shower.'

THEY ORDERED bacon and eggs at the truckstop on the edge of Cromarty. An anorexic girl with a moustache and a pink-caked pimple between her eyebrows brought the food. The eggs lay on tissue-paper bread, the yokes small and pasta-coloured. Narrow pink steaks of meat could be seen in the grey pig fat.

Rebb ate some egg. 'Not from chooks living out the back,' he said. 'You in a position to pay wages?'

Cashin closed his eyes. He hadn't paid Rebb anything for the work done at the house, the fence. It had not entered his mind. 'Jesus, sorry,' he said. 'I just forgot.'

Rebb carried on eating, wiped his mouth with a paper napkin. He reached inside his coat and produced a folded sheet of paper torn from a notebook. 'I reckon it's twenty-six hours. Ten an hour okay?'

'Don't you get the minimum rate?'

'No rent, eating your food.'

'Yeah, well, let's say fifteen.'

'If you like.'

'I'll need your tax file number.'

Rebb smiled. 'Do me a favour. Use Bern's number. Know that by heart, wouldn't you, your cousin, all the transacting you do? Paying the tax on it all.'

Hopelessly compromised, thought Cashin. Just as guilty as any woman with two kids caught shoplifting.

He parked two blocks from the bank. He could have

parked behind the police station but something said that wasn't a good idea. He took money out of the machine and paid Rebb.

'I'll be half an hour,' he said. 'Enough for you?'

'Plenty.'

He walked down wet streets to the station. Hopgood was in, writing in a file, a neat stack to his left awaiting his attention.

'Paperless office,' said Cashin from the door.

Hopgood looked up, expressionless eyes. 'What can I do for you?'

'I'd like to know who ordered the spotlight on Donny's house.'

'That's the Coulter bitch's story, lies, they all fucking lie. It's a way of life. Just a routine patrol.'

'I thought the Daunt was Indian territory? What happened to the Blackhawk Down stuff?'

Bright spots on Hopgood's cheekbones. 'Yeah, well, time to show the fucking flag in the pigsty. Anyway, where do you get off? I don't answer to you. Worry about your own fucking pisspot station.'

Cashin felt the heat in his own face, the urge to hit Hopgood in the middle of his face, to break nose and lips, to see the look he'd seen in Derry Callahan's eyes.

'I'd like to see the Bourgoyne stuff,' he said.

'Why? It's over.'

'I don't think it's over.'

Hopgood tapped a nostril with a finger. He had fat fingers. 'The watch? How does that feel?'

'I'd like to have a look anyway.'

'I'm busy here. Take it up with the station commander when he gets back from leave.'

Their eyes were locked. 'I'll do that,' Cashin said. 'There's something we haven't discussed.'

'Yeah?'

236

'That dud Falcon. You knew it couldn't keep up, didn't you?'

'Didn't know you couldn't drive, mate. Didn't know you were a gutless fucking wonder.'

'And the calls. You heard them.'

'Is that right? There's nothing on tape. You two boongs making up stories now? Like Donny's fucking mother? You related? All fucking related, aren't you? How's that happen, you reckon? All in the one bed fucking in the dark when they've cut the power cause you spent all the money on grog?'

Cashin's vision was blurred. He wanted to kill.

'Let me tell you something else, you fucking smartarse,' said Hopgood. 'You think you can shack up with a swaggie out there and nobody knows? You can let your arsefucker punch out innocent citizens and you look the other way? Is that a thrill for you? You like that kind of thing? Come in your panties, do you?'

Cashin turned and walked. A uniform cop was in the door. The man moved away quickly.

CASHIN WENT down to the esplanade and stood at the wall, the salt wind in his face. There were whitecaps across the bay, a fishing boat was coming in, cresting the grey swells, sinking into the troughs. He did his deep breathing, trying to take control of his nervous system, feeling his heartbeat slow.

After ten minutes, he went back, the only people on foot a group of kids coming down the hill in a rolling maul. He turned right halfway up, went the way he'd walked with Helen Castleman from the court, climbed the steps to her office. The receptionist was a teenager, too much makeup, looking at her nails.

He asked. She spoke on the telephone.

'Down the passage,' she said, a big smile, lots of gum. 'At the end.'

The door was open, her desk was to the right. Helen was waiting for him, looking up, unsmiling. He stood in the doorway.

'Two things,' he said. 'In order of importance.'

'Yes?'

'Donny,' he said. 'I've raised the harassment. They deny it. I'll take it as far as I can.'

'Donny's dead,' she said. 'He shouldn't be. He was a boy who wasn't very bright and who was very scared.'

'We didn't want that. We wanted a trial.'

'We? Is that you and Hopgood? You were fishing. You had nothing.'

'The watch.'

'Being with someone trying to sell a watch is evidence of nothing. Even having the watch means nothing.'

'I'll move on to the fence,' said Cashin.

'You've taken more than a metre from my property,' she said. 'Have your own survey done if you don't accept mine.'

'That's not what bothers you. You thought the property went to the creek.'

'Quite another matter. What I want you to do, Detective Cashin, is to take down the fence you so hastily…'

'I'll sell you the strip to the creek.'

He had not planned to say this.

Helen's head went back. 'Is that what this is about? Are you a friend of the agent?'

Cashin felt the flush. 'Offer withdrawn,' he said. 'Goodbye.'

He was in the doorway when she said, 'Joe, don't go. Please.'

He turned, conscious of the blood in his cheeks, did not want to meet her eyes.

She had a hand up. 'I'm sorry. I retract that. And my outburst on the evening, I apologise for that too. Unlawyerly behaviour.'

The disdain, then the surrender. He didn't know what to do.

'Accept?' she said.

'Okay. Yeah.'

'Good. Sit down, Joe. Let's start again, we know each other in a way, don't we?'

Cashin sat.

'I want to ask you something about Donny.'

'Yes?'

'There's something, it came up, it bothers me.'

'Yes?'

'The pursuit, roadblock, whatever it was, that was because of a watch someone tried to sell in Sydney. Is that right?'

Cashin was going to say yes when Bobby Walshe came into his mind. This was about politics, the three crucified black boys. Bobby wasn't going to let it rest, there was mileage left, miles and miles. She wanted to use him.

'There's the coroner to come,' he said. 'How's Bobby Walshe?'

Helen Castleman bit her lip, looked away, he admired her profile.

'This's not about politics, Joe,' she said. 'It's about the boys, the families. The whole Daunt. It's about justice.'

He said nothing, he could not trust himself.

'Do cops think about things like justice, Joe? Truth? Or is it like your football team, it can do no wrong and winning is everything?'

'Cops think much like lawyers,' said Cashin. 'Only they don't get rich and people try to kill them. What's the point here?'

'Donny's mother says that Corey Pascoe's sister told her mother Corey had a watch, an expensive-looking watch.'

'When was that?'

'About a year ago.'

'Well, who knows what Corey had?' Cashin heard the roughness in his voice. 'Watches and what else?'

'Will you do anything about this?'

'It's not in my hands.'

She said nothing, unblinking. He wanted to look away but he couldn't.

'So you're not interested?'

Cashin was going to repeat himself but Hopgood came into his mind. 'If it makes you happy, I'll talk to the sister,' he said.

'I can get her to come here. You can use the spare office.'

'Not here, no.' That was not a good idea.

'She's scared of cops. I wonder why?'

There had been a Pascoe in his class at primary school. 'Ask them if they know Bern Doogue,' he said. 'Tell them the cop is Bern's cousin.'

Cashin bought the Cromarty *Herald* at the newsagent. He didn't look at it until the lights, waiting to cross.

MOUTH RESORT GO-AHEAD
Council approves $350m plan

He read as he walked. Smooth and tanned Adrian Fyfe was going to get his development, subject to an environmental impact assessment. Nothing about access, about buying the Companions camp from the Bourgoyne estate.

CASHIN SAW them as he rounded the old wool store –
two big men and a woman near the end of the jetty. He
parked, got out, put his hands in the pockets of his bluey
and walked into a wind that smelled of salt and fish, with
hints of burnt diesel.

The jetty planks were old and deeply furrowed, the
gaps between them wide enough to lose a fishing knife
to the sea, see it flash as it hit the water. Only three
other people were out in the weather, a man and a small
boy sitting side by side, arms touching, fishing with
handlines, and an old man layered with clothing,
holding a rod over the railing. His beanie was pulled
down to his eyebrows, a red nose poking out of grey
stubble.

The men watched him coming, the woman standing
between them had her eyes down. Closer, Cashin could
see that she was a tall girl, fifteen or sixteen, snub nose,
bad skin.

'Joe Cashin,' he said when he reached them. He didn't
offer to shake hands.

'Chris Pascoe,' said the man closest, the bigger of the
two. He had a broken nose. 'This's Susie. Don't remember
you from the school.'

'Yeah, well, if you remember Bern Doogue, I was
there.'

'Tough little shit that Bern. All the Doogues. Seen him

242

around, not so little now, he don't know me. Gone white, I reckon.'

The other man stared into the distance, chin up, like a figurehead. He had dreadlocks pushed back, a trimmed beard and a gold ring in the visible earlobe.

'The lawyer says there's something I should know,' said Cashin.

'Tell him, Suse,' said Pascoe to the girl.

Susie blinked rapidly, didn't look at Cashin. 'Corey had a watch,' she said. 'Before he went to Sydney.'

'What kind of watch?'

'Leather strap, it had all these little clock things.' She made tiny circles on her wrist. 'Expensive.'

'Did he say where he'd got it?'

'Didn't know I'd seen it. I was just lookin for my CDs, he pinched my CDs all the time.'

'Why didn't you ask him?

She looked at Cashin, eyebrows up, big brown eyes. 'So he'd know I looked in his room? Shit, not that fuckin brave.'

'Watch your language,' said her father.

'If I showed you a picture of the watch, would you recognise it?' said Cashin.

Susie shrugged inside the anorak, it barely moved. 'Dunno.'

'You had a good look at it?'

'Yeah.'

Cashin thought about the band of pale skin on Bourgoyne's wrist. 'How come you're not sure you'd recognise it?'

'Dunno. I might.'

'The name of the watch?' he said. 'Notice that?'

'Yeah.'

Cashin looked at the men. It gained him nothing. The dreadlocked one was rolling a cigarette.

243

'You remember the name?'

'Yeah. Bretling. Something like that.'

'Can you spell that?'

'What's this spell shit?' said Chris Pascoe. 'She seen the watch.'

'Can you spell it?'

She hesitated. 'Dunno. Like B-R-E-T-L-I-N-G.'

If they'd schooled her, she would have got it right. Unless they'd schooled her not to.

'When was this?' said Cashin.

'Long time ago. A year, I spose.'

'Tell me something,' said Cashin. 'Why'd you only talk about the watch now?'

'Told me mum the day after.'

'After what?'

'After you shot Corey and Luke.'

He absorbed that. 'What did she say?'

The girl looked, not at her father but at the dread-locked man. He opened his mouth and the wind took smoke from it. Cashin couldn't read his eyes.

'She said don't talk about it.'

'Why?'

'Dunno. That's what she said.'

'Got to go,' said Chris Pascoe. 'So she's told you, right? Can't say you don't know now, right?'

'No,' said Cashin. 'Can't say that. Didn't catch your friend's name.'

'Stevo,' said Pascoe. 'He's Stevo. That right, Stevo?'

Stevo sucked on his cigarette, his cheeks hollowed. He flicked the stub, the wind floated it across the jetty. A gull swooped and took it. Stevo's face came alive. 'See that? Fuckin bird smokes.'

'Thanks for your time,' said Cashin. 'Got a number I can ring you on?'

The men looked at each other. Stevo shrugged.

'Give you my mobile,' said Pascoe.

He found the mobile in his jacket and read out the number written on the cover.

Cashin wrote it in his book. 'You'll hear from me or the lawyer,' he said. 'Thank you, Susie.'

'He wasn't a bad kid, Corey,' said Pascoe. 'Could've played AFL footy. Just full of shit, thought he saw a fuckin career in dope. You a mate of Hopgood and that lot?'

'No.'

'But you'll stick with the bastards, won't you? All in together.'

'I do my job. I don't stick with anyone.'

Walking down the uneven planks, looking at the fishermen, at the shifting sea, Cashin felt the eyes on him. At the wool store, he turned his head.

The men hadn't moved. They were watching him, backs against the rail. Susie was looking down at the sodden planks.

'IT'S DIFFICULT,' said Dove, his voice even hoarser on the telephone. 'I'm not a free agent here.'

'This thing's a worry to me,' said Cashin.

'Yeah, well, you have worries and then you have other worries.'

'Like what?'

'I told you about the freezer. The election's coming on. You go on worrying and then you're in charge at Bringalbert North. And your mate Villani can't save you.'

'Where's Bringalbert?'

'Exactly. I have no fucking idea.'

'The difference is that then we thought the boys had done it and you thought someone'd gone soft-cock on Donny, he was going to walk.'

'Yeah, well. Then. Talked to Villani?'

'He told me to get on with my holiday,' said Cashin.

'That'll be coming from on high. The local pols don't want to turn the sexy white hotel staff of Cromarty against them and the federal government doesn't want to give Bobby Walshe any more oxygen than he's getting now.'

It was late morning, a fire going. Cashin was on the floor in the Z-formation, trying to hollow his back, lower legs on an unstable kitchen chair. Silent rain on the roof, drops ghosting down the big window. No working on Tommy Cashin's ruin today.

'If this thing is left,' he said, 'it dies. The inquest will say very unfortunate set of events, no one to blame, it'll pass into history, never be picked up again. Everyone's dead. And then the kids and the families and the whole Daunt have it stuck on them. They murdered Charles Bourgoyne, a local saint. A stain forever.'

'Tragic,' said Dove. 'Stains are tragic. I used to like those stain commercials on TV. Joe, do you get television where you are?'

'And see what?'

'Bobby Walshe and the dead black boys.'

'I may be stuck out here in the arse,' said Cashin, 'but the brain's still functioning. If you don't want to do this, just say it.'

'So touchy. What do you want?'

'Bourgoyne's watch. Did anyone bother to find out where he bought it? It's fancy, I think they have numbers, like car engines.'

'I'll see. That doesn't run to risking the Bumbadgery transfer.'

'I thought it was Bringalbert North?'

'I'm told they're the twin stars in the one-cop constellation. Still doing that lying on the floor business?'

'No.'

'Pity. An interesting practice, a conversation starter. I'll call you.'

Cashin disconnected, stared at the ceiling. He saw Dove's serious face, the doubting eyes behind the little round glasses. After a while, he went into a near-sleep, hearing the rain coursing in the gutters and downpipes. It sounded like the creek in flood. He thought of going down to it after rain when he was a boy, the grass wetting him almost to the armpits, hearing the rushing sound, seeing the water brushing aside the overhanging branches, swamping mossy islands he'd fished from, foaming around and over the big rocks. In places there were whitewater races, small waterfalls. Once he saw a huge piece of the opposite bank break off. It fell slowly into the stream, exposing startled earthworms.

The money Cecily Addison paid out on behalf of Bourgoyne. Cecily's payment records, he had them.

Cashin lifted his legs off the chair, rolled onto his right side, got up with difficulty and went to the table. The thick yellow folder was under layers of old newspapers.

He made a mug of tea, brought it to the table. The first payment sheet was dated January 1993. He flipped through them. Most months were a page, single-spaced.

Start at the beginning and work back? He looked at the top page. Names – shops, tradesmen, rates, power, water, telephones, insurance premiums. Others gave only dates, cheque numbers and amounts. He'd given up the first time he looked at the statements and then things happened and he never went back.

Cashin read, circled, tried to group the items. After an hour, he rang. Cecily Addison was not available, said Mrs McKendrick.

Taking her nap, thought Cashin. 'This is the police,' he said. 'We're terribly polite but we'll come around and wake Mrs Addison if that's necessary.'

'Please hold on,' she said. 'I'll see if she'll speak to you.'

It was several minutes before Cecily Addison came on. 'Yeees?'

'Joe Cashin, Mrs Addison.'

'Joe.' Groggy voice. 'Saw you on television, being rude. Won't get promoted that way, my boy.'

'Mrs Addison, the payments you made for Bourgoyne. Some don't have names. You can't tell who's being paid.'

Cecily began clearing her throat. Cashin held the

telephone away from his ear. After a while, Cecily said, 'That's the regulars, the wages, that sort of thing.'

'There's two grand every month to someone, going back to the beginning of these payments. What's that?'

'No idea. Charles provided an account number, the money was transferred.'

'I need the numbers and the banks.'

'Confidential, I'm afraid.'

Cashin sighed as loudly as he could. 'Been through that with you, Mrs Addison. This is about a murder. I'll come around with the warrant, we'll take away all your files.'

A counter-sigh. 'Not at my fingertips this information. Mrs McKendrick will ring.'

'Inside ten minutes, please, Mrs Addison.'

'Oh, right. Galvanised now, are we? It took the third dead boy and Bobby Walshe.'

'I look forward to hearing from Mrs McKendrick. Very soon. Who was Mr McKendrick?'

'She lost him in Malaya in the fifties. Tailgunner in a Lincoln.'

'A man going forward while looking back,' said Cashin. 'I know that feeling.'

'In this case, falling forward. Off a hotel balcony. Pissed as a parrot, excuse the expression.'

'I'm shocked.'

Inside ten minutes, Mrs McKendrick provided the information, speaking as if to a blackmailer. Then Cashin had to ask Dove to make the inquiries. He rang when Cashin was bringing in firewood.

'I had to suggest, tell half-lies,' Dove said. 'I hardly know you. From now on, I want you to tell your own half-lies.'

'Truth Lite, everyone does it. The name?' The day was almost done, embers behind the western hills.

'A. Pollard. 128A Collet Street, North Melbourne. All withdrawals through local ATMs.'

'Who's A. Pollard?'

'An Arthur Pollard.'

The dogs were nudging him. It was time. 'We have a mystery bloke on the payroll for umpteen years,' he said. 'Needs a bit of work, don't you think?'

Cashin heard a sound. Dove was tapping on his desk.

'Yes, well,' Dove said, 'there's no shortage of things need work around here. And this little inquiry took fucking hours.'

'The extra mile. Force'll be proud of you.'

Three slow knuckle taps. 'I have to say this. I'm unsuited to homicide. It was a mistake. The death of a rich old cunt doesn't move me. I don't care if the guilty walk free. I don't even care if possibly innocent people now dead get the blame.'

Cashin rubbed dog heads in turn, the ridges of bone. 'Bourgoyne's watch?' he said. 'What about that?'

'May I say fuck off, pretty please?'

Time. Cashin put on his father's Drizabone, the short coat, dark brown, wrinkled like the skin of a peatbog man. One day about a year after he came to stay with the Doogues, Bern's father had offered it to him when they were going out with the ferrets.

'Your dad's. Hung onto it for you. Bit big. Mick wasn't small.'

Man and dogs in the rain, going downhill, escaping the worst of the wind. The long dry was over, the creek was filling. The dogs looked at it with amazement, affronted. They tested it with sensitive toes.

Cashin put his hands in the big pleated pockets. Was he wearing this that day? Was it night? Did he take it off and put it on a stone step before he jumped into the Kettle?

Was it the step I sat on with Helen?

He felt cold, whistled for the dogs. They looked around in unison.

RAIN SUITED Cromarty. In the old town, it turned the cobbled gutters to silver streams, darkened the bricks and stones and tiles, gave the leaves of the evergreen oaks a deep lustre.

Cashin parked outside the co-op and sat, wiped the side window to look at the street: a fat damp man pushing a supermarket trolley four blocks from the shop, two skateboarding kids wagging school, two women in shapeless cotton garments arguing as they walked, heads jerking. He didn't understand Cromarty, Cashin thought, he didn't know who had the Grip.

Singo had introduced him to the Grip.

It's the power to hurt, son. And the power to stop anyone hurting you. That's the Grip. There's blokes with millions got it and there's blokes with bugger all. There's blokes with three degrees and blokes can't read the Macca's menu.

The Bourgoynes would have had the Grip when the engine factory employed half the town. Did Charles keep the Grip after it was sold? Did he have any need for it?

Cashin got out. The rain soaked his hair, overran his eyebrows. He bought two big bags of dry dog food, drove to the supermarket and filled two trolleys, bulk buying. Never again could he enter Derry Callahan's shop. No more was there a milk, bread or dog food lifeline. Then he bought some whiting fillets at the fish shop and drove to Kenmare.

The street was empty, a windless moment, straight lines of rain. He went into the butcher. A new person stood behind the counter, a pudgy young man, spotted face, dark hair. They said good day.

'Couple of metres of dog sausage to begin,' Cashin said. 'Where's Kurt?'

'Cromarty. Dentist.'

'Helping out?'

'Permanent. Bit short on the dog, mate.'

'What you've got then.'

The youth weighed the sausage, wrapped it in paper, put it in a plastic bag.

'Plus three kilos of rump,' said Cashin. 'The stuff he hangs.'

He fetched the meat, cut, weighed. 'Take three-thirty?'

'That's fine. Mincer clean?'

'Yeah.'

'Run three kilos of topside, will you? Not too much fat.'

'Need some warning, mate. Come back tomorrow?'

'Too busy, are you?'

'Now, yeah.'

'Tell Kurt Joe Cashin's looking for another butcher, will you?'

The youth thought for a moment. 'Spose I can do the mince,' he said.

Cashin went out, sat in the vehicle, looked at the rain, placed the youth. He was wrapping the mince when Cashin opened the door.

'Local, aren't you?' said Cashin. 'What's the name?'

'Lee Piggot.' Lee was a bad wrapper, his fingers were too big. 'You the Doogues' cousin?'

'That's right. Know the Doogues?'

'Some. When I was at school.'

'Lee Piggot. Hear your name around the Cromarty drug squad?'

Flush, pink turning red. 'No.'

'Must be a name like yours. Butcher's a good job, a career. Honest work. People like their butcher. They even trust their butcher.'

Your police force, Cashin thought. Working with the community to create a better society. Using methods of fear and intimidation.

Last stop, Port Monro. The station was unattended. He let himself in and checked his desk: an envelope of pages faxed by Dove.

Heading home, a man on holiday, five weeks to go. The rain had stopped, the clouds dispersed, the world was clean and light. How much clearing and building could you do in five weeks?

Rebb was at work in the garden. He had found a low drystone wall.

'Jesus,' said Cashin. 'The elves been working here? In the rain?'

'Work's work. Can't let rain stop you.'

'Stops me.'

'You're a cop. You don't know about work. Pulling down the zip, that's work for cops.'

'You'd get on really well with Bern. Soulmates.'

They put in two hours, exposed twenty metres of stacked fieldstone and the remains of a wrought-iron gate.

'Made something to eat,' said Rebb. They walked back to the house and he produced four sandwiches neatly tied with cotton and toasted them under the grill.

'Not bad,' said Cashin. 'Old bushie recipe?'

'Tomato and onion's not a recipe.'

They went back and worked for another hour and then Rebb went to milking. 'Old bloke's taking me for a feed,' he said. 'At the Kenmare pub.'

Cashin carried on for half an hour, then he walked around and looked at the work they'd done in the garden and on the house. He realised that it gave him pleasure to see the progress, that he was proud of his part. It also came to him that he'd laboured for almost four hours without much pain.

Inside, straightening from giving the dogs their bowls, the current went through him. He moved slowly to a kitchen chair, sat bolt upright, eyes closed. It was a long time before he felt safe to rise. Then, tentative movements, he made a fire, opened a beer, sat at the table with the papers from Dove.

There were three medical reports on Bourgoyne. One was on his condition on arrival at the hospital. The second was from a forensic pathologist, who, at the request of the police, examined him as far as was possible in intensive care the next day. The third was the autopsy after his death. Bourgoyne's death was caused by his head striking the stone hearth.

The experts found that the marks on his knees and palms and feet were consistent with walking on hands and knees on rough carpeting. His facial bruises indicated being slapped repeatedly by someone standing above him, slapping with both sides of a hand about nine centimetres wide. The strokes across his back had almost certainly been administered with a bamboo stick of the kind sold by nurseries to support plants.

Cashin opened another beer. He stood at the counter, bottle in hand, pictures in his mind.

An old man roused from his bed, made to crawl down a long passage over a rough carpet.

A half-naked old man on his knees, someone slapping

him, jerking his head from side to side, slapping him with fingers and palm, then backhand with the knuckles.

Then someone caning him across his back. Ten strokes.

Finally, he fell forward, hit his head on the stone hearth.

Cashin opened a can of tomato soup and shook the contents into a pot, added milk. Soup eaten with bread and butter. It had been a standard winter evening meal at the Doogues, home-made soup though, full of solid bits, they emptied their bowls.

He should make some proper soup. How hard could it be?

He thought about catching the bus to Cromarty every school day with Bern and Joannie and Craig and Frank, six of them spread across the back seat, their seat. On the way there, Bern and Barry and Pat mucked around, he finished his homework, Joannie and Craig, the twins, whispered and bickered. On the way home, they were all in high spirits. Then, one by one, Barry, Pat and Bern dropped out and it was just the three of them.

Cashin took the beer back to the chair, wished he had a smoke. How long did the craving last? It would last forever if he kept chipping every chance he got.

He thought about that morning at The Heights – the old man on the floor, the blood, the sour smell. What was the smell? It wasn't one of the smells of homicide. Blood and piss and shit and alcohol and vomit, they were the smells of homicide.

Why was the painting slashed? What was that about? Why would you bother?

He got up, found Carol Gehrig's number in his notebook. It rang for no more than three seconds.

'Hi, Alice here.'

A girl, a teenager, bright voice. She was hoping for a call, hanging out.

'Is Carol Gehrig in?'

A disappointed silence. 'Yeah. Mum! Phone.'

There were sounds and then Carol said hello.

'Joe Cashin. Sorry to bother you again.'

'No bother.'

'Carol, the painting at Bourgoyne's, the cut painting.'

'Yeah?' Another disappointed person.

'Is it still on the wall?'

'No. I got Starkey to take it down.'

'Where is it?'

'I told him to put it in the storeroom.'

'Where's that?'

'Next to the old stables. You go through the studio.'

'Did they ask you about the painting?'

'The cops? No. I don't think so.'

'Why would anyone cut that painting?'

'Beats me. Pretty awful picture. Sad, sort of.'

MRS MCKENDRICK was in her seventies, gaunt, long-nosed, with grey hair scraped back. On her desk stood a computer. To her left, at eye level, was an easel holding her shorthand notebook. To the right, on the desk in two rows, were containers holding paper clips, split pins, pencils, a stapler, a hole punch, sealing wax.

'If she hasn't got anyone with her,' said Cashin, 'it'll only take a few minutes.'

'This firm asks visitors to make appointments,' she said, stroking the keyboard.

Cashin looked around the dark room, the prints of stags at bay, lonely waterfalls and hairy highland cattle grazing in the glens, and he found no patience.

'I'm not a visitor,' he said. 'I'm the police. Would you mind leaving the decision to Mrs Addison?'

The tapping stopped. Grey eyes turned on Cashin. 'I beg your pardon?'

Cecily Addison appeared behind Mrs McKendrick. 'What's all this?' she said. 'Come in, Joe.'

Cashin followed Cecily into her office. She crossed to the fireplace wall and leaned against the small bookcase, moved around, not much flesh to cushion her weight but no great weight to cushion. 'Sit down,' she said. 'What's the problem?'

He handed her the payments statement. 'The ones I've ringed.'

Cecily's gaze went down the list. She frowned. 'Wages, most of these. This I think is the turf club membership. The Melbourne Club this, goes up every year. Credit card bill. Small these days, used to be huge. This is… oh, yes, rates for the North Melbourne property. Wood Street. They go up every year too, don't know why he hangs onto it. The Companions used the place. I did the conveyance for that.'

'What kind of place?'

'It's a hall. They had concerts there in the beginning, I gather. Music. Plays. It was Companions headquarters.'

Cecily began the search for her cigarettes. Today, a quick find, in a handbag. She plucked one, found the Ronson, it fired at the first click. A deep draw, a grey expulsion, a bout of coughing.

'Tell me a bit about the Companions,' said Cashin.

'Well, the money came from Andrew Beecham. Mean anything?'

'No.'

'Andrew's grandfather owned half of St Kilda at one point. Lords of the city, the Beechams. And the country, a huge property other side of Hamilton. It's broken up now, cut into four, five. They had royals there. The English aristocracy. Sirs and the Honourables. Playing polo.'

Cecily looked at her cigarette, turned her palm upwards, reversed it.

'Educated in England, the Beechams,' she said. 'Nothing else good enough. Not Melbourne Grammar, not Melbourne Uni. Andrew never did a day's work in his life. Mind you, he won an MC in the war. Then he married a McCutcheon girl, nearly as rich as he was, half his age. She hanged herself in the mansion in Hawthorn and Beecham had a stroke the same day. Paralysed down one side, gimpy leg, gimpy arm. Ended up marrying a nurse from the hospital. After a decent interval, of course.'

Cashin thought that he could understand marrying the nurse from the hospital.

Cecily was looking out of the window. 'They come to you like angels, nurses,' she said. 'I remember my op, waking up, could've been on Mars, first thing I saw was this apparition in white...'

Silence.

'Mrs Addison, the Companions,' said Cashin.

'Yes. Raphael Morrison. Heard of him?'

'No.'

'He was a bomber pilot, bombed the Germans, Dresden, Hamburg, you know, fried them like ants, women and kids and the old, not many soldiers there. He came home and he had a vision. Teach the young not to make the same mistakes, new world, that kind of thing. Moral improvement. So he started the Companions.'

Cecily covered a yawn with fingertips. 'Anyhow, Andrew Beecham heard about the Companions from Jock Cameron, they were in the war together. Jock introduced Andrew and Morrison to old man Bourgoyne and he got the bug because of his dead older boys, and that's why the camp's where it is. On Bourgoyne land. In the late fifties, I was in the firm then.'

'Bit lost here. Who's Jock Cameron?'

'Pillar of this firm for forty years. Jock got wounded crossing the Rhine. Came out here for his health.'

Cecily stared at Cashin. 'You look a bit like Charles Bourgoyne,' she said.

'So, the Companions.'

'Lovely family, Jock's,' she said. 'Met them in '67, we went to England on the *Dunedin Star*. Never forget those stewards, pillowbiters to a man. They'd come along these narrow passages and rub against my Harry. He didn't take kindly, I can tell you.'

Cashin looked away, embarrassed. 'Something else. Jamie Bourgoyne apparently drowned in Tasmania.'

'Another family tragedy,' she said, not much breath. 'First his mother's death so young.'

'What happened to her?'

'She fell down the stairs. The doctor said she was affected by sleeping pills. Tranquillisers, it might have been tranquillisers, I can't recall. Same night as the Companions fire. Double tragedy.'

'So Bourgoyne brought up the step-kids?'

'Well, brought up's not quite the term. Erica was at school in Melbourne then. Jamie had his own teacher till he was about twelve, I think.'

'And then?'

'School in Melbourne. I suppose they came home in the holidays, I don't know.'

Cashin said his thanks, went out into the day. Ice rain was slanting in under the deep verandahs, almost reaching the shopfronts, soaking the shoes of the few wall-hugging pedestrians. He drove around to the station. Dove's faxes were on his desk and he started reading.

The phone rang. He heard Wexler being polite.

'Look after business for ten or so, boss?' said Wexler, behind him. 'Shoplift at the super.'

'I need the union,' said Cashin. 'On leave, I can't come in here without being exploited.'

He was on the sixth page when Wexler returned, looking pleased.

'Took a while, boss,' he said. 'This woman, she's got no idea the two little kiddies in the cart got stuff up their anoraks, chockies and that. The owners, they jump on her like she's some...'

'Sores?' said Cashin. He couldn't remember her name. He touched the corners of his mouth.

Wexler blinked. 'Yeah. Like little blisters, yeah.'

The first name came. 'Jadeen something?'

Eyes widened. 'Jadeen Reed.'

'Jadeen's just run out of supermarkets in this town. Shopping's in Cromarty from now on.'

Wexler kept blinking. 'Get it wrong, did I, boss?'

'Well,' said Cashin, 'Jadeen might have enough problems without a shoplifting charge.'

He left the station, bought the papers at the newsagent, avoided conversation, walked down to the Dublin. Two short-haired elderly women were at the counter, paying. They nodded and smiled at him. Either they were on the march or they'd seen him on television or both.

Leon thanked them for their patronage. When the door closed, he said, 'So, now retired due to post-traumatic stress caused by the march of toddlers and the aged? Looking forward to a life on the disability pension?'

'Long black, please. Long and strong.'

At the machine, Leon said, 'On that note, I see you and Bobby Walshe are school chums.'

'Kenmare Primary. Survivors.'

'And on to Cromarty High, you two boys?'

'Bobby left. Went to Sydney.'

'So you'll be voting for your other spunky school chum. Helen of Troilism.'

'Of what?'

'Troilism. Threesomes.' Leon was admiring the crema on his creation. 'Try under T in the cop manual. It's probably a crime in Queensland. She's standing in Cromarty for Bobby's all-purpose party?'

'You see that where?'

'The local rag. I've got it here.'

Leon found a copy of the newspaper, opened it to the page. There was a small photograph of Helen Castleman. It did not flatter. The headline said:

'Did it cross your mind,' Leon said, leaning on the counter, 'that our lives are just like stories kids tell you? They get the and-then-and-then right, and then they run out of steam and just stop.'

'You've got kids?' It had not occurred to Cashin.

'Two,' said Leon.

Cashin felt a sense of unfairness. 'Maybe you shouldn't think about your life that way. Maybe you shouldn't think about your life at all. Just make the coffee.'

'I can't help thinking about it,' said Leon. 'When I was growing up I was going to be a doctor, do good things, save lives. A life with a purpose. I wasn't going to be like my father.'

'What was wrong with him?'

'He was an accountant. Dudded his clients, the little old ladies, the pensioners. One day he didn't come home. I was nine, he didn't come back till I was fourteen. Not a single word from him. I used to hope he'd come on my birthday. Then he arrived... anyway, forget it, I get maudlin in winter. Vitamin D deficiency, drink too much.'

'Why can't dentists have a purpose?'

Leon shook his head. 'Ever heard anyone appeal for a dentist to come forward?'

'My feeling,' said Cashin, 'is that you're being a bit hard on yourself.'

CASHIN WAS looking into the fridge, thinking about what to cook for supper when the phone on the counter rang.

'Get anywhere with the matter we discussed?' said Helen Castleman.

'I had the chat with them, yes,' said Cashin.

'So?'

'It's worth thinking about.'

'Just thinking?'

'A manner of speaking.'

Silence.

'I don't know how to take you, detective,' she said.

'Why's that?'

'I don't know whether you want the right result.'

'What's the right result?'

'The truth's the right result.'

Cashin looked at the dogs, splendid before the fire. They felt his gaze, raised heads, looked at him, sighed and sagged.

'You'd be good in parliament,' said Cashin. 'Raise all the standards. The looks, the average IQ.'

'Blind Freddy's dog's got a better chance of getting into parliament,' she said. 'I'm standing to give some choice in this redneck town. Moving on. What are you doing then?'

'Working on the matter.'

'Is that you or the homicide squad?'

264

'I can't speak for the homicide squad. There's no great...'

'Great what?'

'I forget. Interrupting me does that. I'm on leave. Out of touch.'

'And you've no doubt worn a path between your mansion and the illegal fence on my property.'

'There's a pre-existing path. Historical path to the historical boundary.'

'Well, I'm coming up it,' Helen said. 'I want to see your eyes when you talk this vague bullshit.'

'That's also a manner of speaking, is it?' said Cashin.

'It is not. I'll be there in... in however long it takes. I'll be inspecting my boundary on the way.'

'What, now?'

'Setting out this very minute.'

'Dark soon.'

'Not that soon. And I've got a torch.'

'Snakes are a problem.'

'I'm not scared of snakes. Mate.'

'Rats. Big water rats. And land rats.'

'Well, eek, eek, bloody eek. Four-legged rats don't scare me. I'm on my way.'

IN THE FADING afternoon, he saw the red jacket a long way off, a matchflare in the gathering gloom. Then the dogs sniffed her on the wind and took off, ran dead straight. They monstered her but she kept her hands in her pockets, no more scared of dogs than of snakes or rats.

When they met, Helen offered a hand in a formal way. She looked scrubbed, fresh out of the shower, colour on her cheekbones. 'I suppose you could charge me with trespass,' she said.

'I'll keep that in reserve,' said Cashin. 'Let me walk in front, lots of holes. I don't want to be sued.'

He turned and walked.

'Very legalistic meeting this,' said Helen.

'I don't know about a meeting. More like an interview.'

They walked up the slope in silence. At the gate, Cashin whistled the dogs in and they appeared from different directions.

'Highly trained animals,' she said.

'Hungry animals. It's supper time.'

At the back door, he said, 'I'm not apologising for the place. It's a ruin. I live in a ruin.'

They went in, down the passage to the big room.

'Jesus,' she said. 'What room is this?'

'The ballroom. I have the balls in here.'

Cashin shunted the dogs into the kitchen, led the way to the rooms he lived in, cringed at the half-stripped wallpaper, the cracked plaster, the piles of newspapers.

'This is where you go after the balls,' said Helen. 'The less formal room. It's warm.'

'This is where we withdraw to,' he said. 'The withdrawing room.' He had read the term somewhere, hadn't known it before Rai Sarris, that was certain.

Helen looked at him, nodding in an appraising way, biting her lower lip. 'My embarrassment about this visit has been growing,' she said. 'I get so angry.'

Cashin cleared newspapers from a chair, dropped them on the floor. 'Now that you're here,' he said, 'have a seat.'

She sat down.

He didn't know what to do next. He said, awkward, 'Time to feed the dogs. Tea, coffee? A drink?'

'Is that the choice for the dogs? Do I get to choose? Give them tea. And a bickie.'

'Right. What about you?'

'A drink like what?' She was taking off her coat, looking around the room, at the sound equipment, the CD racks, the bookshelf.

'Well, beer. Red wine. Rum, there's Bundy. Coffee with Bundy is good on a cold day, that's every day. With a small shot. A big shot, that's good too.'

'A medium shot. Do you do that?'

'We can try. Tend to extremes here. It's coffee made in a plunger. Warmed up.'

The light caught her hair, shiny. 'Very good. That's a big advance on what I usually drink.'

By the time he'd fed the dogs, the coffee was hot. He poured big hits of rum into mugs and filled up with coffee, picked the mugs up in one hand, sugar in the other, went back.

Helen was looking at the CDs. 'This is heavy stuff,' she said.

'For a cop, you mean?'

'I was speaking for myself. My father played opera all the time. I hated it. Never listened properly, I suppose. I'm a bad listener.'

He gave her a mug. 'A bit of sugar takes the edge off it,' he said.

'I'll be guided by you.'

He spooned sugar into her mug, stirred, did his mug. 'Cheers.'

She shuddered. 'Wow,' she said. 'I like this.'

They sat.

'It's been a sad business,' she said, eyes on the fire.

'No question.'

'I'm feeling bad about this because I think you think I'm trying to use you in some way.'

Barks.

'Mind the dogs?' he said. 'They won't bother you.'

'Let slip the dogs.'

Cashin took her mug, let them in. They charged Helen. She wasn't alarmed. He spoke sternly and they went to the firebox and sank, heads on paws.

'It's not an interview, Joe,' she said. 'I want to talk about what's going on, it's not like I'm wearing a wire. To say what I think, I think the government's happy to see Bourgoyne pinned on these boys if it helps politically.'

'No politics about homicide.'

'No?

'No one's talked politics to me.'

'There should be a taskforce on this. Instead, there's you and Dove, you go on leave, not suspended, on leave. Dove's back in Melbourne. And you tell me you haven't been told this thing's filed under Forget It?'

Cashin didn't want to lie to her.

'I understand the idea is to let things cool down,' he said. 'The man's dead, the boys are dead, we're not pressed for time. It's hard to investigate when you've got people full of rage. Who's going to talk to you?'

'That's the Daunt you're talking about?'

'The Daunt.'

She drank. 'Joe,' she said, 'do you accept that it's possible that the boys didn't attack Bourgoyne?'

The firebox didn't need stoking. He got up and stoked it. Then he put on Björling. The balance had drifted slighty. He fiddled with the controls. 'Yes,' he said, 'that's possible.'

'Well, if it wasn't the boys, you don't have to worry about the Daunt cooling off. You don't have to clear the boys before you look elsewhere, do you?'

'Helen, I'm seconded from homicide to Port Monro. They were stretched and they drafted me. Then things happened.'

'Did Hopgood have any say?'

Cashin sat down. 'Why would he?'

'Because he runs Cromarty. I'm told the station commander doesn't go to the toilet without Hopgood's nod.'

'Well, I'm in Port Monro. Maybe you hear things I don't hear.'

They looked at each other over their mugs. She did a slow blink.

'Joe, people say he's a killer.'

'A killer? Who says that?'

'Daunt people.'

Cashin thought he would believe anything about Hopgood. He looked away. 'People say anything about cops, it's the job.'

'You've got Aboriginal family, haven't they told you?'

'The people I'm related to see me as just another white

269

maggot cop,' he said. 'But you wouldn't understand that. Let's talk about rich white kids who want to run the world.'

Helen closed her eyes. 'Not called for. I'll start again. People say Corey Pascoe was executed that night. You were there. What do you say?'

'I'll say what I have to say to the coroner.'

'You tried to call it off.'

'Did I?'

'Yes, you did.'

'You get that from where?'

'It doesn't matter for present purposes.'

'For present purposes? There aren't any present purposes. Anyway, the coroner will decide what people did and didn't do.'

'Jesus,' she said, 'I can't seem to get this right. Can you relax for a single fucking second?'

He felt the flare, the flush.

'I think you're just spoilt,' he said. 'You come over with all this passion but you're just a rich smart brat. If you can't get what you want, you stamp your little shoe. Well, go to the media. Get the girl to tell them the watch story. You can be on television. It'll help your campaign. Yours and Bobby's both.'

Helen got up, put her mug on the wonky table, picked up her coat. 'Well, thanks for seeing me. And for the fortified coffee.'

'Any time.'

Cashin got up and walked ahead, through the huge room with its sprung floorboards that uttered faint mouse-like complaints. Outside, a three-quarter moon, high clouds, dispersed and running. He said, 'I'll walk with you.'

'No thanks,' she said, pushing an arm into her coat. 'I can find my way.'

'I'll walk to my fence,' said Cashin. 'I want to be a witness to any alleged slips and falls.'

He took the big torch from the peg and went ahead. She followed in silence, down the path, out the gate, across the grassland, into the rabbit lands. Near her fence, he moved the torch and eyes gleamed – four, no, more.

He stopped.

Hares. Transfixed, immobilised hares. The dogs would love this, he thought.

'Dogs would like this,' she said behind him.

He half-turned. She was close behind him, they were centimetres apart.

'No, can't take the dogs out with a light. Hares don't stand a chance.'

She took a small step, put a hand on the back of his head and kissed him on the mouth, pulled back and then kissed him again.

'Sorry,' she said. 'Just an impulse.'

She went around him, switched on her torch. He didn't move, astonished, half-erect, light on her, watched her stoop through the wires of the sagging side fence that met his new corner post, start to climb the slope, fade into the dark, become a moving, rising light. She didn't look back.

Cashin stood there for a time, fingers on his lips, thinking about the night at the Kettle, the other long-ago kisses, two kisses. He shivered, just the cold night.

Why did she do it?

WOOD STREET in North Melbourne was a short dead-end, narrow, blank factory walls on one side facing five thin weatherboard houses. At the end of the street stood a brick building modelled on a Greek temple, no windows, four pillars and a triangular gable. It was a hall of some kind, like a Masonic hall, but the gable was blank.

Cashin drove slowly, angle-parked in front of unmarked roller doors. He didn't get out, thought about driving all the way for no good reason, about how he could agonise about some things for days and weeks and months but do others with no consideration at all.

Vickie had spotted it early, when he'd come home one day driving a second-hand Audi. 'You work it all out intelligently, don't you?' she said. 'Think it through. Then you just do something, anything. You might as well be a total fuckwit, what's the difference in outcomes?'

She was right. That was why Shane Diab was dead, that was why the blood ran out of his mouth and his nose and his eyes and he made terrible sounds and died.

Cashin got out, walked around the vehicle. The floor of the narrow portico of the temple was hidden beneath mouldy dog turds, dumped junk mail returning to pulp, syringes, beer stubbies, cans, bourbon bottles, condoms, pieces of clothing, bits of styrofoam, a rigid beach towel, a length of exhaust pipe.

He went up the two steps, walked over the rubbish to the huge metal-studded double doors. They bore the scars of many attacks. A bell button had been gouged out but the cast-iron knocker had survived. He bashed it against its buffer – once, twice, thrice. He waited, did it again. Again. Again. Then he knelt and pushed back the letterbox flap. Dark inside. He felt eyes on him, stood and turned.

A woman was on the front doorstep of the nearest weatherboard, tortoise head peeping from a shell of garments, the top one a huge floral apron.

'Whaddayadoin?' she said.

Cashin went down the steps, approached her. 'Police.'

'Yeah? Show me.'

He showed her. 'Who looks after this place?'

'Hey?'

'This building.' He pointed at it. 'Who looks after it?'

'Ah. Used to be a bloke. Never come out the front. Never seed him open that door.' She sniffed, wiped a finger under her nose, studied Cashin in silence, unblinking.

'So how did you know he was in there?' he said.

'Merv's got a garage there, he seed him.'

'A garage where?'

She looked at him as if he were slow. 'In the lane. I said that.'

'Right. How do you get to the lane?'

'Next to Wolf's.'

'Where's Wolf's?'

'Well it's in Tilbrook Street. Where'd ya think it would it be?'

'Thanks for your help.'

She watched him three-point turn, drive off. He waved. She didn't respond. In Tilbrook Street, he found the sunken lane, just wide enough for a vehicle. He parked in the entrance and walked along the bluestone gutter running down the middle, looking on the left for the entrance to the back of the temple.

It had to be the plank door with the rotten bottom beside the rusted steel garage doors. Yale lock, no door handle. He put both hands on the door and pushed tentatively. It didn't yield. He tested the right-hand gatepost, it gave a little.

Knocking was required. He knocked, called the name, did it again. Then he looked up and down the lane, stepped into the gateway, braced his back against a gatepost, put a foot on the opposite post, pushed against it and leant on the door.

The door squeaked open and he almost fell in.

Forcible entry, no warrant.

An alley four or five metres long, brick walls on either side, a rubbish bin. Cashin walked to the end. A concreted yard, a rectangle behind a high wall broken only by three small windows and a door. At the left were washing lines, empty.

He went to the door in the building, stood on the top step and knocked, three times, harder each time, hurting his knuckles.

He tried the doorknob. Locked. Another Yale lock, a newer one.

The lane door was one thing, that could be explained away. Forcing entry into a building was another matter. He should ring Villani, tell him what he wanted, what he was doing here.

He examined the door. It had shrunk over the hundred-odd years of its life, no longer fitted snugly into its frame. When you fitted a new lock to an old door, you needed to compensate for the years. That hadn't been done. He bent to look. He glimpsed the lock's tongue.

Go away, said the voice of sense. Leave. Ring Villani. Get a warrant.

That would take forever. Villani would take his guide from Singo, he would cite Singo. He would want a proper case made for the intrusion.

Cashin thought that he wanted to go home, walk the dogs in the clean wind, lie on the floor for a while, sit by the fire and listen to Callas, roll red wine around his mouth while he read some Conrad.

He took out his wallet and found the thin, narrow piece of plastic. For a moment, he held it between thumbs and forefingers, bending it. It was strong, just enough flex.

Oh, well, what the hell, come this far.

The lozenge went in easily, slid around the tongue, pushed it back just enough. He put pressure on the door.

The tongue slipped its lodging.

The door opened.

Light fell on a wide passage, linoleum on the floor, black and white squares, he could see the lines of the boards beneath the covering. He took a step inside. The air was cold and stale, scrabbling noises from above. Birds. They would be starlings, no roof could keep them out. In a few weeks, they could insulate a ceiling with crap.

'Anyone home?' he shouted.

He took a few more steps down the passage, shouted again. No sound, the starlings paused for a few seconds.

Cashin opened the first door on the left. It was a bathroom and toilet, a shower head above the old claw-footed bath. A cabinet above the basin was empty except for a dry cake of soap.

The next door along was open: a kitchen, ancient gas stove, bare pine table, an empty vegetable rack.

Cashin crossed the passage. The room on the other

275

side was a bedroom – a single bed, made with white sheets, a bedside table, a lamp. Two folded blankets stood on a pine chest of drawers. Nothing in the drawers. Cashin opened a narrow wardrobe. It was empty except for wire coathangers.

The next room was the same, a single bed with a striped coir mattress and a table. Across the way, the door opened reluctantly. Clicking the light switch on the right showed an office with a desk and a chair and a grey three-drawer filing cabinet and a wall of wooden shelves holding grey lever-arch files. Cashin touched the bare desk. His fingers came away coated with dust.

He went to the shelves. There were labelled, handwritten cards in brass holders tacked to each shelf: General Correspondence, Correspondence Q'land, Correspondence WA, Correspondence SA, Correspondence Vic. The Vic shelf was bare. Other shelves were labelled Invoices. Nothing on the Invoices Vic shelf. He chose a file from Correspondence WA, flicked through it. Originals and carbon copies and photostats of letters to and from the Companions Camp, Caves Road, Busselton, Western Australia.

Cashin replaced the file, opened a desk drawer.

Used cheque books, in bundles held together with rubber bands, some of which had perished. He took out a book, looked at a few stubs. All the Moral Companions' bills appeared to have been paid from this place.

He closed the drawer, left the room, opened the door at the end of the passage. Darkness. He groped, found the switch, three fluorescent tubes took their time flickering into life. Another passage, transverse, three doors off it. Cashin opened the first one, found switches, one two, three, flicked them all. On the wall opposite, a few lightbulbs lit up around mirrors.

It was a theatre dressing room. He had been in one before, the woman's body was in the toilet. It had been there for sixteen hours. She appeared to have fallen and struck her head against the bowl some time after the last performance of a play by an amateur group. There had been a party. What set the bells ringing was a bruise on the back of her head. The play was written by a doctor. Singo wanted him and they flame-grilled him but in the end there was nothing except an admission that he'd screwed another cast member.

Cashin checked the other rooms. Also small dressing rooms. Two bulbs popped in the second one as he flicked the switches. He walked back, opened a door, went down a long flight of stairs, another door.

A big room, dimly lit by dusty windows high on the walls. He took a few steps.

It was a theatre from another time, longer than it was wide, slightly raked, about thirty rows of seats, all uptilted. To his left, a short flight of steps went up to the stage.

One more time. 'Anyone here?' he shouted. 'Police.'

Starlings up above here too and, from the street, the sound of a car revving, the test-revving of mechanics.

A smell over the dust and the faint odour of damp coming up from beneath the floor. Cashin sniffed, could not identify it. He had smelled it somewhere before and he felt a tightening of the skin on his face and neck.

He walked to the back of the room and pushed open one of a pair of doors. Beyond was a small marble-floored foyer and the front doors. He went back, climbed the stairs to the stage, pushed aside heavy purple velvet curtains. He was in the wings, a dark space, the bare-boarded stage glimpsed through gaps in tall pieces of scenery.

Cashin went to an opening.

Sand had been dumped on the stage, clean building sand, in heaps and splashes.

Sand?

He saw the buckets at the back of the space, three red buckets with FIRE stencilled on them. Someone had emptied the fire buckets onto the stage, thrown the sand around.

Hoons? Hoons wouldn't limit themselves to throwing sand around, they'd trash the whole place, pull down the curtains, shit on the stage, piss off it, jump on the seats till they broke, rip them from their moorings, light fires.

Not hoons, no. This wasn't hooning.

Something else had happened here.

He walked out onto the stage, could not avoid treading on sand, it crunched beneath his feet, a startlingly loud sound. At centre stage, he looked around. Dust motes hung in their millions in the pale yellow glow from the windows

There would be stage lighting. Where?

In the wings, he looked around, found a panel near the stairs with switches – four old-fashioned round porcelain switches, brass toggles. He tipped them all, solid clicks, the stage was illuminated.

He walked back onto the stage. A spotlight above the arch now lit a painted backdrop and perhaps a dozen footlight bulbs were alight. As he watched, two died, a moment, then a third was gone. He looked at the backdrop. It was of a soft rolling landscape, farm buildings here and there, white dots of grazing sheep, a yellow road snaking over the plain and up a hill, a green, softly rounded hill. On its peak stood three crosses, two small ones flanking a cross twice their size.

Cashin went closer. Crucified figures hung from the smaller crosses. But the big cross was empty. It was waiting for someone. He looked at the sand on the floor in front of the backdrop.

Why would anyone throw sand on the stage? To put out a fire? Perhaps someone had started a fire, poured an inflammable fluid on the floorboards, lit it, then panicked, grabbed a fire bucket, smothered the flames.

That was the obvious explanation.

Hoons lit fires.

But they didn't put them out.

He moved sand with a shoe, scraped at it. The bottom grains were dark, stuck together, they came away in clumps. He scraped some more, revealed the boards.

A black stain. He felt a twinge of nausea, the cold in his neck, the back of his head, his ears.

Something bad had happened here.

Time to ring the squad, wait in the vehicle.

He squatted and put out an index finger, touched the floor, looked at his fingertip.

Blood.

He knew blood.

How old? The sand had trapped the moisture.

He stood up, back aching, flexed his shoulders, he was facing the auditorium, the spotlight on, the footlights in his eyes, he could not see the hall clearly.

He saw it.

ALL THE seats in the hall were turned up.

Except for one seat. Six rows back, in the middle of the sixth row.

One seat was down. In the whole auditorium only one seat was down.

Someone had sat on that seat. Someone had chosen that seat. It was the best seat in the house to see something.

To see what?

Nonsense. The seat had probably fallen down, seats did that, everything did that, falling down was a law of nature. You lined up a dozen things that could fall over, at least one did.

Cashin left the stage, went down the stairs, walked down the aisle until he was at the sixth row, took out his mobile and rang homicide.

'Joe Cashin. Is Inspector Villani in?'

'He's on the phone. No, he's off. Putting you through.'

Villani barked his surname. He sounded more like Singo every day.

'It's Joe. Listen, I'm in this hall place in North Melbourne, something's happened here needs looking at.'

Villani coughed. 'Is this Joe from Port Monro? Calling from North Melbourne? On a trip to the big city, Joe? Go ahead, tell us what's on your mind.'

'Here's the address,' said Cashin.

'What the fuck's this?'

'There's blood here, not old.'

'What's this about?'

'Bourgoyne.'

'Bourgoyne?'

'I think so. Yes.'

'In North Melbourne?'

'It's complicated, okay? I'm just reporting this, I'll ring CrimeStoppers if you like. You like?'

'Well that sounds so fucking urgent and imperative I'll drop everything and come myself. What's the address?'

Cashin told him, ended the call. He stood looking at the stage, at the backdrop of an idealised Calvary. Then he walked down the row of seats and up the hall to the stairs on the other side of the stage, climbed them, stood in the dark space beside the stage.

The smell, he knew it. Stronger here. The cold came back to his neck and shoulders and he shivered.

It was the smell in Bourgoyne's sitting room that morning.

He sniffed, looked around, realised he was clenching his teeth. To his left, against the wall, he made out a cast-iron wheel with two handles at right angles. He stepped closer. A cable ran up from behind the wheel, into the darkness. The cable was wrapped around a drum and behind that was a ratchet-wheel with a steel pawl engaged.

It took a moment to work out.

The cable raised and lowered the scenery, the painted backdrops. The ratchet-wheel controlled the process. It ensured that the scenery couldn't come crashing down.

There was something behind the cable, between the cable and the wall. Cashin put out a hand, tugged at it.

A piece of cloth, wadded, stiff but still damp.

The smell. He did not need to sniff the towel. Vinegar. It was a kitchen towel soaked in vinegar.

He held it to the light from the stage. It was dark. Blood.

The questions came without thought. Why was the ratchet-wheel locked? Why was the cable taut?

He pulled back on the iron wheel and the pawl on the ratchet-wheel disengaged. He let the wheel run, the pawl click-clicked, the cable was paying out.

Metallic creaks. A piece of scenery was coming down.

He looked out between the slats, at the piece of stage he could see.

Oh, Jesus.

Bare feet, dark, swollen legs, rivulets of dried blood running down them, striping them, matted pubic hair, a torso dark, the arms upraised, a black hole beneath the ribs, in the side…

Cashin let go the wheel. The pawl engaged, the cable stopped paying out.

The thin, naked, blood-caked body moved gently.

Cashin walked down the hall, into the foyer, unlocked the front door, went out into the cold toxic city air, stood on the top step and breathed it deeply.

A silver car turned into the street, drove down the middle, straight at him, stopped two metres away with front wheels touching the kerb, no concern for angle parking.

The front doors opened. Villani and Finucane got out, pale and black as undertakers, eyes on him.

'What?' said Villani. 'What?'

'Inside,' said Cashin.

THE THREE of them sat in the big untidy room on the seventh floor, desks pushed together, files on every surface, a concert of phone sounds – trings, warbles, silly little tunes.

'Like old times,' said Birkerts. 'Us sitting here. Any minute Singo comes through the door.'

'I fucking wish,' said Villani. He sighed, ran fingers through his hair. 'Jesus, got to get out to see him. Guilt building up on all fronts. The things left undone.'

Cashin thought Villani looked even more tired than the last time, when they drank wine beyond midnight in his son's room.

'Talking undone,' said Birkerts. 'Did I tell you this Fenton bloke's got form for flashing? Out there in the sticks in Clunes, near Ballarat. At Wesley girls.'

'Wesley girls? In Clunes?'

'The school's got something there. Outreach program, the rich kids help the rural poor, give them hints on cooking the cheaper cuts.'

'Freezing place,' said Cashin. 'Check his dick for frostbite.'

'One sick, pathetic case at a time,' said Villani. 'Dr Colley says this bloke on the stage had his hands tied. No clothes on, he's been jacked up on the winch thing and he's been tortured, cut all over, front and back, stabbed, blood everywhere. Gag in the mouth, like a bit, it's a handkerchief, there's another one in his mouth. Then he's been winched right up into the roof. At some point, he died, possibly choked to death. We'll know in the morning.'

'He sat there and watched him hanging,' said Birkerts. 'Bleeding.'

Finucane came in with Dove, who nodded at Cashin. The seated men all looked at Finucane.

'Found the bloke's clothes,' he said. 'In a plastic bag in a rubbish bin. Keys in the pocket.'

'ID?' said Villani.

Finucane showed his palms. 'Nothing,' he said. 'No prints either. No one around there saw anything. Been through the missing reports, no one like him there, not in the last month. We'll hear about his prints soonest.' He looked at his watch. 'His picture's on the news in five minutes, may help.'

Villani turned his head to Cashin. 'So tell everyone.'

'The hall was the headquarters of something called the Moral Companions,' said Cashin. 'A charity. Once they ran camps for poor kids, orphans, state wards. Camps in Queensland and Western Australia. Bourgoyne was a supporter. He owned the land they built a camp on outside Port Monro and he owned the hall.'

'What happened to them?' said Finucane.

'There was a fire at the Port Monro camp in 1983. Three dead. They packed it in.'

'So what's the connection between Bourgoyne and this bloke?' said Birkerts.

'I don't know,' said Cashin. 'But I smelled vinegar that morning at Bourgoyne's.'

'No cloth found there,' said Villani.

'Took it with him,' said Cashin.

'Why'd he leave it this time?'

Cashin shrugged. He was tired, a girdle of pain around his hips, hours spent waiting for forensic to finish.

'Vinegar,' said Birkerts. 'What's with vinegar?'

'They gave me gall to eat: and when I was thirsty they gave me vinegar to drink,' said Dove.

'What?' said Villani. 'What's that?'

'It's from the Book of Common Prayer. A psalm, I forget which one.'

No one said anything. Dove coughed, embarrassed. Cashin registered the ringing phones, the electronic humming, the sound of a television next door, the traffic noises from below.

Villani got up, stretched his arms above his head, palms to the ceiling, eyes closed. 'Joe, this Moral shit,' he said. 'That's religious, is it?'

'Sort of. Started by an ex-priest called Raphael something. Morris. Morrison. After World War II. He had a life-changing experience.'

'I need that,' said Villani.

'Got some nice new suits,' said Cashin. 'Ties too. That's a start.'

'Purely cosmetic,' said Villani. 'I'm unchanged, believe me. The telly, Fin.'

It was the third item on the news. The media hadn't been given much: just a dead man found in a hall in North Melbourne, nothing about him being gagged and tortured, hung naked above a stage.

The man's face was on the screen, clean, almost alive, lights in his eyes. He had been handsome once, longish straight hair combed back, bags under his eyes, deep lines from nose to thin-lipped mouth.

The man is aged in his sixties. His hair is dyed dark brown. Anyone knowing his identity or who has any information about him is asked to call CrimeStoppers on 990 897 897.

'He scrubbed up well,' said Finucane.

'Purely cosmetic,' said Birkerts. 'He's still dead.'

They watched the rest of the news, saw Villani make an appearance to say nothing on the subject of another gangland killing, touch the corner of an eye, his mouth.

'Bit of Al Pacino, bit of Clint Eastwood,' said Cashin. 'Dynamite cocktail, may I say?'

'You may fuck off,' said Villani. 'Just fuck off.'

'Boss?'

Tracy Wallace, the analyst, a thin worried face.

'A woman, boss, transferred from CrimeStoppers. The dead bloke.'

Villani looked at Cashin. 'You take it, skipper,' he said. 'You seem to know what's going on.'

Cashin went to the telephone.

'Mrs Roberta Condi,' said Tracy. 'She lives in North Melbourne.'

He didn't have to write, Tracy had the headphones on.

'Hello, Mrs Condi,' said Cashin. 'Thanks for calling. Can you help us?'

'That's Mr Pollard. The bloke on the telly. I know him.'

'Tell me about it,' said Cashin, his eyes closed.

286

CASHIN PUT the green key in the lock, turned.

'The home of the late Arthur Pollard,' he said and opened the door.

The terrace house was dark, cold. It took him a while to find a light switch.

An overhead lamp came on, two globes lit a sitting room, furniture that was modern in the 1970s. A newspaper was on the coffee table. Cashin went over and looked at the date. 'Four days ago,' he said.

Off the sitting room was a bedroom – a double bed tightly made, no bedspread, a wardrobe with two mirrors, a chest of drawers, shoes in a wire rack. A passage led to another room with a single bed, a desk, a chair and a bookcase.

Cashin looked at the book spines. All paperbacks. Crime novels, disaster novels, novels with golden titles on the spines. Bought from second-hand shops, he thought.

'Neat kitchen,' said Dove from the door.

Cashin followed him down the passage to a 1950s kitchen: a single bare light bulb with a green shade, an enamelled gas stove, an Electrolux fridge with round shoulders and a portable radio on a formica-topped metal table. On the sink stood a blue-and-white striped mug, upside down.

'Like a monk,' Cashin said. He went to the sink and

tried to look out of the window but all he could see was the reflection of the sad room.

Dove clicked switches beside the back door and a powerful floodlight lit the straight rain falling on a concrete yard. It ran to a brick wall with a steel door. Beside the party wall, a single washline held soaked washing: three shirts and three pairs of underpants.

'There's a lane at the back,' said Dove. 'That must be the garage door.'

They went outside, Cashin first, he felt the wet, slippery concrete underfoot. No key on Pollard's ring would unlock the steel door.

'I'll try the door in the lane,' said Dove. He took the keys.

Cashin waited in the house, looked around. In the desk drawers, he found folders with bank statements, power, gas, telephone and rates bills. There was nothing personal – no letters, photographs, no tapes or CDs. Nothing spoke of Arthur Pollard as a human being with a history, with likes and dislikes, except the four cans of baked beans in tomato sauce and a half-empty bottle of whisky and an empty one in the bin.

Dove came in. 'Not a garage anymore,' he said. 'Door's bricked up.'

Dove's mobile rang. He exchanged a few words, phrases, and gave the phone to Cashin. 'The boss,' he said.

'We need the big key here,' said Cashin. 'Sesame. And not tomorrow.'

'How come you give all the orders and you are on long-term secondment from homicide?' said Villani.

'Someone's got to be in charge.'

They waited in the car, streetlights streaming down the windscreen. Cashin found the classical station. His thoughts drifted to home, to the dark ruined house under the wet hill, to the dogs. Rebb would have fed them by now, he didn't have to be asked. They would all be in the shed, the dogs sacked out, drying, the three of them around the old potbelly stove, the rusty shearers' stove not fired for at least thirty years before Rebb, the warmth moving through the building, awakening old smells – lanolin, bacon fat, the rank sweat of tired men now dead.

'This could be coincidence,' said Dove.

'Maybe you should've stayed with the feds,' said Cashin.

A van's lights came around the corner. The driver nosed along, looking. Cashin got out and raised a hand.

The two men in overalls followed them through Pollard's arid house. It was quick.

One man opened a builder's bag and took out an angular piece of metal with a mushroom head. He held it to the garage door jamb, level with the lock. The locksmith tapped it with a sledgehammer, brisk taps, getting harder. When the chisel was wedged, he stood back, flexed his wrists.

'Open Sesame,' he said, swung the hammer like an axe, administered a clean blow to the mushroom, made a sound like a gunshot.

The steel door burst open, hell-dark within.

CASHIN FOUND the switches.

A white-painted room, carpeted floor, windowless. Stale air. Against one wall stood a trestle table with a computer tower, a flat-screen monitor, a printer and a scanner. Next to it were a grey metal filing cabinet and three metal shelf units, four shelves each, the kind sold in hardware shops. The shelves were neat: four for video tapes, four for CDs and DVDs, the others for folders, books, magazines.

Against the door wall was a double bed with a purple sateen quilt and big shiny red pillows. A big-screen television was on a table at the foot, a video player and a DVD player stacked beside it. Beside it stood a tripod. On all the walls were posters – pictures of muscular half-naked men: athletes, bodybuilders, kickboxers, swimmers.

Dove opened the filing cabinet. 'Digital still camera,' he said. 'Digital video camera.'

He closed the drawer, went to the computer, sat down, pressed a button on the tower. 'Give you a feeling, this?' he said.

Cashin didn't say anything. He found a remote control and fiddled with it, switched on the television, got fuzz, pressed buttons.

Vision.

Something filling the screen. It looked like a smooth-skinned vegetable, an eggplant perhaps, the camera moved. An opening, a hole. It was not a vegetable.

The camera drew back.

A face, a young face, a boy. His mouth was open, top teeth showing. There was fear in his eyes.

Cashin pressed the OFF button.

'Look at this shit,' said Dove.

Cashin looked for a minute or two.

'Can't be more than twelve,' said Dove. 'Tops.'

'I'm going home now,' said Cashin. They were at the door when he noticed the two white mugs with yellow spots on the table beside the computer. The tag of a teabag hung over the side of one.

'Had a cup of tea,' he said.

Dove looked back. 'One liked it strong.'

In the car, Cashin spoke to Villani.

'Not surprised,' said Villani. 'Pollard's got form. Sex offences against minors. One gig suspended, done one. Six months. What's there apart from the kiddy-porn chamber?'

'Bank statements, phone bills.'

'Why didn't you stay at home? Stir up all this shit, nobody to do the work.'

'The thought occurred to me.'

'Anyway, I've got a whole house for you to crash in. No one there except me from time to time. You sleep, do you? At some point?'

'Don't project your problems onto me, mate. Any more of that bribe wine?'

'Maybe.'

Before he fell asleep, Cashin saw the vile room, saw on the table the two cheerful spotted mugs, and he put his head beneath the pillow and concentrated on his breathing.

DOVE WAS waiting, reading the *Herald*. He folded it, put it on the back seat. 'Nice to be your driver. I've got something on Bourgoyne's watch.'

'Presumably came in a cleft stick, the runners went via Broome,' said Cashin.

Dove's expression didn't change. 'Bourgoyne bought a Breitling watch from a shop called Cozzen's in Collins Street in 1984. Then six years ago he bought another one.'

Carol Gehrig had described the watch. The girl on the pier, Susie, she had only given the name. Bretling, she said. Why hadn't he asked her to describe the watch? Singo would have closed his eyes, shaken his head: 'You didn't ask? Would you like that engraved on your tombstone? *I didn't ask*.'

Had the pawnbroker in Sydney described the watch the boys offered him that day? Had a cop taken it down? Pawnbrokers had the eye, they knew value, it was their miserable job. 'The shop can describe the watches?' Cashin said.

'Well, I suppose so. I didn't ask.'

'You want that inscribed...' He stopped.

'What?'

'Nothing. Get Ms Bourgoyne?'

'She'll see you in the art gallery at 10.30. The café upstairs. She's on the gallery board. An arts powerbroker.'

'A what?'

'Read it in the *Financial Review* today.'

'I missed that. Just read the Toasty Sugarflakes box. Law, art, politics, the woman's got it covered.'

They drove in silence. In Lygon Street, Cashin retrieved the newspaper from the back seat. Pollard's face was on page five, the story had no more detail than the television news.

'The Pollard calls,' said Dove. 'There's about thirty. Parents, victims. The guy was a very active ped. Sounds like people would have queued to string him up. One bloke says he knows him from a long time ago. Raved on, then he clammed up.'

'I'm going home after this,' said Cashin. 'Handpass the matter to the experts.'

They crossed the city, nothing said until Dove pulled up on the service road across from the gallery. 'You sulking?' he said.

'That's cheeky,' said Cashin.

'What's cheeky mean in homicide?'

'If I was still homicide, it means I outrank you. And that a reject from the Canberra dregs and a proven slackarse should show respect. That's part of what cheeky means.'

'I see. I'll get a description of the watches.'

'You never ran the name Pollard when you checked those Addison payments?'

Dove sucked in his nostrils. 'I was doing you a favour. Anyway, it was three days ago. Pollard was dead.'

Cashin looked at the traffic.

'You're allowed to fuck up,' said Dove. 'Let Hopgood run it that night and kill the boys and you're still okay. The mates look after you.'

'Get the watch descriptions,' Cashin said. 'And see if Sydney got a description from the pawnbroker, whatever he calls himself. Either way, we want it now and that is this very day.'

'Yes, sir.'

Cashin crossed the road to the gallery, dodging traffic and a tram. In the foyer, he looked up and, in the way of it, met the eyes of Erica Bourgoyne. She was leaning on the rail. He went upstairs, found her seated.

'Sorry I'm late,' he said. 'Is this private enough for you?'

'If you don't shout.' She was in dark grey, drinking black coffee, didn't offer. 'What line of investigation is this?'

'Just a chat.'

A downturned mouth. 'I'm not available for chats. What's the point? My step-father's dead, the suspects are dead.'

Cashin thought of Singo, the grey eyes under eyebrows like stick insects. 'Our obligation is to the dead,' he said. 'Your step-father paid money every month to a man called Arthur Pollard.'

'Did he?'

'You don't know Pollard?'

'Never heard of him.'

A group of Japanese tourists were trying to leave the gallery through the entrance. The attendant was redirecting them and they either didn't understand or thought he was an idiot.

'He was murdered a few days ago. In a building owned by your step-father.'

'Christ. What building?'

'A hall in North Melbourne. It used to be a theatre. Did you know he owned it?'

'No. I don't know what he owns. Owned. What has this to do with Charles?'

'There are similarities.'

'Meaning?'

Cashin saw the man, black turtleneck, three tables away, turning a page of a newspaper, a tabloid. 'We're still working on it,' he said. 'Do you know anything about the Moral Companions? The camp at Port Monro?'

'I remember the camp, yes. There was a fire there. Why?'

'This hall was the Companions' headquarters.'

'To be clear here,' said Erica. 'You're saying the Daunt boys didn't bash Charles?'

Cashin looked away, at the water running down the huge plateglass window. Two blurred figures outside were running fingertips across the stream, making wavy transient lines. 'That's possible,' he said.

'What about the watch?'

'Never conclusive.'

'Just because Charles gave this man money doesn't link the attacks,' said Erica. 'Who knows how many people Charles gave money to?'

'I do.'

She sat back, hands on the table, linked them, parted them. 'So you know everything and you say nothing. What can I possibly tell you that you don't know?'

'I thought you might think of something to tell me.'

Erica looked at him, a steady gaze, blue-grey eyes. She touched the slim silver choker around her neck, ran a finger behind it. 'I have nothing else to tell you and I have a meeting to go to.'

Cashin did not know why he had waited to say it. 'Pollard was a paedophile,' he said. 'Fucked boys. Children.'

She shook her head as if mystified. Colour came to her cheekbones, she could not stop that. 'Well,' she said, 'I'm sure that information is useful to you, but...'

'It's not useful to you?'

'Why should it be? Are you scratching around because it's going to be embarrassing if the Daunt boys are innocent?'

'We'll wear that.' He looked away and, at the edge of his vision, he saw the man in the black turtleneck flexing his right hand. 'What are you scared of, Ms Bourgoyne?'

For an instant, he thought she was going to tell him. 'What do you mean?'

'The bodyguard.'

'If I was scared of anything that fell in your area of concern, detective, I'd tell you. Now I have my meeting.'

'Thank you for your time.'

Cashin watched her go. She had good legs. At the escalator, she looked back and caught his eyes, held them a moment longer than necessary. Then the bodyguard blocked his view.

'THE FIRST watch Bourgoyne bought from Cozzen's,' said Dove, 'is this model.' He pointed to a picture in a brochure. 'The receipt is 14 September 1986.'

'Very nice. Time yourself going down the Cresta Run.' It was a technical-looking watch, black face, three white dials, three bevelled winders, recessed, a crocodile strap.

'It's called the Maritimer, still in production.' Dove's speech was clipped, he radiated antagonism. 'Here's the second one he bought, another Maritimer, 14 March 2000.'

It had a plain white face, three small dials, also on a crocodile leather strap.

Cashin thought about the morning at The Heights. A smart watch, Carol Gehrig said. A crocodile skin strap. 'What's the pawnbroker say?'

'He made a statement at the time,' said Dove. 'Sydney sent it but in the excitement it seems to have fallen into a hole.'

Cashin felt as if he had missed a night's sleep somewhere. 'What did he say at the time then?'

'He said, I quote: "It was a Breitling. A Maritimer. It's a collectable. Very expensive. The one with three small dials, black face, crocodile strap."'

Cashin got up, full of pain, went to the window and looked at the school grounds, the public gardens, all soft in the misty rain. He found Helen Castleman's direct number.

'Helen Castleman.'

'Joe Cashin.'

A moment.

'I've tried to call you,' she said. 'Your home phone just rings, your mobile number appears to be off.'

'I'm using another one. I'm in the city.'

'I don't know what I should say. You were so insulting. Arrogant. Dismissive.'

'Got the right person? Listen, I need a description of the watch Susie saw. She gave me the name but I need a description from her. Can you get that?'

'This is because the case is still under investigation?'

'It always has been. Can you get that soonest?'

'I'll see. Give me your number.'

Cashin sat down, looked at Dove. Dove didn't want to look at him.

'Hopgood says there's no record of the messages to him that night,' said Cashin.

Now Dove looked. 'The cunts,' he said. 'They've wiped them. They've wiped the fucking record.'

'It could be at our end, a technical thing.'

Dove shook his head, the overhead light blinked in his round lenses. 'Well, then you can blame me at the inquest,' he said. 'Didn't press the right buttons. Just fucked it up. As a boong does.'

Cashin rose, sitting was worse than standing, went back to the window. He said, 'Hopgood said, and I quote him, "You two boongs making up stories now?"'

'What?'

'He said, you two boongs making up stories now.'

'That's us?'

'I took him to mean that, yes.'

Dove laughed, real pleasure. 'Welcome to Boongland,' he said. 'Listen, bro, want to get some lunch round the corner? Grub sandwich?'

'Had it with round the corner,' said Cashin. 'Had it for six years and I've had it.'

'There's a Brunetti's at the arts centre,' said Dove. 'Know Brunetti's in Carlton?'

'You fucking blow-in, you don't know Brunetti's from Donetti's.'

Finucane joined them in the lift, gave them a ride down St Kilda Road.

'Fin, looking at you,' said Cashin, 'I'm giving you a nine point six on the over-worked, under-slept, generally-fucked-over scale.'

Finucane smiled the small modest smile of a man whose efforts had been recognised. 'Thanks, boss,' he said.

'Want a transfer to Port Monro?' said Cashin. 'Just pub fights and sheep-shagging, the odd cunt nicks his neighbour's hydroponic gear officially used to grow vine-ripened tomatoes. It's a nice place to bring up kids.'

'Too exciting,' said Finucane. 'I've got six blokes to see on Pollard. This one in Footscray, he says he goes back a long way. Probably turn out he rang from his deaf and dumb auntie's house where he isn't and doesn't live.'

At Brunetti's, they queued behind black-clad office workers and backpackers and four women from the country who were overwhelmed by the choices. Cashin bought a calzone, Dove had a roll with duck and olives and capsicum relish and five kinds of leaves. They were drinking coffee when Cashin's mobile rang. He went outside.

'I hear traffic,' said Helen. 'Makes me nostalgic. Where are you?'

'Near the arts centre.'

'So cultured – opera, art galleries.'

'Get hold of Susie?' Cashin was watching a man coming down the pavement on a unicycle, a small white dog perched on each shoulder. The dogs had the resigned air of passengers on a long-distance bus.

'She says the watch had a big black face and two or three little white dials.'

Cashin closed his eyes. He thought that he should say thanks for your help and goodbye. That was what he should do. That was what the police minister and the chief commissioner and the assistant crime commissioner and very possibly Villani would want him to do.

It wasn't the right thing to do. He should tell her that the watch the boys tried to sell in Sydney wasn't the watch Bourgoyne was wearing on the night he was attacked.

'Still there?' said Helen.

'Thanks for your help,' he said.

'That's it?'

'That's it.'

'Well, goodbye.'

They finished their coffee and walked back. Cashin had to wait twenty minutes to see Villani. 'Bourgoyne wasn't wearing the watch the boys tried to sell in Sydney,' he said.

'How do you know?'

Cashin told him.

'Could've pinched that one from the house too. Pinched both watches.'

'No. Corey Pascoe's sister saw the fancy watch about a year ago. Corey had it before he went to Sydney. I've spoken to her.'

'Well that could be bullshit.'

'I believe her.'

'Yeah?'

'She knew the name. She's described the watch.'

'Fuck,' said Villani. 'Fuck. This is not looking good.'

'No. What's showing on Pollard?'

'A woman down the street from the hall's ID'd him. Seen in the vicinity a few times. Once with a kid. About twenty victims to interview. The computer stuff will take forever. Thousands of images. I don't fancy our chances. Just be happy he's dead. Like these drug scumbags we're trying to get justice for.'

'Anyway, I'm off,' said Cashin. 'Going home. I'm on enforced holiday. Over and out.'

'Just when you were settling in again. Want to end this secondment shit? There's fuck all wrong with you.'

'I'm over homicide,' said Cashin. 'I don't want to see any more dead people. Except for Rai Sarris. I want to see the dead Rai Sarris. And Hopgood. I'll make an exception for Hopgood too.'

'Unprofessional attitude. The vinegar smell. You sure about that?'

'Yes.'

Villani walked with him to the lifts. 'I should say,' he said, he looked down the corridor. 'I want to say I've been squeezed on this. I'm not happy with my conduct. Not proud. I am considering my position.'

Cashin didn't know what to say. The lift doors opened. He touched Villani's sleeve. 'Take it easy,' he said. 'Don't obsess.'

LONG BEFORE he'd cleared the city, the mobile rang. Cashin pulled over.

'Boss, Fin. This bloke rang in...'

'Yes. Footscray.'

'You should talk to him, boss.'

'Out of this, Fin, I'm on my way home.'

The traffic was picking up, the early leavers, commuters to the satellite towns, lots of four-wheel-drives, trade utes, trucks.

'Yeah, well, the boss says to ask you, boss.'

'Tell me.'

'Well, this one's pretty fucked up. He drifts off the station, know what I mean?'

'What's the station?'

'He knows Pollard. He hates Pollard. Hates everyone, everything, actually, spit going everywhere, you need a riot shield.'

'How old?'

'Not old old. It's hard to say, shaven head, buggered teeth, maybe forties. Yeah. Major drug problem, no doubt.'

'Get a statement?'

'Boss, this is not statement territory. This is door-punching territory.'

'Door-punching?'

'I was trying to get through to him, he went quiet and

then he came out of the fucking chair and he ran across the room, punched the door, two shots. The second one, his hand's stuck in the door, blood everywhere.'

'His name?' said Cashin.

'David Vincent.'

Cashin expelled breath. 'What's the address? I'm close.'

Finucane was waiting for him, parked in a street of rotting weatherboards, dumped cars and thin front yards silting up with junk mail. Cashin walked over, stood at the car window, hands in his pockets.

'He'll be happy to see you again?'

Finucane scratched his head. 'No. He told me to fuck off. But he's not aggro about me. It's the world that's the problem.'

'Live alone?'

'There's no one else there now.'

'Let's go.'

It took several bouts of knocking before the door opened. Cashin could see a veined eye.

'Mr Vincent,' said Finucane, 'a senior police officer would like a little chat about the things worrying you.'

The door opened enough to show both eyes and a discoloured nose broken more than once, broken and shifted sideways. The eyes were the colour of washing powder. 'Nothing's fuckin worrying me,' Vincent said. 'Where'd you get that crap?'

'Can we come in, Mr Vincent?' said Cashin.

'Fuck off. Said what I wanted.'

'I understand you know Arthur Pollard?'

'That's what I fuckin said. CrimeStoppers. Told the fuckin idiot. Give him the name.'

Cashin smiled at him. 'We're very grateful for that, Mr Vincent. Thank you. Just a few other things we'd like to know.'

'Nah. I'm busy. Got a lot on.'

'Right,' said Cashin. 'Well, we'd really appreciate your help. There's a man murdered, an innocent man...'

Vincent pulled the door open, smashed it against the passage wall, jarred the whole building. 'Innocent? You fuckin mad? The fuckin bastard, shoulda killed the fuckin cunt myself...'

Cashin looked away. He hadn't meant Pollard, he'd been thinking of Bourgoyne.

A woman had come out of the house next door. She was of unguessable age, wearing a pink turban and wrapped in what looked like an ancient embossed velvet curtain, faded and moulting.

'Dint I tell you to bugger off last time?' she shouted. 'Comin around with yer bloody Yank religion, yer bloody tower of Pisa, leanin bloody watchtower, whatbloodyever.'

'Police,' said Finucane.

She went backwards at speed. Cashin looked at Vincent. The rage had left his face as if the outburst had drained some poison from him. He was a big man but stooped and gone to fat, rolls at his neck.

'Woman's mad,' said Vincent in a calm voice. 'Completely out of her tree. Come in.'

They followed him into a dim passage and a small room with a collapsed sofa, two moulded plastic restroom chairs and a metal-legged coffee table with five beer cans on it. A television set stood on two stacked milk crates. Vincent sat on the sofa and lit a cigarette, holding the lighter in both hands, shaking badly. Blood was caked on the fingers and knuckles of his right hand.

Cashin and Finucane sat on the plastic chairs.

'So you know Arthur Pollard, Mr Vincent?' said Cashin.

Vincent picked up a beer can, shook it, tested another one, found one with liquid in it. 'Many fuckin times you want me to say it? Know the cunt, know the cunt, know the...'

Cashin held up a hand. 'Sorry. Where do you know him from, Mr Vincent?'

Vincent drank, looked down at the floor, drew on the cigarette. His left shoulder was jerking. 'From the fuckin holidays.'

'What holidays, Mr Vincent?'

'The fuckin holidays, you know, the holidays.' He raised his head, fixed his gaze on Cashin. 'Tried to tell em, y'know. It wasn't just me. Oh no. Nearly, poor little bugger, saw em. Saw em.'

'Tell them what, Mr Vincent?'

'Don't believe me, do you?'

'What holidays are you talking about?'

'Givin me that fuckin look, I know that fuckin look, HATE THAT FUCKIN LOOK.'

'Steady on,' said Cashin.

'Piss off. Piss off. Got nothing to say to you cunts, all the same, you're all fuckin in it, bastards kill a kid, you, you... you can just fuck off.'

'Spare a smoke?' said Cashin.

'What?'

Cashin mimed smoking. 'Give us a smoke?'

Vincent's eyes flicked from Cashin to Finucane and back. He put a hand into his dirty cotton top and took out a packet of Leisure Lights, opened it with a black-rimmed thumbnail, offered it, shaking. Cashin took. Vincent offered the box to Finucane.

'No thanks,' said Finucane. 'Trying to give up.'

'Yeah. Me too.' Vincent gave the plastic lighter to Cashin.

Cashin lit up, returned the lighter. 'Thanks, mate,' he said. 'So they wouldn't listen?'

'Wouldn't listen,' said Vincent. 'Copped a thrashin

from the bastard Kerno. Thrashed me all the time. Thin as a stick, I was. Broke me ribs, three ribs. Made me tell school I fell off me bike.'

A long silence. Vincent emptied the beer can, put it on the table. His shaven, scarred head went down, almost touched his knees, the cigarette was going to burn his fingers. Cashin and Finucane read each other's eyes.

'Didn't have a bike,' said Vincent, a sad little boy's voice. 'Never ever had a bike. Wanted a bike.'

Cashin smoked. The cigarette tasted terrible, made him glad he didn't smoke. Smoke much. Vincent didn't look up, dropped his butt on the carpet, aimed a foot at it, missed. The smell of burning nylon fibres rose, acrid and strangely sweet.

'I'd like to hear about when you were a kid,' said Cashin. 'I'll listen. You talk, I'll listen.'

Another long silence. Vincent raised his head, startled, looked at them as if they'd just appeared in the room. 'Got to go,' he said breathlessly. 'A lot on, blokes.'

He rose unsteadily and left the room, bumped against the door jamb. They heard him muttering as he went down the passage. A door slammed.

'That's probably it,' said Finucane. He stood on Vincent's cigarette.

Outside, in the rain, Cashin said to Finucane, 'The holidays. He's talking about a Moral Companions camp, Fin. His whole life, we need his whole life. That's ASAP. Tell Villani I said that.'

'Not staying then, boss?'

'No. Also the files at the hall. Someone needs to pull out everything that refers to Port Monro. Call me with what you get. Ring me, okay?'

'Okay. First to know, boss.'

'And for fuck's sake get some sleep, Fin. You're a worry to me.'

'Right. They stay dead, don't they?'

'You're learning. It's slow but you're learning.'

It was long dark by the time he switched off and saw the torch beam coming down the side of the house, saw the running dogs side by side, heads up, big ears swinging. They were at the vehicle before he could get out. He had to fight their weight to open the door. A spoke of pain ran down his right thigh as he swung his legs out.

'Thought we'd lost you,' said Rebb, a hulk behind the light.

Cashin was returning the dogs' affection, head down, allowing them to lick his hands, his hair, his ears. 'Got stuck in the city,' he said. 'I reckoned you might do the right thing by these brutes.'

'No brute food left,' said Rebb. 'I took the little peashooter of yours for a walk. Okay?'

'Good thinking.'

'The other bunny's in the oven. Used the olives in the fridge. Also a tin of tomatoes.'

'What do you know about olives?' said Cashin.

'Picked them in South Australia, worked in a place they pickled them. Ate olives till they came out of my ears. Swaggies eat anything. Roadkill, caviar.'

'I need a drink,' said Cashin. 'You left anything to drink?'

'I'm leaving in the morning.'

Cashin felt tiredness and pain expand within him, fill him. 'Can we talk about that?'

'I'll drop in if I come this way again.'

'Come in and have a drink anyway. Farewell drink.'

'Had a drink. Knackered. I'll shake your hand now.'

He put out a hand. Cashin didn't want to take it. He took it.

'I owe you money,' he said. 'Fix it up tomorrow. Promise.'

'Leave it on the step,' said Rebb. 'Haven't got it, I'll pick it up next time. Trust you, you're a cop. Who else can you trust?'

He turned and walked. Cashin felt a loss for which he was not prepared. 'Mate,' he said. 'Mate, fucking sleep on it, will you?'

No reply.

'For the sake of the dogs.'

'Good dogs,' said Rebb. 'Miss the dogs.'

A DARK DAY, the vehicle climbing a rainslicked road towards a hilltop lost in mist. In the gate of The Heights, up the driveway, the poplars dripping.

Cashin took the left turn, the road that wound around the house at a distance, ended at the redbrick double-storey building. He parked on the paving in front of the wooden garage doors, switched off, wound down his window. The cold and wet blew in. He sat in the quiet, engine clicks the only sounds, thinking about why this was a pointless thing to do.

He thought about Shane Diab's parents coming to see him in hospital, when he was out of danger. They didn't sit, they were awkward, their English wasn't good. He didn't know what to say to them, he knew their son was dead because of him. After a while, Vincentia saved him and they said goodbye. Shane's mother touched him on the cheek, then, quickly, she kissed him on the forehead. They left a white cardboard box on the cabinet beside the bed.

Vincentia opened the box, held it up, tilted it to Cashin. It was a square cake, white icing, a cross in red. It took him a while to see that names formed the bar of the cross: Joe+Shane.

He gave the cake to Vincentia. Later she told him the nurses on the shift shared it, a fruit cake, very good.

Cashin got out, walked around the building to the double doors in the centre. The mist was turning to rain.

There were about a dozen keys on the ring Erica Bourgoyne had given him. The seventh one worked. He unlocked the door, went down the corridor. The pottery room was dark, the shutters closed. He found the light switches and high up tubes flickered, lit the room. The door was directly opposite.

The lights showed a swept brick floor, gardening tools pinned on a pegboard, arranged on shelves like exhibits. A ride-on mower, a small tractor and a trailer stood in a line, showroom clean. A prim room, it spoke of organisation and discipline.

To Cashin's right, the painting leant against the wall, face averted, its slashed V held in place with masking tape. It was bigger than he remembered.

He went to it, gripped the frame and awkwardly lifted it, turned and settled it back against the wall. He could not see the painting properly before he had taken several steps back.

It was a painting of a moonlit landscape, a pale path running through sand dunes covered with coastal scrub towards a group of buildings in the distance, hints of lights in windows. Most of the canvas was of a huge sky of wind-driven grey-black clouds lit by a near-full moon.

Cashin knew the place. He had stood where the painter stood, on the top of the last big dune, looking towards the now-ruined buildings and the highway and the road that snaked up from the highway, went up the hill to the Kenmare road and driveway to The Heights.

He went closer. In the path were what appeared to be figures, a short column of people, three abreast, walking towards the buildings. Children, they were children, two taller figures.

The painting was unsigned. He turned it around. In the bottom left corner was a small sticker. On it was written in red ink:

Companions Camp, Port Monro, 1977.

'THE COMPANIONS camp,' said Cashin. 'At the mouth.'

There was a long silence. Cecily Addison, standing at the mantelpiece, staring at him. He never knew how long to meet Cecily's gaze because it was possible that she was not seeing him.

'You seem like a good person to ask,' said Cashin.

Cecily's head tilted, her eyelids fluttered. She took on the look of someone having her feet massaged. 'May I ask what this is about?'

'Charles Bourgoyne.'

'I thought that was over.'

'No.'

A last long draw on her cigarette, a raised eyebrow. 'Well, what do you want to know, my dear?

'What kind of camp was it?' Cashin said.

'For boys. Orphans and the like. Boys in homes. Foster children. The Moral Companions gave them a holiday, a bit of fun. Lots of Cromarty people helped out, including my Harry. It was a good cause.'

'And it burned down.'

'In 1983. Tragic. Mind you, it could've been worse. Just three boys there on the night. And the man in charge. The Companion, that's what they called themselves. He couldn't save them. Overcome by fumes, that was the coroner's verdict.'

'Where were the other kids?'

'On some cultural jaunt.' She stretched an arm, dropped her cigarette into the vase on the mantelpiece. 'They used to take them to Cromarty. Music, plays, that sort of thing. Still a lot of that then. People didn't sit at home in front of the television watching American rubbish.'

'What caused the fire?'

'I think they said it was the boiler in the dormitory building, the double-storey. A timber building. The boys were sleeping upstairs.'

Cashin thought about the blackened brick foundations, the charred floor joist. He had stood where the boys had died.

'Apart from owning the land, did Bourgoyne have anything to do with the camp?'

Cecily frowned, deep lines. 'Well, I don't know. He took an interest, of course. Following on from his dad. Lots of people took an interest. Public-spirited place then, Cromarty. People did good works, didn't do it to get their names in the paper either. Virtue is its own reward. Are you familiar with that expression, detective?'

'My reward is the award wage, Mrs Addison.'

She narrow-eyed him. 'You are a cut above the dull boys couldn't find another job, aren't you?'

'So that was the end of the camp?' said Cashin.

'The camp, the Companions too. It was all over the papers. I think they just packed it in. It was the last Companions camp left. Charles gave the manager bloke a job. Percy Crake. A cold fish, Percy Crake.'

There was a knock on the half-open door.

'Yes,' said Cecily.

Mrs McKendrick. 'Your appointment will be twenty minutes late, Mrs Addison,' she said. 'Car trouble is the excuse they offer.'

'Thank you, my dear.'

Mrs McKendrick turned like a teenage ballerina, reaching behind her to close the door she had found open. It was a message.

'She was in love with Jock Cameron,' said Cecily. 'All those years. Sad, really. He never noticed. Often wondered if he'd taken a bit of shrapnel in the tackle.'

'I'm told there are no Companions' records for Port Monro at the hall in Melbourne.'

Fin had rung while he was driving from The Heights.

'All the other camps' records are there,' said Cashin. 'Could they be somewhere else?'

'No idea. Why would they keep them somewhere else?'

On the mantelpiece, the vase was emitting smoke like a fumarole. Cashin got up and took it to the window, pushed up the bottom sash and shook the container, sent the smouldering contents to float on the sea wind.

'Thank you, Joe.'

'I'll go then. Thank you for your time, Mrs Addison.'

'My pleasure.'

It was cold outside, no one loitering. Cashin felt the need to walk, went down the street, past the empty clothing boutiques, the aromatherapist, the properties in the window of the estate agent. He crossed Crozier Street and passed the pub lounge, saw three people watching a greyhound race on the television, the old man coughing as if he could die there, on his feet. Beyond the pub were houses, mostly holiday rentals, curtains drawn.

As Cashin walked, the singing from the bluestone church on the rise became louder. He turned the corner on the faltering and cracking last lines of a hymn.

Heaven's morning breaks, and earth's vain shadows flee;
In life, in death, O Lord, abide with me.

314

There was a time of silence, then an attenuated Amen that stood in the cold air, hung in the branches of the pines.

Cashin felt the sudden withering ache of loss and mortality and he turned and went back the way he had come, into the wind.

HE WAS CROSSING a rope bridge in a gale, water far below. The bridge was swaying and creaking and groaning and slats were missing. He looked down and it was the Kettle, a huge wave coming in, he was fighting to hold his footing, clinging to the side ropes, he couldn't hold on, he was losing his grip, he was going into the Kettle.

In his sweat, Cashin lay wide awake, heart like a speedball, relief coming over him. He knew what the sounds were: the television aerial was loose again, being pushed around by the wind, chafing against the strapping. The sounds had triggered the Kettle dream. How did dreams work?

He turned the clock around: 6.46 am. Seven-hour sleep, the longest unbroken sleep he could remember. Just twinges of pain in getting up, a good morning, let in the dogs, fed them, drank juice, showered.

It was a grey day, no wind to speak of. When the dogs came back from looking for Rebb, he chose the circular route, up the hill. The European trees were bare now, standing in their damp leaves, a hundred and more generations of leaves. They went down the slope and across the big clearing, no hares today. Cashin stepped from rock to rock to cross the creek, still turbulent. Then, no sign of the dogs, he turned westwards, towards Helen's property, the painting on his mind – the moonlit plain, the little procession of boys going towards the buildings, the lights in the windows. The Companions camp. He thought about Pollard hanging in the Companions hall, crucified, dying while someone sat as if watching a play or a concert, something to enjoy, to applaud.

When did Pollard lose consciousness? Did the watcher listen with pleasure to his sounds, to his agony? Did he ask for mercy? Was that what the watcher wanted?

Bourgoyne's payments to Pollard. Bourgoyne the patron of the Companions.

The Companions kept records for the camps in Western Australia, Queensland and South Australia, camps closed before Port Monro. What happened to the Port Monro records?

The belt the dogs found that day.

Be Prepared.

No bigger than a dog collar, adult hands could span a waist that small.

Work was in progress on the Castleman house. New corrugated iron on the roof, what looked like a weather-board extension, pink primed boards, big windows, a platform sticking out, a deck when finished. It would be a place to loll, looking down at the creek, up at the hill. Looking at his property.

Why did he offer to sell her the creek strip? Because she was cross with him and she was the rich and beautiful and sophisticated girl who kissed him when he was a shy, gangling boy whose aunt cut his hair?

Offer permanently withdrawn.

It was a good fence, taut. Rebb's fence. How far could you walk in a day? Rebb wouldn't ask for lifts, people would have to ask him. Every tool Rebb had used was lined up inside the shearing shed, cleaned and oiled. His mattress was leaning against the wall, the blankets were on the bed springs, folded square, the pillow on them and the washed pillowslip on top.

Cashin was chewing porridge cooked in the microwave when the phone rang.

'Tuesday arrived down there yet?' said Dove.

'Of what week?'

'I should've said the year. Done the full sweep on this David Vincent.'

'Yes?'

'It's a brick high.'

'The summary. You've done that, of course.'

'Of course. Born Melbourne 1968, taken into care 1973, lived somewhere called Colville House 1973 to 1976. Then foster family number one until 1978, number two until 1979, ran away, found, number three until 1980, ran away. Still with me?'

'Keep going.'

'Next record is an arrest in Perth in 1983 for theft of a handbag. Age fifteen. After that it's a list of petty stuff, sent to juvenile in '84 for six months, again in '86, nine months. That's it for form.'

'The rest?'

'It's a sad story. Institutions. It says here, on this one report, clinical depression compounded by multiple addictions. Four years in Lakeside, Ballarat. That sounds nice. By the lake. I read the problem as smack, ampheta-mines, methadone, dope, booze, gets in fights and sustains injuries to many parts of the body.'

Cashin had not noticed the cloth of sunlight unroll across the old room's boards. 'Thank you,' he said. 'Listen, I need the number Dave Vincent called CrimeStoppers from. Tracy's got it.'

'I thought talking to Vincent was a problem?'

'Sometimes it's people looking at you that's the problem.'

An observation from Singo. Early in the piece, in the first year, the Geelong man who wouldn't say anything, his hands clenched, his neck a fence of tendons. Singo wrote his extension number on a pad and gave it to the man. They left and waited in Singo's office. The phone rang inside a minute and Singo talked to him for almost an hour.

'Well, I'm glad you can look at yourself so objectively,' said Dove. 'Over the phone, that is. For my education, may I ask what you want from Vincent?'

'I think he was at the Companions camp at Port Monro.'

'Yes? Where does that get you?'

'Just having a sniff.'

'Ah, the sniff. I keep hearing about it. A trade secret. Hang on.'

Dove was back with the number inside two minutes.

'Back to work then,' said Cashin. 'Go around to whatever the drug squad is now called and arrest the first prick you see.'

'So old-fashioned, so out of touch with modern policing.'

David Vincent's number rang out. Too early for him, Cashin thought. His day would probably begin when most people were thinking about lunch.

'UNEMPLOYED,' said Carol Gehrig, shifted on the chair, pulled at the crotch of her tracksuit. 'Sixteen weeks pay, how's that for twenty-six years on the job?'

The cheap timber house stood in the teeth of the wind on a low hill looking over Kenmare. Behind it was a big shed, open in front, a truck shed with just an old yellow Mazda in it.

'Who sacked you?' said Cashin.

'The lawyer. Addison. Place's going on the market some time. She wants me to clean up when the time comes.'

She sucked on her stub, ground it out among the five or six already in the abalone shell on the table. She offered Cashin the packet. He shook his head.

'Coffee?' she said. 'Tea? I should've asked. Caught me without my face too. Not used to being here at this time of the morning.'

He'd had to wait minutes, didn't knock again after he heard movements inside.

'No thanks. Ever heard of someone called Arthur Pollard?'

'Pollard? No.'

The sagging foam chair made his back hurt. Cashin sat up straight, tried to extend his spine. He took out the doctored, sanitised photograph of Pollard. 'Know this man?'

She looked at it, held it away. 'Something familiar... don't know. Local?'

'No. Tell me about Percy Crake.'

'Well, he came after the fire at the camp. Little moustache. His sister arrived, a bitch. Face like an axe, moustache too. Bigger than Crake's. Called herself Mrs Lowell. Christ knows how she got Mr Lowell. She used to come behind me with a tissue looking for dust.'

'What did Crake do?'

'Took over, marched around like a dork. He used to make us stand outside his office for our wages, keep us waiting like he was busy inside. Then he'd open the door and he'd say: Now then, line up in alphabetical order.'

The voice she imitated wasn't loud and commanding. It was thin and grating. 'Five people. In alphabetical order, I ask you? Pommy shit. Fucking scoutmaster.'

Be Prepared.

Cashin saw the stiff and cracked little belt, the round rusted buckle. 'That was in 1980,' he said.

'Year I started, full-time in 1978. Mrs B was there with the kids. She was nice, gave him about twenty years. Real tragedy that, falling down the stairs.'

'How did they take it, the kids?'

'The boy never said a word. Erica followed Mr B around like he was a pop star. She was in love with him. Girls can be like that.'

An intake of smoke, a blowing, a tapping into the abalone shell. 'They used to have parties. Garden parties, cocktail parties, dinner parties, all the Cromarty money, people from Melbourne. For the autumn races, there'd be people staying. I got help. There was a cook and a waiter come from Melbourne.'

Carol sucked her cheeks hollow. 'Anyway, old times. History. What's this about?'

Cashin shrugged. 'Just curious.'

'Thought the black kids did it?'

'What do you think?'

'No surprise to me. Daunt's a fucking curse on this town.'

'You must know a lot about the Bourgoynes.'

'Not that much. Cleaning up behind people, that's the job. Washing, ironing. Twenty hours a week the last ten years or so. That's it.' More smoking. 'Head down, bum up around there, mate,' she said. 'Unless you're Bruce Starkey.'

'He got special treatment?'

'Well, in the old days, Crake was always checking. He caught you havin a smoko, he'd dock your pay quarter of an hour. Can you believe that? Bloody Starkey, he never went near him, didn't have to line up for his pay, the big prick.'

'How'd Bourgoyne and Crake get on?'

'Pretty good. Only time I ever heard Crake laugh was when Mr B was in his office. Crake helped him with the pots, the kiln. They used to do it at weekends. Burn it all weekend.'

'You saw that?'

'No. Mrs Lowell told me. Burn through the night. Starkey used to be chainsawing and chopping for a week before.'

'How often was this?'

'Jeez, it's been a long time. I suppose twice a year. Yeah.'

'Those pots in the gallery room. Nine pots. That's all he kept?'

'He used to smash em up. Starkey took the bits to the tip. Half a ute load at a time.'

Cashin looked at the barren green view, thought about how nice it would be if this had never begun, if he had never received the call that morning.

'Sure you don't want coffee? I'm going…'

'No thanks,' said Cashin. 'Erica says she knows almost nothing about her step-father's affairs. What do you think?'

Carol frowned, aged ten years. 'Well, wouldn't surprise me. I can count on one hand the times I've seen her there since she was about fourteen. Fell out of love with her step-dad.'

She came with him to the vehicle, hugging herself against the cold. The dogs liked the look of her and she had no fear of them, scratched their chins.

'Twin buggers,' she said. 'What kind's this?'

'Poodles.'

'Nah. Poodles are sooky litle things. Rough buggers, these.'

'Neglected,' said Cashin. 'Short of haircuts and brushing.'

'Bit like me.' She was fondling big dog ears, not looking at him. 'You married?'

'Not anymore.'

'Kids?'

He hesitated. 'No.'

'Kids are good, it's bloody jobs that's the problem. My ex went to Darwin, don't blame him. Fisherman. I couldn't hack it, never saw him, he just slept here.'

'Thanks for the help,' said Cashin.

'Any time. Come again. Have a beer.'

'That'd be good. Starkey get the boot too?'

'Dunno. Place'll need some keeping up if it's on the market.'

Cashin was in the vehicle when he thought to ask. 'The Companions camp. Know anything about it?'

Carol shook her head. 'Not much. Starkey used to work there before the fire.'

THE CROMARTY *Herald*'s editorial office was in an ugly yellow-brick 1950s building on the edge of the business area.

Cashin went through glass doors into an area with a long counter staffed by two young women. A glass wall cut them off from a big office, half a dozen desks, five women and a man, all with heads down. He had to wait for three people to pay bills, one to lodge a classified advertisement.

'I'd like to see back copies of the paper, please,' he said.

'Through that door,' the woman said. 'There's about six months.'

'For 1983.'

'Jeez. Don't think you can do that.' She wasn't interested, looking at the person behind him.

'Is there a library?'

'Library?'

'Where you keep your files.'

Puzzled brow. 'Better ask editorial,' she said. 'In there.'

Another reception room, an older woman behind a desk. He asked the same question. This time, he said police. She spoke on the phone. In seconds, a door opened and a man in his fifties, bald, florid, big belly, came in. Cashin introduced himself, showed the badge.

'Alec Clarke,' the man said. 'Assistant editor. Come through.'

It was a big room, six or seven people at desks, looking at computers, three men doing the same at a cluttered table in the centre. It was not unlike a squad room. Clarke led Cashin to the first office in a row of four cubicles. They sat.

'How can I help?'

Cashin told him.

'That far back? Looking for something in particular?'

'A fire. At the Moral Companions camp near Port.'

'Right, yes. Big news that, the boys. Very sad. What's the interest now?'

'Idle curiosity.'

Clarke laughed, held up his hands, palms out. 'Message received. I'll have a check, back in a minute.'

He went out, turned right. Cashin looked at the workers. They were all young women except for the three at the middle table, seedy older men, pale, moulting and flaking. The ginger one who appeared to be in charge was methodically fossicking in his nostrils, from time to time studying the finds. A painfully thin young woman came in and went to the prospector, spoke in a respectful manner. He pulled a face, waved his right hand dismissively. She nodded and she went to a seat at the back of the room. Cashin saw her shoulders slump, her chin go down.

'Sorry to be so long, detective,' said Clarke. He sat behind the desk.

'Always a pleasure to watch a well-oiled machine,' said Cashin.

A tight smile. 'Now there's a problem here,' said Clarke. 'We went modern in '84, put everything on microfiche. You're probably too young to remember microfiche.'

'I know microfiche.'

'Yes. Well, we had a fire in '86, a cigarette someone

325

dropped in a bin, but we lost the fiche for about ten years from 1976.'

'What about the actual papers?'

'Destroyed in '84, unfortunately. No concern for heritage then. In retrospect, we should never...'

'The State Library would have them?'

'Worth a try. Certainly.'

Outside, Cashin walked to the vehicle in a cold morning, looked up at a sky deep as heaven, pale as memory. The dogs beat each other with their tails at the sight of him.

THE STATE Library did not hold the Cromarty *Herald*. Cashin put down the phone and thought about Corey Pascoe and Bourgoyne's watch. Did it matter now?

He closed his eyes, put his head back. The boys were dead because of a Bourgoyne watch. The whole terrible business turned on the watch.

How did Corey come to have a watch belonging to Bourgoyne? Chris Pascoe said something that day on the pier, it hadn't registered as important. *He wasn't a bad kid, Corey. Could've played AFL footy. Just full of shit, thought he saw a fuckin career in dope. You a mate of Hopgood and that lot?*

A career in dope. Was he talking about Corey smoking dope? That wouldn't be remarkable on the Daunt, it wouldn't be remarkable anywhere in the country. Dope was like beer in the 1960s. People then didn't say the beer kept them from playing professional footy.

No, Pascoe didn't mean smoking. He meant growing, dealing.

He watched the dogs patrolling the backyard, complaining to each other of sensory deprivation. They didn't like the place, they wanted to be somewhere with Rebb. What kind of memory did dogs have? Did they miss Rebb?

The Piggots were drug people. Billy Piggot was dealing to schoolkids. Debbie Doogue had been a customer.

Kendall behind him. 'Am I allowed to say I'd like you back in that chair permanently ASAbloodyP? I am so bored by these boy wonders I could face a charge any time now.'

'I'm back soon,' said Cashin. 'Never heard of anyone missing me.'

'Staging for compliments, that's not allowed,' she said. 'What I appreciate is that you don't go on about reality crap on television and how many slow curls for the maximum upper-body benefit.'

'Actually, I've been thinking about curls. This kid came in about the hairdresser girlfriend took his ute to Queensland. He says the Piggots are getting rich. Been busted to your knowledge, the Pigs?'

'In my time, no.'

'Why's that?'

'Don't know. It's Cromarty's business.'

'Yes, but someone has to tell Cromarty.'

'I don't think they need telling. I think they know.'

'This come up before I arrived? When Sadler was in charge?'

'We had complaints.' Kendall looked away. 'Sadler said he'd talk to Cromarty. Anyway, work to do.'

'Just hold a sec, Ken. The day of the march, I asked you about Billy Piggot, you said something about a Ray Piggot. What was it again?'

'Ripped five hundred bucks off a rep staying at the Wavecrest. He said he gave Ray a lift from outside Cromarty, invited him to his room for a beer. Later the money was gone. Just two thirsty blokes, you understand, one's about fifty, the other one looks like he's fourteen.'

'He had Ray's full name?'

'Yes. Sadler rang Cromarty. Hopgood and that Steggles arrived. Parked in the back. Ray Piggot was in the car. Must've picked him up on the way. They left him there, talked to the rep in the interview room. He left, they left. Never heard any more.'

'Piggot not charged?'

'Nope. He got off a charge in Melbourne too. Stole a stereo and a laptop from a bloke he met in the park. Streetkid then.'

'What does all this say to you?'

Kendall smiled her small sad, comprehending smile, eyes down. 'I'm just happy to have my job,' she said. 'When I was physically stuffed, people didn't push me away, get me out of sight, pension me off. They were family to me. You'd know about that. Not so?'

She left. Cashin put his head back, heard the messages from his tired places. The morning at the court, Greg Law had given him a message about Hopgood. Head-kicking, grass-growing Gaby Trevena wasn't the most dangerous person in town, he said. Had Law been delivering a threat from Hopgood? Or had he been saying he wasn't a Hopgood man?

You a mate of Hopgood and that lot?

Hopgood and Lloyd. And Steggles, presumably.

Steggles vomited that night. In the pouring rain, face down, his gun pointed at the sky, a tube of vomit sprang from his mouth. The hamburger he had been eating at the briefing, the greasy yellow chips with sauce-red tips, they exited his body after he shot the boy.

Didn't have the stomach for it, Steggie.

Cashin rang Helen Castleman.

'I want to talk to that Pascoe again,' he said.

'Your bedside manner needs some work. Has anyone told you that?'

'I'll talk to him in your office. You can be there.'

'This is official, is it? An official interview?'

'No. Just a chat.'

'Well, I don't represent Pascoe, so I have no standing when it comes to chats. Also I have no desire to assist the police in their chatting work.'

'I'll start again. I'm trying to clear the boys. Clear your client.'

'My late client.'

She was silent. Cashin waited.

'I'll get back to you,' she said. 'Where are you?'

Cashin went outside, walked around the block in the wind, only a few people in the main street, moving between vehicles and shops. Leon's place was empty.

'Police,' said Cashin loudly. 'This business open?'

'Open to bloody suggestions,' said Leon, coming out of the kitchen. 'Open to offers of any kind. Limited menu today. Soup, that's all I'm offering, a proper minestrone made with a ham bone.'

'To take away?'

'Seven-fifty eaten on premises. For removal, I'll accept four-fifty. Three-fifty because you're the police.'

'You can keep the bone.'

'Three-fifty. I'll chuck in a slice of bread. Proper bread. Buttered. With butter.'

'Two slices.'

'Stood over. I'm being stood over. What kind of music do you like?'

Cashin was eating the soup at his desk when the phone rang.

'He doesn't want to come here,' said Helen. 'He's a very uninterested person, he's not interested in chatting.'

'That's it?'

'He says if you want to chat, you can come to his house tonight. He would like to point out that he owes the police nothing. I'm paraphrasing and editing here so as not to offend your tender sensibilities.'

So smart. Cashin thought he could read books for

another ten years and it wouldn't help. 'I'll do that then,' he said. 'Thank you and goodbye.'

'I have to drive you, come with you. He doesn't want the squad car outside his place. And so, since you're trying to do something about a major injustice, I'm willing to do that.'

He looked at the dogs in the yard and he thought about her mouth, the kisses. Kisses from nowhere. Separated by twenty years.

CASHIN AND Helen sat at a kitchen table in what had been the garage of a house. Now it was like a small pub with a bar and a full-size snooker table and an assortment of chairs. A television set was mounted on a side wall.

Chris Pascoe brought a six-pack of beer from behind the bar and put it on the table. He sat down, took one and popped it. 'Help yourself,' he said. 'So what's this about?'

'The watch Corey had,' said Cashin.

'Suse told you.'

'I'm keen to know how he got it.'

'Thinkin of chargin him with theft? Well, he's had the fuckin death penalty. Slipped your mind?'

'No. What we want is to find out who bashed Bourgoyne. It wasn't the boys, I'm pretty sure about that.'

'Since when?'

'Since I decided to believe Susie about when she saw the watch.'

Pascoe drank, wiped his lips, found a cigarette. 'Yeah, well, Suse don't know where he got it, his mum don't know.'

'His mates might know though.'

'Mates mostly dead.'

Helen coughed. 'Chris, I said on the phone, I'm here because of Donny. I want his name cleared, the names of all the boys. And the Daunt. The Daunt shouldn't have to wear this.'

Pascoe laughed, a smoker's ragged laugh-cough. 'Don't worry about the Daunt. Wearin the blame's nothin new for the Daunt. Anyway, how's it help to find where he got the watch? Bloody thing must've been pinched some time.'

'If it turns out Corey pinched it, that's it,' said Cashin. 'We'll just leave it there, call it quits.'

'I hear Hopgood doesn't like you,' said Pascoe.

'How would you hear that?'

Pascoe shrugged, smoked, little smile. 'Walls got ears, mate. You'd be sleepin under the bed these days, right?'

The side door opened violently, banged the wall. The other man from the pier, the gaunt-faced man with dreadlocks. Cashin thought he looked bigger indoors.

'So what's the fuckin party?' he said.

Pascoe held up a hand. 'Havin a talk, Stevo.'

'Talk? Beer with the cops? Things fuckin changin around here, mate. Havin the fuckin trivia nights with the cops next.'

'Gettin the Corey watch stuff sorted,' said Pascoe. 'That's all.'

'Yeah, well,' said Stevo. 'It's sorted. Who's the lady?'

'The lawyer,' said Pascoe. 'Donny's lawyer.'

Stevo stepped across, stood behind Pascoe, reached over and picked up the six-pack, ripped out a can, looking at Cashin, at Helen, back at Cashin, blood in his eyes. 'Not drinkin?' he said. 'Don't drink with boongs?'

Pub fight shit, thought Cashin, no answer would defuse it. He looked at Pascoe. 'Listen, if your mate here's in charge, I'm gone.'

'So piss off,' said Stevo.

Pascoe didn't look around. 'Settle down, Stevo,' he said, a briskness to his tone.

'Settle down? Don't you fuckin tell me to settle down, where the fuck you…'

Pascoe shoved his chair back, took Stevo by surprise, knocked him off balance. He was upright in one quick movement and walking Stevo backwards, barrel chest bumping, three steps, pinned him against the bar. In his face, their chins touching, Pascoe said something to Stevo, Cashin couldn't catch it.

Stevo raised his hands. Pascoe stepped back, gestured. Stevo went behind the bar, leaned on it, didn't look at them. Pascoe went back to his chair, drank some beer.

'What I'll say is this,' he said as if nothing had happened. 'What I'll say is Corey coulda got the watch in a trade like, y'know.'

'For what?' said Cashin.

'Jeez, how'd I know? What do you reckon?'

'So who'd be on the other side?'

'Big ask, mate.'

'That's useful. Got any other stuff you'd like to tell me? Other people don't like me? How about Steggles? Wall ears hear anything about Steggie?'

'Dead man walkin. The fuckin prick.'

'Do it myself,' said Stevo, slurring. 'Fuckin tonight. Blow the cunt away.'

'Shut up, Stevo,' said Pascoe. 'Just fuckin shut up.'

Cashin took a can, ripped the top. He glanced at Helen. She had the air of someone watching a blood sport, lips parted, smears of colour on her cheekbones.

'Listen,' said Cashin. 'You want something, tell me quick, I'm thinking about food now. I eat around this time of the day, the night.'

'Corey done some stupid stuff, will of his own,' said Pascoe. 'Couldn't tell him a fuckin thing, just go his own way.'

Cashin said, 'This's dope you're talkin about?'

Pascoe waved a big hand. 'People grow a bit of weed, make a few bucks. No work around here.'

'So what did he do?'

'Well, y'know, there's ways of doin business. I'm not talkin fuckin truckloads, you understand, just beer money. Anyway, I hear Corey did these private deals, him and Luke, he's another kid wouldn't listen, bugger all respect.'

Pascoe offered the cigarettes. Cashin took one, the lighter, lit up, blew smoke at the roof, his instinct told him to make the leap. 'Piggots,' he said. 'This is Piggots?'

Pascoe looked at Helen, looked at Cashin. 'Not all asleep in Port, are you? Yeah, Piggots. They got ambitions, the fuckin Piggots, such dickheads but they reckon they're headin for the big time, they're gonna be players.'

'Fuckin Piggots,' said Stevo. He had a Jim Beam bottle in his hand now. 'Blow the cunts away. White fuckin maggots.'

'Stevo,' said Pascoe. 'Shut the fuck up. Watch TV. Find the fuckin cartoons.'

Helen said, 'Chris, correct me, you're saying Corey traded for the watch with the Piggots?'

'That's, that's possible, yeah.'

'Tell me how the Piggots got the watch,' said Helen.

Pascoe was looking at Cashin. 'Can you imagine?' he said. 'These Pigs got the idea this shit's easier than poachin abalone. Don't even want to grow it themselves, don't want to move it. All reward and no risk.'

'That's very ambitious,' said Cashin.

'My fuckin oath. And I hear they got someone to do a cook for em, too. This bloke, he's like a travellin speed cook.'

'Is that right?'

'Shouldn't be allowed, should it?'

'No.'

Pascoe leaned forward, put his face as close to Cashin's as he could. 'Can't expect fuckin Hopgood and the local boys to do anythin, can you? Be unreasonable since Hoppy's got a share in the horse. Whole leg, I hear.'

'Something'll have to be done about that,' said Cashin.

'Fuckin right.' He sat back. 'Hearin me.'

Cashin nodded. 'Hearing you.'

Helen coughed. 'About how the Piggots got the watch,' she said. 'Can we get on to that?'

Cashin thought that he knew the answer, delivered to him by some process in the brain that endlessly sifted, sorted and shuffled things heard and read, seen and felt, bits and pieces with no obvious use, just clutter, litter, until the moment when two of them touched, spun and found each other, fitted like hands locking.

'Ray Piggot,' he said.

'You're so fuckin quick,' said Pascoe. 'Yeah, the bumboy. That's what I hear.'

The complaint against Ray Piggot. Hopgood and Steggles at the station, Ray in the car outside. Ray who looked all of fourteen.

'Ray Piggot stole the watch from Bourgoyne?' said Helen, uncertainly.

'Well, wouldn't have been a present.'

'I don't understand what's going on here,' said Helen. 'Who's Ray Piggot? Am I just…'

Cashin said, 'So to clear this up, we're not talking about Ray and a burg?'

Pascoe laughed. 'Hopgood woulda dropped him off up there for old Charlie Bourgoyne. This cunt Ray knew what he was in for but he's not the first kid been fed to Charlie and his mates. That's one of Hoppy's jobs. That's the way it's always been.'

THEY DROVE in silence to the forecourt of the service station where Cashin had parked. 'Thank you,' he said, made to go.

'Wait.'

There were no cars at the pumps. The windows of the small cashier's cabin were steamed up by breath.

'I need some things explained to me,' said Helen. 'What the hell was going on there?'

Cashin thought about what to say to her. She had no further part to play in this shit, she didn't have a client. 'Pascoe's growing,' he said. 'Also, he delivers, he does the tightarse run. The Piggots get other people to grow, make tablets, deliver. Pascoe says Hopgood and the mates are in it, building up their super.'

'Why's Pascoe telling you?'

'He wants me to take care of the Piggots. For telling me how the boys got the watch.'

'This is another watch, an earlier one?'

'That's right. Different model.'

'So it was a stuff-up from the beginning?'

'It was.'

'And you believe the story about this Ray Piggot?'

Cashin looked at her. A car turned in and the headlights splashed her face and he felt again the full sad stupidity of teenage lust for someone beyond reach. 'Ray's a quickpick,' he said. 'Rips off the punters if he can.'

'A quickpick?'

'Drivethrough, a hitchhiker. One size fits all.'

'Joe, I was in corporate law until a year ago.'

'It doesn't matter,' he said. 'There's nothing left for you to do. Just a mess for us to clean up. Of our own making.'

'Joe.'

'What?'

'Give me a break. You wouldn't know what you know if I hadn't pushed you to see Pascoe. Pascoe says Hopgood delivered Ray Piggot to Bourgoyne. And other boys. Nobody's ever said this about Bourgoyne.'

'In your circle.'

'What's that mean? In my circle?'

'Maybe you Bayview Drive people don't talk about stuff like that. Too vulgar.'

Helen tapped second knuckles of both hands on the steering wheel. 'Not rising to that bait,' she said, a pause between each word.

'Got to go,' said Cashin. 'I'll get back to you.'

It was cold and damp outside, a sea mist. He ducked his head to say thanks.

'Are you often in pain?' said Helen.

'No.'

'Well, you fooled me. Anyway, I'm in the house, we're neighbours. Care to stop off for a drink? I can microwave some party pies. I gather people in your circle enjoy them.'

He was going to say, no thank you, I'll give that a miss, but he looked into her eyes. 'I'll follow you,' he said.

'No,' she said, 'you go first. You know the road better.'

The driveway to the Corrigan house ran between old elms, many dead. It was newly graded, the earth white in the headlights. Cashin parked to the left of the homestead gate and switched off. Helen parked beside him. He got out, uneasy. The moving sky opened and a full moon appeared in the wedge, lit the world pale grey. They went down the long path in silence, climbed new timber steps to the front door.

'I'm still a bit spooked out here,' she said. 'The dark. The silence. It may be a mistake.'

'Get a dog,' said Cashin. 'And a gun.'

They went down a passage. She clicked lights, revealed a big empty room, two or three of the old house's rooms knocked into one, a new floor laid. There were two chairs and a low table.

'I haven't got around to furniture yet,' said Helen. 'Or unpacked the books.'

He followed her into a kitchen.

'Stove, fridge, microwave,' she said. 'It's your basic bed-and-breakfast establishment. No personality.'

'Party pies are just right then,' said Cashin. 'Very little personality in a party pie.'

Helen hooked her thumbs in her coat pockets. She lifted her chin. Cashin saw the tendons in her throat. He could feel his heartbeat.

'Hungry?' she said.

'Your eyes,' said Cashin. 'Did you inherit that?'

'My grandmother had different coloured eyes.' She half-turned from him. 'You were a person of interest at school. I like that term. Person of interest.'

'That's a lie. You never noticed me.'

'You looked so hostile. Glowering. You still glower. Something sexy about a glower.'

'How do you glower?'

'Don't question your gift.' Helen crossed the space and took his head in her hands, kissed him, drew back. 'Not too responsive,' she said. 'Are cops intimate on the first date?'

339

Cashin put his hands inside her coat, held her, inhaled her smell, felt her ribs. She was thinner than he expected. He shivered. 'Cops generally don't have second dates.'

There was a long moment.

Helen took Cashin's right hand, kissed it, kissed his lips, led him.

In the night, he awoke, sensed that she was awake.

'Do you still ride?' he said.

'No. I had a bad fall, lost my nerve.'

'I thought the idea was to get on again.'

She touched him. 'Is that a suggestion?'

THE HOUSE could be seen from a long way, the front door dead centre at the end of a drive of pencil pines. As Cashin drove, the weak western sunlight flicked unnervingly through the trees.

A thin, lined woman wearing a dark tracksuit answered his knocks. Cashin said the words, offered the ID.

'Round the back,' she said. 'In the shed.'

He walked on the concrete apron. The place had the air of a low-security prison – the fence around the compound, the building freshly painted, the watermelon scent of newly mown grass in the air. No trees, no flowers, no weeds.

The shed, big enough for a few light aircraft, had an open sliding door on the north side. A man appeared in it when Cashin was ten metres away.

'Mr Starkey?' said Cashin.

'Yeah?'

He was wearing clean blue overalls over a checked shirt, a huge man, fat but hard looking, head the shape and colour of a scrubbed potato.

'Detective Senior Sergeant Cashin. Can we talk?'

'Yeah.' He turned and went inside.

Cashin followed him. Mrs Starkey's kitchen would be this clean and neat, he thought. Power tools in racks. Two long benches with galvanised iron tops shone under the fluorescent light. Behind them pegboards held tools – spanners, wrenches, pliers, metal snips, hacksaws, steel rulers, clamps, calipers – arranged by size in laser-straight rows. There was a big metal lathe and a tiny one, a drill stand, two bench grinders, a power hacksaw, a stand with slots and holes for files and punches and other things.

In the centre of the space, under chain hoists, four old engines in stages of disassembly stood on square steel tables.

A tall thin youth, dressed like Starkey, was at a vice, filing at something. He glanced at Cashin, looked down at the work, a lock of hair falling.

'Go talk to yer mum, Tay,' said Starkey.

Tay had an oily cloth in his back pocket. He took it out and carefully wiped the bench, went over to a stand, wiped his file and put it in its place.

He went without looking at Cashin again. Cashin watched him go. He held one shoulder lower than the other, walked with it leading in a crab-like way.

'Working on these engines,' said Cashin.

'Yeah,' said Starkey. His eyes were slits. 'Bourgoyne & Cromie engines. What can I do for you?'

'You fix them?'

'Restore em. Best ever made. What?'

Cashin realised there was nowhere to sit. 'The watch Mr Bourgoyne was wearing,' he said. 'Can you identify it?'

'Yeah, I reckon.'

Cashin took out a colour copy of the brochure, folded to show only the watch with the plain white face, three small dials.

'Yeah, that's it,' Starkey said.

'He was wearing that watch that day?'

'Wore it every day.'

'Thanks. Just a few other questions.'

'What's the problem? Daunt coons bashed him.' Impassive face, grey marble eyes.

342

'We're not sure of that.'

'Yeah? That fuckin little Coulter took the Kettle dive to have a swim? Guilty as shit.'

Starkey walked to the door and spat, wiped his lips, came back, planted himself, questioning head angle.

'At home that night?' said Cashin. 'You and Tay?'

Starkey's eyes narrowed, full of threat. 'Answered that question already. What's your fuckin problem?'

'Come down to the station,' said Cashin. 'The two of you. Bring the toothbrushes, just in case.'

Starkey exercised his jaw, up and down, back and forth.

'Know a cop called Hopgood?' he said. 'I know him. Mate.'

Cashin took out his mobile, held it out. 'Ring him,' he said.

'In my own fuckin time.'

'Want me to ring him? I'll ring him for you.'

Starkey put his hands in his pockets. 'We was at home, ask her. Don't go out at night much. Just footy stuff.'

'Still working at The Heights?'

'Till it's sold, yeah.'

'Well-paid job, The Heights.'

'That right?'

'About four times what your gardener gets around here. Five, maybe.'

'Two of us.'

'Twice as much then.'

'Twice as much fuckin work as anywhere else.'

'You drove him around too.'

Starkey put a huge hand to his neck. 'Didn't drive him around. Took him to the bank, to the city. He didn't like to drive anymore.'

'Know someone called Arthur Pollard?'

'No.'

343

'Know this man?' He showed him the full-face mugshot of Pollard, watched his eyes.

'No.'

Cashin considered where to go, took the soft route. 'Mr Starkey, I'll tell you we don't think the Daunt boys attacked Mr Bourgoyne. So if you can tell me anything you saw or heard, any feeling you might have...'

'You don't think?'

'No.'

'Why?'

'Some things don't add up.'

'Charged that Coulter, didn't ya?'

'We thought he was involved, it was a holding action.'

'What's that mean?'

'What did you think when you heard about it?'

There was an instant, something in Starkey's muddy eyes. 'Well, shock, that's it, yeah.'

'That's all?'

'What else? Don't happen around here that kind of thing, does it?'

'Did you like him?'

'He was all right. Yeah. Not likely to be mates, were we, him and me?'

'Who could want to harm him?'

'Apart from thievin scum?'

'Yes.'

'No idea.'

'Had any visitors recently, Mr Bourgoyne? Apart from the step-daughter?'

'Nah. Not that I saw.'

'What about burglaries at The Heights before this happened?'

'Not in my time. Had some horses pinched once. They cut the wire, pinched three horses from the bottom paddock. You'd have the records, wouldn't ya?'

'If it was reported.'

'Why wouldn't it be reported?'

'Crake. How'd you get on with him?'

Starkey shrugged. 'Okay. Had his ways he wanted things done. I did em that way.'

'He helped Bourgoyne with the kiln, didn't he?'

'Can't remember that well.'

'You worked at the Companions camp.'

Starkey scratched his head again, an uncertain look, averted his eyes. 'Long time ago,' he said.

'So you knew Crake from the camp?'

'Yeah. He was the boss.'

'What was your job?'

'Maintenance. Bit of footy coaching. Showed the kids the ropes.'

'There on the night of the fire?'

The big hands were expressive now. 'Nah. At the pub in Port.'

'Tell me about driving him to the city. Where'd you go?'

'The flat in Relly Street. He took taxis from there.'

'Stay over?'

'Hotel in St Kilda. Gedding's Hotel.'

Cashin went over to the engines. 'This one a generator?' he said.

'Made in '56. Better than anything you can buy today.'

'How much ground you got here?'

'Thirty acres.'

'Farm it?'

'Nah. Put the house in the middle of the block. Didn't wanna hear neighbours. Now the one bastard's complaining about the engines.'

'Well,' said Cashin, 'tell him you'll connect him up if the power fails. I could use a generator. Sell them?'

'Don't sell, not a business,' said Starkey. 'Only restore

ones my granddad and my dad finished off. They punched their initials under the number.'

'How do you find them?'

'Advertise, Queensland, WA, Northern Territory. I got auctioneers keep a lookout at clearing sales, that kind of thing. Found one in Fiji, rusted to buggery. Cost a bit to bring it home.'

'And you've found four?'

'Thirteen. Got another shed for em.'

'Where do you stop?'

'Stop?'

'Collecting them.'

'Don't have to stop.'

There was no point in asking why. It was a pretty useless question most of the time. The answer was either obvious or too complicated to understand. Cashin looked for the engine number. 'Ever drive Bourgoyne to a house in North Melbourne?'

'North... no. Only took him to Relly Street.'

The fortress had a crack, a hairline fracture. He didn't look at Starkey. 'A hall in North Melbourne, you drove him there.'

'A hall? Just Relly Street.'

'The Companions hall. You know it, don't bullshit me, Mr Starkey.'

'No, don't know it.'

Cashin went to another engine. They were simple machines, he could probably learn to fix one. Easier than making a decent soup. 'Your dad, he'd have been pretty pissed off when they sold the factory.'

Silence. Starkey coughed, off balance. 'Never said a word. Mum told me that.'

'What'd he do afterwards?'

'Nothin. Died before the payout. Some serious brain thing.'

'That's sad.' Cashin didn't look at him. 'I'll tell you what's a serious brain thing, Mr Starkey. Bullshitting me. That's a seriously bad brain thing. Tell me about the hall.'

'Don't know no hall.'

'I'll need to talk to Tay,' said Cashin. 'By himself.'

'Why?'

'He might have seen something. Heard something.'

Starkey stared at Cashin. 'He wouldn't know nothin, mate. Always with me.'

Cashin shrugged. 'We'll see.'

'Listen,' said Starkey, a different voice. 'Boy's not the brightest. She dropped him on the lid when he was tiny. Short-circuited the little bugger. No use at school.'

'Get him in here.'

Starkey scratched his scalp, slowly, urgently. 'Do me a favour, mate,' he said. 'Let him alone. Gets nightmares. Screams.'

The felt moment of power. Cashin could see Starkey's fear. 'That's really tough. Get him.'

'Mate, please.'

'Just get him.'

'I'm gonna ring Hopgood.'

'Listen, Starkey,' said Cashin. 'Hopgood can't protect you. This is a city matter. And now, because you're so fucking obstructive, I'm not going to talk to Tay here, not going to talk to him at the station. I'm taking him to Melbourne. Pack his toothbrush and his jarmies and a couple of biscuits. What kind of bickies does he like?'

He saw hate in Starkey's eyes, and he saw pure shining fear, fear and panic.

'Can't do that, mate. I ask you, please, I ask you...'

'North Melbourne. The house in Collett Street. You drove him there?'

'No, I didn't, you gotta...'

'Wasting my time. Got a trip ahead of me. Tell me the truth or get Tay. Now.'

Starkey looked around the shed as if the answer might be written on a wall, he could read it out. 'Okay. Took him there.'

'When last?'

'Five, six years, I dunno.'

'How many times?'

'Few.'

'Every time you went to Melbourne?'

'I suppose.'

'How often was that?'

Starkey swallowed. 'Four, five times a year.'

'And the hall?'

'Don't know the hall.'

Cashin caught the tinny sound in the big man's voice.

He took out the mugshot of Pollard, didn't show it. 'I'm asking you again. Do you know this man?'

'I know him.'

'What's his name?'

'Arthur Pollard. He used to come to the camp.'

'Where else do you know him from?'

'Collett Street. I seen him there.'

Cashin walked to the work bench, ran a finger over the piece of metal Tay had been filing. It was a part of some sort. 'Pollard's a perv,' he said. 'Know that? He likes boys. Small boys. Fucks them. And the rest. Lots of the rest, I can tell you. Know about that do you, Mr Starkey?'

Silence. Cashin didn't look at Starkey. 'Didn't drop your boy off in Collett Street, did you, Mr Starkey? Feed him to Pollard?'

'I'll kill you,' Starkey said slowly, voice thick. 'Say that again, I'll fuckin kill you.'

Cashin turned. 'Tell me about Bourgoyne.'

Starkey had a hand on his chest. His face was orange, he was trying to control his breathing. 'Never saw anything. Nothin. So help me, I never saw anythin.'

'What about the hall?'

'Just the once. Picked up a lot of stuff, files and that. He said to burn it.'

'Bourgoyne?'

'Yeah.'

'So where'd you burn it?

'Nowhere to burn there. Brought the stuff back here to burn.'

'Dad.'

Tay was in the door, chin near his chest, looking through a comb of pale hair that touched the bridge of his nose.

'What?'

'Mum says spaggy bol okay for tea?'

'Tell her to go for it, son.'

Tay went. Cashin walked to the door, turned. 'Don't go anywhere,' he said. 'There's plenty more we want to know. And don't mention this little talk to anyone. You go running to fucking Hopgood, running anywhere, I'm coming back for you and Tay, you'll both rot in remand in Melbourne. Not together either. He'll be in with blokes fuck dogs. And so will you.'

'Didn't burn the stuff,' said Starkey quietly.

CASHIN SAT at the table and sifted through the contents of Starkey's cardboard boxes. It was half an hour before he came upon the clipping of a photograph from the Cromarty *Herald*. The date at the top of the page was 12 August 1977.

A strapline above the picture said:

CLEAN AIR IS A KICK FOR CITY BOYS

The caption read:

Coach Rob Starkey, North Cromarty star half-forward, fires up the Companions Camp under-15 side at half-time in their game against St Stephen's on Saturday morning. The city boys, having a much-needed holiday at the Port Monro camp thanks to the Moral Companions, went down 167-43. But the score didn't matter. The point was to have a good run around in the bracing air.

The black-and-white photograph showed boys in muddy white shorts and dark football jumpers facing a big man. He was holding the ball horizontally and he was saying something. The boys, hair close-cut back and sides, were eating orange quarters – sour oranges, said the nearest boy's puckered face, his closed eyes.

In the background were spectators, all but two of them men, rugged up against the cold. To the right were two men in overcoats and, in front of them, a small boy. The men were smoking cigarettes.

Cashin got up from the table and took the clipping to the window, held it to the dying light. He recognised the man in the centre wearing a camel overcoat from the photographs at The Heights: Charles Bourgoyne. He had long fingers. The man on his right could be Percy Crake – he had a small moustache.

Cashin looked at the other spectators: middle-aged men, a sharp-nosed woman wearing a headscarf, a laughing woman of indeterminate age. The face behind Bourgoyne was turned away, a young man, short hair combed back, something about him.

Was the boy with Bourgoyne and Crake? He was frowning. He seemed to be looking at the camera. Something in the small face nagged at Cashin. He closed his eyes and he saw Erica Bourgoyne across the table from him at the gallery.

James Bourgoyne. The boy with the sad face might be the drowned Jamie, Erica's brother, Bourgoyne's step-son.

Cashin went back to the papers and looked for other photographs. In a folder, he found more than a dozen 8x10 prints. They were all the same: boys lined up in three rows of nine or ten, tallest at the back, the front row on one knee. They wore singlets and dark shorts, tennis shoes with short socks. The man with the moustache was in all of them, dressed like the boys, standing to the right, apart. His arms were folded, fists beneath his biceps, bulging them. He had hairy legs, big thighs and muscular calves. At the left stood two other men in tracksuits. One of them, a stocky dark man wearing glasses, was in all the photographs. The other one – tall, thin, long-nosed – was in five or six.

He turned a photograph over: *Companions Camp 1979.*

The names were written in pencil in a loose hand: back row, middle row, front row. *At left: Mr Percy Crake. At right: Mr Robin Bonney, Mr Duncan Vallins.*

Vallins was the tall man, Bonney the dark, solid one.

Cashin looked for the name and he found it in 1977.

David Vincent was in the middle row, a skinny, pale boy, long-necked, his adam's apple and the bumps on his shoulders visible. His head was turned away slightly, apprehensively, as if he feared some physical harm from the photographer.

Cashin read the other names, looked at the faces, looked away and thought. He fetched the telephone and dialled, listened, eyes closed. David Vincent was out or out of it. He rang Melbourne, had to wait for Tracy.

'Two names,' he said. 'Robin Bonney. Duncan Vallins. Appreciate and so on.'

'You are Singo's clones,' she said. 'You and the boss. Have people told you that?'

'They've told me young Clint Eastwood. Does that square with you?'

'And so on. You going to actually speak to me the next time you come in here? As opposed to acknowledging my existence?'

A dog rose on the sofa and, in an indolent manner, put its paws on the floor and did a stretch, backside high above its head. The other dog followed suit, an offended look.

'Preoccupied then,' said Cashin. 'I'm sorry. Still married to that bloke in moving?'

'No. Divorced.'

'Right. Moved on. Well, next time I'm in we can exchange some more personal information. Blood types, that kind of thing.'

'I'm holding my breath. Got a Robin Gray Bonney here. Age fifty-seven. Possibility?'

'About right.'

'Former social worker. Form is child sex offender. Suspended sentence on two charges. Then he did four years of a six.'

'More and more right.'

'Well, he's dead. Multiple stab wounds, castrated, mutilated and strangled. In Sydney. Marrickville. That's, that's two days ago. No arrest.'

Cashin tried to do the front stretch exercise, the opening of the shoulderblades, felt all the muscles resist.

'Here we go,' said Tracy. 'Vallins, Duncan Grant, age fifty-three. Anglican priest, address in Brisbane, Fortitude Valley but that's 1994. Child sex form, suspended sentence 1987. Did a year in 1994–95. I presume he's a former priest now.'

'Why would you presume that? Trace, three things. All the details on Bonney. The mutilation. Two, on Vallins, beg Brisbane to check that address and stress we don't want him spooked. Three, tell Dove we need the coroner's report on a fire at the Companions camp, Port Monro, in 1983.'

He was at the window. Ragged-edged ribbons of pink ran down the sky, died on the black hill.

Same night as the fire. Double tragedy.

Cecily Addison's words. Bourgoyne's wife fell down the stairs on the night of the fire. Tranquillisers blamed.

'Now that I think about it,' he said, 'I might come to town. Pass that on to the boss, will you?'

'I'll pass it on to all the lovesick in this building. Dove's here, want to talk to him?'

'No, but put him on anyway.'

Clicks.

'Good day,' said Dove. 'The CrimeStoppers log on Bourgoyne. You looked at it?'

'How the fuck would I have looked at it?'

'I don't think anyone's looked at it. On the night it was on television, a woman rang. She saw it, rang straight away. Mrs Moira Laidlaw. Her words are, I suggest you investigate Jamie Bourgoyne.'

'That's it?'

'That's it.'

'Well, Jamie's dead. Drowned in Tasmania.'

'You don't have to drown to be dead in Tasmania, but I thought this was worth a sniff. Is that it? Sniff? Snuff?'

'You've talked to her?'

'This is ten minutes old. I rang but you were busy.'

'Get the full sweep on the dead Jamie. Tracy'll tell you what else. I'll see you tomorrow.'

Cashin knew he should go immediately, tell Villani, get in the vehicle and go. He knew he wouldn't. What did it matter now?

354

'I SAW HIM quite clearly,' said the old woman in a dry and precise voice. 'I was waiting at the lights in Toorak Road and they changed and a car stopped. For some reason, I looked and Jamie was in the passenger seat.'

'You knew him well, Mrs Laidlaw?' said Cashin.

'Of course. He's my nephew, my sister's child. He lived with us for a time.'

'Right. And you saw him when?'

'About six weeks ago. On a Friday. I go shopping and have lunch with friends on Fridays.'

It was just past 4 pm but Cashin thought that it felt much later in the sitting room, the light dim outside, a row of raindrops waiting to fall from a thin branch framed in the French doors. 'And you know that Jamie is said to have drowned in Tasmania in 1993?' he said.

'Yes. Well, obviously he didn't because I saw him in Toorak Road.'

Cashin looked at Dove, passed to him that there was no point in questioning the identification.

'May I ask why you thought we should investigate Jamie over the assault on his step-father?' said Dove.

'Because he's alive and he's capable of it. He hates Charles Bourgoyne.'

'Why's that?'

'I have no idea. Ask Erica.' She turned her head and the light made her short hair gleam.

'When last did you see Jamie?' said Dove. 'Before Toorak Road, I mean.'

'He came to my husband's funeral. Turned up at the church. God knows how he knew. Didn't talk to anyone except Erica. Not a word to his step-father.'

'He liked your husband?' said Cashin.

She picked at nothing on her cardigan. 'No. And my husband certainly wasn't fond of him.'

'Why was that?'

'He didn't like him.'

Cashin waited but nothing came. 'Why didn't he like him, Mrs Laidlaw?'

She looked down. A dove-grey cat had come into the room and was leaning against her right leg. It was staring at Cashin, eyes the colour of ash. 'My husband never forgot his nephew's death. Mark drowned in the pool when he was ten. Jamie was here. No one else.'

'Was there a suspicion that Jamie was involved?'

'No one said anything.'

'But your husband thought he was?'

She blinked at Cashin. 'Jamie was three years older than Mark, you see.'

Cashin felt the silken ankle-winding of the cat. 'Was that important?'

'He was supposed to be looking after Mark. We loved Mark very much. He'd been with us since he was six. He was like a son to us.'

'I see. And Jamie came to your husband's funeral?'

'Yes. Out of the blue and dressed like some sort of hippy musician.'

'When was that?'

'In 1996. The twelfth of May 1996. He came here the next day.'

'Why?'

'He wanted a photograph of Mark. He asked if he

could have one. He knew where the photographs were too, where we kept Mark's things. He said he'd thought of Mark as a brother. Quite unbelievable, frankly.'

'And you never saw him again?'

'No. Not until Toorak Road. A cup of tea? I could make tea.'

'No thank you, Mrs Laidlaw,' said Dove. 'How long did Jamie live with you?'

She took off her glasses, touched the corner of an eye carefully, replaced them. 'Not very long. Less than two years. He came after he stopped boarding at the college. His step-father asked us.'

'And that was here?'

'Here?'

'You lived in this house then?' said Cashin.

Mrs Laidlaw looked at him as if he were not the full quid. 'We've always lived here. I grew up here, my grand-parents built this house.'

'And after Jamie finished school…?'

'He didn't finish school. He left.'

'He left school?'

'Yes. And he left here. He was in year eleven and one day he just left.'

'Where did he go?'

'I don't know. Erica told me he was in Queensland at one point.'

A telephone rang in the passage.

'Excuse me.'

Cashin and Dove stood up with her. She walked slowly to the door and Cashin went to the French doors and looked at the garden, at the big bare trees – an oak, an elm, a tree he couldn't identify. Their leaves had not been raked and they lay in soggy drifts. A stone retaining wall was leaning, blocks loose. Soon it would collapse, the worms would be revealed.

'These charity calls,' said Mrs Laidlaw. 'I don't really know what to say to the people. They sound so nice.'

She sat down in her chair. The cat elevated itself into her lap. Cashin and Dove sat.

'Mrs Laidlaw, why did Jamie stop boarding at the school?' said Cashin.

'I didn't hear the details. The school could tell you, I suppose.'

'And the reason he left here?'

'You might ask the school about that too. I'd be lying if I said his departure wasn't a great relief.'

She stroked the cat, looking at it. 'Jamie was a strange boy. He was very attached to his mother and I don't think he got over her death. But there was something else about him...'

'Yes?'

'Silent, always watching, and somehow scared. As if you might hurt him. Then he'd do these horrible things. Once when he was here for the weekend from school he made a bow and arrow and shot the cat next door. Through the eye. He said it was an accident. But there was a dog set on fire down the road. We knew it was Jamie. And he drowned Mark's budgies in the pool. In their cage.'

She looked from Cashin to Dove. 'He used to read my husband's medical books. He'd sit on the floor in the study and look at anatomy texts for hours.'

'Do you know anyone he might be in contact with?' said Cashin.

She was stroking the cat, her head down. 'No. He had a friend at school, another problem boy. They expelled him, I gather.'

'What school did he go to, Mrs Laidlaw?'

'St Paul's. The Bourgoynes all went to St Paul's. Gave it a lot of money.'

'You said he hated Charles Bourgoyne.'

'Yes. I didn't realise how much until I suggested he might like to spend a holiday with Charles. He'd been spending them here. He ran into the front door with his head. Deliberately. And he sat there on the floor screaming no, no, no, over and over. Sixteen stitches in his scalp, that's what it took.'

'Thank you for your help, Mrs Laidlaw.'

'You're not what I expected.' She was looking at Dove.

'We come in all types,' Cashin said.

She smiled at Dove, an affectionate smile, as if she knew him and thought well of him.

They went down the passage to the front door. Cashin said, 'Mrs Laidlaw, I have to ask you. Is there even the slightest doubt in your mind over the man you saw in Toorak Road? Is it possible that it wasn't Jamie?'

'No doubt at all. I'm perfectly sane, I had my glasses on and it was Jamie.'

'You told Erica you'd seen him?'

'Yes. I rang her as soon as I got home.'

'What did she say?'

'Nothing really. Yes, dear, that sort of thing.'

A thin but steady rain fell on the men as they walked down the balding gravel path and along the pavement to the vehicle. The gutters were running, carrying leaves and twigs and acorns. In some dark tunnel, they would meet the sordid human litter of the city and go together to the cold slate bay.

It came to Cashin as they reached the car. 'Be back in a sec,' he said.

Mrs Laidlaw opened the door as if she'd been waiting behind it. He asked her.

'Mark Kingston Denby,' she said. 'Why?'

'Just for the record.'

In the car, Cashin said, 'The school. The expelled friend.'

THE DEPUTY headmaster was in his fifties, grey-suited, tanned and fit-looking like a cross-country skier. 'School policy is that we do not disclose information about students or staff, past or present,' he said. He smiled, snowy teeth.

'Mr Waterson,' said Cashin, 'we'll ruin your evening. We'll be back inside an hour with a warrant and a truck to take away all your files. And who knows, the media might show up too. Can't keep anything secret these days. So St Paul's will be all over the television news tonight. The parents will like that, I'm sure.'

Waterson scratched his cheek, a pink square-cut nail. He wore a copper bracelet. 'I'll need to consult,' he said. 'Please excuse me a moment.'

Dove went to the office window. 'Dusk on the playing fields,' he said. 'Like England.'

Cashin was looking at the deputy headmaster's books. They all seemed to be about business management. 'We fucked this thing up,' he said. 'So badly. I'm glad Singo's not around to see it.'

'Thank god it's we,' said Dove. 'Imagine what it would be like to have fucked it up all by yourself. Even mostly.'

The door opened. 'Follow me please, gentlemen,' said Waterson. 'I caught our legal adviser on her way home. She works here two days a week.'

They went down the corridor and into a big wood-panelled room. A dark-haired woman in a pinstriped suit was at the head of a table that could seat at least twenty.

'Louise Carter,' said Waterson. 'Detective Cashin and Detective Dove. Please sit down, gentlemen.'

They sat. Carter looked at them in turn.

'This school jealously guards the privacy of its community,' she said. She was about fifty, a long face, taut skin around her eyes, a slightly startled look. 'We don't accede to requests for information unless requested to do so by the community family or the community family member concerned, if that person is in a position to make such a request. And, even then, we reserve the right to exercise our own judgment on acceding to any requests.'

'You've got that written in your hand,' said Dove. 'I saw you look down.'

She was not amused.

'The community family I'm talking about is in serious shit,' said Cashin. 'Just yes or no, we're in a hurry.'

Carter moved her mouth. 'You can't bully St Paul's, detective. Perhaps you don't realise the position it occupies in this city.'

'I don't give a bugger either. We'll crawl all over the place. Inside an hour. Believe me.'

She didn't blink. 'What is it you want to know about these students?'

'Why Jamie Bourgoyne was kicked out as a boarder, the name of the friend he had here who was expelled and why.'

A head movement of refusal. 'Not possible. Please understand that the Bourgoyne family has a long and close association with the school. I'm afraid we can't...'

'Don't loosen your seatbelt,' said Cashin. 'We'll be back soon. You might want to check the lippy, you're going to be on television.'

Cashin and Dove stood.

'Wait,' said Waterson, getting up. 'I think we can meet this request.'

He left the room and the woman followed him, heels clicking. There was a brief exchange outside and she came back and stood at a window. Then she sat down and there was silence until she coughed and said, 'Have I seen you two on television?'

Cashin had his eyes on the big painting opposite, vertical bars of grey and brown. It reminded him of a jumper Bern wore, knitted by some old relative, a person with self-respect would compost it.

Once he would have wanted this woman to think well of him.

'You may have seen me,' said Dove. 'I'm the undercover cop. Sometimes I have a beard.'

Waterson came in. He put two yellow folders on the table and sat. 'I'll deal with all your inquiries in a narrative,' he said, businesslike. 'Feel free to interrupt.'

The woman said, 'David, can we...'

'James Bourgoyne and a boy called Justin Fischer were in the same class and in the boarding house together,' said Waterson.

He looked at the woman, at Cashin. 'I feel compelled to say that I considered James to be a seriously disturbed young man. And Justin Fischer is the most dangerous boy I've encountered in my thirty-six years in education.'

The lawyer leaned forward. 'David, there's absolutely no call for this kind of candour. May I...'

'What happened?' said Cashin.

'Among other things, they were suspected of lighting two fires. One burnt down a sports equipment store, the other was lit in the boarding house.'

'David, please.'

'Police matters,' said Cashin.

'The police were called in, of course,' said Waterson, 'but we didn't pass on our suspicions and they could find nothing. Instead, we asked James's step-father to remove him from the boarding establishment. This was an attempt to separate the pair.'

The lawyer held up her hands. 'This may be the moment...'

'In retrospect,' said Waterson, 'we should have told the police everything and expelled both students. In that order.'

The woman said, quickly, 'David, before you say another word, I must insist that the headmaster be consulted.'

Waterson didn't look at her, kept his eyes on Cashin. 'Louise,' he said, 'the headmaster has the moral sense of Pol Pot. Let's not now compound our earlier atrocious judgments.'

Cashin saw in the tanned man's eyes the relief he had seen in people who were confessing to murder. 'Go on,' he said. He had the feeling now, the cough tickle in the mind.

'After Bourgoyne left the boarding establishment,' said Waterson, 'there were hedge-burnings locally. Three or four, I can't remember. Then in Prahran a boy, he was seven or eight, was taken to a quiet spot by two teenage boys and tortured. There's no other word for it. It was brief and he wasn't badly hurt but it was torture, sadism. One of our students came to us, he was a boarder, and he said he'd seen Bourgoyne and Fischer near the scene around the time.'

'You told the police?'

'To our eternal discredit, we did not.'

'The student wasn't told to go to the police?'

'David,' said the woman, 'I must now advise you to...'

'He was discouraged from doing so,' said Waterson.

'On instructions from the headmaster, I discouraged him.'

'Is that the same as telling him not to?' said Dove. 'Discouraged?'

'Pretty close,' said Waterson. 'We then expelled Bourgoyne and Fischer. That day. It was the only right and proper thing we did in all our dealings with the pair.'

'I'd like copies of the files, please,' said Cashin.

'These are copies,' said Waterson. He pushed them across the table.

'Thank you,' said Cashin. He got up and shook hands with Waterson. He didn't look at the lawyer. 'There won't be any reason that I can see for us to mention the school.'

Going down the stone stairs, Cashin opened a file. 'Get Tracy,' he said to Dove. In the entrance hall, Dove handed him the mobile.

'Tracy, Joe. This is top of the list, front burner. Everything on a Justin David Fischer. That's an S-C-H-E-R. The last address is for an aunt, Mrs K. L. Fischer, 19 Hendon Street, Albert Park. Ask Birk to see if someone can chase that.'

'We've got the Jamie Bourgoyne sweep and the inquest on the Companions fire. Fin's looking at them.'

'Ask him to ring me, will you?'

'And Brisbane checked that Duncan Grant Vallins address. He left there two years ago. They don't have anything more recent.'

'Bugger.'

'The neighbour says a bloke was asking for him last week. Long hair, beard. Another one in the car.'

In the twilight, they crunched softly down the gravel driveway. Boys in green blazers and grey flannels were coming along a path to their right. The pale one in front was eating chips out of box. A boy behind him put a headlock on him, pulled his head back. Another boy walked by and casually took the chip box, kept walking, put one in his mouth.

'Year ten mugging class,' said Dove. 'Been out on a prac.'

'WHAT'S HE SHOW?' said Cashin. They were at lights in Toorak Road. Three blonde women were crossing, damp combed hair, no makeup, flushed from an after-work gym class.

'My oath,' said Dove. 'These things are sent to try us.'

'Never on the electoral roll,' said Finucane. 'Never registered for Medicare, the dole, anything. A driver's licence issued Darwin 1989, you get that in a show bag. Then he's on the move. Minor drug stuff in Cairns, arrest for assaulting a kid age twelve in Coffs Harbour. Not proceeded with. Suspended sentences for assault in Sydney in 1986. In a park, victim age sixteen. Possession of heroin in Sydney in 1987. Two years for aggravated burglary in Melbourne in 1990.'

The lights turned green. Without a glance either way, an old woman, small and hunched, head down, wearing a transparent plastic raincoat, pushed a pram-like homemade trolley into the crossing.

'Like Columbus,' said Dove. 'She has no idea.'

The car behind them hooted, two long blasts.

Dove waited until the woman had crossed to safety before he pulled away slowly, held the speed, an act of provocation.

'Go on,' said Cashin.

'That's it. Jamie came out in '92 and he's presumed drowned in Tassie in '93.'

Cashin said, 'Fin, Tracy's on this Fischer bloke. Get whatever and ring me, okay? Also she's got a Duncan Grant Vallins. He's a ped, former Anglican sky pilot, address unknown, see if he's in our system, see if the church knows anything about him. Tell the choirboy who does the church's spin to co-operate or they'll turn in the fucking wind. On *The 7.30 Report* tonight.'

'Boss.'

'And one other thing. Try the name Mark Kingston Denby. Ring Dove if you get anything.'

'Boss.'

Cashin closed his eyes and thought about Helen Castleman naked. So smooth. Nakedness and sex changed everything. No bacon and onion and tomato sandwich would ever taste like that again.

'Where to?' said Dove.

'Queen Street. Know that?'

'Memorised the map, that's the first thing I did.'

'Then there'll always be a job for you driving cabs. Probably sooner than later.'

In Queen Street, Dove said, 'Accepting that I might have come on a bit like...'

'Here,' said Cashin. 'Park in there. I want to talk to Erica Bourgoyne.'

'Bit late in the day, isn't it?'

'She's a lawyer. They don't go home.'

Cashin had the door open when Dove's mobile rang. He waited while Dove answered, held up a finger. 'Putting him on,' said Dove, offered the phone.

'Boss, I got through to this church bloke, he gave me Duncan Grant Vallins straight off,' said Finucane. 'Living in a place in Essendon, St Aidan's Home for Boys. It's shut down but this bloke says church people in need sometimes stay there.'

'In need of what?' said Cashin. 'The address?'

The night was upon them now, rain blurring the lights, dripping from the street trees, the pavement a parade of pale faces above dark garments.

'Also Mark Kingston Denby, found him. Came out of jail nine weeks ago. Six years for armed robberies. There's a co-accused here.'

'Yes?'

'A Justin Fischer,' said Finucane. 'He got the same.'

Cashin thought of calling Villani, changed his mind, told Dove where to go.

THE HEADLIGHTS lit the pillars and the double gates: cast-iron, ornate, fully two metres high, once painted, now an autumn colour and flaking. Beyond them was a driveway, and the lights threw the gates' shadows onto dark, uncontrolled vegetation.

'If the prick's at home, we're taking him into protective custody,' said Cashin. His whole torso was aching now and the pain slivers were going down his thighs.

Dove switched off, cut the lights. The street was dark here, the nearest lamp on the other side, fifty metres down. They got out, into the cold evening, the rain holding off for a while.

'What do we do?' said Dove.

'Knock on the front door,' said Cashin. 'What else is there to do?'

He tried the gate, put his hand through an opening and found a lever, raised it with difficulty, a screech of metal. The right-hand gate resisted his push, then swung easily. 'Leave it open,' he said.

They walked up the drive side by side, trying not to brush the wet bushes. 'You armed?' said Dove.

'Relax,' said Cashin, 'it's one old ex-priest ped, not party night at the Hell's Angels.' He knew he should be carrying. He'd got out of the habit, lost the instinct.

The building came into sight, double-storeyed, brick, arched windows, steps up to a long porch and a front door with leadlight windows on either side. A slit of light showed in a window to the left, a curtain not fully drawn.

'Someone home,' said Cashin. 'Someone in need.'

They climbed the stairs, he pulled back a solid ring of brass, pounded a few times, waited, hammered again.

The leadlight on the left glowed dimly – red and white and green and violet, a biblical scene, a group of men, one haloed.

'Who's there?' A firm male voice.

'Police,' said Cashin.

'Put your identification through the letter slot.'

Cashin gestured to Dove, who took out his ID card, pushed it through the slot. It was taken. They heard two bolts slide. The door opened.

'What is it?' A tall unshaven man in black, many-chinned, round glasses, thin grey hair combed back, oily, curling at the tips.

'Duncan Grant Vallins?'

'Yes.'

'Detective Senior Sergeant Cashin, homicide. Detective Dove.'

'What do you want?'

'Can we come in?'

Vallins hesitated, stood back. They went into a marble-floored entrance hall with a staircase rising in the centre, branching left and right to a gallery. Six metres up hung a many-tiered crystal chandelier.

'This way,' said Vallins.

They followed his pear shape into a room to the left. It was a big sitting room, one dim unshaded bulb above, one standing lamp near a fireplace. The furniture was old, shabby, unmatched chairs, a sagging chintz sofa. The smell was of damp and mouse droppings and ancient cigarette smoke trapped in curtains and carpet and coverings.

371

Vallins sat in the chair next to the lamp, crossed his legs, adjusted them. His thighs were fat. Next to a white cup, a filter cigarette was burning in a brass ashtray and he picked it up and drew deeply, long thin fingers stained the colour of cinnamon sticks. 'What do you want?' he said.

'Do you know an Arthur Pollard?' said Cashin, looking at the room, at the high ceiling, at the group of bottles on a side table, whisky bottles, seven or eight, empty except for two.

'Vaguely. Years ago.'

'Robin Gray Bonney. Know him?'

Vallins sucked on the cigarette, spat smoke, waved a hand. 'Also a long time ago. Donkeys' years. Why?'

'Charles Bourgoyne,' said Cashin. 'You probably know Charles. Vaguely. From a long time ago. And Mr Crake of course.'

Vallins didn't say anything, found a cigarette in a packet, lit it from his stub, had trouble docking, a shake in both hands. He ground the donor in the ashtray. 'What is this nonsense?' he said, high, proper voice. 'Why have you come here to bother me?'

'You may want to be in protective custody,' said Cashin. 'You may want to sit around and tell us about the Companions camps, those golden days. You looked really fit in the photographs. Took a lot of exercise then, did you, Mr Vallins? With the boys?'

'There's nothing I want to tell you,' said Vallins. 'Not a single thing. You can go now.'

'Bit of a hermit here, are you, Mr Vallins? All alone in this place for Anglicans in need?'

'None of your business. You know the way out.'

Cashin looked at Dove. Dove didn't seem happy, he was scratching his skull. Did scalps still itch without hair? Why was that?

'Fine,' said Cashin. 'On our way then. We'll leave you to think about how your friends Arthur and Robin were tortured. Robin's was nasty. Had something hot shoved up him. The knife sharpener. Know that thing? The steel? They think it was heated over the gas ring. Red hot. Came out the front.'

Vallins' face screwed up. 'What?'

'Tortured and killed,' said Cashin. 'Bourgoyne, Bonney, Pollard. We'll find our own way out then, Mr Vallins. Good night.'

Cashin walked. He was at the door when Vallins said, 'Please wait, detective, I'm sorry, I didn't know…'

'Just stopped by to keep you informed of the mortality rate among people like you,' said Cashin. 'Offer extended and refused. That's on record. Good luck and sleep tight, Mr Vallins.'

They were in the entrance hall, Cashin in front, then Dove, Vallins a pace behind.

'I think you might be right, detective,' said Vallins, high voice. 'Do I need…'

'I know what you need, Duncan,' said a voice from above, from the gallery. 'You need to repent your filthy life and die at peace with the Lord.'

CASHIN COULDN'T see the man. The light from the sitting room was too feeble.

'Who is it?' he said.

He knew.

Someone laughed, not the speaker. 'Cops,' he said. 'I can smell cops, filthy stinking, rotten cops.'

Cashin looked at Dove. His eyes were on the gallery, he was pushing back his overcoat with his right hand, Cashin saw the spring-clip holster, the butt, Dove's reaching fingers.

Bangs, bright red muzzle-flash.

Dove went backwards, spun around to face Cashin, Cashin saw his glasses glint, saw Dove's open mouth, his hands coming up to his chest, he was falling sideways.

'ONE DOWN!'

Cashin saw the fusebox on the wall beside the stained glass window. He went for it, two paces, dived, clawed at it with his left hand, off-balance, going down, saw the flash at the edge of his vision, felt a knife slice across his back below the shoulderblades.

'TWO DOWN!'

Coal dark. He was on his knees, his whole back seemed to be on fire.

Shit, he thought, I've taken one.

'Please!' shouted Vallins. 'I'll give you money, I've got money!'

Cashin put out a hand and found Dove's shoulder, the feel of cloth, touched his face. He was breathing. He crawled across, heard Dove's small snoring noise. He felt for Dove's holster, slid his hand down his body.

Empty.

Jesus, he got the gun out, dropped it. Where?

'COMING FOR YOU, BOYS!'

The squeaking voice.

Cashin was groping frantically, the marble floor was ice-cold.

'Please!' shouted Vallins. 'Pleeease!'

'First you must repent, Duncan,' said the deeper, calmer voice.

Cashin was crawling fast, there was a door to the right of the stairs, he needed to get there before they switched on the mains, they'd seen him switch off, they'd find it, you never went unarmed, you never needed the fucking thing until you needed it so badly that your teeth ached.

He crawled into a wall, stood up, went left, groping, knocked over something, a table, an object hit the floor, smashed.

Bang, gun-flash. From half-way down the stairs.

Cashin found a deep recess, found the door, found the doorknob, twisted, the door opened, he was inside.

A scent. A faint, sickly perfume.

Don't close the door, they'll hear the click.

He was feeling light-headed. He walked into something solid, thigh-high, turned right, felt his way, it was the back of something, it went on, it ended, a post, carved, he put out a hand and touched a wall.

A pew. This is a church. A chapel. That's the smell.

Right hand on the wall, he took a step, felt something, knocked it off its mounting. It hit the floor, a loud noise, he stopped.

'Over there,' said the first voice. 'He's over there. He doesn't have a gun.'

'Blow this cop away,' said the high voice. 'Blow his head off.'

'No, get the other cop, Justin. We'll let this one bleed out. He's a lamb of God. I'll pray for him.'

Cashin heard a whimpering, a terrible sound, fear and pain combined.

He was trying to become accustomed to the dark, he was blinking, trying to blink quickly, but he couldn't, his eyelids were too heavy. Loss of blood? He put his right hand under the overcoat, felt his back.

Wet. Warm.

He felt the need to sit. He put out his hand, found the back of a pew, leaned against it, urgency gone, it didn't matter. He was going to die here, in this ice-cold and sickly-sweet room.

No. A way out of here. Find the door. Follow the wall.

His eyes weren't working. He was underwater, black water, not water, something thicker. Blood. Trying to move in blood. Water and blood. Diab and Dove, he'd killed them both. He couldn't feel his toes move. Couldn't feel his legs. Couldn't breathe. He took his hand off the pew and he felt himself falling, saw something, a pole, tried to grab it.

It was loose, fell with him. Something hit his head. Terrible pain, then nothing.

HE WAS IN the hospital, something cold on his face, they wiped your face with wet towels, it was someone speaking loudly. Not to him. It wasn't close, it was the radio, the television…

Cashin didn't open his eyes. He knew he wasn't in hospital, he was lying on something stone hard. A floor. An icy marble floor. Everything came back.

'Do you remember what you did to me, Duncan?' said the voice. 'How I cried out in pain? How I asked for mercy? Do you remember that, Duncan?'

A silence.

I'm alive, Cashin thought. I'm lying on the floor and I'm alive.

'I was so happy when I found out you'd become a priest, Duncan,' said the voice.

Jamie Bourgoyne. Except he was now his dead cousin, Mark Kingston Denby.

'We've both given ourself to the Lord, Duncan,' said Jamie. 'It changes everything, doesn't it? I was a sinner. I've done bad things, Duncan. I've caused terrible suffering to some of God's creatures. You'll understand that, won't you? Of course, you will. You didn't come to the Lord with a pure heart either.'

A sound of agony.

'The little children, Duncan. Do you think about what our Saviour said? Answer me, Duncan.'

Words, a burbling of words.

'Duncan, our Lord said, Suffer the little children to come unto me. What a wonderful thing to say, wasn't it, Duncan? Suffer the little children to come unto me, and forbid them not, for of such is the kingdom of God.'

The scream filled the chapel, filled Cashin's head, seemed to enter his ear from the marble floor.

'Can I?' said the high voice. 'Give me a chance, Jamie.'

'Soon, soon. I must prepare Duncan. Duncan, the word suffer, what an important word it is. The word *suffer*. In both its meanings. Speak to me, Duncan. Say *Suffer the little children to come unto me*. Say that, Duncan.'

Cashin realised that his eyes were working, there was light. It was candlelight, it moved, flickered, shadows on the wall, they hadn't bothered to switch on the lights, they had lit candles, Dove was dead, they thought he was dead too, or dying quickly. Bleeding out.

Bleeding out.

Vallins was croaking something, trying to form the sentence.

'A child,' said Jamie. 'Duncan, a little boy. Did you ever feel any regret? Any remorse? I don't think so. You and Robin and Crake. I was so sad to hear Crake died while I was in jail. The Lord wanted me to minister to Crake too.'

'Give me a go,' said Justin. 'C'mon Jame.'

Cashin tried to raise himself, he had no strength in his body, he could not move, he should lie here, they would kill Vallins, then they would go. He could hold his breath. Jamie didn't care about him, didn't hate him.

'And in those days shall men seek death,' said Jamie, 'and shall not find it, and shall desire to die, and death shall flee from them. I had to go to prison and live with bad people before I understood those words. Do you understand them now, Duncan?'

'Please, please, please...' Groans, wretched and terrible sounds.

'I often wanted to die and I couldn't, Duncan. Now I know that the Lord wanted me to live with my torment because he had a purpose for me.'

'Let me, Jame, let me,' said Justin.

'I am he that liveth, and was dead, and behold, I am alive for evermore, Amen, and have the keys of hell and of death. Do you know those words, Duncan? St John the Divine. *The keys of hell and death*. The Lord has given them to me. Is this hell for you, Duncan? Is this?'

I just lie here, thought Cashin. I've killed Dove, they're torturing a man to death. If I live, what'll I say to Singo? Never mind Singo. To Villani. Fin. Birkerts. I'm a policeman, for Christsakes.

'The Lord wants you to know the meaning of pain, of pain and fear, Duncan,' said Jamie. 'He wanted Charles to know that too because of what Charles did to me. And your friend Robin. Do you know, I never forgot your faces, you and Robin? They say children don't remember people. Some do, Duncan, some do, they see them in their nightmares.'

A shriek, a pure scarlet spear of pain.

'Courage, Duncan. Robin didn't have any courage, he was lucky we were so rushed. And Arthur Pollard. I didn't know about Arthur, but in prison the Lord brought me together with a man, a very sad person, and he told me about Arthur.'

'Please, Jesus, ah, ah...'

'I looked for some to have pity on me but there was no man, neither found I any to comfort me,' said Jamie. 'They gave me gall to eat, and when I was thirsty, they gave me vinegar to drink. Duncan's thirsty, Justin, give him a drink.'

A sound, a gurgling sound, coughing, choking.

'There, that's better, isn't it?'

Silence.

'All done, Duncan, you can't make any more noise now, can you? You look like a pig, Duncan. Are you saying a prayer in your mind? To the beast? You can only pray to the beast, can't you? Here Justin, the Lord wants you to send Duncan to meet his king the beast.'

Cashin pushed himself to his knees, lifted his head, heavy.

Flickering yellow light. A thing was on a bare stone altar, a pink fleshy thing tied with rope, trussed like a piece of meat for roasting. It was bleeding everywhere, blood was running down it in streams.

Two men were standing at the altar. The short one on the right was holding up a knife, the candlelight played on the blade. The other man, taller, was holding the thing, Vallins, holding his head, Cashin could see it was his head, the man, Jamie, was holding Vallins' head by the ears, the hair and the ears, he seemed to be kissing Vallins' head...

No.

Cashin shook his head, he didn't ask his system to shake his head, it shook his head. He tried to stand up. There was something on the floor, a pole, no... yes, a pole with a cross at the top, a brass cross with pointed tips, not arrowheads.

No. Not arrowheads.

Diamonds, yes, diamonds.

He put his hand on it, tried to grasp it, he had no grip, he could not quite feel it.

He grasped it and he stood up, he surprised himself, he was upright and he had the pole with the cross in his right hand.

He was looking at them.

They weren't looking at him. They hadn't heard him.

'Go to the eternal fires, Duncan,' said Jamie. 'Send him, Justin.'

'No,' said Cashin.

They turned their heads.

Cashin threw the pole with the brass cross. It hung in the air. Justin turned, the long knife in his right hand.

The diamond-shaped tip entered his throat, in the hollow, between the clavicle bones. It stuck there, fell back. He raised his hands to his throat, embraced the holy spear, took a step, uncertain step, his left leg abandoned him, he fell, his feet slid on the cold hard floor.

'Under arrest,' said Cashin, thick tongue.

Jamie was holding the head of Vallins, looking down at Justin. 'Justie,' he said. 'Justie.'

He let go of the pig-tied Vallins, went to his knees.

Cashin could see only the top of his head.

'Justie, no,' he said. 'Justie, no, Justie, no, no. Justie no, my darling no, Justie, no, no, nooo…'

Cashin walked back the way he had come. It seemed to take a long time to reach the chapel door. He crossed the entrance hall to the switchboard, found the mains switch.

The sitting room light came on.

Dove's pistol was lying almost at his feet. He bent to pick it up, fell over, got up, tried again, reached the weapon. He didn't look at Dove, walked back to the chapel, through the door, found a light switch, walked down the central aisle, stopped three or four metres from the altar.

Jamie was hunched over Justin. There was blood everywhere. He looked at Cashin, stood up, the knife in his hand.

'Under arrest,' said Cashin.

Jamie shook his head. 'No,' he said. 'I have to kill you now.'

Cashin raised Dove's pistol, aimed at Jamie's chest, you aimed for the broadest part, he pulled the trigger.

Jamie cocked his head like a bird. Smiled.

Missed him, Cashin thought. How did I do that? He couldn't see Jamie properly, the gun was too heavy, he couldn't hold it up.

'The Lord doesn't want me to die,' said Jamie. 'He wants you to die because you took Justin from me.'

He took a pace towards Cashin, held out the knife. Cashin saw the light on it, saw the blood. His legs were going, he couldn't stand any longer, he was going down...

The knife, Jamie's eyes above it, so close.

'Now you must pray to your father who art in heaven,' said Jamie.

'Our father,' said Cashin.

'SURE YOU don't need a hand with that?' said Michael.

'No,' said Cashin. The small bag was almost weightless – toothbrush, razor, pyjamas, the things his brother had brought to the hospital. They stood waiting for the lift, awkward, shoulder to shoulder.

'I've got a new job,' said Michael. 'In Melbourne. A small firm.'

'That's good,' said Cashin. He had dreamed about Dove, walking down a street with Dove, and then Dove's face had become Shane Diab's.

'Start in a fortnight. I thought I might come down for a week or so. I could help you build. Not that I've ever built anything. I've got some gym muscles though.'

'No experience necessary. Just brute strength.'

The lift came, empty. Inside, they faced the door.

'Joe, I want to ask,' said Michael, eyes on the floor indicator panel. 'It's been on my mind…'

'What?'

'Going there unarmed. That wasn't a self-destruction thing, was it? I mean…'

'It was a colossal stupidity and arrogance thing,' said Cashin. 'That's my speciality.'

'There's something else,' said Michael. 'I talked to Vickie, Mum put her on to me.'

'Talked about what?'

383

'She says to tell you you can see the boy. She's told her partner he's your child.'

Short of breath, Cashin said, 'She's told the boy?'

'Yes.'

The lift stopped, the door opened, Villani was there.

He shook hands with Michael. They went through the sliding doors, down the ramp and along the side of the building. It was between showers, big jagged holes blown in the clouds, a sky to eternity.

'See you in a few days,' said Michael.

'Buy some gloves,' said Cashin. 'Work gloves.'

Finucane had parked the vehicle behind Villani's. He came to meet them.

'G'day, boss,' he said. 'Feelin okay?'

'Fine,' said Cashin.

'Get in for a minute,' said Villani. 'And you, Fin.'

Cashin got in the passenger side. The cop car smell.

'You look like death,' said Villani. 'Are you telling me they don't have those tanning machines?'

'I was shocked too.'

'Anyway, pale or not, you and Dove, you're a charmed fucking pair,' said Villani. 'That's charmed, not charming. He's coming out next week. Clotting power of a lobster, the doc says.'

'A lobster?' said Finucane from the back. 'A lobster?'

'That's what he said. Listen, Joe, stuff to tell you. First, Fin's got some sense out of that loony Dave Vincent. On the phone, mark you. Fin's got his notebook. Speak Fin.'

Finucane coughed. 'He was at the camp the night of the fire,' he said. 'Called Dave Curnow then, the name of his foster family. He says he was supposed to go to some concert thing but he was planning to run away and he hid. Then two men arrived and they took a body out of the back of the car. Small body, he says.'

Cashin was looking at the road, not seeing the traffic.

'They took it into the building where the boys slept. Then they left and he says he saw flames inside the building. He ran away and he slept on the beach and the next day he hitched a lift and he was gone. Ended up in WA, a boy age twelve.'

'What did the autopsies on the dead boys show?' said Cashin.

'Local doctor did them,' said Finucane. 'I gather that's the way it was then. Smoke inhalation killed them.'

'All three.'

'That's right.'

'No mention of anything else?'

'Nothing, boss.'

Cashin regretted eating breakfast, a sick feeling rising in him. 'Remember the doctor's name?'

'I've got it here. Castleman, Dr Rodney Castleman. Signed Bourgoyne's wife's death certificate too. A busy GP.'

Helen's father. Cecily Addison said:

Lots of people took an interest. Public-spirited place then, Cromarty. People did good works, didn't do it to get their names in the paper either. Virtue is its own reward.

'Here's something weird,' said Villani. 'Dave Vincent remembers the car that night.'

'Got a thing about cars, Dave,' said Finucane. 'He says it was a Merc station wagon. He knows that because it was the first wagon Mercedes made. 1979.'

'Was that useful?' said Cashin.

'I tracked it.'

'Let me guess. Bourgoyne.'

'Company car. Charles Bourgoyne and someone called J. A. Cameron were directors.'

'Jock Cameron. Local solicitor. Who was the Companion there that night?'

'Vallins,' said Villani.

'Got a smoke?' said Cashin.

Villani took out a packet and pushed in the lighter. They waited in silence, lit up.

The nicotine hit Cashin like a headbutt, he couldn't speak for a while, then he said, 'Jesus, how did they get away with it? Ran the camp as a brothel, murdered at least three boys, not a murmur. What kind of fucking investigation was there?'

Villani ran down the front windows, a smell of exhaust fumes, of newly spread bitumen. 'Something else to tell you. Singo died two days ago. Another stroke. Big time.'

'Shit,' said Cashin. 'Well. Shit.' He felt tears coming, turned his head away from Villani, blinked rapidly.

'Singo did the Companions fire,' said Villani. 'He was number two then.'

Cashin saw Singo in his exhausted riven raincoat, saw the burnt ruins in that place, the goalposts in the grass, the little belt. Singo had never mentioned Cromarty. Late at night, drink taken, he talked about jobs in Stawell and Mildura and Geelong and Sale and Shepparton, about the travelling prostitute murders in Bendigo, the man who killed his uncle and aunt on the tobacco farm near Bright, planned to turn them into silage and feed them to the pigs.

Singo never spoke of Cromarty.

'I got a bad feeling,' said Villani. He shifted, uncomfortable. 'We pulled his bank records. I never thought that day would come, not if I lived to… anyway, nothing. Just his pay and dividends from some Foster's shares.'

'He wouldn't drink their beer,' said Cashin. 'He hated their beer.'

Villani looked at him in a hopeless way, opened his window and flicked his butt, almost hit a seagull, caused it to hop. Cashin thought about the meeting on the pier, the gull catching the stub in mid-air.

'Three years ago,' said Villani, 'Singo inherited a million bucks from his brother. Derek. Derek left the whole family rich. About fourteen million in the estate.'

'Yes?' said Cashin.

'Singo's like a fuckin parrot on my shoulder, I'm where I am because of him. Think the job's done, son? Well, go the extra yard. Ninety-nine times, it's a waste. But then there's the one. So I went the yard, we went the yard.'

Fat raindrops on the windscreen. Cashin thought that he wanted to be home now, in the buggered old house, in the buggered old chair, he wanted the dogs burrowing their noses into the cushions beneath his thighs, the fire going, the music. He wanted Björling. It would be Björling first. Björling and then Callas.

'Someone paid two hundred thousand dollars into brother Derek's three bank accounts in 1983,' said Villani. 'Three days after the Cromarty fire. Then, after the inquest, Derek got another two hundred grand. He bought land on the Gold Coast. No cunt, Derek.'

Cashin looked at Villani. Villani held his gaze, deep lines between his eyebrows, nodded, small nods, drew on his cigarette, tried to blow smoke out of the window. It came back.

'Singo took money from Bourgoyne?'

'Paid from a company bank account. You have to go back through three other companies to find it's a Bourgoyne outfit.'

Cashin thought that there was no firm ground in life. Just crusts of different thicknesses over the ooze. They sat in silence, watching three nurses going off duty, level as cricket stumps, the one in the middle moving her hands as if conducting an orchestra.

'It's like two deaths to me,' said Villani. 'I woke today, something's missing, something's gone.'

'Anything else?' said Cashin. 'Any other bits and pieces I should be aware of? No? I'll be on my way home then, thank you for coming.'

'Fin's driving,' said Villani. 'Birkerts's down there, he's finished, he'll bring him back. Don't like that, you can take a cab, take a fucking walk.'

Cashin wanted to argue but he had no strength.

'There is something else,' said Villani. 'Singo's lawyer rang. We're in the will, you and me and Birk.'

'Last untainted place in the force, homicide,' said Cashin. 'The Salvos can have my share.'

When they were on the road, Cashin said, 'Fin, I need to go to Queen Street. Won't take long.'

ERICA BOURGOYNE, handsome and severe in black, was standing behind a glass-topped desk. 'I really don't have time today,' she said. 'So can we keep this as brief as possible?'

'We can,' said Cashin.

He took his time, looked around the big wood-panelled office, at the glass-fronted bookshelves, the leather client chairs, the fresh violets in a cut-glass vase on the windowsill, the bare plane branches outside.

'Very nice office,' he said.

'Please get on with it.' Head on one side, the voice and face of a schoolteacher with a dim pupil.

'I thought I might put a few things to you. Propositions.'

She looked at her watch. 'I can give you five minutes. To the second.'

'Your brother was sexually abused by your step-father and you know that.'

Erica sat down, blinking as if something had lodged in her eyes.

'Jamie and Justin Fischer tortured and killed Arthur Pollard and I think you know that. Jamie and Justin murdered a man called Robin Gray Bonney in Sydney and you may or may not know that.'

Erica held up her hands. 'Detective, this is absolutely...'

'Why didn't you tell me, tell anyone, that Mrs Laidlaw had seen Jamie?'

A vague gesture. 'Moira's getting on, she can't be relied upon...'

'Mrs Laidlaw appeared to me to be in complete command of her faculties. She had no doubt that she saw Jamie. And you believed her, didn't you? That's when you hired the security. It was before Charles was bashed.'

'Detective Cashin, you've overstepped the mark. I can see no point in going on with this.'

'We can do it in a formal interview,' said Cashin. 'Put the day on hold and come down to St Kilda Road. It's probably better that way. You're the one who's overstepped a mark. You're looking at conspiracy.'

Silence. She held his gaze but he saw the sign.

'You spoke to Jamie, didn't you?' said Cashin.

'No.'

Erica closed her eyes. He could see the tracery of veins. Cashin said what had been on his mind for a long time. 'Just the two of you after your mother's accident. All alone at night in that big house with Charles. What happened at night, Erica?'

'Joe, please, no.' Her chin was on her chest, a piece of hair fell across her brow. 'Please, Joe.'

'What happened to you in that house, Erica?'

Silence.

'Did you become Charles's little wife? Was it before or after your mother's death? You followed him around. You worshipped him. Did you know those men were fucking Jamie? Did you know Charles was?'

She had begun to shake. 'No, no, no...' It was not a denial. It was a plea for him to stop.

'Still believe your mother's death was an accident, do you, Erica? The same night as the fire at the Companions camp, remember that? Three boys died that night.

Charles killed one of them with his own hands at The Heights. Did your mother see something? Hear something?'

'Joe, no, please, I can't...'

Cashin looked at her bowed head, saw the pale skin of her scalp, her hands clenched at her throat.

Erica did not raise her head, she was saying something inaudible, saying it to herself, again and again and again, saying a mantra.

Cashin knew about mantras. He had said a million mantras, against pain, against thought, against memory, against the night that would not surrender its dark.

She straightened in her chair, she was trying to regain her composure.

Cashin waited.

'What does it matter now, Joe?' she said, voice drained of life, an old voice. 'Why do you want to drag this from me? Do you get pleasure from this?'

'The bodyguard,' said Cashin. 'What was that about?'

'A client threatened me.'

'I don't believe you. I think you always knew Jamie was alive. You were protective of him but you were also scared of him. That's right, isn't it?'

No reply.

'You watched them torture Pollard, didn't you? There was one seat down in the hall. Just one. You sat there, Erica.'

She was crying silently, tears gouging her makeup.

'Did Charles hand you on to Pollard, Erica? Pollard liked young girls too. We found the pictures in his computer. You wanted Jamie to kill Charles and Pollard, didn't you? You couldn't be there for Charles but you weren't going to miss Pollard. That's right, isn't it.'

Erica began to sob, louder and louder, her head down, her upper body shaking.

'Did you stay to the end, Erica? Did you clap when they raised him? Did it cleanse you?'

A woman crying, her whole body crying, her whole being crying.

Cashin stood.

'You're a sick person, Ms Bourgoyne,' he said. 'Sickness has bred sickness. Thanks for your time.'

Solid rain was falling on Queen Street. Fin was double-parked, obstructing the traffic, reading the paper.

'How was that, boss?' he said.

'Pretty ordinary,' said Cashin. 'Take me home, son.'

THE DOGS were unrecognisable.

'What have you done to them?' said Cashin. 'Look at those ears.'

'They've been properly clipped and groomed for the first time in their lives,' said his mother. 'They loved it.'

'They're in shock. They need counselling.'

'I think they should stay here. They're happy here. I don't think they want to go back to that ruin.'

Cashin walked to the vehicle and opened a back door. The dogs looked, didn't move.

'See, Joseph,' said his mother. 'See.'

Cashin whistled, one clear whistle, and jerked his thumb at the door. The dogs raced for the vehicle, managed to get through the doorway abreast, sat bolt upright, looking straight ahead.

Cashin closed the door. 'I'll bring them to visit,' he said.

'Often,' said his mother. 'Bonzo loves them. They're his best dog friends.'

Cashin thought he saw a tear. 'I'll drop them off to see Bonzo when I go to town,' he said. 'Provided there's no dioxin spraying going on.' He went over and kissed her.

'You should think about counselling, Joseph,' she said, holding his head. 'Your life is the most awful litany of horrors.'

'Just a run of bad luck.' He got in.

She came to the window. 'They like chicken, have you got chicken?'

'They like fillet steak too. They get dead animals I find by the roadside. Bye, Syb.'

Driving home with the last pink in the west, the night taking the land ditch by ditch, hollow by hollow. At the crossroads, he switched on the lights and, five minutes later, they panned across the dark house and a man leaning against the wall, smoking a cigarette, holding a torch.

Rebb came to the vehicle, opened the back door for the dogs. 'Sweet Jesus,' he said, 'you traded the dogs?'

They leapt on him, ecstatic.

'Don't blame me,' said Cashin. 'My mother did it. I thought you'd gone?'

'Went, nothin there, come back this way,' Rebb said. 'Old bloke not walking too good. So I thought I might as well give him a hand, do a bit of work on the cathedral in between.'

They walked around, looked by torchlight at what Rebb had done.

'Bit,' said Cashin. 'Call that a bit?'

'Bern come around, give me a hand. Bad mouth on him, Bern, but he works.'

'The works part is news to me. He's got a good memory, that I know.'

'Yeah?' Rebb shone the light on a new wall, walked over and ran a finger along the pointing.

'The day he brought the water tank. He remembered you from all those years ago, when you were kids. Played footy against you. Against the Companions camp.'

Rebb said, 'Well, that's news to me. Never heard of the Companions camp.' He turned the torch on the dogs.

'I've got a picture of you,' said Cashin. 'Eating an orange slice. Age about twelve.'

'Never been twelve,' said Rebb. 'I could make a bunny pie. Took the popgun again.'

'Anything happen to you there?'

Cashin thought Rebb smiled.

'Just stayed the one day,' Rebb said. 'Didn't like the food.'

'I've got steak,' said Cashin. 'How's that?'

'That'll do. The neighbour was here. Left something for you. Wrapped like a present.'

'I need a present,' said Cashin. 'Long time since anyone gave me a present.'

'Being alive's a present,' said Rebb. 'Every minute of every hour of every day.'

IN THE late afternoon, Cashin took the dogs. They put up the first hares close to the house, the creatures grown bold in their absence. Then, in the meadow, they interrupted a communion of rabbits. The dogs ran themselves to exhaustion, put not a tooth on fur.

At the creek, the dogs strode in, got wet to the shoulder, stood in holes, scrambled, alarmed. Cashin got wet too, up to the knees, water inside his boots. He didn't care, slopped up the hill, thinking about what he should do. In the end, he didn't have to make a decision, he saw her coming down the slope from her house.

They met at the corner post, Rebb's corner post, said hello. She looked thinner, better looking than he remembered.

'They're tired,' she said. 'What've you done to them?'

He summoned up saliva to speak. 'Unfit,' said Cashin. 'Too fat, too slow. Spoilt. That's going to change.'

'How are you, Joe?'

'Fine. I'm fine. Flesh wound. Plus I'm really brave and I never complain.'

Helen shook her head. 'I wanted to come and see you but I thought... well, I don't know what I thought. I thought you'd be surrounded by your family and your cop friends.'

The dogs took off, talk was boring, they wanted action.

'Good thinking,' said Cashin. 'That's the way it was, night and day. They worked shifts, family, cop friends, family.'

'You prick. See Bobby Walshe on television?'

'No.'

'He said you and Dove deserved medals.'

'For stupidity? I don't think they've got that.'

Helen shook her head. 'And the news about the resort?'

'No.'

'Erica Bourgoyne decided not to sell the Companions camp to Fyfe. She's giving it to the state to be part of the coastal reserve. So there's no access to the mouth and the whole resort project collapses.'

Cashin thought about the seat in the Companions hall, Erica in her office, the marks of tears on her cream silk shirt, the sobbing.

'That's good,' he said. 'Leaves you free to concentrate on winning the election.'

'I'm counting on getting at least one cop vote.'

'Depends on a number of things falling into place. But we cops aren't allowed to talk politics.'

'Allowed to drink?'

'My liver is in near-new condition. Nothing to do for weeks.'

They looked at each other, he broke away, saw the dusk in the creek hollow, the treetops moving on the hill. 'I always meant to ask. When did your dad die?'

'In 1988. He didn't take a bend on the coast road. The year after we finished school. Why?'

'Nothing. He signed Bourgoyne's wife's death certificate.'

'Signed hundreds, I imagine.'

'Yes.'

'So. Come up for a drink? I could feed you.'

'Is that party pies?'

'We didn't get around to them last time.'

'Feed these beasts first,' he said. 'I'll be back.'

'Don't get waylaid,' she said.

'Waylaid. I've never heard anyone say that word.'

'You're a work in progress,' she said. 'There are words to come.'

He set off up the rise, legs like logs, whistled the dogs, and he looked back and she had not moved, she was watching him.

'Go home,' he shouted. 'Why don't you just go home and put on the party pies.'

He woke lying on his side. Above the window blind was a line of daylight, the colour of smoke. He could feel her warmth against him and then she stirred and he felt her breath on the skin between his shoulderblades and then her lips moved against his spine, and then she pressed them to him and she kissed. The world opened, the day began, he felt that he was alive again, forgiven.

'JOE?'

'Yes.'

'Carol Gehrig. Early for you?'

'No.'

'Joe, this is rubbish but last night, had a few wines, it came into me head.'

'What?'

'There was chockie wrappers in the bin a few times. Twice.'

'Yes?'

'Well, he didn't eat em,' Carol said. 'Nothin sweet in the place. Didn't even have sugar in his tea.'

'You saw chocolate wrappers in the kitchen bin?'

'Not the kitchen bin. The big one outside. Saw em when I put the stuff in. Mars bars and that shit.'

'Well, someone staying?'

'No. Not then.'

'Twice?'

'Well, I remember twice. Wastin your time with rubbish?'

Rebb came into sight, coming home from Den's cows, a dog on each flank, looking around like bodyguards, alert for assassins hiding in the grass.

'Never,' he said. 'Any idea when?'

'I know the one, it was Kirstie's birthday the day before and I'd had this... anyhow, the day. A Monday, twenty-three seven and it's 1988. That's for sure. Yes.'

23.07.88.

'Interesting,' said Cashin. 'Think about the other time. A month would help, a year. Even winter or summer.'

'I'll think.'

They said goodbye and he stayed where he was, in his mind the image of Bourgoyne's nine pots, all the pieces the perfectionist had thought worth keeping. Into the base of one was scratched a date: 11/6/88.

Was that the day it was made? Could you upturn a newly-thrown pot that size and scratch a date on the bottom? Or did that come later?

He went to the telephone, looked at it for a while, thinking about being upstairs in the old brick building at The Heights, looking back and registering the bolt on the bedroom door.

If you walked up the hill on a night when the kiln was burning, you would hear it before you saw it – it would be a powerful sound, a vibrating, a thrumming. And when you rounded the woodpile, you would see the fire holes glowing white hot, they would light the clearing, and you would feel on your face the force of the sea wind that was blowing into the kiln's mouth.

He dialled the direct number. It rang and rang and then Tracy answered, more reprimand than greeting.

'It's Joe,' he said. 'Do me a favour, Trace. Kids missing in June, July, 1988. Boys.'

'No end to it,' she said.

'Not on this earth.'

A morning of sunlight on the round winter hill, above it cloud strands fleeing inland, and the wind on the long grass, annoying it, strumming it.

A bark at the door, another, more urgent, the dogs taking turns. He let them in and they surrounded him and he was glad to have them and to be there.

Keep reading for an extract from Peter Temple's forthcoming novel *Truth*, which will be published in hardback by Quercus in January 2010.

ON THE Westgate Bridge, behind them a flat in Altona, a dead woman, a girl really, dirty hair, dyed red, pale roots, she was stabbed too many times to count, stomach, chest, back, face. The child, male, two or three years old, his head was kicked. Blood everywhere. On the nylon carpet, it lay in pools, a chain of tacky black ponds.

Villani looked at the city towers, wobbling, unstable in the sulphurous haze. He shouldn't have come. There was no need. 'This air-conditioner's fucked,' he said. 'Second one this week.'

'Never go over here without thinking,' said Birkerts. 'What?'

'My grandad. On it.'

One spring morning in 1970, the bridge's half-built steel frame stood in the air, it crawled with men, unmarried men, men with wives, men with wives and children, men with children they did not know, men with nothing but the job and the hard, hard hangover and then Span 10–11 failed.

One hundred and twelve metres of newly raised steel and concrete, two thousand tonnes.

Men and machines, tools, lunchboxes, toilets, whole sheds – even, someone said, a small black dog, barking – all fell down the sky. In moments, thirty-five men were dead or dying, bodies broken, sunk in the foul grey crusted sludge of the Yarra's bank. Diesel fuel lay everywhere. A fire broke out and, slowly, a filthy plume rose to mark the scene.

'Dead?' said Villani.

'No, taking a shit, rode the dunny all the way down.'

'Certainly passed on that shit-riding talent,' said Villani, thinking about Singleton, who couldn't keep his hands off the job either, couldn't stay in the office. It was not something to admire in the head of Homicide.

On the down ramp, Birkerts' phone rang, it was on speaker.

Finucane's deep voice:

'Boss. Boss, Altona, we're at the husband's brother's place in Maidstone. He's here, the hubby, in the garage. Hosepipe. Well, not a hosepipe, black plastic thing, y'know, like a pool hose?'

'Excellent work,' said Birkerts. 'Could've been in Alice Springs by now. Tennant Creek.'

Finucane coughed. 'So, yeah, maybe the scientists can come on here, boss. Plus the truck.'

'Sort that out, Fin. Might be pizza though.'

'I'll tell the wife hold the T-bones.'

Birkerts ended the call.

'Closed this Altona thing in an hour,' he said. 'That's pretty neat for the clearance.'

Villani heard Singo:

Joe Cashin had thought he was doing the job properly and it took the jaws to open the car embedded in the fallen house. Diab was dead, Cashin was breathing but no hope, too much blood lost, too much broken and ruptured.

Singleton only left the hospital to sit in his car, the old Falcon. He aged, grey stubble sprouted, his silken hair went greasy. After the surgery, when they told him

Joe had some small chance and allowed him into the room, he took Joe's slack hand, held it, kissed its knuckles. Then he stood, smoothed Joe's hair, bent to kiss Joe's forehead.

Finucane was there, he was the witness, and he told Villani. They did not know that Singleton was capable of such emotions.

The next time Cashin came out of hospital, the second time in three years, he was pale as a barked tree. Singo was dead by then, a second stroke, and Villani was acting boss of Homicide.

'The clearance rate,' Villani said. 'A disappointment to me to hear you use the term.'

His phone.

Gavan Kiely, deputy head of Homicide, two months in the job.

'We have a dead woman in the Prosilio building, that's in Docklands,' he said. 'Paul Dove's asked for assistance.'

'Why?'

'Out of his depth. I'm off to Auckland later but I can go.'

'No,' said Villani. 'I bear this cross.'

HE WENT down the passage into the bedroom, a bed big enough for four sleepers, mattress naked, pillows bare. Forensic had finished there. He picked up a pillow with his fingertips, sniffed it.

Faintest smell of perfume. Deeper sniff. The other pillow. Different perfume, slightly stronger smell.

He walked through the empty dressing-room into the

bathroom, saw the glass bath and beside it a bronze arm rising from the floor, its hand offering a cake of soap.

She was on the plastic bag in a yoga posture of rest – legs parted, palms up, scarlet toenails, long legs, sparse pubic hair, small breasts. His view was blocked by the shoulder of a kneeling forensic tech. Villani stepped sideways and saw her face, recoiled. For a terrible heart-jumping instant, he thought it was Lizzie, the resemblance was strong.

He turned to the wall of glass, breathed out, his heart settled. The drab grey bay lay before him and, between the heads, a pinhead, a container ship. Gradually it would show its ponderous shape, a huge lolling flat-topped steel slug bleeding rust and oil and putrid waste.

'Panic button,' said Dove. He was wearing a navy suit, a white shirt and a dark tie, a neurosurgeon on his hospital rounds.

Villani looked: rubber, dimpled like a golf ball, set in the wall between the shower and the head of the bath.

'Nice shower,' said Dove.

A stainless-steel disc hung above a perforated square of metal. On a glass shelf, a dozen or more soap bars were displayed as if for sale.

The forensic woman said, 'Broken neck. Bath empty but she's damp.'

She was new on the job, Canadian, a mannish young woman, no make-up, tanned, crew cut.

'How do you break your neck in the bath?' said Villani.

'It's hard to do it yourself. Takes a lot to break a neck.'

'Really?'

She didn't get his tone. 'Absolutely. Takes force.'

'What else?' said Villani.

'Nothing I can see now.'

404

'The time? Inspired guess.'

'Less than twenty-four or I have to go back to school.'

'I'm sure they'll be pleased to see you. Taken the water temperature into account?'

'What?'

Villani pointed. The small digital touchscreen at the door was set at 48 degrees.

'Didn't see that,' she said. 'I would have. In due course.'

'No doubt.'

Little smile. 'Okay, Lance,' she said. 'Zip it.'

Lance was a gaunt man, spade beard. He tried to zip the bag, it stuck below the woman's breasts. He moved the slider back and forth, got it free, encased her in the plastic.

Not ungently, they lifted the bag onto the trolley.

When they were gone, Dove and Weber came to him.

'Who owns this?' said Villani.

'They're finding out,' said Dove. 'Apparently it's complicated.'

'They?'

'The management. Waiting for us downstairs.'

'You want me to do it?' said Villani.

Dove touched a cheekbone, unhappy. 'That would be helpful, boss.'

'You want to do it, Web?' said Villani, rubbing it in to Dove.

Weber was mid-thirties, looked twenty, an unmarried evange-lical Christian. He came with plenty of country experience: mothers who drowned babies, sons who axed their mothers, access fathers who wasted the kids. But Old Testament murders in the rural welfare sumps didn't prepare you for women dead in apartments with private lifts, glass baths, French soaps and three bottles of Moët in the fridge.

'No, boss,' he said.

They walked on the plastic strip, passed through the apartment's small pale marble hall, through the front door into a corridor. They waited for the lift.

'What's her name?' Villani said.

'They don't know,' said Dove. 'Know nothing about her. There's no ID.'

'Neighbours?'

'Aren't any. Six apartments on this floor, all empty.'

The lift came, they fell thirty floors. On the sixth, at a desk, three dark suits, two men and a woman, waited. The plump fiftyish man came forward, pushing back limp hair.

'Alex Manton, building manager,' he said.

Dove said, 'This is Inspector Villani, head of Homicide.'

Manton offered his hand. It felt dry, chalky.

'Let's talk in the meeting space, inspector,' Manton said.

The room had a painting on the inner wall, vaguely marine, five metres by three at least, blue-grey smears, possibly applied with a mop. They sat at a long table with legs of chromed pipe.

'Who owns the apartment?' said Villani.

'A company called Shollonel Pty Ltd, registered in Lebanon,' said Manton. 'As far as we know, it's not occupied.'

'You don't know?'

'Well, it's not a given to know. People buy apartments to live in, investment, future use. They might not live in them at all, live in them for short or long periods. We ask people to register when they're in residence. But you can't force them.'

'How was she found?' said Villani.

'Sylvia?' said Manton. 'Our head concierge, Sylvia Allegro.'

The woman, dolly face. 'The apartment's front door wasn't fully closed,' she said. 'The lock didn't engage. That triggers a buzzer in the apartment. If it isn't closed in two minutes, there's a security alert and they ring the apartment. If that doesn't work, they go up.'

'So there in four, five minutes?' said Villani.

Sylvia looked at Manton, who was looking at the other man, fortyish, head like a glans.

'Obviously not quite,' said the man.

'You are?' said Villani.

'David Condy, head of security for the apartments and the hotel.' He was English.

'What's not quite mean?'

'I'm told the whole electronic system failed its first big test last night. The casino opening. Orion. Four hundred guests.'

'The open door. The system tells you when?'

'It should do. But what with . . .'

'That's no?'

'Yes. No.'

'Panic buttons up there.'

'In all the apartments.'

'Not pressed?

Condy ran a finger in his collar. 'No evidence of that.'

'You don't know?'

'It's difficult to say. With the failure, we have no record.'

'That's not difficult,' said Villani. 'It's impossible.'

Manton held up a pudgy hand. 'To cut to the whatever, inspector, a major IT malfunction. Coinciding with this matter, so we look a little silly.'

Villani looked at the woman. 'The bed's stripped. How would you get rid of sheets and stuff?'

'Get rid of?'

'Dispose of.'

The woman flicked at Manton. 'Well, the garbage chute, I suppose,' she said.

'Can you tell where garbage has come from?'

'No.'

'Explain this building to me, Mr Manton. Just an outline.'

Manton's right hand consulted his hair. 'From the top, four floors of penthouses. Then six floors, four apartments each. Beneath them, it's fourteen floors of apartments, six to a floor. Then it's the three recreation floors, pools, gyms, spas, and so on. Then twelve more floors of apartments, eight to a floor. Then the casino's four floors, the hotel's ten floors, two floors of catering, housekeeping. And these reception floors, that's concierge, admin and security. The casino has its own security but its systems mesh with the building's.'

'Or don't.' Villani pointed down.

'Under us, the business floors, retail, and hospitality, ground floor plaza. Five basement levels for parking and utilities.'

In Villani's line of sight, the door opened. A man came in, a woman followed, even height, suits, white shirts.

'Crashing in,' said the man, loud. 'Introductions, please, Alex.'

Manton stood. 'Inspector Villani, this is Guy Ulyatt of Marscay Corporation.'

Ulyatt was fat and pink, cornsilk hair, tuber nose. 'Pleasure, inspector,' he said. He didn't offer a hand, sat down. The woman sat beside him.

Villani said to Manton, 'This person's got something to tell us?'

'Sorry, sorry,' said Ulyatt. 'I'm head of corporate affairs for Marscay.'

'You have something to tell us?' said Villani.

'Making sure you're getting maximum co-operation. No reflection on Alex, of course.'

'Mr Manton is helping us,' said Villani. 'If you don't have a contribution, thank you and goodbye.'

'I beg your pardon?' said Ulyatt. 'I represent the building's owners.'

Silence in the big room. Villani looked at Dove. He wanted him to learn something from this. Dove held his eyes but there was no telling what he was learning.

'We Own The Building,' said Ulyatt, four distinct words.

'What's that got to do with me?' said Villani.

'We'd like to work with you. Minimise the impact on Prosilio and its people.'

'Homicide, Mr Elliot,' said Villani. 'We're from Homicide.'

'It's Ulyatt.' He spelled it.

'Yes,' said Villani. 'You might try talking to some other branch of the force. Impact minimisation division. I'm sure there's one, I'd be the last to know.'

Ulyatt smiled, a genial fish, a grouper. 'Why don't we settle down and sort this out? Julie?'

The woman smiled. She had shoe-black hair, she'd been under the knife, knew the needle, the dermabrasion, detailed down to her tyres like a saleyard Mercedes.

'Julie Sorenson, our key media person,' said Ulyatt.

'Hi,' she said, vanilla teeth, eyes like a dead deer, 'It's Stephen, isn't it?'

'Hi and goodbye,' said Villani. 'Same to you, Mr Elliot. Lovely to meet you but we're pushed here. A deceased person.'

Ulyatt lost the fish look. 'It's Ulyatt. I'm trying to be helpful, inspector, and I'm being met by hostility. Why is that?'

'This is what we need, Mr Manton,' said Villani. 'Ready?'

'Sylvia?' said Manton.

She had her pen ready.

'All CCTV tapes from 3pm yesterday, all lifts, parking,' said Villani. 'Also duty rosters, plus every single recorded coming and going, cars, people, deliveries, tradies, whatever.'

Ulyatt whistled. 'Tall order,' he said. 'We'll need a lot more time.'

'Got that down?' said Villani to Sylvia Allegro.

'Yes.'

'Also the CVs and rosters of all staff with access to the thirty-sixth floor or who could allow anyone access. And the owners of apartments on the floor and other floors with access to the floor. Plus the guest list for the casino function.'

'We don't have that,' said Ulyatt. 'That's Orion's business.'

'The casino function was in your building,' said Villani. 'I suggest you ask them. If they won't co-operate, let Detective Dove here know.'

Ulyatt was shaking his head.

'We'll show the victim on television tonight, ask for information,' said Villani.

'I can't see the necessity at this stage,' said Ulyatt.

Villani delayed looking at him, met the eyes of Dove, Weber, Manton, Allegro, not Condy, he was looking away. Then he fixed Ulyatt. 'All these rich people paying for full-on security, the panic buttons, the cameras,' he said. 'A woman murdered in your building, that's a negative?'

'It's a woman found dead,' said Ulyatt. 'It's not clear to me that she was murdered. And I can't see why you would go on television until you've examined the information you want. Which we will provide as speedily as we can, I can assure you.'

'I don't need to be told how to conduct an investigation,' said Villani. 'And I don't want to be told.'

'I'm trying to help. I can go further up the food chain,' said Ulyatt.

'What?'

'Talk to people in government.'

Awake at 4.30am, Villani was feeling the length of the day now, his best behind him. 'You'll talk to people in government,' he said.

Ulyatt's lips drew back. 'As a last resort, of course.'

'So resort to it, mate,' said Villani, pilot flame of resentment igniting the burner. 'You're dealing with the bottom feeders, there's nowhere to go but up.'

'I certainly will be putting our view,' said Ulyatt, a long sour look, he rose, the woman rose too. He turned on his black shoes, the woman turned, they both wore thin black shoes, they both had slack arses, one fat, one thin, the surgery hadn't extended to lifting her arse. They left, Ulyatt taking out his mobile.

'No garbage to leave the premises, Mr Manton,' said Villani. 'I've always wanted to give someone that instruction.'

'It's gone,' said Manton. 'It goes before 7am, every day except Sunday.'

'Right. So. How do you get up there?'

'Private lifts,' said Manton. 'From the basements and the ground floor. Card-activated, access only to your floor.'

'And who's got cards?'

Manton turned to Condy. 'David?'

'I'd have to check,' said Condy.

Villani said, 'You don't know?'

'There's a procedure for issuing cards. I'll check.'

Villani moved his shoulders. 'Getting into the apartment?' he said. 'How's that work?'

'Same card, plus a PIN and optional fingerprint and iris scanning,' said Condy. 'The print and iris are in temporary abeyance.'

'Temporary what?'

'Ah, being finetuned.'

'Not working?'

'For the moment, no.'

'So it's just the card?'

'Yes.'

'Same card you don't know how many people have.'

Villani turned to Dove.

'I'm off,' he said. 'If we don't get the fullest co-operation here, I'll be on television saying that this building is a management disaster and a dangerous place to live and residents should be alarmed.'

'Inspector, we're trying to be . . .'

'Just do it, please,' said Villani, rising.

In the ground-floor foyer, he said to Dove and Weber, 'One, get Tracy onto the company that owns the apartment. Two, ID's the priority here. Run her prints. See what vision they've got, get someone to take down every rego in the parking garage. And get that casino guest list.'

Dove nodded.

Weber said, scratching his scalp, 'Fancy set-up, this. Like a palace.'

'So what?' said Villani.

Weber shrugged, awkward.

'Just another dead person,' said Villani. 'Flat in a Housing Commission, this palace, all the same. Just proce-dure. Bomb it to Snake.'

'Excuse, boss?'

'Know the term, Mr Dove? Honours degree of any use here?'

'I'd say it's a technical Homicide term,' said Dove.

He was cleaning his rimless glasses, brown face vulnerable.

Villani looked at him for a while. 'Follow the drill. The procedure. Do what you've been taught. Tick stuff off. That way you don't have to ask for help.'

'I didn't ask for help,' said Dove. 'I asked Inspector Kiely a few questions.'

'Not the way he saw it,' said Villani. His phone tapped his chest.

'Please hold for Mr Colby,' said Angela Lowell, the secretary.

The assistant commissioner said, 'Steve, this Prosilio woman, I've had Mr Barry on the line. Broken neck, right?'

'They say that.'

'So he understands it could be an accident. A fall.'

'Bullshit, boss,' said Villani.

'Yeah, well, he wants nothing said about murder.'

'What's this?'

'Mr Barry's request to you. I'm the fucking conduit. With me, inspector?'

'Yes, boss.'

'Talk later, okay?'

'Yes, boss.'

Ulyatt hadn't been bluffing. He'd gone close to the top of the food chain. Perhaps he'd gone to the top, to Chief Commissioner Gillam, perhaps he could go to the premier.

Dove and Weber were looking at him.

'Media out there?' said Villani.

'No,' said Dove.

'No? What happened to media leaks? Anyway, if they show up, say a woman found dead, cause not established, can't rule out anything. Don't say murder, don't say suspicious, don't say anything about where in the

413

building. Just a dead woman and we are waiting for forensic.'

Dove blinked, made tiny head movements, Villani saw his anxiety. His impulse was to make him suffer but judgment overrode it.

'On second thoughts, you do it, Web,' he said. 'See how you go in the big smoke.'

Wide eyes, Weber said, 'Sure, boss, sure. Done a bit of media.'

Villani passed through the sliding doors, the hot late afternoon seized his breath, his passage was brief, no media, down the stairs, across the forecourt, a cool car waiting.

On the radio, Alan Machin, 3AR's drive man, said: 'Radio okay, boss?'

'Fine.'

So how far's the nearest police station, Gerry?

Craigieburn Road, isn't it? Too far's all I can say. Twenty-five minutes for the ambos to get here, they say the one kid's dead already. And the ambos load them up and they're gone before the bloody cops get here.

So it's what, more than an hour all-up before the police respond, is that . . .

Definitely. You notice they find hundreds when some dork gets lost bloody bushwalkin? That sorta thing?

Thanks for that, Gerry. Alice's been waiting, go ahead, Alice.

It's Alysha, actually, with a y. I wanted to talk about the trains but your caller's bloody spot on. We get riots around here, I'm not joking, riot's the only . . .

Where's that, Alisha, where's around . . .

'They don't like cops much, do they, boss?' said the driver.

'They can't like cops,' said Villani. 'Cops are their better side.'